BLACK DRAGON

B

L

A

C

K

DRAGON

KIRK MITCHELL

A THOMAS DUNNE BOOK

ST. MARTIN'S PRESS
NEW YORK

All the characters in this novel—with the exception of the historical personages, whose public records speak for them—are fictitious, and any resemblance to actual persons, living or dead, is purely coincidental.

Design by Robin Malkin

Library of Congress Cataloging-in-Publication Data

Mitchell, Kirk.
Black dragon / by Kirk Mitchell.
p. cm.
"A Thomas Dunne Book"
ISBN 0-312-01774-X
I. Title.
PS3563.I7675B5 1988
813'.54—dc19 87-36695

First Edition

10 9 8 7 6 5 4 3 2 1

BLACK DRAGON

CHAPTER 1

The sentries in the eight watchtowers had gotten the word. They took their searchlights off the automatic patterns on the perimeter fence and began manually sweeping the interior of the camp.

Barrack after barrack had been blacked out, although it was not long after the nightly head count. Usually, a few naked bulbs were left burning here and there in the blocks. But now, other than the searchlights, the only illumination came from *Hakujin* Country, the Caucasian enclave in the southeast corner of the camp.

Maybe the evacuees had gotten the word as well.

Hunkering down behind the windshield of the open jeep, Jared Campbell tried to light a Lucky Strike without searing his fingers. Still, an unruly blue flame snaked out of his Zippo. It coiled around his hand, biting him. "God Almighty!"

"Lieutenant?" Elwayne, a corporal, asked without taking his eyes off the street, which was dusty-looking in the weak headlamps and empty now of Japanese.

Jared shook his fingers in the air. "You know, I was reading in the *Times* this morning . . ." His drawl trailed off into resentful silence.

"Reading what, sir?"

"Right now—I mean this very *hour*—we're liberating Guam in your Pacific Theater and pushing on toward Paris in your European . . ." Jared didn't have to finish that, meanwhile, here they rotted, out nowhere in the high desert of California, with castoffs from the last war—down to doughboy helmets and Enfield rifles. Elwayne—his dogrobber, or boy Friday—had heard this gripe often enough for Jared to feel a bit ashamed. "Swing by Block Twenty-eight first," he suddenly said without really understanding why himself. Just a dim hunch.

"Sir?"

"Elwayne—do what I say for once. Just for ducks."

The jeep slewed around the corner near the outdoor theater. The headlamps rippled over the sandy firebreak that, earlier in the evening, had been dimpled by thousands of sandaled feet, circles of shuffling and clapping dancers, Noh actors leering at the *hakujin* staff from behind demon masks—all in celebration of *obon*, some festival to honor the dead, as best Jared understood it. And, in truth, the softly glowing paper lanterns strung on wires over the scene *had* seemed like restless spirits as they trembled in the hot wind.

And now there would be one more oblivious soul to remember next summer, what if the war wasn't over by then and Manzanar War Relocation Center not shut down. He wondered how long it would take the sagebrush and rattlers to reclaim the site, although Captain Snavely said it might be 1950 before the Jap resistance expected on the home islands was put down. And, as long as Japs were fighting Americans anywhere in the world, Manzanar would stay in business.

Jared flicked away his cigarette.

Never in those cockamamie days following Pearl Harbor had he imagined that the *duration* might mean this. And he knew that six more years on top of the two he had already wasted here would be more than he could take. And salt was being rubbed into the bedsore Manzanar had worn in his patience by reports trickling back from France: in their first brush with the Krauts, green GIs weren't firing their weapons. They were cringing in their holes instead, waiting for the elephant to go away.

Jared knew as well as any man can know that he wouldn't do this. He had killed three men before his thirtieth birthday—two of them at arm's distance. Head shots. One of the poor fools had taken his own child hostage, clung to the baby as if she were a Bible, but Jared had still found a way to kill him. So he had already seen the elephant in all its guises, a thousand more times than the pimply kids FDR was funneling into the craw instead of J. Campbell, who'd never had any illusions that it would be anything but a lousy business over there, made bearable only by its necessity. He figured he still believed in the necessity of it all—even the need for this godforsaken wallow.

From the midst of the fourteen identical tar-paper barracks in Block 28, a solitary bulb shone defiantly from a window. In the backwash of the headlamps, anger could be seen slowly rising to the surface of Jared's face. He began working his thick jaw muscles as he watched. No silhouettes showed through the amber-lit shade—and he was thankful for that. He had half-expected to see the reunited lovers entwined, but he knew they were more modest than that. All of them in this sweltering hole were modest, just as they were polite and industrious and as canny-looking as weasels.

He motioned for Elwayne to slow the jeep. "Why *his?* Thousands of windows, and only his is lit."

"Whose, sir?"

"Don't matter. Turn back for the judo *dojo*."

"Lieutenant . . . ?" Elwayne looked uncertain, queasy even.

"What?"

"Okay if I don't go inside with you?"

"Why?"

"Well, I seen a deer gutted once. It made me sick."

"You sure as hell ain't a farm kid."

"No, sir. I don't like blood."

♦ ♦ ♦

The hands of the judo *sensei* were shaking.

Jared knew the man's file: he had been nabbed in the roundup of Group C aliens—those watched before the war because of their "pro-Japanese inclinations and propagandist activities"—that had come weeks after the known dangerous aliens had been picked up on the night of December 7. Still, he had spent some months at the enemy alien internment camp in New Mexico before being cleared to join his citizen children here at Manzanar.

"I no here, *chui-san*," he blurted, addressing Jared by rank as he barred the steps to the judo pavilion with his wiry body, desperate to have a word with the lieutenant before he slipped across the covered platform into the adjoining office and *saw*. "I come back close up *dojo* after *obon odori*."

"Settle down, nobody's saying otherwise."

The *sensei* was flanked by two patrolmen from the internal police department. No taller than five-three, and no heavier than a hundred and twenty pounds, they looked like overaged Boy Scouts in their brown-and-tan uniforms. Evacuees themselves, each earned sixteen bucks a month for listening to family squabbles in a hodgepodge of English and Japanese and searching half-heartedly for moonshine distilled from mess hall rice or canned fruit. Jared couldn't stomach the swill, which the Japanese cops jokingly called "yellow lightning." Nearly all of them were *nisei*, the American-born offspring of the immigrant generation, the *issei*.

"The *sensei* was away from the *dojo* between four and nine-thirty, Lieutenant," one of the little cops said. "We have multiple witnesses."

"Multiple witnesses?" Jared echoed. He had never heard the expression before but liked it. He would try to remember it for after the war when he went back to the San Bernardino Police Department. It was a dandy turn of bullshit, and cops got promoted by turns of bullshit.

"Yes, sir—I have five names."

Standing beside Elwayne, who had positioned his six-and-a-half-foot frame on the steps, vintage Enfield held lackadaisically at port arms, the *nisei* patrolman looked like a dwarf. In that moment Jared realized why the elfin cop got sixteen bucks a month and Elwayne several times that for doing what was really the same job: in enforcement work a man gets paid for the space he threatens.

"Chief Fukuda's already inside the office, sir." The *nisei* nudged the *sensei* aside so Jared could make his way across the pavilion.

The rubberized wrestling mats felt spongy under his heels. There was a roof but no walls to the *dojo,* so he could see the busy searchbeams, whose glare always looked cold to him—like winter moonlight.

He knocked on the office door.

"Enter," a voice said from the other side.

Jared stepped inside.

The first thing he noticed was the smell. It wasn't really offensive yet. It reminded him of the blood sausage a squarehead neighbor named Klaus had dropped off at the Campbells' farm in Oklahoma now and again. It had started during the First World War, when Klaus was scared to silly grins that local folks would think he was for the Kaiser.

Hank Fukuda seemed in control of himself, but his face had paled. As usual he was in civvies, sporting a white shirt, tan cotton trousers, and a pair of cordovan loafers, which he wore even when compelled to put on his uniform. "Lieutenant."

"Evening, Chief."

From their tones of voice it was clear that race eclipsed rank at Manzanar.

"Who is it?" Jared asked.

"The warehouseman, Shido."

Jared whistled softly. "Masao Shido? You sure?"

The chief gave a quick nod.

"Your desk sergeant said something about suicide."

"Yeah, but I've got problems with that."

Jared let that sink in for a moment. From someone like

Henry Fukuda it was more than idle speculation. Prior to evacuation he had been a criminalistics technician with the Los Angeles PD, and before that, a coroner's assistant. He was intimate with the mechanics of death and could read a body with greater accuracy than Jared, who himself was no stranger to violent passings.

When the Manzanar Police Department had been formed, Hank Fukuda was found to be the only evacuee with any kind of law enforcement background. The lack of *nihonjin* cops was mostly due to the height requirement every police outfit in the country had, but also partly because no chief or sheriff believed that a Jap patrolman would have "presence"—whatever they imagined that to be. If anybody had presence, it was Hank Fukuda. A stocky man with a gray fringe around his bullet-shaped head, Fukuda refused to be intimidated by anyone, which was more than could be said for Jared's own chief back in San Bernardino.

And the lieutenant felt close to trusting him. Fukuda was third generation; his father's family had been in California a half-century longer than Jared's. However, when the day's work was done, Fukuda couldn't retire to *Hakujin* Country, couldn't enjoy a game of pool and knock back a couple of beers at the Caucasian recreation club. He had to go back to a tar-paper barrack in Block 2. He couldn't be completely trusted because he was still an evacuee. Simply put, Hank was a kind of trusty if only because Manzanar was a kind of prison—and the test of that was the simple fact the residents weren't free to walk out the armed gates.

So, while they were amicable toward each other, Jared and Hank Fukuda were in no position to be friends.

"Well, what's bothering you about this one?" Jared asked, realizing that his drawl, which he consciously had to tone down, was rampant tonight—he was uneasier than he'd thought. "You come across a defensive wound?"

"I wish it were that simple. I'll have to show you."

The small office was lit by a low-wattage bulb, and directly beneath it stood two triptyches of rice-paper screens, forming a translucent pen around the outlines of a body. The smell of blood sausage became stronger, turned sour from a trace of fecal odor—as Jared followed Hank up to the panels, their shoes crackling over the straw *tatami* mats on which the students meditated. The lieutenant took a breath and held it.

They halted, and Fukuda moved aside one of the screens. "These were like this when I arrived. The *sensei* says he didn't do it."

"They belong in here?"

"Yeah, but they're usually stacked over in that corner till the girls hold an *odori* class on the platform. You know, so the judo boys can't see them dance, laugh at them."

There was lots of blood. It had radiated out at least five feet from the corpse, staining the underlying mat. "Abdominal?" Jared had to ask, because Shido was sitting cross-legged, his torso slumped down between his yawning knees.

"Clean across the guts, your B-flat *seppuku*."

"Not mine, hoss."

Hank gave a meaningless shrug.

Then Jared repeated what he had done first at each of the more than three hundred deaths he had attended as a civilian cop: he seized the lifeless left hand and pinched the thumbnail hard between his own fingers. It worked better than trying to take a neck pulse—especially when his own pulse was swishing wildly with the realization that *this could be me . . . this is how I'll look when it's my turn.* A white impression showed under Shido's jaundiced nail. However, blood didn't flow back in to erase it, even after thirty seconds. The warehouseman was as dead as a pharaoh—there were even some mottled blushes of postmortem lividity at the elbows. But Jared had known at once that Shido was gone. The fingernail thing was just a trick that dispelled the shock and got him working, thinking about things other than his own death.

He shifted his stance to study the body from another angle. "God Almighty!"

"Right," Fukuda whispered.

Both men said nothing for a long moment. The searchlight

from the nearest tower flashed across the windows. Absently, Jared reached for one of the toothpicks he kept in the pocket of his wilted khaki shirt, then decided not to chew it. "I've seen defensive wounds on the hands, the arms—even on the feet, Hank. But a quarter-ways through a fella's neck?"

Fukuda was studying him, carefully. "How much do you know about *seppuku?*"

"Hara-kiri?"

Fukuda gave another slight shrug. "Whatever."

"Probably nothing."

Giving a wide berth to the bloodstain, which was already browning, the chief lowered his chest to the mat and motioned for Jared to join him. From this vantage, they could see the handle of the dagger that was still thrust into the right side of Shido's abdomen. A cadaveric spasm had cleaved the fist to the hilt—a kind of instantaneous rigor mortis that was all but impossible for a murderer to fake. So the instant of death had come while Shido was slicing from left to right across his own belly. A loop of intestine was protruding from the wound, bulbous and dove-colored, the membranes already dry-looking from contact with the desert air. From this level Jared could also lock gazes with the dead man's eyes, which were bulged by the first instant of agony—a horrified shouting of eyes that would have seemed more insistent had not the brown-rimmed corneas clouded into a milky, uncaring gray.

"Ritual suicide comes in two parts," Fukuda said quietly, his breath at close quarters musty from yellow lightning, which Jared, as usual, ignored. "First, the guy gives himself the stomach-cut. Actually, that's the *hara-kiri*, which just means belly-cutting. It's usually done with an *aikuchi*." He answered before Jared could ask: "A kind of dagger with no hilt guard."

"Is this one?"

"Yeah, I can tell by the diamond design on the hilt."

"I thought we confiscated all the cutlery at intake."

"Obviously not. The second part of *seppuku* is called the *kaishaku*."

"You mean there's *more* to this than gutting yourself?"

"Yeah. *Hara-kiri* is so painful the guy picks somebody he trusts, a friendly second, to end his suffering with a sword. The blow to the neck's supposed to come right away. But Shido did a helluva lot of suffering—look at all the blood—before his pal finally obliged him. He lived several minutes after starting the stomach-cut. Shido's friendly second wasn't all that friendly."

Jared winced as his eyes measured the depth of the neck wound, made all the more visible by the slumping of Shido's head. "You sure it was a sword? Maybe he cut himself there first before turning to his belly?"

"Yeah. There's a ring of contusion injury here." Hank pressed the flesh beside the wound. It was rigored, although Jared had just determined that Shido's left hand was still flaccid. Rigor mortis starts in the muscles of the jaw and neck, then works downward. Death within two or three hours then, Jared guessed, but not out loud; he was afraid Hank might correct him.

"This means something heavier than the dagger," Fukuda went on. "And if you look close, you can make out some crushing effect on the clavicle. Sword—had to be."

Jared came to his feet, noting the blood spattered across the screen as he rose.

Fukuda read his thoughts. "Already photographed."

"Good." Jared could see it plainly: the chief was champing at the bit to use his skills, one of the few chances he'd had since being evacuated—not that there hadn't been other violent deaths in camp. Almost to the day of the first anniversary of Pearl Harbor, the MPs had opened fire on a mob in front of the police station, killing two Japanese and wounding eleven. Since the *hakujin* had done the shooting and no evacuee was going to pass judgment on anything done by the MPs, the chief had been excluded from the investigation.

It was one of many things Jared and Fukuda never discussed.

The chief now opened the scarred medical bag he had deposited in a corner of the enclosure. When he took out his meat thermometer, Jared turned away. He feigned preoccupation with lighting a cigarette until Fukuda had rolled the corpse onto its back, parted the bloodsoaked linen *gi*, and stabbed the temperature probe into Shido's slowly cooling liver.

Out of the corner of his eye, Jared noticed how brusquely Hank had done it. The chief had never wasted any courtesy on the muscular and gruff-spoken alien who'd gone out of his way to bait any evacuee who helped enforce the dictates of the *hakujin* administration. Like many, Shido had called Fukuda an *inu*: "dog" in literal Japanese, but so much more than that—informer, collaborator, traitor, scum.

But Masao Shido had also been an object of suspicion. He was believed to have been a practicing Shintoist, the only religion prohibited by War Relocation Authority regulations because it involved worshiping the emperor in addition to spirits hiding in woods and rocks and ponds. Some *issei* said that Shido had distinguished himself as an imperial marine in the 1905 war with Russia; others insisted that he had fled Hokkaido in 1910 to avoid prosecution for smuggling. Whatever the case, he had made statements in camp block meetings to the effect that one day the victorious Imperial Army would liberate Manzanar and that all *inu* would be beheaded in front of the administration building.

Yet in 1943, when fifteen hundred evacuees suspected of having pro-Japanese sentiments had been trucked up to the segregation camp at Tule Lake on the California–Oregon border, Masao Shido was not among them.

Jared had never gotten a straight answer as to why Shido eluded transfer to Tule Lake when rumors were rife that he had taken over the leadership of the secret Black Dragon Society, a handful of militarist thugs who donned masks and tried to intimidate loyal evacuees at night. Others had been sent to Tule on less suspicion. When asked why Shido continued to remain at Manzanar, Project Director Morris Wenge had passed the buck to Associate Director Montgomery Lee, and Monty's best answer had been that the staff was already onto Shido's tricks. If he were shipped up to Tule, another but less predictable *issei* would take over the Black Dragon. At that point

Jared had quit beating his head against the wall: Shido was probably somebody's pet informant; the FBI and the Office of Naval Intelligence were said to have several planted among the evacuees. Campbell knew that nobody was what he seemed at Manzanar; nobody was above one kind of suspicion or another.

But now what did it matter? Shido, lying on the bloody mat, no longer seemed cunning and dangerous. He looked small and old, his musculature deflated by the gaping wounds.

"Ballpark—he died about three hours ago." The chief jotted down the temperature of Shido's liver on a clipboard. "You know, there are only two ways to screw up the *kaishaku*—and this is one of them."

"How's that?"

"The guy wielding the sword should almost sever the head—but only *almost*. He's supposed to leave a strip of muscle and skin. This cut's way too shallow." Fukuda mopped his face with an olive-drab handkerchief.

For the first time since entering, Jared realized that the day's heat, which for the past week had broken a hundred and five, was still trapped inside the office. Death Valley was only one desert basin to the east.

"Ninety-two in here," the chief said.

"I believe it. And what's the other wrong way to do this *seppuku* thing?"

"To completely lop off the head."

Jared nodded, his eyes remote for a moment. "Well, don't let me hold you up." Then, making sure his stride didn't seem too eager, he started for the door—and the night air, which he knew would seem deliciously cool in contrast. "I'll be breaking this to the director. Give a holler if you need anything."

"What about body storage in this heat?"

Jared paused. The morgue at the camp hospital wasn't refrigerated. The only cold storage was inside the military police compound to the immediate south of Manzanar. "All right, I'll tell them to make space in the reefer."

"Thanks."

Jared emerged into a darkness pungent with burnt orange

peel, which the evacuees smudged in one-gallon cans to ward off mosquitoes. Still, he inhaled, deeply and gratefully; he was rejoining the living.

♦ ♦ ♦

Long ago, before he recognized what was possible and what was not, Hank Fukuda had dreamed of becoming a street cop. But his applications went unanswered. And, when he looked around at other Japanese Americans his age—graduates of Berkeley and UCLA, not lowly L.A. City College like himself—and saw that they were either gardeners or clerks in Little Tokyo stores, he made his peace with reality and eventually came up with a way to salvage a torn scrap of his dream. He started as a night attendant in the city morgue, then moved up to coroner's assistant, and finally was accepted as a technician at the police criminalistics lab.

He liked his vocation, even though it was but an echo of the dream, a compromise. Still, there was a delicacy to dusting for fingerprints that appealed to him. This occurred to him as if for the first time while he worked on the surfaces of a paper screen. He halted the camel-hair brush in mid-stroke and studied his blunt fingers as if they belonged to another man. An appreciation of grace and beauty in ordinary things—was this the only vestige of Henry Yoshio Fukuda's Japaneseness to survive integrated public schools and Benny Goodman and stainless steel forks? He chuckled to himself, but without humor: The fingers seemed to belong to a man caught on the margins of identity, his physicality scarcely familiar even to himself.

Then he went back to work, bringing the latent friction ridges into definition with applications of the jet-colored volcanic powder. Patterns emerged in heretofore invisible smudges on the rice paper, each the distinctive signature of an evacuee: this whorl perhaps from a *nisei* girl in white bobby socks, chewing Wrigley's as she helped set up the screens for the *odori* class her *issei* parents made her attend so she would have grace enough to snare a *nice* Japanese boy; this loop from a youth mastering jujitsu so that reentering the *hakujin* world would seem that much less fearful (would these Manzanar kids ever be normal again?); and a palm impression, perhaps from the *sensei*, who longed for a Meiji Japan that no longer existed, and privately hoped for a victory that was no longer possible.

Also, among these, was evidence left by the man who had helped Masao Shido die.

He had worn gloves. Cotton perhaps. Hank had discovered the fabric impressions only by shining his flashlight obliquely across the rice paper. The wearer had probably been confident he was leaving nothing behind that might identify him; but his warm hands had secreted oil into the material, which then deposited the weave imprint on the screen. More fragile than impressions left by bare fingers, these Hank would preserve by taking the entire panel down to the station for storage.

Shido's friendly second had already erred, although only slightly.

Hank lifted the first friction ridge impression with adhesive tape, then affixed it to a three-by-five card. He tried to frame it in words: that there was something bigger and uglier here than the contempt one man can feel for another. Why had he been unwilling to discuss it with Jared Campbell? Was it because of his own prejudices against the MP lieutenant's exasperating drawl, those shoulders made bullish by farm labor? Still, Hank suspected Campbell to be one of those sly rustics whose words come purposely slower than his thoughts. His light blue eyes were calculating; they seldom lost their incisiveness, even when he bared his teeth in laughter. And, unlike most of the *hakujin* staff and all of the MPs, he seemed to make the distinction between American Japanese and those little yellow devils doing Tojo's bidding in Asia. This, the Lost Distinction, sometimes flashed in Campbell's eyes like the light of truth, before dimming to indifference again. But, all things being equal, the lieutenant seemed like a hick to Hank Fukuda, whose loafers had always trod concrete until evacuation. Fourth Army was not about to waste its brightest officers on guard duty; any *baka* could understand these were second-rate troops at Manzanar.

One of Hank's eyelids twitched. I really should pass along word of Shido's death before someone else does, he told himself. I must not appear to be withholding information.

But no, he decided after a few minutes. He would wait and see what the lieutenant would accomplish on his own. He wanted to trust the Okie. There was something in the big sandy-haired plowboy that begged to be fulfilled with trust, although Hank—perhaps alone in the camp—knew of an important trust Campbell had already violated. But this shred of intelligence had not been passed along. Sexual misdemeanors have little meaning in a global war.

From the direction of the main gate came the rumbling of the MP's Dodge two-and-a-half-ton truck, the same one that made the rounds every morning, dropping off enough perishable food at each mess hall to feed three hundred evacuees that day. The only sizable refrigeration unit in the camp was located inside the MP compound, and it was into that reefer that Masao Shido would now go until the county coroner could see fit to pick him up.

The quiet of the office was disturbed by a soft but inhuman gasp from the body. It was already giving off its gasses of putrefaction. Hank didn't startle: he had rubbed elbows with the dead for too long.

Shido had been a formidable man. Hank would grant him that much.

And before the bored, insouciant MPs arrived, the chief did something that seemed strange, even to himself: he set down the brush and jar of powder, then steepled his stubby hands together before his chest. Slowly, in the manner of his great-grandfather, he bowed deeply from the waist toward Shido's remains.

Curiously, if only for a moment, the turmoil that had become Hank Fukuda's inner life abated in the serenity of the gesture—but only briefly, for then two soldiers burst inside the *dojo* office. "Hey, Fukuda, you got a fucking stiff for the cooler?"

CHAPTER 2

Tonight, as on each of the ten nights since the major's return from Europe, the Nitta family had retired an hour earlier than usual.

This, Kimiko Nitta realized, was so that Tadashi and she would have darkness in which to make love. But even this sham privacy was being jarred every sixty seconds by the searchlight from Watchtower 2, which for some reason was scanning the interior of the camp. Each time it penetrated the shade, she had a lightning glimpse of Eddie—as everyone except his parents called Tadashi Nitta—lying on his steel cot across from her. His right hand was dangling within inches of the floor, cupped around the glow of a cigarette. Pulled up over his left shoulder was a GI blanket, although it was stifling in the barrack apartment and two or three more hours might pass in heavy stillness before the breezes would slide down off the Sierra.

He had drunk too much, again. This time it had been at the *obon*. Clan after clan had begged him to sample their homemade sake, but the alcohol had done nothing to melt the contempt that had solidified in his eyes over the past few days.

Hand in his trouser pocket, he had strolled down the crowded firebreaks, his back stiff, as if he wished to accentuate his six-foot height. That he said little was taken by the older evacuees to be a form of manliness; he was, after all, a *bushi*, a warrior.

But the pregnant quality to his silence was terrifying her. To everyone's shame, he had already exploded once. The explosion would come again—the lights deep in his eyes burned like little fuses.

Does he know? she kept asking herself. The unanswered question had already cost her five of her ninety-seven pounds, and her ribs had begun to show like stripes beneath her breasts. Several times over the past ten days she had vomited shortly after eating: the Block 28 mess hall seemed to be serving her the rancid leftovers of her own betrayal. And, as if that was not enough to sap her strength and spirit, Jared Campbell could be seen each dusk running the four miles around the perimeter fence, his eyes sunk back far into his large head. She had not believed him capable of such unhappiness. On all fronts she had created misery.

Earlier this evening, in a now vapid ritual, she had waited until the women's bathhouse was empty but for herself, then slipped into the pink satin baby-doll nightgown she'd ordered from the Sears and Roebuck catalogue outlet in camp. Somehow, it would have seemed brazen to do this in the company of her husband's family—even behind the olive-drab blanket partition: everything that involved touching her own body now seemed so in their presence. Covering herself with her Navy-surplus pea coat, which hung to her knees, she hurried back to the barrack, holding her toothbrush conspicuously before her as she swept past the apartment stoops of the 120-foot-long tar-paper structure, each porch crowded with *issei*, many in kimonos. They murmured in Japanese to one another—seemingly about her, as if they had guessed that she wore nothing beneath her nightie again tonight, needlessly, and that her heart was so hopelessly twisted her husband would not touch her. Thankfully, there was no wind to fold the hem of the coat back up over her bare legs, although she was ordinarily quite proud of them. Only an inch taller than five feet, she nevertheless had *gobo ashi*—long slender legs so called because they resembled the willowy brown roots of the *gobo* vegetable—whereas most of the women in her family were cursed with *daikon ashi*, shaped like the stubby bulb of the Japanese horseradish plant.

Kimiko Nitta was beautiful, but took no pleasure in it. And lately, she had begun to wish that she were the plainest woman in camp.

A crack of hickory had caused her to glance over the top of Barrack 5 in time to see a baseball arc up against the violet twilight, then, inexorably, be sucked back to the firebreak grit again.

Nothing seemed to escape Manzanar, not even baseballs.

During Eddie's absence, she had shared an apartment with his parents. Now, she expected him to apply for their own quarters, but so far he had not, nor did he give any indication that he intended to move out. At twenty by twenty-four feet, it was the largest apartment in the barrack, but it was also the least comfortable. Stubbornly, her *issei* father-in-law had refused to improve it. When the camp administration offered plasterboard to cover the rough pine boards, he refused, saying that the government had stolen his tuna boats and he wasn't going to take plasterboard in return. When linoleum was made available, he said again that the government had stolen his boats and he wasn't going to take linoleum in return. At this point, he was beyond accepting any kind of compensation, and if the *hakujin* pushed him too far, he would simply die at their expense.

Through the thin wall Kimiko could hear her sister-in-law Mae in the adjoining apartment trying to shush her six-month-old daughter. But the baby's screams went through the entire barrack like skewers. Mae's husband had recently arrived in Italy with the 442nd Regimental Combat Team, which had then linked up with the largely Hawaiian 100th Infantry Battalion, Eddie's former outfit. In addition to her own child, Mae cared for her twin nephews, age nine and uncontrollable. Their mother,

Eddie's youngest sister, had died in childbirth last autumn at the camp hospital, her infant stillborn.

Kimiko turned over on her cot, and the chain springs groaned.

With a self-amused look Kimiko had found offensive—God, but some of these *issei* possessed a crude, phallic humor—her father-in-law had tacked two blankets to the overhead beams, creating a private sleeping space for Eddie and her. Yet she couldn't move on her cot without everyone in both apartments knowing it—and she had hoped, a little desperately, this was why Eddie refused to come to her, because of the noises their coupling would make. Yet one evening after he'd been back a week, the wind rose off the desert and the barrack creaked and moaned like a wooden ship in a storm, covering all human sounds. Still, he hadn't crossed the floorboards, whose wide cracks puffed out tiny billows of dust from the unskirted space beneath the building.

It was then she tried to convince herself it was his wound.

His left arm was missing from the shoulder. Even now he persisted in wearing a bandage, although she knew somehow that the scar had already formed and there was no need to cover it.

He wouldn't come tonight, she finally decided. She tried to sleep, although the bedsheet tucked under her chin stank of dust. Everything here smelled of alkaline dust, especially the hair of the children, who groveled in it searching for Paiute arrowheads.

Her father-in-law coughed in the darkness. Too many cigarettes. Until evacuation, his hands had been kept busy with fishing lines and nets—the sea.

A mosquito whined somewhere up near the peak of the ceiling.

She slipped into drowsiness, knowing it would not coast her the full languorous distance into sleep. In a few minutes, twenty at the most, she would snap wide awake and be more conscious and exhausted than before. Yet, sliding through this brief torpor, she could take a hand in her own dreams, direct them almost, compelling them to persuade her that Stanford was still real, that Peter was still there on campus—and not soaring across tropical skies, sending Japanese pilots with little-boy faces to their deaths. Cringing even now, she heard him whisper something about her "seductive" eyes. She had never told him that she didn't care for their seductive shape; for a time as a teenager she had even slept with Scotch tape contorting her fleshy eyelids, pulling them upward in a futile attempt to create the Caucasoid fold.

With such a fold, everything was possible, her sleep-voice explained.

When Peter began to laugh at her confession, it was not the serene Brahman chortle of the law student she had adored. She suddenly realized it was Jared Campbell's sad chuckle. They were both large men with sandy hair, Peter and Jared; both the ideal of a male beauty her *issei* mother would have found too coarse and pinkish—had she lived to find out.

Puzzlement: How had these thoughts meandered all the way from Stanford to Jared Campbell?

Oh, yes, she murmured inwardly, and the wakeful half of her mind secreted the time-connective membrane. . . .

Sunday afternoon in Peter's apartment a block off campus, looking beyond Peter's flushed face through the slightly parted curtains of his bedroom window onto Stanford's oaks, she imagined how nice it would be to make love outside. She was thinking this when Peter came with a shudder that began at the base of his spine and ended with a hunching of his shoulders. Afraid of drawing another accusation of being unexpressive, she told him she loved him, but he was too consumed by his moment of pleasure to hear, perhaps.

A shout from the direction of campus—something about pearls. And Japs. At first she couldn't believe that the word had been used by anyone at Stanford, and so viciously, too.

Peter swung his legs over the side of the bed and tuned in NBC from San Francisco. His hand fumbled for a cigarette. And when he heard what had happened that morning while they lay entwined, oblivious to the world, he rasped, "Jesus."

Then he slowly turned and looked at her as if she were a stranger, an invader naked in his bed.

The Scotch tape had remedied nothing. It was only from her own perspective that the view seemed round; the world looked back upon her with an icy narrowness. She was indelibly *nihonjin*.

Tanforan Racetrack Assembly Center. The blows had come in such stunning succession after Pearl Harbor that it seemed strangely fitting somehow that one morning she should find herself warehoused with other Bay Region *nisei* college students in horse stalls that still reeked of manure and mildewed hay. A way station along a confused process of evacuation. Only one conclusion made sense: she, in careless ignorance of the *hakujin* order of things, had done something deserving of this humiliation. In time, when the shock wore off, she would understand what it had been. Then she could begin again.

Peter left school in March for naval aviation training in Florida. He soon stopped writing, and she found perverse satisfaction in the fact that her only pregnancy scare had come and gone without conception the summer before, rather than after, Pearl Harbor, when the thing possibly taking root within her might have been hateful to him. In April, like a dozen other *nisei* co-workers, she was fired from her part-time job with the California Department of Justice—something about the inbred disposition of all Japanese to obey the emperor, although she herself felt no allegiance to the reclusive forty-year-old marine biologist living in a foreign country called Nippon. And then, the first week in May, the Western Defense Command exclusion posters sprouted like lichens on telephone poles all over Palo Alto, instructing ALL PERSONS OF JAPANESE ANCESTRY to report to a civil control station for evacuation to an assembly center. Her first thought, as a law student, had been to file a writ of habeus corpus, calling the government's bluff, demanding to know the justification for her detainment. She was a *citizen*, for the love of Jesus.

But Eddie Nitta, a self-assured engineering major and former ROTC cadet from Stanford, who would have been class salutatorian had he been permitted to graduate, talked her out of it. He had gotten word from a Caucasian buddy with Fourth Army headquarters' staff at the Presidio of San Francisco—troublemakers would be segregated in a more severe internment camp.

Leaning against the whitewashed rail of the inside track at Tanforan, Kimiko had wept—not for her fate, which she deserved for some ineffable reason, but for her lack of courage, which made her punishment seem all the more appropriate. She feared the segregation camp, although she had no idea what an ordinary permanent camp would be like. Eddie had held her in his two strong arms with just enough tenderness to make her feel ashamed: for her affair with Peter; for the willingness she'd felt to bear his baby; and for knowing with such obstinate certainty, even as he held her, that she could never really love the handsome and consoling *nihonjin*, who wanted only to reassure her that she had not been singled out for *hakujin* contempt, that she was not alone.

In those days, she had feared being alone more than anything. Now she longed for it.

She had arrived at Manzanar knowing only one person, Eddie Nitta. They were married six weeks later in a joint Christian-Buddhist ceremony.

The floor creaked once, tentatively, then again. Instantly, Kimiko was awake.

She felt a rush of coolness as the sheet was lifted back over her body, but closed her eyelids. It was cowardly, but she didn't want to see him, to be caught by his grim eyes as she appraised the damage to his once supple and balanced wholeness when the searchlight burst across the window again.

He entered her, abruptly, his touch not as she remembered it from their month of marriage before he shipped out. He caused her some pain, and she hoped that it was not intentional. Unable to rise above her on two arms, he lay heavily across her small breasts. The heat in the apartment quickly brought on copious sweating; she found the slippery sensation between their bodies unpleasant.

Then he froze, almost as if he had at last coupled with an immensely gratifying death, before rousing himself with a flexing of his haunches. He withdrew from her without a word, a gesture, a kiss.

"Eddie?" she whispered, rising on her elbows.

He dressed in the darkness and went out, banging the door.

The baby whimpered, then began screeching. "Setsuko . . . Setsuko," her mother whined, close to tears herself.

Kimiko lay back down, a tissue clenched between her thighs.

♦ ♦ ♦

Jared Campbell rousted the sleepy-eyed buck sergeant on duty inside the orderly room at MP headquarters. "Send a couple troops in the deuce-and-a-half to the judo *dojo*."

"What do we got, Lieutenant?"

"A corpse. Wake Cookie and have him make space in the reefer."

After a quick iced coffee, Jared decided to make one more check before disturbing Director Wenge. Anything left undone in the first hours of this investigation would surface like a pustule in his next efficiency report. The captain would make sure of it. Morton Snavely had been turned down by every police outfit on the Coast—a heart murmur, he claimed, although the same defect hadn't kept him out of the Army. He loved sniffing out picayune omissions in Jared's procedure, partly because the lieutenant had been a real cop, and partly because Snavely detested Okies almost as much as Japs. Born to money, a powerful fruit-growing family in the San Joaquin Valley, he'd had a brief career as a "special deputy" hired by the growers to keep the migrants in line. Rumor had it he had shot a picker for no good reason, shot him in the back, running away. He was never prosecuted for it—the growers owned those counties lock, stock, and barrel—but it was probably the reason law outfits wouldn't take him on. No chief wants a man with a hair trigger.

Snavely was away at the Presidio, and he could stay there for all Jared cared.

Allowing Elwayne to turn in, he ambled outside to his jeep and sat heavily behind the wheel. The cooling breeze off the mountains was late tonight. He fired up the engine and pampered the worn clutch as he accelerated out of the compound.

Returning the salute of the private in the pagoda-roofed sentry house at the main gate and then the wave of Hank Fukuda's man inside the police inspection post, he made his way through the darkened blocks to Sixth Street and followed it west. The lane was flanked on the south by barrack after barrack, and, on the north, by a belt of orchards and truck plots. These people could make land yield, even piss-poor land. And they had the prettiest damn ways of tying down the dust outside their doorsteps with little lawns, patches of flowers, or rock gardens.

He flicked off his low beams and used the desert starshine, hoping to catch somebody darting across the asphalt in front of him. But he knew it would never be that easy.

The sentry at the west gate unlocked it for him, and Jared inched through, bringing up his lights for a moment to locate the outer perimeter road. His beams passed over the cemetery out in the sage, the big obelisk—or "soul-consoling tower," as the evacuees called it—glistening as he veered off toward Tower 4.

As soon as he killed the engine, he could hear the radio voice drifting down from the observation platform: *"Music-maker Harry James and his trumpet section head for home with a number known far and wide in the world of jazz . . . it's a favorite among James's fans everywhere . . . 'Trumpet Blues' . . ."*

The searchlight, on manual, rippled out across the brush and froze on Jared, briefly, before whisking back toward the center of the camp. The radio clicked to silence, leaving him a bit disappointed as he continued on toward the base of the tower. The brass had sounded nice floating thinly across the desert; it had somehow seemed in tune with the big, pendulous stars.

He wouldn't put the sentry on report for sneaking a table radio into the tower, as the captain demanded. Snavely didn't understand the boredom a man felt while waiting for his relief, especially after it dawned on him that the *issei* were too old and arthritic from a lifetime of stoop labor to run away, and the last thing the *nisei* wanted was to appear disloyal to the *hakujin* staff. Besides, Manzanar's perimeter fence was more mesh than it was wire—five strands of barbed wire a foot apart; anybody could wriggle through if he had a mind to.

Jared wasn't challenged as he began climbing the wooden ladder inside the tower bracing—tedium had long since done away with such martial tomfoolery. He didn't look down; he didn't like being up off the ground. The first trapdoor swung back onto the floor of a small enclosure with dirty pitted windows on all four sides. This was where the sentries withdrew at the first hint of wind. In winter, the desert gales could cause frostbite; and, in the dry months, they bore clouds of grit that could sandblast the paint off a soldier's tinpot. In fair weather, the sentries usually went up on the flat roof of the enclosure and leaned against the railing while they gazed down on the camp spread out below.

A Thompson submachine gun was propped against a corner of the enclosure—kept out of sight of visitors in accordance with Morris Wenge's wishes.

Jared went through the second trapdoor and crawled out onto the roof. The radio was nowhere in sight. He pretended not to know that the sentry had dangled it over the dark side of the tower by its electric cord until all was clear again.

"Lieutenant." The PFC, a Mexican kid, saluted. The hint in his voice was unmistakable: he had no use for unblooded officers. At nineteen, he already wore the Combat Infantryman Badge and a Purple Heart.

Jared had his own resentments to mask. Had he known in early 1942 that, because of his six years of cop experience—two of them as a homicide detective—he would be shanghaied out of combat readiness training and then dumped in a stateside MP company, he would never have volunteered. "Everything okay, soldier?"

"Yes, sir." He stood with his shoulders hunched forward, just slightly, as if it would hurt to throw them completely back. Shot in the chest on Bougainville, he was an infantry convalescent being rotated through the company until fit to return to his own outfit—or he went over the hill, as two of them already had rather than return to the Pacific.

Jared felt certain that, before the war, the boy had been a *pachuco*. He had tussled with enough zoot-suiters to recognize one by the smoldering in his eyes. "You been on duty here since eight?"

"Yes, sir."

"This tower's got the best view of the judo school, wouldn't you say?"

"I guess so. What's been going on down there, sir?"

"Warehouseman killed himself inside the office."

"Oh." There was no inflection to his voice. Like the other convalescents, he seemed to have no attitude toward the Japs. No hatred. Nothing. Maybe war just left you exhausted—and scared of loud noises.

"You see anything unusual?"

"Nips jitter-bugging all over the firebreaks. It's been crazy." He began working the searchlight again. "I could barely keep an eye on the wire."

Jared hesitated before asking, "You ever notice the *nisei* major with only one arm? The tall fella?"

"Sure."

"Did you see him go inside the *dojo* tonight?"

"I don't think so."

"What about anybody else?"

"Really, sir, I barely had time to watch the perimeter."

"All right . . ." Jared rested his forearms on the sun-curled paint of the top rail. He stared out across the night: the Owens was a deep valley, some said the deepest in America, hemmed in by two ranges running north and south of the camp as far as the eye could see. The Sierra Nevada, to the west, had been clawed jagged by glaciers, some of which were still tucked in its higher clefts; the Inyo Mountains, to the east, were rounder than Sierra and calico instead of ash-colored, but nearly as tall as the western range.

Jared lowered his gaze to the blocks of barracks.

The camp resembled a flotilla of Biblical arks anchored in a lucent bay that had been bulldozed out of the darker sagebrush, the *hakujin* arks painted white and the more numerous *nihonjin* ones tar-paper black. It was only from the tower that he realized over again that Manzanar was the biggest city in five hundred miles of arid nothingness between L.A. and Reno. And, sooner or later, despite the submissiveness of most of the evacuees, it had been bound to dish up some real crime.

Jap traditions be damned—it was a felony in California to help somebody kill himself. If he were back at his old desk in the San Bernardino PD dick bureau, Jared knew what he'd do: treat Shido's death like any other homicide. But in these circumstances he had no clear idea who had jurisdiction. Did the case belong to the War Relocation Authority, its overseer, the Western Defense Command/Fourth Army, or the Inyo County Sheriff's Office? Chances were all three agencies would let well enough alone. After all, nobody but a Hirohito-worshiping alien had come to the end of his days, and that was what this war was all about: deep-sixing folks like Masao Shido. Even some evacuees, Major Tadashi Nitta for one, had warned Shido to keep a lid on his fascist politics, or pay the price; supposedly, it had been only a shade less than a death threat. So nobody was going to shed any tears at the old man's funeral.

Still, a crime had been committed. And, at the very least, a suspect who had tried to decapitate his victim deserved some watching.

"Carry on, soldier."

"Yes, sir."

Jared lowered himself through the trapdoor.

CHAPTER 3

By day, camouflage netting was woven by evacuees in the factory. But sometimes, as soon as it was dark, Yuki Ota found her own purposes for the building, even though it was off-limits after five o'clock until seven the next morning.

She waited on the shadowy side of her Block 3 barrack for the searchbeam to roll past. It made no sense, the tower lights being turned inward on the camp tonight. But little of what the MPs did made sense.

Hiking her skirt over her knees, she bolted across First Street. She didn't bother to check for the roving patrol: at this hour, the civilian watchmen hired to guard the warehouses and war production complexes were at the coffee urn inside the police station. Sometimes, she longed for the thrill of a chase along the loading docks; but she also trusted that these two *hakujin,* who'd been here since 1942 and had only enormous beer bellies to show for it, would never fire their revolvers at her. Chuck and Jerry had probably forgotten how to shoot by now. The fact was, they spent most of their patrol looking for *sushi* handouts, or for dark corners to piss in.

Long ago, right after she had finished servicing a net worker in her noisy barrack, he had mentioned that the swing-out window on the east wall of the factory had a busted latch and couldn't be secured. This was the side that, as chance would have it, neither Tower 6 nor 7 could cover with its beam. Their next appointment was conducted there, and after that she used the factory for clients who wanted more privacy than what the block offered, or were afraid of being seen entering her apartment.

Now, as always, Yuki was careful not to scuff her red patent leather shoes or snag her Ike jacket—which she wore both summer and winter to protect her smooth skin—as she clambered up onto the fifty-gallon oil drum and eased her stocky frame through the window and onto the workbench within. Her first breath inside the darkened interior made her swear softly—the body odor of the workers from two days before still mingled in the stale air with the smell of hemp and camouflage dye. Nets dangled from their drying frames like vines in a Tarzan movie.

She'd slit her wrists before she'd work forty-eight hours a week in this sweatshop.

Sprawling atop one of the net bundles, a scratchy but serviceable bed, she waited for the timid knock on the sliding door, which she would then unbolt.

Director Wenge always boasted to the press that everybody worked at Manzanar, meaning that his *yabos* weren't getting a free ride at government expense. Well, everybody worked except Yuki Ota. She had refused by laughing in the clerk's face. In the first place, after promising "going wages" in a leaflet passed out at the assembly centers, the WRA had reversed itself and offered only from twelve to nineteen dollars *a month* for volunteer work. She made that much even on the rare evenings when the MPs, for some bogus reason, locked down Manzanar. Secondly, she preferred to sleep during the day. It wasn't easy, what with the racket the kids in the next apartment made; with old man Higashi, who'd gone off his rocker, plucking at his banjo-like *samisen*; and with the high school band marching up and down the windblown streets playing Sousa. But a mason jar of sake with breakfast helped in all but the hottest weeks of summer; then she relied on barbiturates pilfered from the hospital pharmacy.

Yuki had nearly escaped evacuation altogether.

Bainbridge Island, because of its naval installations, was the first area on the Coast to be cleared of its Japanese. The Army put out Exclusion Order Number One on March 24, 1942, calling for the Bainbridge evacuation to take place five days later. Although Yuki had resented being evicted from the spacious mossy-roofed Victorian she shared with six Caucasian girls, she was sharp enough not to stick around and argue, particularly when her sailor friends—who'd sworn up and down they'd vouch for her loyalty—failed to deliver on the promise. It had been the booze talking, because it wasn't too bright for an enlisted man to help an eighteen-year-old *nisei* blackout girl—not when Jap subs had been reported in Puget Sound and MacArthur had just shown up in Australia with his tail between his legs.

Nobody could afford to help Yuki Ota—except Yuki Ota. Had it ever been any different? So, she put on a pair of jade earrings, hopped the night ferry across the sound to Seattle, and convinced a hawk-nosed woman who ran a brothel on the top floor of a waterfront hotel that she was Cindy Lee. The Army was harping about voluntary relocation. She'd done one better than that: a voluntary ancestry change. Being Chinese was like being an honorary Caucasian, the pearliest shade of yellow. And nobody seemed to recognize the often hairsplitting differences between Chinese and Japanese features, even sailors and Marines who had served in the Orient. In fact, she could recall a potted lance corporal reeling in his beer-soaked skivvies as he toasted her: "Baby, here's to Chinese-American friendship!"

"*Banzai!*"

"*Banzai* my ass!" he said, choking on a mouthful of brew. "You're a fucking card, Cindy!"

Miss Lee had squirreled away five grand by the time the volunteerism suddenly fell out of the bottom of relocation and

110,000 *yabos* were trundled off to ten camps in some of the worst badlands in the West. But she might have gone on enjoying the wartime benefits of being Chinese had there not been a changing of the guard in city government. Before her madam could come to terms with the new chief of police, the brothel was raided and everybody was given a jovial paddy wagon ride down to the station—nothing more than a brief shutdown until the wrinkles in the new patronage system could be ironed out, she believed.

Sure enough, the charges against the girls were dismissed within twenty-four hours, and all were released—except Cindy Lee.

One of the cops had worked in nearby Everett before the war and thought he remembered her from a bust there at an American Legion Monte Carlo Night that had gotten out of hand. He took it upon himself to send Cindy Lee's fingerprints to the Bureau of Criminal Identification in Olympia; and, naturally, they had come back matched to one Yukiko Ota, an American Japanese formerly of Bainbridge Island with six prior solicitation offenses. She was remanded to the FBI, who hollered about prosecuting her for violating something called Public Law 503 and Roosevelt's Executive Order 9066. But in the end, the agents only turned her over to a pair of fat goons with MP armbands and admittedly unloaded rifles, who escorted her all the way to the main gate at Manzanar War Relocation Center, a thousand miles from any Washington-state friends or former clients she might have had in the camp at Minidoka, Idaho.

That was in August of 1942. Manzanar looked like a slum on the surface of the moon. A dusty wind kicked up that afternoon and blew for a week straight. Yuki was given a mattress cover, shown how to fill it with straw ticking, then lay on it for two days without rising, not even for water.

To her, coping had always meant the freedom to move on. It had started when she ran away from home in Portland at sixteen, mostly because her stepfather—who, more than any *hakujin* she had ever encountered, deserved to be called a *keto*, or hairy ape—couldn't keep his hands off her when he drank, and partly because nothing interesting ever happened in Portland. Now she could go nowhere beyond the barbed wire. It was like being home again. And her skin, decidedly her best asset, became parched and flaky after only a week of exposure to the desert wind.

But Yuki had not survived this long by feeling sorry for herself.

Gradually her spirits were lifted by the realization that the WRA had landed her in the midst of over a thousand unattached males. True, cash was scarce in Manzanar, and discreet working space scarcer; yet, in the relative terms of evacuation, she knew that she could prosper here.

There had been adjustments, of course—like the first time she did an old *issei* who probably hadn't been laid since leaving Yamaguchi prefecture in his teens. Smiling gratefully, he took an object from his neatly bundled clothes. It proved to be a rubber ring, which he snugged around his somewhat flaccid penis. A *himinikawa*, he explained when she looked confused, a pleasure ring to keep him erect all night long—if she so desired. She did not so desire, but couldn't bring herself to tell him: to please men is to survive, that much she remembered from her mother, a "picture bride" who got off the boat in Portland only to discover that her groom, a virile twenty-five-year-old in the photograph she was clutching, was pushing sixty.

Then a *kibei*, a *nisei* educated in Japan, acquainted her with *hiroguki*, dried stalks of taro that he wrapped around his member to enlarge its proportions. Surprisingly, the stalks felt light and soft yet created a pleasant burning sensation inside her. When she professed a liking for his *hiroguki*, the same *kibei*, who was assigned to Manzanar's experimental guayule-rubber farm, proudly presented her with her first *harigata*, that life-sized appliance that is both like a man and better than a man.

So, Yuki adapted to the ways of her new *issei* customers,

whom she found to be more artful and inventive at love than their *hakujin* counterparts—although the few *nisei* she had bedded were as predictable as any *keto*.

Recently, a prewar millionaire had begged her to marry him, although she had gently reminded him that everything he was offering her now belonged to the Caucasians. He had been foolish enough to imagine that he was the same man without the big tuna cannery. A common enough delusion in camp. December 7 had split each life into irreconcilable halves, one prewar and one evacuee. But Yuki somehow felt superior in that, by virtue of persisting in her old ways, she alone, of all the shuffling mouse-faced thousands, had kept herself whole. She was the same person she had always been.

A jeep accelerating in approach now brought her to the window. She thought that her client was finally arriving.

But it was only the MP lieutenant. The light from a bulb over a warehouse dock shone across his rugged profile as he passed by and continued down First Street. Briefly, she wondered what it would be like with him: he was quiet, yet with something of the roughneck in him. He was also very big, a foot and a half taller than most evacuees, but didn't seem intimidating like some of the taller *hakujin*.

How much time had passed? A half hour? An hour? Whatever—it was time to give up and go back. Tonight's client had apparently found some other way to satisfy his strange itches. She patted the *harigata* in her coat pocket, not her personal one but one she had ordered from her *kibei* friend to use in her work. There were a few men who preferred to be gratified in this way. And thinking of unusual requests: she had a midnight appointment with three elderly men who would ask her to blanch her plain broad face with rice powder and pretend to be some elegant geisha they had worshiped in the storybook land of their youth. After they had drunk enough (while she hid her yawns behind a fan), they would half sing, half sob through "*Kimi ga yo*"—a morose Japanese "Star-Spangled Banner," as best as she understood the words. Finally, they would get down to discussing her "pillowing price," only to haggle like pig farmers.

Still, it was better than working forty-eight hours for four dollars in the camouflage net factory.

♦ ♦ ♦

Jared parked the jeep in front of the white clapboard house. As he'd expected, all the windows were darkened.

He had something of a soft spot for old Morris Wenge. But to a man, the other MPs despised him—for his Quaker ways, his habit of referring to the evacuees and himself as "we," even for his brushy gray eyebrows, which unraveled off the sharp ledge of his brow like smoke. Reluctantly, Wenge had wound up with the directorship because of infighting between the Justice and War Departments early in the war—it still wasn't clear who really ran the show.

From the beginning, the Justice Department boys, liberal attorneys for the most part, were scared stiff that when anti-Japanese feeling eventually died down they would be left holding the evacuation bag, which by then would be riddled full of constitutional holes by the likes of the American Civil Liberties Union. The War Department boys, who had few lawyers and even fewer liberals in their ranks, wanted camp bosses who wouldn't coddle the Japs. What it boiled down to for Manzanar was a tired old Quaker from the Agriculture Department being made director, with a former Navy officer appointed his exec to make sure Brother Wenge didn't get carried away with this "we" business.

The associate director, Montgomery Robert Lee, had his damaged side, but he also had a sweet-natured facet that shone, almost dazzled, through his bouts of melancholy. Virginia-born and bred, he had a gentility to his Southernness that Jared, whose sharecropper ancestors had abandoned Alabama at the turn of the century for the Oklahoma land rush, secretly envied.

Yet, in having a natural affection for Monty, Jared couldn't bring himself to dislike Morris Wenge, Lee's implacable foe. The thing Will Rogers had said about himself was just as true of his fellow Sooners: It was a good man's failing to like everybody. How many times had Jared watched his brother whip some poor fool half senseless in a tavern brawl, then smooth down the guy's hair and buy him a beer, treating him from that point on like his long-lost cousin? Maybe his kin just couldn't stand seeing somebody so hurting and licked. Once, during a precious hour alone with Kimiko, Jared had brought this up, and she'd whispered back, "Your brother was acting out a ritual."

He had smiled. "What's that?"

"Well, it's like a key to understanding what goes on inside a people."

A little peeved all at once, he said that he'd never thought of his folks as being a *people*, that he didn't even know what an Okie was the first time a Californian called him one. But, patiently, she went on in that satiny college-girl voice of hers to explain what losing the Civil War—after so much courage and sacrifice—had done to Southerners: how they glorified lost causes, how they almost took pleasure in losing. It wasn't easy to hear these things from her lips. Which was usually a tip-off that something was true, he admitted to himself. Sometimes he had to wring the truth's neck before he could embrace it; but she had a point—there was poetry in losing.

She had also said that he was sentimental, that he often did things purely for sentimental reasons—as if there was something wrong in that.

A bright green meteorite plunged out of the thick of the Milky Way and disappeared behind Director Wenge's house.

Stars—he'd never seen so many until coming to this country.

From under the eaves of the house came a tinkling of windchimes. Manzanar High School kids had made them for a few of the staff—the best-liked ones, he supposed. Jared had mailed his to his mother in San Bernardino, who then wrote that they sounded real pretty when the breezes pushed through the orange groves, and weren't *the Japs clever with their hands?* Morris Wenge's chimes continued to clink against one another—cool air was finally flowing down off the Sierra. Jared wanted to luxuriate in it for a while, but it was time to wake the man.

He crushed his smoke underfoot, then strode to the front door. "Mr. Wenge . . . ?"

There was no answer, even after a second knock.

He was on the verge of saving his report about Shido's death until morning when a voice of caution reminded him that the director would want to know about it right away so he could prepare a briefing for his superiors and even the press, who might be rattling his cage first thing in the morning. Wenge would be hopping mad, and justifiably too, if the Presidio brass or the FBI rang him at dawn, demanding to know why the hell his Japs were chopping each other up with swords and he didn't have a clue as to what they were talking about. Both Fourth Army Intelligence and the FBI had a knack of finding out about camp goings-on without being informed through official channels. Wenge suspected Monty Lee, and Monty accused evacuees of being on the FBI payroll. Jared was beyond caring, but didn't want Wenge to suffer any embarrassment come morning.

Treading softly, he made his way around the house, careful not to blunder across the rock garden as he had once before. An *issei* gardener raked the gravel in graceful patterns around boulders that jutted up like islands from a calm bay, and Wenge would spend hours in a lawn chair before the miniature vista. With no family, he had loads of empty hours to fill.

But for the bad feelings between Wenge and Lee, Jared would have never wound up with the headache of supervising the evacuee police department. In the other camps the associate director was charged with this duty, but Wenge had refused to let Lee ramrod Hank Fukuda, afraid that Monty's past profession would put a martial stamp on internal security. At last, a compromise had been hammered out by the civilian and Army bosses in San Francisco: Lieutenant Campbell, with his civilian police experience, would keep tabs on the Japanese cops *in addition to continuing to serve as executive officer of the MP company, whose mission remains to provide external security to the project.*

Everybody was pleased with the arrangement except Lieutenant Campbell.

It was dark on the small cement patio behind the house. He started to rap on the screen frame, but then realized that the door behind it was shut—unusual for a summer night, when everybody kept doors and windows open to the breezes.

He went to the bedroom window and scratched the screen twice with a fingernail. "Mr. Wenge?"

The lower sash had been propped up with a stick, but it made it no easier to see inside the room, which seemed black in contrast to the grayness outdoors.

"Jared Campbell here, sir."

He wondered if the fresh experience in the judo *dojo* was tricking his senses: he had just imagined catching a coppery whiff of blood. Some odors have a way of clinging to the hairs inside a man's nose, like those given off by a charred body. He dismissed the faint smell as just that—Masao Shido's death was lingering inside his nostrils; it would do so until he could shower.

"Sorry to bother you, sir, but we've got a problem."

Nothing.

No, wait—Jared pressed his ear against the brittle fabric of the screen. A fan was going in the living room. Why hadn't Wenge set it on his nightstand to stir the air where he slept?

Jared stood there listening and the murmuring began to suggest a sound more like running liquid than the whirring of fan blades.

"Mr. Wenge, you awake, sir?"

Static. Jared realized it was the static from a radio tuned to a station that had gone off the air for the night.

His nostrils suddenly flared. He had caught it again—more strongly now: the rich metallic stench of blood.

Sidestepping back to the door, he unholstered his Colt .45 pistol, rammed a cartridge into the chamber. Then he tested the latch—and was glad he had before deciding to kick in the door. It was unlocked.

He kept his finger outside the trigger guard should Morris

Wenge suddenly step from a room and groggily ask what he was doing prowling around his house brandishing a sidearm. Morris Wenge hated guns. He had often said so.

Fumbling in the dimness of the living room, Jared discerned the curved top of the radio. He found the knob and flicked off the loud hissing. Now in his late sixties, Morris Wenge slept so fitfully his lights were ordinarily guttering across *Hakujin* Country two hours before dawn. He could never sleep through such loud rasping.

The abrupt silence roared in Jared's ears. He had to hold his breath to hear anything over his own pulse.

A gasp came from an open door. He spun toward the bathroom, froze, then slowly exhaled between clenched teeth. It had been the leaky toilet tank, sighing as it leveled off. He slid his sweaty finger off the trigger once again.

The hallway floorboards carped under his weight. Hesitating outside the partially open door to the bedroom, he prayed that he'd hear the rhythmic swells of breathing coming from the faint outlines of the four-poster bed. But he had to force himself to turn on the wall switch without benefit of such assurance.

A sound escaped him—but he didn't realize it. It wasn't a scream or a shout or a moan or like any noise he had ever made before. It was just the sound, barely human, of air being expelled from from his lungs as he clenched his guts in his arms. He didn't know if he was standing or collapsing; he seemed to be suspended in horror, floating in a ball of lightning from which bizarre questions snapped:

Why was Morris Wenge using a red woolen blanket in heat like this?

No—Jared's eyes struggled to inform his oxygen-starved mind: it was a bed sheet, its top portion so blood-soaked that little of its whiteness remained.

And why was the director hiding beneath the sheet like a frightened child?

But no—Wenge's naked shoulders and half of his neck could be seen above the sheet. The jarring incompleteness of the scene grayed out Jared's vision for an instant. Sounds like a board being sawed confused him until he realized they were his own labored breaths.

Then his dazed eyes began darting around the room in search of Morris Wenge's severed head.

"Jesus—no!"

It had come to rest on the far side of the four-poster.

The one thing about the moment Jared knew even then that he would always recall, and with perfect clarity too: the gaping expression on the director's waxen face suggested that he wanted to broach something vital but had forgotten what it was he wanted to say.

CHAPTER 4

Nicholas Bleecher reached for his wristwatch on the nightstand. It was several seconds before his eyes could focus the two phosphorescent smears into hour and minute hands: ten after one. The shade was half-raised to admit some air, and he could see the Golden Gate Bridge, black and skeletal against a sheen of stars. No fog would be rolling in this morning.

Rising on an elbow, he lit a cigarette and caught her in the flaring of the match. Seeing her like this—lying on her side, the curvature of her hip swelling the sheet, her breasts squeezed together by her pale arms—he could almost feel affection for her. Almost. Large areolas were said to be the badges of a passionate temperament, but Bleecher was beginning to wonder if those big pink rosettes were hers by mistake. She was so wooden, so dull, it was a wonder she could correct his spelling and grammar as well as she did.

And now the usual problem was cropping up.

She assumed that physical intimacy gave her the right to express her silly little thoughts, bare her peanut of a soul. This evening over dinner atop the Mark Hopkins Hotel, she had actually asked him if he thought she more resembled Laverne Andrews than Rita Hayworth. He had been on the verge of marshaling a patronizing chuckle, but then something else seized him—a malicious feeling for her so sudden and intense he was more surprised than she when he reached across the table and slapped her face. She wept. He apologized, of course, and they quickly left. Thank God they'd both been out of uniform.

Perhaps his anger had exploded from knowing exactly what was coming, step by dreary step, the hints only a child would imagine to be discreet, all adding up to: When did he intend to abandon his middle-aged wife palatially ensconced across the bay in Berkeley? At forty-seven, he had no intention of separating himself from Gracious's money; he had even put some properties that had come his way by windfall in her name, so as to throw any muckrakers from the *San Francisco Chronicle* off the scent.

Bleecher smiled, a bit sadly, as he studied the sleeping girl in the wan light. Twenty years old. A sassy-looking little tart, especially when suited up in her WAC uniform, her red hair pulled up under a tan kepi.

Soon he would have to come down hard on her delusions. But not too hard. Otherwise, she might look elsewhere for protection in the male dominion of the Presidio. He had made a considerable investment of time in her. And he had only recently conditioned her to fellatio. While still somewhat clumsy in her ministrations, she was improving with each effort. She was even beginning to pretend to enjoy it.

"Vickie?"

She snuggled her face deeper into the pillow.

"Victoria . . ." He slid his hand between her thighs, then up to the moist apex of her legs.

Her eyes startled open—an instant of confusion before she realized where she was.

"I've got a call coming in, baby."

She groaned. "Okay." Swinging her legs over the side of the bed, she sat slope-shouldered for a few moments, the complexion of her back china-white, not freckled like the other

California redheads Bleecher had bedded. When she finally rose, he once again appreciated her pouty haunches.

"Don't forget to run the water in the tub."

"Okay," she mumbled, then closed the bathroom door behind her.

He checked his watch again: it was time.

Through the closed door came splashing sounds as she dutifully opened the taps. He snuffed out his smoke in the crystal ashtray and padded to the window. Before lowering the sash and shade, he glanced down on the parking lot behind the brick headquarters of Fourth Army Intelligence. The roving sentry was nowhere in sight, not that it really mattered.

The colonel had not requested one of the handsome officers' houses set among the eucalyptus and Monterey pines on this parklike post at the tip of the San Francisco peninsula. That would have meant that Gracious could then join him. Instead, he had established himself in small but comfortable bachelor quarters on the second story of the Civil War-era building. Ostensibly, this was so he could coordinate G-2 operations around the clock; but it also provided him with a convenient means of summoning members of the secretarial pool to his quarters at hours that otherwise might seem improper to their WAC officers.

At last the phone rang.

Bleecher waited until the fourth ring so as not to seem too anxious. "Yes?"

"I have something to report. . . ." The soft voice trailed off into shallow breathing. Bleecher had heard the panic in it, but reassured himself that, even under the calmest of circumstances, this was a high-strung personality he was dealing with. But there was something else in the timbre of the voice, something unmistakable to a man who had been a prosecuting attorney in civilian life—guilt.

"Go on," Bleecher said.

For several seconds, only static came across the line. Then, "Something unfortunate has happened here."

"It's aborted then?"

"No, no—nothing like that . . ." The man laughed quietly, ineffably, then fell silent.

"Talk to me, dammit."

Ice clinked in a glass. "Nothing is changed. Except . . . to take advantage of the unexpected is consistent with the principle of *Tai No Sen*—"

"What the hell are you talking about?" Bleecher interrupted.

"The Way of the Sword. A code for warriors."

"Are you alone?"

"Terribly."

"Go to sleep."

"I don't think I can right now. Everything's still going to happen. I want to get out."

"No."

"I need ever so much to leave here."

"I can't let you do that. Stay in your quarters. I'll fly over in the morning." Bleecher hoped there would be no thunderstorms over the Sierra Nevada. Already that week, the surly granite hump had claimed another B-26 being ferried across the country by a female pilot. "Are you still there?"

A long sigh. "Yes. Whatever happens, I always seem to be here. This hell was planned with me in mind. Good night."

Bleecher sat for a moment with the receiver propped under his chin, making a quick assessment. Caution on the phone had deprived him of all the facts, but it was clear that something had gone wrong.

"Nick?" Vickie's face was thrust through the crack between the bathroom door and its jamb. "Can I come out now?"

"No."

The door slammed shut.

He tried exhaling the irritation out of his voice as he dialed an inter-post number. There would be no more sleep tonight, perhaps none for a few days.

It was picked up on the sixth ring; the man was getting old. "Yes?"

"Colonel Bleecher here, sir. Sorry to disturb you."

"That's quite all right, my boy," Lieutenant General James Van Zwartz lied.

◆ ◆ ◆

There were easier and only slightly less accurate ways to sketch Masao Shido's death scene than the coordinate method. But Hank Fukuda insisted that his men run a string from opposite corners of the judo *dojo* office. To this imaginary line on his plot he connected everything inside the room, no matter how seemingly trivial, and carefully recorded the distances that he himself determined with a metal tape measure.

Shido had lost a great quantity of blood. Hank estimated four quarts. This was only further indication that the alien had experienced two lifetimes: one from birth to age fifty-nine; and a second, eternally longer one that began when he inched the *aikuchi* into the softest part of his body—and ended only when his second brought down the tardy sword.

Hank glanced up at the bare light bulb, realizing that this dusty little sun was the last thing Shido had fixed his eyes on before the onset of oblivion. Then the chief squared the tape over the center of the bloodstain in which Shido had writhed. "Ready to copy?" he asked Patrolman Wada, who was holding the clipboard for him.

"You betcha." Over the past twenty minutes, the enormous young man had been slipping tangles of dried cuttlefish strips out of his uniform shirt pocket, chewing them whenever he thought the chief wasn't watching.

"Thirty-seven inches." Hank took another measurement. "And jot down twenty-two inches and a quarter to the eastern extremity of the stain."

"You betcha."

"What you got in your mouth?"

"*Nanchu* say?"

"You heard what I said."

Wada's multiple chins stopped jiggling. "Nutting."

Hank fought back a smile. They were a different breed, these Hawaiian-bred *nisei*. For one thing, he had overheard Wada boasting about the big cedar *ofuro* his family had outside their shanty on the sugar plantation. A California *nihonjin* would be mortified to have one of the traditional soaking tubs in his backyard. What the hell would the *hakujin* neighbors think? It was bad enough they suspected Japanese families of getting naked together for some kind of pagan fertility rite. City-bred, Hank had never even been in an *ofuro* until he came to camp. But Hawaiian Japanese seemed less inclined than their mainland cousins to conform, to blend in, to please the *hakujin*—maybe the carefree spirit of aloha had toned down these frenetic and essentially Nipponese compunctions.

Hank glanced at Wada's feet. The man's white socks showed beneath his baggy trousers. "What happened to your shoes?"

"Nutting."

"Then where the hell are they?"

"On porch, I betcha."

The Fukudas had skipped the mid-Pacific steppingstone to the United States. While most immigrants worked as contract laborers on Hawaiian sugar plantations before stealing away to better opportunities on the mainland, Sentaro Fukuda, a samurai displaced by the collapse of the feudal system, had sailed directly from Honshu to San Francisco in 1869, testing the sincerity of an imperial edict that allowed Japanese to leave their homeland for the first time in over two centuries. Inland at Gold Hill, he helped establish the Wakamatsu Colony, the Nipponese Plymouth on the North American continent, which eventually failed because of drought, its thirty members scattering—some back to Japan, some staying in America.

At first Californians welcomed the few Japanese to reach their shores as being superior to the Chinese, who were believed to be violent and vice-ridden. Yet, within a few decades, the Oriental exclusion societies saved their worst venom for the Jappers, who all at once were held to be twice as brutal and profligate as the Celestials. Additionally, it was believed that the Japanese race was capable of rodent-like prolificness, although census information never supported this fear. A rash of laws made it impossible for these *issei* to own the land they had reclaimed from desert and swamp, or to become citizens after decades of legal residency—even after service in the Spanish-American and First World Wars, in some cases.

In thinking back on that half century of orchestrated bias, Hank Fukuda could recognize the seeds of internment.

In Hawaii, which had proved on the morning of December 7 to be a bona fide war zone, fewer than a thousand Japanese were interned. In fact, Wada's uncle was still working for the Navy shipyards as a pipe fitter. Yet, in California, Oregon, and Washington—a paper fantasy of a war zone—110,000 men, women, and children of any Japanese ancestry down to a sixteenth part were trundled off to ten camps in the most godforsaken wastelands imaginable.

This was one of the inconsistencies of the Great Evacuation that could drive an evacuee mad, if he dwelt on such riddles. Even the words used by the government to mask the realities were riddles: Hank knew himself to be an inmate, not an *evacuee*; and Manzanar was a concentration camp, not a *relocation center*. Although established on a model seemingly designed by the Junior Chamber of Commerce and administrated by an uneasy coalition of social workers and armed guards, Manzanar was nonetheless a dustbin in which the distrusted and unwanted were stored—by force, if necessary. The barbed wire and machine guns were not formalities, as much as Morris Wenge pretended them to be.

Hank shook his head. Poor Wada. He might now be gamboling across Waikiki's sands had his parents not encouraged him to give up sumo wrestling and go to a trade college in San Diego.

Hank's pulse had quickened. He took a few deep breaths, then shrugged: *shikata ga nai*—nothing can be done. An expression suitable for all occasions, but none as apt as internment.

Suddenly, the light blinked off in the office. Then a loud wail undulated out of the south, a sound so unfamiliar it took several seconds for him to realize it was the hand-operated air-raid siren in the MP compound. Letting the tape snake back onto its spool, he glanced at Wada, who was wearing an insipid grin, as if to say: Is somebody actually going to bomb *us?*

Another patrolman raced in through the door, squeezing his cap in his fist. "Chief—!"

Hank quieted him with a gesture, then strode out under the pavilion.

The night was wildly kaleidoscopic, although the power had been cut to the camp. The searchlights cross-stitched the darkness, probing facilities that had never been disturbed before, like the orphanage diagonally across the firebreak from the judo school. A pair of Maryknoll sisters had come outside to see what was wrong, their Japanese faces seeming all the more moon-shaped for being framed by the headdresses of their habits. A half-breed child, one of several sent to the camp by their Caucasian mothers, joined the nuns to gawk at the dizzying array of light but was finally noticed and scolded back inside.

Hank tried to filter out the caterwauling of the siren to listen for something droning across the huge sky. But no aircraft engines hummed in approach, nor did the searchlights leave the camp and stretch up toward the stars.

Wada was now standing at his side, breathing shallowly. "What you think, maybe?"

"I don't know."

"An escape, I betcha."

"No," he said quietly.

"You think maybe this it?"

Hank chuckled. "What the hell do you mean by *it?*"

"You know, Chief," Wada said solemnly.

Yes, he knew. But he wasn't about to ratify this fear, which was intensified, not diminished, the longer internment went on. *The next logical step beyond mass detention was mass execution.* The notion was ridiculous, but it was also irradicable, first infecting him while he had languished in the assembly center at Santa Anita Racetrack. He had just strolled over to the paddock—where in another life he'd studied the thoroughbreds over a cold beer—only to be challenged by a kid in khakis, all of seventeen and brandishing a tommy gun, who barked, "Get your fucking yellow ass back to the housing area!" And, on the bus ride to Manzanar, the fear hit him with such certainty he had to open the window for air: the coach would not arrive at a newly built camp. The existence of such a camp was a lie. The driver would simply pull off into some clearing in the Joshua trees. Everyone would be piled out by unusually nervous MPs, who would not be able to bring themselves to make eye contact with the evacuees. A covered truck would back up to within fifty yards of the small uncertain crowd, and the guards would step aside, quickly. The rear canvas flap would be raised from within, revealing a machine gun manned by two soldiers with bright blond hair and steel-blue eyes. . . .

"Here come a jeep," Wada whispered.

The driver could be heard going through his gears like a demon—Morris Wenge abhorred hot-rodding on Manzanar's streets. And then a second vehicle, the MPs' heavy truck, halted at the fenced end of the firebreak to offload a sentry before lumbering out of sight again with its cargo of restless troops.

Bayonets. The MPs had fixed bayonets, something they hadn't done in a long while.

At last, the jeep turned the corner nearest the *dojo,* cutting too sharply and bouncing over the furrows of a victory garden. Hank didn't realize how keenly he had been hoping for Jared Campbell's return until he saw that it was Osler, the first sergeant, who was sitting in the passenger bucket, his burly arms folded over his chest. Noticing Hank and his men on the *dojo* steps, he motioned for his driver to stop.

Rising from his seat but not stepping down, Osler nudged his helmet back off his glistening forehead. "What do you think you're doing?"

Hank figured Osler hadn't recognized them to be evacuee police. "We're wrapping up a death investigation, Sergeant."

"Inside—and stay there."

"I don't think you understand. Lieutenant Campbell—"

"It don't matter if I understand, Fukuda! This is a lockdown!"

Hank hiked his chin toward his department's worn vehicle, a Ford station wagon. "Can we drive back to our PD?"

"Nothing unauthorized moves."

"How about if we stay out here on the platform?"

"Get inside that fucking door!"

The jeep roared away.

Slowly, Hank turned and led his men back into the office. Too benumbed to feel his own humiliation, he saw it reflected in their faces. He stood apart from them, hands clasped behind him.

The miasma of Shido's death seemed stronger after his brief absence from the stifling room. The beams rummaged across the windows with a disturbing lack of rhythm. Until this moment, the metronomic sweeping had seemed like the ticking of a cuckoo clock, something only peripherally apparent. But now that the entire universe had been somehow thrown out of kilter, Hank wondered how he could possibly hope to sleep in the wash of such fitful lights. He wanted to sleep.

"Chief?" It was Wada, his voice a low growl.

"Yes."

"That buggah Osler. He jam me up all the time. I go fix him someday." He made a twisting gesture with his fat hands.

Hank's lips tightened. "Enough." He couldn't let his men disparage the MPs, as much as he agreed that the first sergeant—who had been reprimanded by Lieutenant Campbell for whipping an evacuee with a spring-loaded sap and then cleared of any wrongdoing by Captain Snavely—was indeed a "buggah." Yet, he had no illusions about his own meager sway: it emanated from the *hakujin*, and to undermine their authority was to sabotage his own. His personal feelings, the gnawing sense of outrage that never let go of him, had nothing to do with it.

The siren finally wound down to silence.

No one said anything inside the office for forty-five minutes.

Eventually, a few of the men, made weary by not knowing what was going to happen next, slumped down onto the mats, heads bowed. Snapping his fingers, Hank signaled them to stand again: he couldn't bear to see them so defeated-looking.

At last, Campbell's man, Elwayne, arrived by jeep and called the chief out. Hank strolled through the door into an unexpected coolness—the nightly breeze had begun flowing off the Sierra. "What's up, Corporal?"

"Hell if I know. You're to grab your gear and come with me on the double."

"What about my men? They've been stuck in here for nearly an hour."

"I got orders to take just you to our compound."

Hank looked puzzled; in two and a half years he had never stepped inside the military police enclave.

He ducked back into the office to tell his men to sit tight for as long as it took him to find out what was going on. He would get permission from the lieutenant for them to return to the station, or even back to their barracks, if possible.

Then Elwayne stomped on the pedal, and they sped toward the main gate at fifty miles an hour.

Into the praetorium, Hank thought.

CHAPTER 5

Osler loomed at the distant end of the corridor, his hands fisted on his pistol belt. The waxed linoleum captured his reflection and stretched it all the way down to Hank Fukuda's loafers.

His tour of the lockdown complete, the first sergeant had rolled his sleeves up to his biceps, a hint of the informality the MPs enjoyed in their own nest, or maybe only a loosening of the regs in Captain Snavely's absence—Hank had no idea which. He was a stranger here.

Osler's lips puckered as if he intended to spit; he probably thought he was smiling.

The chief continued down the corridor, two paces behind Elwayne. An MP brushed past him, adjusting his helmet chin strap as he hurried out, but Hank kept his eyes firmly on Osler's. *He hates me only for my face. There's nothing more to it than that.*

"What's he doing in here?" Osler asked Elwayne.

"Lieutenant's orders, Top."

The first sergeant sucked in a long breath and held it as

he glared at Hank. Then, whistling tunelessly, he turned and sauntered inside the gun-rack room, from which a clash then echoed, that of a rifle bolt being opened and driven shut.

Elwayne rapped on Captain Snavely's door, and Jared Campbell's muffled voice came from within: "Enter."

He was sitting on a corner of the captain's desk, as if unwilling to take the company commander's chair. The telephone receiver was scrunched between his ear and shoulder. Unsmiling, he motioned for Hank to be seated, then dismissed Elwayne with a careless salute that became a cup-gesture, meaning coffee for the chief.

Hank waved off the offer, and the corporal withdrew.

"If you can't find Captain Snavely," Campbell said into the phone, "I need to talk to Colonel Bleecher right away." He paused, listening with a frown. Hank could hear a faint squawk on the other end, but couldn't make out the words. "No, I'm not leaving any message except this: I want the colonel or one of his people to phone me. That's Lieutenant J. Campbell, the 319th MP Escort Guard Company, at the number I've given you twice in the last five minutes. . . ."

Hank realized that, with a few more years, the already pronounced lines in the lieutenant's face would deepen into gullies, and then he would be more gaunt-looking than angularly handsome—a typically weathered, rawboned cropper. But it also struck the chief that whatever had happened this evening, it had visibly aged Jared Campbell. His cheeks were sunken, the skin like gray flannel.

"This *is* an emergency," Campbell went on, hoarsely now. "Otherwise, why would I even *think* of asking you to disturb the colonel? No, I can't tell you that. So you get somebody to wake Bleecher, you hear?" He slammed down the receiver.

Hank expected him to cuss or at least grumble a bit. But Campbell just slumped there, his eyes fixed absently on his bony chapped fingers, which he had steepled together.

First things first, Hank decided. "My boys are still stuck inside the *dojo* office."

Campbell glanced up, pulling himself out of his trance. "Shit." Stiffly, he got up, cracked the door, and hollered, "Elwayne!"

The corporal trotted in, chrome bayonet in one hand and a sharpening stone dripping oil in the other. "Lieutenant?"

"Let the towers know what you're doing, then grab my jeep and escort the chief's crew back to the PD. But before you do that, tell Osler to man the phone in here. I'll be in BOQ. And *if* Mr. Lee turns up, send him over." Campbell strapped on his holster, then inclined his head for Hank to follow him out. "Got to talk with no interruptions."

But a buck sergeant delayed Campbell in the corridor. "Getting calls from staff, sir—they want to know when the power's coming back on."

The breath whistled out the lieutenant's nose. "How the hell do I know?! I didn't pull the goddamned master switch!"

The sergeant looked sheepish. "It's in lockdown circular, sir. Everything blacked out except us and the towers. What should I say to them?"

"Tell them the electrician's trying to fix what we fucked up."

"Like *that*, sir?"

"Christ Almighty. Come on, Hank."

They stepped out the front door onto an expanse of gravel that crunched underfoot. A footpath marked by whitewashed stones led to a hutment that looked like a low-rent duplex near the shipyards in Long Beach. Hank couldn't recall it being visible from the camp, and when he'd arrived in '42 the MPs had been living in conical tents.

Campbell unlocked one of the hutment's two doors, shuffled inside, and tugged on the chain to an overhead fixture.

It was his personal room, stuffy from having been closed up all evening. Hank stood awkwardly in its sparse midst, feeling as if he were spying on a part of the man's life that had always been closed to him.

"Get comfortable while I pour," Campbell said. "Toss your kit anywheres."

Hank sat on the bed because it seemed only fitting that the lieutenant take the straight-back chair at the small desk. On its dusty surface was a stack of books, and he really felt like a spy as he scanned the titles: a Bible, of course; Webster's dictionary, its spine more flaked from opening than the Bible's; an English grammar, also well used; John Steinbeck's *The Grapes of Wrath*; and Tolstoy's *War and Peace*—something of a surprise, although the pages were cleaved early in the peace by a red ribbon, the kind county fairs hand out as prizes. He believed the framed photograph on the green plasterboard wall to be of the president, but knew he couldn't meet that warm, benevolent gaze without feeling betrayed. He too had once had a portrait of Franklin Roosevelt on his bedroom wall.

All in all, Campbell's quarters were neat, but not Army neat. Like Hank, he had been a bachelor too long before the war caught up with him.

Campbell handed him a tumbler with four fingers of whiskey in it. Hank took a careful sip. Sour mash bourbon. He smiled as an inane tune ran through his head: "It's Been a Long, Long Time." When he nodded his thanks, he saw in the other man's eyes that the drink had been to prepare him for bad news. The lieutenant hadn't touched his own glass.

"Hank," he began softly, "I need your help on something that could blow the lid off this place. Even the troops don't really know what's up—except Osler. Can I count on you?"

Briefly, Hank felt a wave dizziness—Campbell's tone of voice was that unsettling. "Sure."

"I appreciate it . . . I really do." He polished off his bourbon in three quick bobs of his Adam's apple. Then he told Hank what had happened to Morris Wenge. When he was done, nothing was said between the men for at least a minute, although they continued to watch each other.

Finally, Hank had to clear his throat. "The scene is secured, I'm sure."

"Full perimeter guard. Nobody's been inside the house except me and Osler. And I made sure he touched nothing."

"Fine," Hank said, then looked down. "The director was a good man."

"Yes, I was damn proud to know him."

"I mean, it took somebody *hateful* to kill him."

Campbell rose abruptly out of his chair: he had forgotten to open the window, and the two men men were lathered in sweat. "We both know who comes to mind first."

"Shido?"

Campbell dipped his head once as he savored the cool sage-scented air that gushed in. "Any thoughts on him as our boy?"

"Well, it's shot through with a lot of ifs."

"Such as?"

"It's possible, I suppose, but how'd he slip in and out of *Hakujin* Country without being noticed?"

Campbell hunched his shoulders as if to admit it was a good point: *Nisei* were known to call on their Caucasian friends on the camp's staff in the early evening, but Masao Shido could have never ventured across First Street, Manzanar's line of racial demarcation, without raising eyebrows. Particularly as night was falling.

"But it's a start," Hank went on, afraid that he had somehow ridiculed the lieutenant's idea. "And we can assume Shido died around ten tonight."

Campbell brightened. "Then if your thermometer says Wenge died an hour or two earlier—say eight or nine—we got ourselves a peg to hang a case on."

"But if not?"

Campbell fell silent. That he had a suspect other than Shido in the back of his mind was betrayed by a restless sweep of his hand through his light-colored hair. This other suspect had to be the sword-wielder, Hank surmised.

"Feel like one more for the road, hoss?"

"No thanks, the sooner I get to work the better."

"You bet. Let me walk you over."

As if there's a choice, thought Hank, but without rancor. He appreciated Campbell's way of putting things: it was nice not to be reminded at every turn that he was a prisoner.

"I've got to wake Mr. Lee while I'm over in that neighborhood," Campbell said. "Siren didn't do the trick, I guess."

Neither man had to say it—the associate director was usually too far gone by midnight to be roused by anything less than a dousing with ice water. Even then, it was an uphill battle to goad him into full consciousness. Monty Lee had to be on his last leg with the San Francisco brass, having recently caved in the corner of a barrack while careening around the darkened camp in his jeep.

Outside, the searchbeams were still on manual. It was disconcerting, this frenzy of light. Hank glanced at Campbell to see how it was affecting him, but the lieutenant kept his eyes on the orange fan-shaped beam his flashlight was spilling across the ground.

Hank badly wanted to say something. But he found it impossible to share what he was thinking: that tomorrow might be like December 8, 1941, all over again. Once more the specter of the truck with the machine gun seemed dismally real to him. His fear prevented him from seeing the absurdity in this notion. His fear didn't know that this was America . . . Hank Fukuda's America.

♦ ♦ ♦

Just like the Army.

A latrine resting on a stained concrete slab. Against one wall a twelve-foot-long trough, its leaky spigots softly drumming the galvanized metal. A lower trough on the adjoining wall for a urinal. And eight toilet bowls without partitions for privacy. Eddie Nitta sat on one of the stools, his trousers up, a midden of cigarette butts between his bare feet. He had slipped off his straw *zoris* to scratch his soles on the rough cement. The hard yellow calluses raised by the Italian countryside were gradually flaking off, and his feet were going soft again, itching as they grew more sensitive with each day he was away from the war.

If anything, he felt puzzlement, not joy, not even a vague sense of relief, that he was still alive. This is what he thought about as he sat there, alone.

He got ready to light another smoke.

It was no mindless trick, not with only one hand. First he tucked the cigarette in the corner of his mouth, then laid the book of matches across his palm. He flipped back the cover with his thumb and pinched off a match with his middle finger and thumbnail. Some of the amputees in the hospital had been able to dispense with the next step and complete the entire operation with the matchbook in hand from start to finish, but Eddie told himself with a raw grin that he was gifted in other ways—like getting *nisei* kids killed by the bushel. He dropped the book to the floor and held it steady with his big toe, the abrasive strip facing up. Then he struck the match and lit his cigarette.

Why not use a Zippo? Because it was a challenge this way. And so few challenges remained.

He shouldn't have gone straight to making love tonight. He should have just lain beside her. Making love this soon had been the same as skipping the floor step, and he'd burned his fingers trying. Yet, sweating across from Kimiko in the hot stillness, he had felt certain that this, at last, was the night to try. He had even had an appetite for the first time since returning. Oh, there were a dozen things he could blame for coming like a rabbit. It had been his first ejaculation in over a year. The lack of privacy in that breathlessly hot shanty. And the loss of his arm. Even if it meant nothing to her—as she pretended so well—the simple and undeniable indignity of his injury was making him suspect her of things. Bad things, things unconscionable for a Japanese wife.

And, more and more, he wanted to trust Kimiko to be just that: his *yome*, a typically double-edged Japanese word that meant both young wife *and* daughter-in-law—just to remind her of *all* her obligations. He laughed to himself. A year ago, the very notion would have seemed ridiculously *bootchie*—Japanesey in *nisei* slang. Kimiko and he were Americans, weren't they? And hell, he was so far from being samurai he had nearly been tagged by the FBI as a PAF, a Premature Anti-Fascist, something Hank Fukuda had managed to doctor out of his camp records so his Army enlistment wouldn't be held up. Eddie had nearly forgone Stanford for the Spanish Civil War and the *Abura hamu Lincoln* Battalion, as his confused parents had called it. Nobody had been more anti-mikado than Ed Nitta.

He flicked his cigarette through the bathhouse portal and into the stagnant-looking waters of the *ofuro*. His eyes grew grim.

Now he wanted to take refuge in Kimiko's and his Japaneseness, however little of it remained. The bonds of fidelity ran through it like threads of steel. Look at his parents and the other *issei* couples—adultery could not penetrate the bulwark of their tightly knit obligations. He had tried to say this to Kimiko with his body, his urgency. But he had failed.

Lastly, Eddie blamed tonight on his outburst at his testimonial dinner.

His parents had not yet forgiven him. He had smeared their faces, as they would put it. The next morning, his mother took down her flag with its single blue star from the sand-scored window. It had damned near killed him to see that star come down. It was him—his spirit, his fucking *kami*—that star.

The day of the dinner had started well enough. Eddie and his father called on family friends, their shoddy little apartments spruced up for the arrival of Major Tadashi Nitta, who found an antidote to his unease in the delicate cups of sake that were passed to him, one after another.

"Tadashi has been suggested for a medal," his father announced in Japanese. So it had begun: that *bootchie* counterpoint to self-deprecation, formalized boasting; Terminal Island fishermen carrying on as if they were *shōgun*.

Eddie hid his frown behind the cup—either his fourth or fifth at that apartment; later he couldn't recall which. Booze had never been his ally.

"*Hai?*" their host exclaimed. "A medal for what?"

His father turned to Eddie with a grin. "Tell Tanaka-*san* for what you will get this cross."

"For being a *kotonk*."

Everyone blinked at him, smiling. "What kind of word is this?" his father finally asked.

"Hawaiian word."

"Most of Eddie's men were *buta*-heads," his father explained. Pig-heads—Hawaiian *nisei*.

The derisive laughter made Eddie look down, but his expression remained detached. "Yes, and a *kotonk* is the hollow sound a coconut makes when it strikes the ground." He seemed unaware of the bewilderment this created. Rising without explanation, he set down his lacquered cup and went to the window. "Jesus Christ . . ."

"What is it, Tadashi?"

"The wind still peels the tar paper right off the roofs."

Silence.

"Nothing has changed," he went on.

"*Hai*, it's all the same," his host said lightly, reaching to fill Eddie's cup again.

"This *kotonk* really cracked the whip, you know. I encouraged them to sacrifice themselves. It got to the point my *hakujin* colonel had to read me the riot act. He must have known. Wasting them wasn't going to change anything back here." Eddie smiled and shook his head. "The roofs still leak."

He was only dimly aware of his father's embarrassment, his host's silence; both seemed insignificant. Time had lost its structure, its predictability, and before he could understand where the afternoon had gone he found himself seated on a dais with an explosion of red, white, and dyed-blue carnations in front of him on a linen tablecloth. Just at the instant the high school glee club began singing "My Country, 'Tis of Thee," the sherbet light of sunset flooded the far end of the mess hall. Eddie had to squint for several seconds before realizing it was Masao Shido standing in the open door with several silhouettes arrayed behind him. Briefly, he thought that Shido had brought along some of his Black Dragon thugs just to intimidate everyone; but the gradual shifting of the light etched faces on the silhouettes, and Eddie was amazed to see Shido's retinue consisting of the young GIs he had ordered to their deaths in Italy. They were all comporting themselves as samurai. It was crazy.

When Shido waved for Eddie to follow, he knew somehow that it was to the Yasukuni Shrine in Tokyo, the receptacle for the souls of departed warriors. It was all Eddie could do to keep from shouting, "You and I will die soon enough, Shido-*san!*"

The door swung shut on the wind with a slam that startled the guests and left them chuckling at their own timidity.

Morris Wenge was pontificating at the lectern with the WRA monogram shining down on the evacuees in their prewar suits and evening gowns. His warm voice was seductive in the ears of a people who took the slightest *hakujin* courtesy as a harbinger that the nightmare might soon end, and they nodded their heads to the soothing tempo of his words. His white eyebrows suggested Santa Claus, and he kept dipping into his bag brimming with solicitudes—especially his habit of referring to the evacuees and himself in the collective we: "*We* have made great strides since December of 1943 . . ." Which was as much as the director ever referred to the MP shooting spree. ". . . and we should have every confidence our population will be further reduced as more and more of us resettle to jobs elsewhere in the country. . . ." As domestics, gardeners, stoop laborers—Eddie suppressed a desire to laugh maniacally. "It pleases me to divulge what I intend to testify before a select congressional committee next month—that, by virtue of the patriotism and constructive attitude of its residents, Manzanar has outlived its usefulness and should be dismantled, its detachment of military police freed for duties more vital to the national defense." Applause. The old man beamed. "And now we come to the purpose of tonight's festivities. . . ."

Eddie realized that, somehow, he had been brought to his feet. More applause, and a big golden key jigsawed out of plywood was thrust into his hands. The key to Manzanar—he tried to fight down a smirk, found it irrepressible, then hoped everyone would mistake his expression for shy gratification. *The fucking key to Manzanar: guaranteed to unlock any door except those opening outward!* He wanted to howl.

He peered out into the well-scrubbed *bootchie* faces. He began speaking, but his voice didn't seem to be his own. "North of Naples . . . we liberated an Italian POW camp. The Germans had cleaned out most of these, hauled all the prisoners north. But we enveloped this one before they could do that. . . ." Smiling, Wenge skidded his chair around so he could face Eddie. "This afternoon, I noticed the tar paper on the chicken coops we call our homes . . . and I realized how much better that Italian camp was than Manzanar. There were slate shingles on the roofs . . . real roofs."

Eddie's eyes had begun to shine, but then he grinned as if to put down the rising murmur in the hall. "I keep looking for my sister out among you." He cupped his hands and shouted, "Emiko?!" Then choked from an attempt to laugh. "Which is kind of drippy, I guess. She's gone. And there's nothing I can do about it. Gone because the hospital didn't have a special pair of forceps for pregnant women. That's the best they can tell me . . . forceps." Then the words surged out of him with such vehemence he looked more surprised than anyone as he glowered down his finger at Morris Wenge. "But I'm not holding the hospital responsible. I'm holding you! I'm holding—!"

Someone had seized him from behind, touching his wound. He winced, although unsure if he actually felt any pain.

His father's stricken face was only inches from his own. "No more—we go."

Reeling against the insistence of his father's grasp, Eddie saw Kimiko helping his mother out the side door, the old woman looking tiny and hunched in the black dress she'd bought for Emiko's wedding. The fair-haired MP lieutenant held the door open for them, and, oddly enough, it looked as if he tried to touch Kimi's forearm as she swept past.

Wenge was talking again, smiling compassionately as always. "I'm sure we understand how you feel, Major Nitta. And let's all pray that by this time next year there shall remain no argument for Manzanar to exist. . . ."

Eddie stopped resisting his father's tugging. Then they were outside in the pinkish dusk, setting off across a firebreak that stretched sandily before them like the Gobi. "Well, I guess I finally got to give my salutatorian speech."

"Shut up, Tadashi," his father hissed.

And that freed the sob that had been lodged in Eddie's chest for months. He wept all the way back to their barrack, the kids halting their baseball game to watch him stagger past on his father's arm. He had laughed as he cried—the stunned, dusty faces of Manzanar's kids had done it to him.

Now, suddenly, the lights in the latrine blinked and then went out. A siren started.

Eddie got up off the toilet and strolled outside, smiling quizzically. From opposite directions two searchlights pounced on him in the same instant. He gave a slight wave toward the towers that left him feeling mousy, but something told him not to move until the beams let go of him.

In less than a minute, a jeep had raced through the narrow space between two barracks and sprayed gravel against his forelegs as it skidded to a halt. An MP first sergeant leaped out and demanded to know Eddie's name and the six-digit number that indicated his block, barrack, and apartment. Shading his eyes with his hand, Eddie told him, and the driver scribbled the information into a notebook. The sergeant then approached on foot and, without warning, grasped Eddie's arm and turned the wrist so he could inspect the fingernails with his flashlight.

"What the hell are you doing, Sergeant?"

He was slipping a leather billy out of his back pocket when he noticed Eddie's khaki trousers and web waist belt. He smiled with one corner of his mouth; it was no less menacing than his scowl. "You in?"

"My ID, which is in my barrack, would inform you that I am *Major* Nitta."

After a long moment, he released Eddie's wrist and saluted. "My apologies, sir."

"Who are you?"

"Sir, First Sergeant Osler."

Eddie turned his ear toward the siren for a moment. "What's going on?"

"I'm not at liberty to say, sir. For the log, may I assume the major was returning to his residence from the latrine when observed?"

"You may."

"The major may find it convenient to remain inside the rest of the night. Good night, sir."

Without being dismissed, the sergeant about-faced and strode back to the jeep. He shared an inaudible wisecrack with his driver as they backed out of the block, and they drove away laughing quietly.

Eddie tried to make nothing more of it—a couple of rear echelon soda jerks looking for a chance to throw their weight around. Yet, despite his intention, he did make something more of it, feeding his resentment by reminding himself that the *hakujin* had made a mistake: they had conditioned him to feel damned little remorse after killing other *hakujin*. Germans and Americans looked alike, as far as he was concerned.

CHAPTER 6

Glancing skyward, Jared turned away from Director Wenge's house for the second time since midnight. The desert stars were wide-eyed, seemingly dabbed up there by that one-eared Dutchman. He couldn't recall the painter's name. Which only convinced him that his self-improvement efforts over the years had gone bust: two semesters of junior college night classes and, later, for no good reason, the correspondence course in long-drawer's music—he figured he was the only Okie alive who knew there was a cow in Tchaikovsky, or gave a damn. Maybe the chief at San Bernardino PD had summed him up when he hired him for a patrolman's slot back in '35. Jared was ten minutes late to the interview: he had gotten into a fistfight with some idler on a street corner who'd made fun of his white shirt and four-in-hand necktie; his only jacket, denim with more white threads showing than blue, had been left at home. When the chief asked him why he was late, Jared told him, straight. The old man nodded. "Who won?"

"Me, sir."

"Good—because that's why I'll hire you, if I do. You're a big ol' muley Okie kid. You grew up on a farm, so you know how to work. You'd probably tell the truth even if I offered you a hundred dollars not to. But one thing, son. You'll have to do something about that accent. Except when you're with your own kind. And I won't mind you doing that—rubbing elbows with the migrants now and again. Keeping an eye out for red agitators."

Jared had no idea what the chief was talking about. But when at last he understood, he quietly said no to spying on union organizers who came into the county. Hell, his cousin Duane was one of them. Nothing came of Jared's resistance, though. By the time he was off probationary status, he was well liked by the rest of the brass; he had proved himself a reliable man with both his fists and a gun, a good door smasher, too. "But otherwise," the chief went on that first day with his shit-eating grin, "the accent—it breeds disrespect. Folks figure anybody what talks like that is stupid. *Are* you stupid?"

Jared's face had remained expressionless. "If I am, I reckon I'm the last person to ask, sir."

He chuckled to himself now, remembering, but then sobered again. For a moment he had forgotten the scene only a few minutes behind him.

Hank Fukuda had paled as he whispered, "Good God." That had shaken Jared more than anything: Hank's blanching at Morris Wenge's decapitated corpse. Yet, somehow, he'd come up with the outward calm to say, "Take your time, Hank. We both know there's no reason to rush. I'll be breaking it to Mr. Lee."

Now he hesitated before crossing the street to Monty's bungalow. The power had come back on at last, and all the lights in the white clapboard apartments of the Caucasian staff were on—all except the associate director's. He shook his head. The siren had awakened every living thing within ten miles—even the sheriff had phoned to gripe, forcing Jared to lie that it was only a security drill. The siren had been Osler's idea; the former speakeasy bouncer was champing at the bit to announce to the world that the Japs had murdered their chief guardian.

Knocking on Monty's door would accomplish nothing.

Jared made certain it was locked before taking a small leather case out of his back pocket. A warded lock, one of the easiest in camp to pick—but then he paused, the tension tool poised in his right hand. He held his breath, hoping to hear sounds of life from within.

Silence, other than a shrill cricket cadence.

Sidestepping around the house, he checked the sills for signs of a forced entry. Nothing was disturbed. The living room drapes were parted a few inches. He slanted his flashlight against the glass so the beam would be dimmed less by its own reflection, and the faint blush skimmed over some disorderly bookshelves, a scabbarded samurai sword on the wall, a bottle of bourbon and a glass on the ebony tea table, and finally onto Monty himself, spread-eagle on the floor. His left leg was cocked at an odd angle across the sofa cushions, suggesting that he had been driven to the floor.

For an instant Jared thought of smashing the glass to reach inside for the latch, then crawling through the window. Instead, he ran back to the front door. He chambered a cartridge, tucked the pistol in his moist armpit, then broke out his pick set again. It was really a simple trick—jiggling the tension tool past the wards at the mouth of the keyhole and then nudging back the bolt. But his fingers were trembling enough to tempt him to stave in the door. He was on the verge of doing just that when the lock snicked open.

Clutching the .45 with his right hand, he threw back the door with his left forearm. Once inside, he immediately ducked around the wall so he wouldn't be backlit by the tower searchlights.

The air was stale with tobacco smoke and whiskey breath. He inched across the living room, keeping to the oval rug to muffle his footfalls. Then he knelt beside Monty and ran the beam over his body. No apparent wounds. He was pinching Lee's thumbnail when the man groaned and withdrew his hand.

"Damn"—Jared exhaled, holstering the .45—"but you can be hard on a friendship." Gently, he kicked the man's veiny foot. "Hoss, it's Jared . . ." It was useless: he was out for the count.

Sadly now, Campbell smiled down on the associate director, his own age within a month, but of slight build and with those delicate yet masculine features the Southern aristocracy fancied to be its mark of Cain. His dark brown hair seemed almost black in comparison to his pasty skin; his avoidance of the sun was nearly a mania.

The telephone lay overturned on the floor beside him. Jared dialed the MP switchboard and asked for Osler, who reported no word yet from the Presidio. "All right," he said wearily, "I'll be at Mr. Lee's residence the next hour or so."

"Very good, Lieutenant." As always, the first sergeant's tone of voice was too accommodating to be sincere.

Jared turned on a lamp and studied the associate director for a moment. "Mr. Lazarus, I recommend you get your ass up, *now*."

An eyelid twitched, but refused to open.

"Lieutenant General James Van Zwartz himself might be ringing any minute. I'm sure he'll want to talk to that flower of Confederate manhood, Montgomery Robert Lee." Jared rolled the sweaty head between his palms. It was the face of a boy, an overly sensitive one at that. "This ain't no way to get it all out, Monty . . ."

His first few months at Manzanar, Jared had thought Lee to be a stuffed shirt, what with his la-di-da affectations that belonged only in the parlor at Tara. And there was the glittering irritant of his Annapolis graduation ring on top of that—Monty rarely spent a gesture without waving it in somebody's nose. Like everybody else, Jared doubted if the associate director had truly sprung from the loins of the moneyed Lees of Richmond, who were a cut above even the redoubtable Custis-Lees of Arlington. It all smacked of a put-on, especially to an Okie whose kin had sprung from the loins of sharecroppers.

Then late one spring night Jared had been in his office at the police station, finishing up the monthly report, when a *nisei* cop burst in without knocking. "Lieutenant, come quick! Mr.

Lee's running around the flagpole in his jeep, shouting for you to come out!"

"What?"

"And he's got a colored man in the back playing the piccolo!"

Seeing Jared come out on the steps, Monty braked hard, then coughed as his dust caught up with him. "Mr. Campbell?"

"Mr. Lee?" Jared had to smile: the associate director and his Negro passenger, the assistant steward, each raised a bottle to salute him and then the Stars and Bars they had just hoisted up the pole.

"Mr. Campbell, what *are* you doing?"

"Working, Mr. Lee."

"Do you have any idea what day this is?"

"Monday."

"No—the *first* Monday in *June!*" Monty's grin slowly faded. "Didn't you tell me your people were originally from Alabama?"

"Oh, dang me—Jeff Davis's birthday!"

"Dang you indeed, Mr. Campbell. Life in California has dulled your sense of tradition. Now, if you care to join us, Mr. Jackson and I are going into Independence to celebrate." Then Monty lowered his voice to a stage whisper. "It would greatly cheer me if you might attend. Mr. Jackson is excellent company, and will no doubt be served in this Unionist country. But I fear he's an abolitionist at heart." Jackson laughed good-naturedly, and Monty slapped the empty front seat. "Besides, Mr. Campbell, you are a blossom among briers, an amiable man." So Jared caved in, and the three of them roared past the main sentry house out onto the highway with Jackson piping "The Bonnie Blue Flag."

Liquor unhinged Montgomery Lee's normally reserved self, permitting a sweet, often funny, and engagingly sad man to slip out. However, the evening's gaiety was cut short by a harmless question, and in impenetrable silence Monty drove them back to camp. Jared had asked him nothing more that night than why he had resigned his commission.

Now, in the bungalow, Monty's eyelids parted into watery slits.

"Hoss, you with me?"

His voice was a croak. "The official . . ." His eyes drooped shut again.

"Stay with me, Monty. Talk to me, Monty."

"The official court of inquiry . . . in Shanghai, it was . . . only reiterated what I said all along. The attack was predicated in most wanton detail . . ." It had been another night of reliving the sinking of the USS *Panay* for Ensign M. R. Lee, retired.

Jared peeled Monty's perspiration-soaked T-shirt over his head. The associate director didn't resist, but moaned softly as if Jared had hurt him somewhere. The deeply indented scar, most of the purple bleached out of it by seven years of slow healing, started in a crater atop the floating ribs of his left side and curved down into his trousers. As soon as Jared touched the top button of Monty's fly, the man shuddered awake, his hands coming together over his groin. He glared at the lieutenant, then relaxed as he recognized him. "What's afoot?"

"I'm going to throw your skinny ass in a cool soak. Then we've got to talk—something's happened."

"Allow me but a few more winks."

"No way." Jared pulled off the man's trousers, and his boxer shorts, in which he had urinated, came away with them.

Monty had already confessed the severity of his wound to Jared, so it was less shocking now to see the wrinkled bud of scar tissue—all that remained of Monty's penis, although his scrotum hadn't been damaged by the bomb casing fragment that, but for inches, would have torn his body completely in two.

"I fear I shall be sick."

"Go ahead." Jared turned the man's face to the side so he wouldn't choke.

A terrible concentration came into Monty's eyes, but then he smiled. "This too has passed."

◆ ◆ ◆

While the tub filled with cold water, Monty recounted the death throes of the *Panay* back in '37: how the treachery was realized by the gunboat's crew only as the first bombs unleashed by the Japanese naval aviators struck the port bow, destroyed a three-inch gun, then boiled up the tan waters of the Yangtze. Even then there were those aboard who couldn't believe it was happening. The American flag was clearly visible, and the United States was not at war with the Empire of Nippon. Monty laughed bitterly as he recalled how the ammunition boxes had been locked and the gunner's mate refused to open them until he got orders from an officer. Monty, at that moment, was groveling for breath in a pool of his own blood inside the wrecked pilot house, and the captain lay nearby, delirious from a shattered leg.

"Now, should anyone still doubt their perfidy," Monty said, sprinkling more bubble powder into the water around him, "I will say only this. I have it on authority—Naval Intelligence intercepted and decoded a message to the Jap combined fleet . . ." He paused to frown at Jared. "Are you listening to me? I expect no less from a friend who's ordinarily courteous."

"I'll make some coffee. Where do you keep it?"

"In the ice box. And please bring me a cigar from the humidor in there."

Jared had *not* been listening. Helping Monty stagger into the bathroom minutes before, he had been taken aback to find the tub's porcelain beaded with water. Yet it was apparent from Monty's sharp odor that he hadn't bathed today.

The samurai sword in the living room.

As Monty droned on about the worst day of his life, Jared's thoughts had focused on the antique blade. Now, noiselessly, he lifted it out of the scabbard, fingering no more than the sides of the hilt guard, and inspected the seam where the blade was joined to the handle. He looked for traces of blood or, more probably, stains from a recent washing. Heavily mineralized, camp water left spots on everything it touched. But the metal was clean. Had it been wiped down with a soft cloth? He ran his thumb down the flat of the blade. A thin film of dust, invisible before, became evident in contrast to the gleaming swipe his thumb had left.

Jared nodded to himself—in relief.

Then the sound of Monty rising in the tub made him slip the sword back into the scabbard and rush for the bathroom before the man fell.

"It's awfully quiet in there. Ah, here you are. You, Mr. Campbell, are a burglar—don't deny it. I know certain well I locked my doors before retiring this evening. . . ." Steadying himself with one hand on the sink, Monty reached for the West Point bathrobe hanging on the back of the door.

Jared helped him into it. "I can't find the coffee."

"Do you know the history of this robe?"

"No," Jared lied.

"It once belonged to an insufferable cadet named . . ." Monty paused while knotting the terry-cloth sash. "My God, I've forgotten his name. And it was such a delight to mispronounce it. Anyways, he had no idea when he gave me points in the autumn of 'thirty-four that we gallant middies—"

"Did you play ball at Annapolis?"

"Of course not. I barely made the height requirement." He scowled. "You knew that. It would have been impossible . . . impossible . . ." Then, without warning, his eyes turned glassy. He tried to push past Jared in his haste to escape to the living room, but the lieutenant gently restrained him before helping him to the sofa.

"Oh, my dearest friend . . . my friend . . ." Monty began to weep. "She was an angel. And you can't imagine what it was like to hear those words from the lips of an angel: 'Our going on as man and wife is impossible . . . and it'd be unrealistic of us to ask too much of our friendship.' " He smiled miserably as he wiped his cheeks. "I would have given worlds for that friendship to go on. I took my sword, broke it over my knee, and threw it into the Rappahannock. I was that ruined. That devastated. You know I'm speaking the God's truth, don't you?"

Jared clenched the man's bony shoulder. "Let me look for that coffee again."

◆ ◆ ◆

After four cups, Monty seemed lucid enough to listen to how Masao Shido and Morris Wenge had died. But it robbed him of what little color there had been in his face. He set down his cup and came to his feet, then seemed to realize that he was too weak and dizzy to pace up and down the room. Slowly, he sank back into the cushions. "This . . . this is *appalling*."

"I left a message at the Presidio. But so far nobody's called back."

Monty appeared not to have heard him. He tugged at his underlip with his fingers, then sighed. "You know, this puts me in an awkward position."

"How's that?"

"Well, I'll be expected to express regrets for the passing of a man for whom I had neither respect nor affection."

"Oh, Monty, he wasn't a bad old boy—"

Lee raised his hand adamantly. "Morris Wenge failed to understand the one fact the director of this project absolutely must. Let's be charitable about it—obedience to emperor is not a choice for these people. It's a biological imperative. And this only proves it. After the humane treatment we've offered them—despite what our own boys are suffering at their hands—this is how they show their gratitude. By murdering the man who coddled them."

"Whoa, hoss—I have no idea whose work this is."

"It's obvious to me. As someone who has traveled extensively in the Orient, I can assure you this entire episode has the Nipponese temperament written all over it. Assassination followed by *seppuku*—a common expression of *Bushido*."

"What's that?"

"Their warriors' code—a twisted reflection of our concepts of chivalry and duty. Their officers live and breathe it."

"Where'd you run across Jap officers? In China?"

Monty reached for his cup and took a quiet sip. "No, in Japan."

"I didn't know you'd been."

"Only briefly." A sweep of his eyes took in the sword and the other Japanese appointments. "Where'd you think I acquired all this?"

"I thought maybe you got it off the evacuees at intake."

Monty's laugh was brittle. "I am not a purloiner, Mr. Campbell. I want nothing from these people. And the point I'm trying to make is this—Shido murdered Wenge, then purified his motives by taking his own life. In this way he proved that the killing wasn't for personal gain. Clearly, a reenactment of their most famous legend, that of the Forty-seven Ronin, who avenged their lord's death, then committed—"

Both men glanced toward the open front door as a jeep arrived. A moment later, Elwayne trotted up the cement path to the porch, his bayonet tapping against the back of his helmet. "Lieutenant?"

Jared met him at the threshold. "What's up?"

"Fukuda's done. He wants to talk to you."

The chief could be seen in silhouette, waiting in the back of the jeep.

"All right, see what if Mr. Lee here won't offer you a cup."

"Why, it'd be my pleasure, Corporal. . . ."

Jared motioned for the chief to walk with him across the street. They halted in the middle of the motor pool's gravel yard, just outside the tepee of bug-riddled light thrown by a pole lamp.

Jared offered a cigarette to the chief, who inhaled the smoke hungrily. He spoke first. "Who's going to do the postmortem?"

Jared clicked his Zippo shut. "Don't know—it's something I got to talk over with the Presidio. County coroner's nothing but a mortician. What about the camp doctor?"

"No evacuee will touch this."

"Then what do you suggest?"

"A fresh post performed by a competent pathologist. The sooner the better."

"You mean bring somebody in from L.A.?"

"If need be. I've got a few names. Strictly the best."

Jared saw the hesitancy in Fukuda's eyes. "Hank, I'm not doubting this is the way to go. But an autopsy just ain't mine to okay. All I'm asking for right now is your opinion. And I'll give you the same right I'm giving myself."

"Which is?"

"To wind up with egg all over my face. I'm a cop, not a mind reader."

The chief's smile remained uneasy. "Okay."

"Does it look like the same weapon?"

"Maybe—but only maybe. Say the edge of a sword blade was gouged or nicked. You might be able to match the deformity to marks left in bone. But, for it to hold water in court, the deformity would have to be *really* pronounced."

"And that ain't the case here?"

Fukuda nodded. "And as far as the rate at which a body cools, we both know it depends on a lot of things."

"Would decapitation have to figure into it?"

"Common sense tells me so. Wenge's liver had to cool down faster than normal if only because of reduced body mass. But, hell, I don't know . . . I just don't know." The chief's eyes brightened a little. "I will say that it took two, maybe three blows to sever the head."

"What about prints?"

"Fresh-looking smudges on the back door and radio."

"They'll be mine." Jared exhaled a cloud of smoke. "Hank, trails grow cold fast. I got to make a decision in the next few minutes. And I understand there's no such thing as chapter and verse in your line of work. . . ."

"But you still want me to tell you who died when."

Jared said nothing.

"Just between us, Lieutenant?"

"At this point, I can agree to that. If the situation changes, I'll talk to you first."

Fukuda sighed loudly. "Morris Wenge died *at least* an hour after Shido did tonight."

"Goddamnit!" Jared hurled his cigarette to the ground, startling the chief.

"What's wrong?"

"Come on, Hank—we got an arrest to make."

CHAPTER 7

Jared told Hank Fukuda to take the front seat beside Elwayne. He didn't want to feel the chief's eyes burning on the back of his head as they left *Hakujin* Country for the evacuee side of the camp.

Two possibilities had been quashed. The first, that Shido killed Morris Wenge before taking his own life, had been ruled out by the slowly cooling livers of the two dead men. And the temperature of Shido's most likely ruled out the second possibility, that a Caucasian, acting as the alien's friendly second, had helped or even forced him to die between eight and half past this evening. How could a white man have wended his way unnoticed through the mobbed firebreaks of the *obon odori* in the bright desert twilight?

As Elwayne drove ever deeper into the rows of barracks, the chief reared taller in his seat.

"Where to now, Lieutenant?" the corporal asked, idling at the intersection to which Jared had ordered him.

"Block Twenty-eight."

Fukuda froze, the backwash of the headlamps glancing off

the side of his face. Jared knew that the chief's own hope for a *hakujin* suspect had just died. It now seemed inescapable that an evacuee had attended Shido's final minutes, then used the first darkness to slip into *Hakujin* Country—unless the two deaths had nothing more in common than the same date of occurrence. But a coincidence this profound didn't wash, not when Jared could come up with a man who had reasons to kill both Shido and Wenge.

He had been tempted to send the chief and a couple of his cops to make the arrest. But that would have been cowardly: he was about to lock up the husband of a woman he had made love to, a woman he still loved. This was something he had to do himself; otherwise she might never forgive him.

Besides, Major Tadashi Nitta had put his own head in the noose at his testimonial dinner.

Three sheets to the wind, alternately seething and morose as he swayed at the podium, Nitta had first hissed Shido's name—for no apparent reason—then lambasted poor old Morris Wenge for his sister's death. The next morning, Jared took it upon himself to find out what had happened to Emiko Nitta-Miyakoda. He came away from the hospital believing that the evacuee staff, which lacked for even ordinary supplies like diapers and pabulum, was bound to have trouble with a breech stillbirth and should not be blamed. But Eddie wasn't faulting the Japanese doctor, he was blaming the internment that had dumped his family here, stripping them of a lucrative fishing business that would have made the best medical care on the Coast affordable for Emiko. And Morris Wenge's was the *hakujin* face to that internment.

Jared looked skyward, wishing that a transfer out of Manzanar would tumble down out of the big rock-candy stars, sparing him what was only seconds away.

♦ ♦ ♦

In July of 1942, a young *nisei* woman applied to the police department for work. A former law student, she also had clerical experience with the state justice department. The chief hired her in a minute, even before asking Jared what he thought. So, thanks to the chief's eagerness, the interview was just a formality.

And that first time Jared saw Kimiko a warm stillness came to his face. "Why do you want this job, Mrs. Nitta?"

"To keep busy while my husband's away."

He told himself that she was coolly beautiful in the way of smart women, and he had never especially cared for overly smart women. "Where's Mr. Nitta?"

"Camp McCoy in Wisconsin. He was in ROTC at Stanford, so the Army assigned him to the 100th Infantry Battalion."

"Isn't that an all-Hawaiian outfit?" For once, he was careful not to say *ain't*.

"Yes, but a few *nisei* officers are being recruited here on the mainland."

"I see." Jared came to his feet and shook her hand. It was small and cool. "Well, I hope you'll like working here."

"I'm sure I will."

When she had left the room, the chief's expression turned both triumphant and foolish. "What do you think?"

"Fine, Hank," Jared muttered. But he had a hunch he wasn't going to find it easy spending his afternoons in close proximity to the willowly young woman. His inkling was well founded. He soon began stealing the day's images of her back to his hutment to savor in the privacy of his loneliness. He turned her face over in his mind a thousand times. Then he tried to ignore her as much as common courtesy permitted, but she was not as shy as the other *nisei* clerk-typists. And one afternoon, as he lounged at his desk eating the box lunch the MP mess hall prepared each morning for him, she came in to deliver the Presidio teletypes.

"What are you reading, Lieutenant?" she asked quietly.

His mouth full of apple, he showed her the cover: *War and Peace*. She looked a bit surprised, so he quickly swallowed and explained, "I cut this article out of the *Times*—the twelve books every thinking man oughta read."

"Oh, what are they?"

He took the clipping from the back of *War and Peace* and handed it to her with an embarrassed grin.

"These are very fine books," she said after a moment. "Especially *Madame Bovary*. Have you read it yet?"

"No, I'm just down to number three."

She studied him, a funny look in her eyes, almost as if she were peering right through him. "What do you want to be, Lieutenant?"

As soon as it escaped his mouth, he realized it to be the strangest thing he'd ever said. "Somebody else, I suppose . . . just somebody else."

She withdrew, smiling, and he came close to pitching Tolstoy into the wastebasket. *I've got to learn how to talk to people.*

Sometimes, when they traded glances, there was accusation in her face, and it withered his confidence. But on other occasions her eyes seemed to entreat his—as if she were looking to him for something he could never hope to offer. The chief mentioned that living with her *issei* in-laws was driving her nuts, although she never brought it up with Jared.

Her loveliness continued to torture him, sweetly, night after night as he lay in his hutment. He drilled himself into thinking that Japanese women seemed prettier, more feminine than Caucasian girls, only because they were new to his way of *seeing*. And, to put the skids on his growing infatuation, he spent a boozy weekend in San Bernardino with an old flame, a big blonde and former Fred Harvey girl he'd gotten defrocked by returning her late to the dormitory once too often.

Yet, on the hungover bus ride back to Manzanar, with a woolly sky spitting the first snow of the season, Jared finally admitted to himself that he was falling in love with an evacuee. A devotedly married one at that. And, even under the pressures of camp life, these people weren't much for adultery.

He simply had to get away.

Once again, he asked the captain to shake a few branches over at the Presidio and see if a replacement lieutenant wouldn't drop out. But, once again, Snavely denied the transfer.

Jared began behaving crossly toward her, hoping she could

be goaded into revealing a side he wouldn't care for. He knew it to be childish and unlike him, but he kept it up for a month until late one afternoon, sultry with Indian summer, he growled for a file and she didn't move away from his desk. He glanced up: she was sobbing.

"I'm sorry," she whispered, quickly recovering herself. "I'm just tired today."

There followed a long moment in which he didn't know what to say, and she had just turned to go when he blurted, "I hate this place more than you do."

She halted at the door. The oscillating fan on his desk lifted the silky black down on her nape. He wanted to brush it with his lips. They were killing him, these little but forbidden things he kept imagining.

"Do you really?" She sounded unconvinced.

"Reminds me of a goddamned Hooverville."

Her eyes said that she knew what the migrant camps had been like, and with that he ran out of things to say. Instead, he pretended to be absorbed with the report before him, his cheekbones singed red. As she went out, he knew that for the third night that week he would join Monty Lee in getting blind drunk.

There would have been no affair but for the shooting a week later.

It had been building for months, crackling over Manzanar like electricity—ten thousand volts waiting for a fuse to blow. And this fuse turned out to be a rumor that the *hakujin* staff and their *inu* pals were stealing sugar out of the warehouses and selling it on the black market. Passed from barrack to barrack, the story took on a nasty twist: the two latest infant deaths had come from saccharin being mixed in their formulas instead of sugar. A former bigwig in the Japanese American Citizens League was accused of being an FBI informant and beaten within an inch of his life by six hooded men, allegedly of the Black Dragon, who then tried to torch the co-op general store before the fire department drove them off with hoses. At that point, with the militarists having the run of the camp and openly warring with the *aka*—or self-avowed reds, who urged support for Wenge's administration—Captain Snavely astonished Jared by ordering the arrest of a peaceable-enough *kibei* whose only offense had been to organize a mess hall workers' union. From his fondly recalled days as a special deputy in the San Joaquin Valley, Snavely equated unions with communist agitation. Jared argued in vain that the handful of bona fide Bolsheviks in Manzanar were urging *restraint*, all because Uncle Joe Stalin wanted a second front, and it was their natural enemy, Masao Shido, who was fanning the flames of unrest. The captain smiled bitterly and said, "I knew I wouldn't be able to count on you, Campbell, when the chips were—"

"Captain, please, you're punishing the innocent with the guilty. And you just can't push these folks this way."

"Return to your quarters."

"You can't push people with nothing left to lose!"

"Are *you* pushing for a court-martial, Lieutenant?"

At last, Jared remembered himself. "No, sir." He turned on his heels and then shame tightened his face: Kimiko had witnessed the confrontation from a police station window.

He returned to the compound.

The winter sun paled down through the clouds, and he lay on his cot, listening to the clanging of the mess hall bells and the cries of *banzai* that drifted through his open window. Darkness brought the crackling of huge bonfires and finally the roar of a crowd thousands-strong. "God Almighty!"

Disregarding Snavely's orders, Jared jumped in his jeep and raced back to camp, where at least three thousand Japanese—the loyal and disloyal alike—had gathered outside the police station, demanding the release of the popular kitchen worker. The captain stood behind a human barricade of troops, wheezing inside his gas mask and stupefied by the size of the angry gathering, although he seemed relieved that the lieutenant had returned. Waving a Thompson submachine gun around, Osler had just told the men to lob tear gas grenades—with no thought given to the company's World War I masks, most of which leaked like colanders, and to the stiff breeze, which folded the stinging clouds back and forth between the MPs and the *nihonjin*, who so far instead of advancing were dancing in something like a conga line and singing a boisterous Japanese song. Choking for breath and half-blinded, Jared thought he saw the evacuees break and run in the same instant a driverless pickup truck careened out of Block 1 toward the jail, the first rank of soldiers scrambling to either side to avoid being run down. The truck stalled a short distance later, and Jared had just removed the kitchen scale weight that had been propped against the accelerator when a shotgun barked twice. A rifle joined in, and then a tommy gun, which meant that Osler was firing, too. Jared started batting down muzzles as he cried, "Cease fire—nobody's shooting at *you!* Sling arms!"

But it was too late: the dead, the dying, the wounded lay among the last sputterings of the gas grenades.

In his account of the incident, Jared noted that all of the gunshot wounds were to the backs and sides of the evacuees. But this observation never appeared in the final report issued by the Presidio. Jared protested, but then Colonel Bleecher personally phoned him. "If Tokyo somehow finds out our boys shot unarmed Jap civilians who were running away from them, the bastards will butcher every last American prisoner of war they hold. You want that on your conscience, Lieutenant?"

A month later, after Manzanar had returned to its listless normalcy, Jared looked in on a mess hall dance and was surprised to find Kimiko Nitta in the dimly lit vestibule, swaying to the music of the Jive Bombers—until she became aware of him. Her hands flew halfway to her face before she restrained them.

"Evening, Kimiko." He struggled to keep the hunger out of his eyes. Turn around and go *now*, he told himself. "What're you doing here?"

She held a finger to her lips, then whispered, "Chaperone."

As he looked past her into the hall filled with teenagers locked in each other's arms for the "Tennessee Waltz," he thought he could feel the warmth in her eyes on the side of his face.

"Thank you . . ."

He hiked an eyebrow. "Pardon?"

"I saw that evening . . . from the station."

Somehow it was communicated to him without words: she meant the shooting. "Well, two dead and eleven wounded is nothing to get congratulated for."

"You tried, Lieutenant."

"We're away from work. How about calling me Jared?"

She nodded. "Jared."

He sensed her fear, but it only intoxicated him, and she didn't move away when he stepped closer. A skinny *nisei* crooner, a hint of Sinatra's vulnerability in his smile, clasped the microphone. Jared knew it would be "Serenade in Blue" from the opening bars. She didn't resist when he took her left hand and slipped his right around her waist. But she did pull him back a few feet so they couldn't be seen from inside the hall.

As soon as she rested her head on his shoulder, he realized that they had crossed the line—and might never find their way back over. If caught, it would be bad enough for him: he would face a general court-martial; romantic fraternization had been the first thing the Lamb Committee asked about when it investigated Manzanar, and General Van Zwartz would have a fit if one of his men could be linked to a Japanese woman. But for her it could prove a thousand times worse—ostracism by her family, perhaps disfigurement or even death at the hands of the faceless thugs of the Black Dragon. And where could she run? Nowhere, for as long as the war lasted.

Yet he kissed her.

He wanted to bite her lower lip, her neck, but was frightened he might hurt her. The waiting had made him want to hurt her a little.

"I suppose you've already gathered this," he heard himself whispering over the sudden roar of blood in his ears, "but I love you . . . God Almighty, I love you." He felt the sudden tension in the small of her back, and that was enough to make him let go of her. "I'm sorry," he said, then rushed out the door to his jeep. He sped off without looking back to see if she'd followed him out onto the steps.

The next day he would rather have deserted than show up at the station. The chief, at their one o'clock briefing, even asked him if he'd caught the influenza that was ripping through the barracks. And when Kimiko brought in the Presidio traffic, he quietly thanked her but kept his eyes on his work—until he heard the door click shut. When he looked up, his sigh of relief was cut short: she was leaning on her hands against the door, frowning at him. When finally she spoke, her voice was tremulous. "Last night, you didn't ask me how I feel."

"I didn't figure it was any of my business."

"Well, it is." She brushed her fingertips across her forehead—a gesture full of sadness and exhaustion; she'd probably slept no better than he had.

"Then how do you feel?"

"Awful. Dirty, I think." Tears threatened her eyes. "But I want to become someone else, too. And I'm too weak to do it alone here."

He went to her, hesitated, then seized her, kissed her. "Me too . . . me too . . ." Within moments, his fingers were fumbling for the hem of her skirt. "I can't take this place without you."

She closed her eyes and smiled. "Oh, Jared . . ."

He entered her standing. It was too frenzied and hastened by fear to be good; he was terrified that it wasn't good for her, although she said that it was, that it had been tender and that he was a tender man.

However, the next afternoon she declined to let him do it again, saying that it was the place, the station. He certainly understood that, but still, his eyes smarted and he groaned as he held her. But then she said that she loved him and that they could love each other in every other way—and he laughed, softly. She was smarter than he was; she'd come up with a way for them to proceed safely, without destroying each other. Over the next fourteen months, he never took her again but always believed that she was securely his—until that windy afternoon when a telegram was hand-carried by Morris Wenge from the administration building to the police station:

WASHINGTON DC 845P APR 1–44
MRS KIMIKO NITTA
MANZANAR WAR RELOCATION CENTER INYO
COUNTY CALIF
REGRET TO INFORM YOU YOUR HUSBAND WAS SERIOUSLY
WOUNDED IN ACTION IN ITALY SIXTEEN MARCH UNTIL
NEW ADDRESS IS RECEIVED ADDRESS MAIL FOR HIM
QUOTE MAJOR TADASHI NITTA SERIAL NUMBER
HOSPITALIZED CENTRAL HOSPITAL DIRECTORY APO 640
CARE POSTMASTER NEWYORK NEWYORK UNQUOTE YOU
WILL BE ADVISED AS REPORTS OF CONDITION ARE
RECEIVED.
WITSELL ACTING THE ADJUTANT GENERAL

Kimiko had no idea of the extent of her husband's injuries until a week later, when a photostatically reduced V-mail letter arrived from a hospital chaplain in Naples. A mortar blast had blown off Tadashi's left arm a few inches above the elbow, but since his first operation the surgeons had "revised" the stump because it had failed to heal properly, sawing through half the shoulder joint. The chaplain finished with: ". . . The major is stoical about his wound, but I sense that he is deeply worried about its effect on you. Although he declines to write at this point, I believe that supportive letters from you and other members of the family—but particularly from you, Mrs. Nitta—will hasten his recovery. . . ."

Jared could not decide which was worse that final afternoon together: to hear Kimiko's words as she gave him her neatly typed resignation from the department—and pity himself for the bleakness those words promised in his life—or to watch how she agonized over them. "I'll never forget you," she said, hiding her eyes, her nostrils flaring moistly in the shadow of her hand. "I've never felt closer to anyone . . . but I can't do this anymore. Do you understand?" She looked at him, her eyes shining.

He nodded, unable to speak. Yet, in order to forgive her, he had only to realize the the news from Italy was more than her fragile guilt could bear. He *understood*, and that was the hell of it.

When she was gone from his office, he did something he had not done since twisting around in the bed of his father's truck for a last glimpse at the farmhouse, which, crazily, looked like a beach cottage in the midst of all that wind-humped sand: Jared had driven his fist into his palm, clutched it to the point of trembling, and wept.

♦ ♦ ♦

Elwayne parked beside the Block 28 ironing room.

Jared sat in silence for a moment, his hand tight on the collapsed canopy bar that ran around the back of the jeep. Then he said, "Let's get this over with—Hank, cover the east side."

CHAPTER 8

The siren was dying away as Kimiko's mother-in-law opened the door for Eddie. "Tadashi!" she cried, then began babbling hysterically in Japanese.

"No yake up!" Eddie's father snarled—don't get your dander up.

"Dad's right—it's nothing. The MPs just want to play soldier. Everybody go back to bed. Kimiko?"

For the first time since his return, affection softened his voice. The sweep of a tower floodlight passed over his face, and she saw that he was smiling at her, the unexpected warmth in his eyes making her hand drift to her throat.

His father told him the power was out. He said it was no matter.

Taking her hand, Eddie led her into their blanket-partitioned space and sat her down on his cot. But, instead of sitting beside her in the darkness, he ducked back out through the slit in the blanket. A moment later, he could be heard opening the storage cabinet his father had made from castoff apple crates.

A match sizzled to life. His mother muttered something, and he whispered, *"No shimpai."* Don't worry.

When he returned to Kimiko, a *chochin* was flickering redly in his hand. He hooked the paper lantern to the overhead fixture, and the candle flame grew steady. She joined him in smiling at its glow. Somehow, the *chochin* had a way of making the searchlights fade away.

They said nothing for perhaps a half hour. He ran his thumb over the back of her hand and touched her nape hair from time to time.

When he finally spoke, he surprised her once again. "Kimi-*chan* . . ." He had called her this only once before, and they had busted up laughing then: it had struck them as being too quaint, too *bootchie*. But now his expression remained strangely solemn as he brushed her cheek with his fingertips. "My God, you're beautiful."

She seized his hand and held it to her face. "It must be the *chochin*."

"No."

He was torturing her with kindness, but she didn't want him to stop, to become distant toward her again.

"We've got to talk. Make plans." Withdrawing his hand, he turned business-like but remained cheerful. "I think we should resettle."

She glanced down in confusion. They had been over this ground before—and never with any success. "What about your discharge from the Army?"

His eyes darted angrily toward his bandaged shoulder, but quickly mellowed again. He rose and put on his khaki shirt. "It's mine when I want it."

WRA regulations required them to secure promises of employment before they could board the train east. "Where do you think we can find work?"

"What about Boston and that *hakujin* roommate of yours from Stanford?"

"Jean?"

"Yeah—doesn't she want you to clerk for her old man's law firm?"

"I don't know, Eddie. She made that offer almost two years ago."

He frowned as he held out his right sleeve for her to button; the left was already pinned up. "So what? You're still friends, aren't you?"

"I suppose."

"Then what the hell is bothering you?"

She grasped his hand before he could withdraw into himself. "What would you do? You're a brilliant man, Eddie, a Stanford man. And you've always said the jobs back there are so menial, so—"

They both turned away from the wash of harsh light—the power had come back on. He reached for the draw chain and gave it a tug. The softness of the *chochin* enveloped them again. "I don't know," he said. "And I don't really care. All I know is that this dump is going to kill us. If not that, it'll drive us apart."

She avoided his eyes.

"Let's get out of here. What do you say, girl?"

She kissed his hand. He was showing her the way back from aberration, and the gratitude she felt at that moment was every bit as strong as love. Why couldn't she be like her mother, or Eddie's mother, or poor Emiko had been—satisfied with a relationship of tolerance and "fellow feeling," if not love? At least Eddie was communicative when not depressed, and, unlike his father, didn't demand to be indulged at every turn.

Harder and harder she kissed his hand, hating herself more with each press of her lips against his skin.

If her behavior hadn't been exactly aberrant, at the very least her Weltanschauung, her world view, was twisted. Like the other self-absorbed coeds in her dormitory, she had eagerly sought a reflection of herself in the faddishly popular works of Freud. But the writings disquieted more than amused her, and she was left wondering if in loving Peter she was confusing image with object. And, more recently, had she made the same mistake with Jared, whom she had loved all the more because he so openly admired her? Could she lift the hem of her Western skirt and see the Achilles' heel of transplanted Japanese everywhere: *amae*, the obsessive need to be cherished, to be found worthy of love by others?

Freud, a Jew, an outsider himself, would have understood the anxiety that comes from never quite feeling accepted, as well as how a young *nisei* woman might confuse the American Dream, the rampant possibilities, with large fair-haired men who nested her in their warm arms and whispered that they loved her. Yet, in the end, wanting her might not have been the same as accepting her, particularly in Peter's case. Now, Tadashi, by bringing out the *chochin*, was lighting her way back to acceptance—a husband cut from the same flesh. The *hakujin*, even those who nested her in their arms, would always betray her—this camp was proof of that. But she would learn to live with it. She would find peace with the husband who, long ago, had watched Peter and her together with uncomprehending eyes.

"Yes, Tadashi," she said at last, "let's apply tomorrow. As soon as the resettlement office opens."

She lay back across the cot. He reclined beside her, came to her more gently and patiently than before.

And it seemed perversely appropriate to her, so much in keeping with the labyrinth of dead ends that was Manzanar, for someone to knock insistently on the door at that moment.

"*Hai?*" her father-in-law asked gruffly, as he spoke to all *hakujin* now.

Kimiko closed her eyes as she listened to Jared Campbell clear the unease out of his throat. "Sorry to disturb you, Mr. Nitta, but I got to talk to the major."

"What say?"

"That's between us, sir."

Eddie squeezed her shoulder as he rose and went through the blanket. "May I help you, Lieutenant?"

"Yes, sir—you're to come with me."

"Why?"

"I'm not at liberty to say."

Kimiko threw on her robe and hurried to the door.

Jared glanced at her, his jaw muscles rippling under the bristle of a day's growth. "Mrs. Nitta."

"Lieutenant?" She surprised herself by how adamant she sounded, though her heart was racing: she could feel bold with Jared, but never with Eddie. "Is my husband being placed under arrest?"

"Detained—for questioning."

"I see no legal difference. On what charge is he—"

"Kimiko, please." Eddie was glaring at her.

She lowered her eyes.

Handcuffs rattled, and she saw that Elwayne had produced his set. But the corporal hesitated, unable to figure out how to manacle a one-armed man. Trust Jared to know: he snapped one cuff onto Eddie's wrist, then attached the other to her husband's belt at the back loop. "I'm sorry, everybody," he said quietly. "This should be cleared up shortly."

Hank Fukuda, who had been lingering in the background after belatedly coming around the corner of the barrack, stepped forward and touched her arm. "He'll be okay, promise."

Kimiko said nothing. She knew when the chief was lying. He too was sometimes confused by the difference between what he desired from the *hakujin* and what they were really offering.

♦ ♦ ♦

While Elwayne brought a stainless steel pitcher and three coffee mugs into Captain Snavely's office, Eddie Nitta and Jared Campbell studied each other. Hank Fukuda felt strangely god-like. He knew things neither man did, and other things they would never imagine he knew. It was a feeling of power he didn't relish.

It was apparent from Campbell's apologies that he felt morally disadvantaged. Hank believed this awkwardness spoke well of him. After all, he had been so reckless as to have had an affair with the major's wife—everyone at the station knew about it; two people in love betray themselves with every glance they share. And Nitta's obvious ignorance of the matter wasn't helping Campbell feel any cleaner. It was the only interrogation

Hank could recall in which the interrogator looked more guilty than the suspect. The atmosphere in the office reminded him of the silent Japanese movies his grandparents had dragged him to every Friday night at the Nippon Theatre in Little Tokyo, movies that were rife with pained sensibilities and misfired noble intentions; the only thing missing was the jabbering of *benshi*, the narrator, as he beat his drum to heighten the pathos.

Campbell sighed. "Major, I got to ask you some questions—"

"About what?"

"Your whereabouts since noon today—" Campbell corrected himself with a shake of his head. "I mean yesterday."

Eddie looked to Hank. All at once he was no longer a combat soldier. He was just a slender *nisei* kid, searching for the guideposts through *Hakujin* Country.

Hank nodded for him to go ahead and answer. Immediately, he was disappointed with himself. There was nothing safe about this situation for an evacuee, particularly one as outspoken as Tadashi Nitta.

"Hell, Lieutenant," Eddie said, "I don't know. Let's see—napped all afternoon in my apartment. . . ." Campbell's eyes narrowed with pain for a moment. "Dinner at five in our mess hall."

"Did you mess hall hop?"—meaning did he try his gastronomic luck at a hall other than his own in Block 28.

"No."

"Did you go to the festival?"

"No."

"Why not, Major?"

"Just didn't feel like it. I took a long cool shower in the bathhouse, say from eight to nine."

"Was anybody with you?"

"No, I had the place to myself because of the *odori*."

"And after that?"

"I don't know—a stroll along I Street, so I could see the sunset on the mountains."

"Alone again?"

Eddie nodded, a bit irked now. "Anything wrong with that?"

Campbell ignored the challenge. "Did you pass Watchtower Four on your walk?"

"Sure, I had to if I used I Street. I walked out to where Bair's Creek comes in under the wire. Had a smoke or two. Waited for the sun to go down before heading home."

"What time did you get back to your apartment?"

"A little before ten. I made the head count, if that's what you mean."

Hank noted the keenness in Campbell's eyes. It couldn't be repressed in a cop—the hunt was on. After two years of benumbing boredom, he was stirring to life again. He would chase down the truth, probably regardless of the personal consequences. In that moment, Hank found himself pitying Jared Campbell as much as Eddie Nitta.

◆ ◆ ◆

Sheriff Bertie Coy's indigestion made lying down impossible—two fried venison steaks and four diced potatoes with red onions, hadn't it been? Yes, and with nothing left over for his beagles. He reached for the flashlight on the nightstand and briefly lit the face of the alarm clock. Three-thirty. "Sugar, I'm just dying. Where's the bicarbonate?"

His wife mumbled something from her side of the bed.

"What?" Silence. "Shit—I'll find it myself."

Two full glasses did little to relieve his discomfort, so he decided on a drive. That usually worked when the bicarb didn't. Maybe it was the jiggling. He would also try a warm beer. The fizz.

Remembering to top off his radiator after yesterday's Death Valley patrol, he searched the overgrown grass for the garden hose, then turned it on. Summer or winter, the snow-fed waters of the Owens Valley were cold right from the spigot. In fact, it was the abundant water trapped in the snowpack of the Sierra Nevada that made Inyo the only county in California with an absentee landlord—the City of Los Angeles.

Coy let the chunky-looking Mercury station wagon roll

down the sloping driveway and out onto the street before turning over the engine: his wife claimed she was a light sleeper. He switched on the lights—thank God that blackout folderol had never been imposed this far inland. The week following Pearl Harbor he had taken it upon himself to tape blue cellophane over the headlamps of the patrol cars, but then it hit him: What self-respecting Jap would bother to bomb Independence, California? Three hundred souls gathered around a courthouse, a tavern, a hotel, the valley headquarters of L.A. Water and Power, and a poured-concrete jail—whose glass front door he now crept past, trying to catch his deputy napping. But Waldo, his scuffed Acmes propped up on the front desk, was reading—and mussing—the department's gratis copy of the *Times*. Later in the morning he would swear up and down that no hands had touched it prior to the sheriff's. Waldo was useless; the war had taken Coy's best deputies.

The town ended in a blink, and he drove south through desert, keeping to the wartime speed limit of 35 miles per hour, although there were no lights on the two-lane highway as far as the eye could see. The board of supervisors had threatened to put governors on his patrol cars like the military vehicles had to keep his deputies from speeding. But Coy had stopped them dead in their tracks by asking if the goddamned crooks had governors on their jalopies. It was a moment he still savored, the way their faces went purple.

Years before, this stretch of road had been lined by alfalfa fields, and on a warm night like tonight a driver would slip in and out of pockets of coolness that had been trapped by the irrigated grass. But farming in the Owens Valley had been dried up, the parched fields gone back to sage and greasewood. Back in the teens, Los Angeles had bribed the U.S. Reclamation Service agent, who had then hornswoggled the locals into pushing Congress for a dam, which the city then appropriated for its own uses. Next, L.A. had turned its greedy eye on the ranches themselves, gobbling them up one by one. The Coy place had been among the last to hold out, but then the city's bullyboys forced the sale of the spread above theirs, and the sheriff's father had found himself cut off from his water, checkmated on the first move of a game he could never win. After foreclosure, the Coys had walked away from Rancho Manzanar and its one hundred and sixty acres of creek-fed orchards and fields with a grand total of forty dollars in the family coffer—a dented Folger's can.

Coy groped for the church key in the glovebox, then cracked the bottle of Pabst. He'd give a month's salary for one hearty belch.

The highway cut through a screen of locust trees, and the sheriff shook his head at the jackstraw blaze of Manzanar's searchlights. The expense of running this Jap resort—on land that was rightfully his family's no less—had to be tremendous. How long would it go on? He had written his congressman on official letterhead about this very issue and received a report by the Committee for the Investigation of Un-American Activities. The long and the short of it was that the panel—headed by Representative Maurice Lamb of Texas—was worried about the same thing the sheriff was, and they were working on legislation to deport the more than 120,000 Japs on the U.S. mainland and the 160,000 in Hawaii back to their ancestral homeland as soon as the war was won. The note his congressman had paper-clipped to the cover of the report admitted that it was going to be a close vote because the eastern politicians just didn't understand the problem. They didn't have Japs in their states putting white farm laborers and fishermen out of work. But, with the support of concerned citizens like Bertrand Oliver Coy, mass deportation would be pushed through.

Driving past the one mile of camp fronting the highway, he wondered again why the siren had been sounded tonight, awakening him six miles away in Independence. The Okie or Arkie or whatever he was lieutenant had been less than informative. Coy would phone Captain Snavely in the morning and demand a little consideration for the local population. He could do business with Snavely.

From the last tower in line, a sentry gave him a bored wave. The sheriff ignored it.

The discomfort was getting worse. He wondered if it might be the onset of a heart attack. Reaching under his roll of belly fat, he unhitched his belt before draining the last of the Pabst.

He had just passed the intake to the Los Angeles Aqueduct when his vision fogged. For a moment he thought he was fainting, and his foot flew to the brake pedal. A heartbeat later, he was stunned by a concussive *thump* that reverberated in his chest. He gnashed his teeth together to keep from crying out, while from behind the car a dazzling orange flash fanned out across the sky, reflecting on the lustrous black paint of the hood as it turned night into day.

All this was followed by a deathly roar.

◆ ◆ ◆

Jared Campbell was no longer acting apologetically toward Eddie Nitta. "What do you think of Masao Shido?"

The major shrugged. "What can I say?"

"Do you hate him? Respect him?"

The inaccurate use of the present tense concerning the dead warehouseman was not lost on Hank Fukuda, who poured himself another cup of coffee, even though the last one had gone down like lava.

"Both hate and respect, I guess," Nitta answered after a thoughtful pause. "Does all this have something to do with the Black Dragon?"

Campbell lit two cigarettes and handed one to the major. "Let me ask the questions. Have you had any go-arounds with Shido?"

"Sure."

"Over what?"

"When I volunteered for the 100th, he got nasty, threatened to take it out on my family."

"And what'd you say to that?"

Nitta blew smoke out his nose. "Told him I'd kill him." He smiled at Hank. "The chief knows all about this. I asked him to keep an eye out for my folks while I was overseas."

Hank rubbed his eyes with his hands.

"Explain what you mean by both hating and respecting Shido," Campbell said.

"He's one helluva man, Lieutenant. Ask the Russians who faced him at Port Arthur. But it's because of loudmouths like him that my family and I are here."

Campbell stared at Eddie for a long moment. "Something you said, Major, at your testimonial dinner. . . ."

Nitta wiped the corners of his mouth with his fingers, but refused to look away.

"What'd you mean by holding Director Wenge responsible?"

Suspicion came into Eddie's eyes. He was beginning to sense the parameters of the trap: something had happened to Shido and Wenge, something fatal. Smirking now, he was on the verge of answering Campbell when a flash lit up the window. Hank's first thought was *searchlight*, but then he realized the MPs in the towers never swept their own compound. Next he wondered if a transformer box on one of the poles had blown. But that was ruled out when an orange explosion mushroomed up out of the south, its shock wave rumbling against the panes of glass.

All three men came to their feet, their faces vermilion with the last of the fiery glow.

Campbell was first to move, and ran for the door. "Elwayne!"

"Yo."

"Put Major Nitta in our guardhouse!"

The corporal appeared in the corridor, seemingly oblivious to the blast that had just died away. "*Ours*, Lieutenant, and not *their* cage at the station?"

"Just do it, Elwayne!" Outside, the siren was starting to wail again. "And tell Osler to cut that goddamned thing!"

As Elwayne hustled Eddie out the door, Campbell grabbed Hank by the arm. "Pick up your bag and come with me!"

♦ ♦ ♦

The scene reminded the chief of the grunion hunts of his youth. His father would drive their Model A roadster onto the darkened beach and park just short of the high-tide line. Then he would aim the headlights out across the foamy shallows, and Hank and his cousins would race out to catch the slippery little darts of silver with their bare hands.

But now the headlights belonged to Jared Campbell's jeep, and the frothy torrent of water was flowing across a desert highway south of Manzanar, not Santa Monica Beach.

The county sheriff was standing in the midst of this flood, the water humping over the tops of his boots as he glared toward the aqueduct. The six-foot-diameter iron conduit had been twisted like a pipe cleaner. Its split seams were disgorging tons of water down a sandy slope and over the road in a swift tea-colored sheet. A peculiar smell, like carbolic fumes or something, was hanging in the air.

"What's he doing here?"

Campbell seemed genuinely confused. "Sheriff?"

"The Jap!"

Gesturing for Hank to follow, the lieutenant waded out to the lawman. "We're from the camp—"

"I know that."

"—and this is Hank Fukuda, chief of police."

"I know that, too," the sheriff said in a low voice. "Get him out of here."

"We'd like to help, if we can."

His eyes shifted to the aqueduct. "You already have."

"I don't catch your drift, Sheriff."

He let out an infuriated laugh, then scowled. "Now valley folks'll be blamed for what your Japs gone and done. Tell Wenge thanks a bunch."

"You saw somebody here prior to the blast?"

The sheriff laughed in the same humorless way, then fell silent as he locked gazes with Hank. The water gurgled around the legs of the three men. "I don't need no help. You bastards got no jurisdiction here."

Campbell's eyes went cold. The muscles of his right arm flexed under his sleeve, and Hank thought he was on the verge of Sunday punching the sheriff. But then the lieutenant patted Hank on the shoulder.

"Let's go, Chief, before this crime-fighter finds out that what he's made of floats real good."

CHAPTER 9

The VIP command transport plummeted as if the bottom had fallen out of the sky.

It had been bouncing and yawing through air curdled by updrafts when an ominous stillness came over the plush C-41A. And then the plunge. Colonel Nicholas Bleecher was belted into his leather swivel seat, but the colored steward cried out as he suddenly found himself levitating in the forward passageway. Although terrified himself, the colonel came close to laughing as he watched the man's head bounce along the curved ceiling; but then he had to duck as a silver pot lifted off the fold-up table and spewed coffee onto the Fourth Army insignia woven into the carpet. Bleecher closed his eyes. The twin Pratt and Whitney engines were still rumbling, so it had to be a downdraft, and downdrafts usually came to an abrupt end: hopefully sometime before the plane slammed into the dark forests and granite of the Sierra Nevada below.

Then it came—a shudder so jarring Bleecher thought for an instant that they had indeed crashed. Opening his eyes, he saw the steward in one piece, but flat on his back and nursing his right forearm. "Broken?" the colonel asked.

"No, sir, I don't think so."

"Then clean up the mess in here."

"Yes, sir." Grabbing a white towel, the steward staggered into the main compartment and knelt at the big brown stain in the carpet.

The co-pilot cracked the cockpit door and asked if everyone was all right.

Bleecher glared down the length of the passageway at him but didn't reply. Then, yawning to unplug his ears, he parted the window curtains and gazed down: the plane's toylike shadow was rippling across an azure-colored lake. He detested flying over the Sierra. This time of year, huge thunderheads boiled up from the crest by late afternoon. Fortunately, he would conclude his business at Manzanar by one o'clock and be back in the air before the skies turned even surlier. The consequences of flying through an electrical storm could not be appealed. And Nicholas Bleecher believed that most everything in life could be appealed. Nineteen years spent in criminal law, thirteen of them as the Alameda County DA, had convinced him not to believe in the certainty of catastrophes. Surprises—yes. There were always surprises. But these had a way of opening into opportunities as long as one followed Mr. Kipling's advice and kept his head.

That's why early this morning, upon returning the call to the MP lieutenant with the moronic twang and the third-grade grammar, the colonel had not surrendered to panic. Instead, he had calmly taken stock of the night's events: Wenge slain, an evacuee named Shido an apparent suicide, the aqueduct blasted four miles south of camp, and finally—most promisingly, perhaps—a *nisei* war hero arrested as the kingpin behind it all.

Lieutenant Campbell—a homicide detective before the war, according to his file—claimed to have probable cause to detain Major Tadashi Nitta for questioning. Unexpected but interesting. Bleecher had assured the bumpkin not to worry, that he had wider latitude to arrest and hold a suspect than he'd ever enjoyed as a civilian cop. Campbell hadn't seemed convinced, leaving Bleecher to wonder if the man was as beetle-headed as he sounded, in spite of the puzzling anomaly in his personnel jacket: he had blown the lid off the quantitative reasoning portion of his Army General Classification Test but then botched the verbal section, which meant, most likely, that his inflated math and mechanics scores were clerical errors.

Campbell *had* to be slow.

This had given the colonel an idea, which he mulled over as he showered. By the time he was toweling himself dry, he could smile. Actually, he had not been thrown a curve; he had just been paid a bigger dividend than expected. And this is how he'd explained it to Lieutenant General Van Zwartz as they breakfasted on the old man's veranda, the bay shining below. The general, a timid soul beneath his West Point severity, needed reassurance—he hadn't touched his eggs Benedict. "Where's this all leading, Nick?"

"Into waters we've already charted, sir. . . ." And so he had laid out how this new twist meshed with the original plan. The general had considered his words in glum silence, but at least began nibbling at his breakfast. Then, keeping his tone of voice offhand so as not to further alarm the old man, the colonel had asked if he might have another look at the Pinkerton file, which Van Zwartz kept with the most sensitive materials in his personal safe. This was in his study, and while the old man was upstairs Bleecher had lit a cigarette and let out a long jet of smoke. Van Zwartz might crumble under enough pressure, he had told himself; from this point on, it would be wise to insulate him as much as possible. He could survive only in parade-ground sunlight, whereas Bleecher found his sustenance in the shadows of the war. He was an intelligencer, after all.

Now, as the pilot found a patch of smoother air on the desert side of the Sierra, Bleecher ordered a fresh pot of coffee. Only after his steward had gone forward to the small galley did the colonel unbuckle his restraining belt and retrieve his briefcase from overhead storage. From it he took an unmarked manila jacket. The contents had originally come into his hands from the Office of Naval Intelligence, but not gratuitously by any means. Fourth Army Intelligence had been sitting on something of vital interest to the Navy: a stolid balding Midwestern patrician, who happened to chair the Senate Naval Affairs Committee, liked to frolic under an assumed name at a Santa Cruz nudist club that catered to Bay Region queers. Bleecher's agent had snapped some hilarious shots of the honorable chairman cavorting through the redwoods, his big white fanny flashing in the sun as he clasped hands with a not-quite-famous but instantly recognizable actor under contract with MGM. Needless to say, ever since a swap of intelligence goodies with Bleecher in early 1942, the Navy had been getting all it asked of the Senate.

In return, the colonel was slipped a valise under the table at a Chinatown restaurant in which were photostats of everything the Navy had on Japanese espionage in America, the names of its own operatives as well. Included was the Pinkerton file that Bleecher had specifically requested, surprising the Navy that he knew anything about it. The ONI code name had a significance: B. F. Pinkerton was the dashing young lieutenant who had devastated Madame Butterfly. This had pricked Bleecher's professional sensibilities. A code name, even a tongue-in-cheek one, should never offer a riddle. With persistence, riddles are solved. Still, securing the file from Naval Intelligence had been something of a coup, for it documented an operational failure.

In 1939 the ONI planted a civilian intelligence specialist in Tokyo. Overtly, he was a trade coordinator with the U.S. embassy, but his real job was to assist the naval attaché. It's no secret that a military attaché is simply a spy with diplomatic immunity; and, because he knows that his slightest move is being monitored by his host's counterintelligence boys, he must rely on an innocent-looking embassy staffer to do his legwork for him. Enter Pinkerton. A retired naval officer but utterly lacking in martial bearing, he was singularly qualified for this mission. And he did a bang-up job for several months—until one morning the chief of Tokyo police paid a discreet call on the ambassador.

After some typical Jap beating around the bush, the chief came to the point: a prostitute had been found hacked to death in the Yoshiwara, Tokyo's paper-lantern, or red-light, district. He had "incontrovertible proof" that an embassy employee had committed the atrocity. When the ambassador demanded to see the proof, the chief switched tactics and started talking about how one more strain on Japanese-American relations might lead to a complete diplomatic breakdown. Would it not be better for all concerned if the culprit were quietly spirited out of Japan?

This sudden persona non grata, of course, was Pinkerton, who pled innocence in a star-chamber court before the ambassador and the naval attaché. He might have been telling the truth: there was a chance the Japanese had gotten wise to his junkets to Yokosuka, site of their sprawling navy base, or to his sightseeing cruises on Tokyo Bay, invariably in the vicinity of the empire's newest capital warships, and were using the accusation to boot him out of the country without having to reveal that they had fingered him as an intelligencer.

Whatever the case, Pinkerton was shipped home, where he languished until Pearl Harbor. He applied again to the ONI and was refused, then to the soon-to-be disbanded Corps of Intelligence Police and was also turned down, and finally to Bleecher, who promised to consider him for "some delicate domestic espionage work, pending a background investigation." He thanked the colonel with tears in his eyes, but, as he was shaking hands in parting, blurted, "Sir, there's something else we should discuss in all candor . . . something that happened in Tokyo. . . ."

Bleecher had known nothing about the affair. Nor would he have discovered anything about it. Each intelligence fiefdom jealously guarded its own information, and the ONI was not about to reveal one of its own snafus—not without good reason.

The file and photos on Senator Nature Boy eventually provided such a reason.

Pinkerton got the job, gratefully accepting it as the vindication of his blamelessness. However, unbeknown to him, the colonel had hired Pinkerton on the premise that he had indeed carried some kind of bladed instrument into the Yoshiwara—and there dismembered a diminutive whore.

"Colonel, sir?"

Bleecher slapped the file shut so his steward couldn't see its contents. "What is it, Emmanuel?"

"The pilot says we'll be landing in a few minutes, sir. You still want that coffee?"

"No, bring me a shot of Scotch instead."

"Very good, sir."

Then, to keep his mind off the crosswinds that could lash Manzanar's airstrip without warning, he returned the file to his briefcase and took out a chart, which unfolded into a three-by-four-foot rectangle. It could have been the blueprint for an army post, except that there was no headquarters building, no post theater, no parade ground, and none of the dwellings looked large enough to be a barrack. Some of the streets ended in cul-de-sacs after winding quite unmilitarily around what appeared to be a golf course. Before the war, the acreage had been a strawberry farm owned by California Japs. Ordered to evacuate within seventy-two hours, they had entrusted their holdings to the Farm Security Administration, and the FSA had turned them over to a property management corporation, which had operated the farm so deeply in the red that the land had recently gone into foreclosure. The colonel smiled; he had just read in the *San Francisco Examiner* that this year alone a million people would pour into California. A *million* people!

The transport plane banked sharply: the saw-toothed profile of the Sierra was replaced by a gray-green expanse of sagebrush, and that in turn by a dun-colored square crowded with neat rows of dominoes—Manzanar War Relocation Center.

Perhaps it was good that events were beginning to assert

themselves. After glowing white-hot in the months after December 7, the fervor had gradually cooled. It was no longer believed that an attack on the West Coast was imminent, let alone possible—even in the halls of the War Department, which had just dismantled Fourth Army's interceptor squadron, leaving a single worn-out P-40 to protect the Presidio from, say, a Jap seaplane attack.

No, it was clear that the American people, having slipped back into their habitual lassitude, would have to be awakened once again.

The wheels touched down with a gut-wrenching jolt.

◆ ◆ ◆

The bench in the corridor of the administration building was as hard as a Southern Baptist pew. Changing positions for the tenth time in as many minutes, Jared tried once again to get comfortable. It was no use. Doubtless, it had something to do with the fact that he hadn't slept in thirty hours now. His stomach was coffee-scorched, his eyes inflamed. Instead of gore or even death, he associated homicides with his own fatigue. In the last few minutes his ears had started ringing, a sure sign that he was washed-up until he could get a few hours' rest.

A little boy occupied the far end of the bench, his high-top shoes dangling halfway to the floor. He had a *chawan*, a rice-bowl haircut, parted down the middle, and suspicious comet-shaped eyes that kept darting toward Jared. His mother had gone into the settlement office twenty minutes earlier, after needlessly telling him to behave himself while she tried to wrest a ticket for them out of Western Defense Command.

Jared tried a wink on him, but the boy's gaze dropped to the floor and he squirmed up against the armrest.

"Hey, bub, look here . . ." Jared began snipping two fingers together as if they formed a pair of scissors. "Okay?"

He agreed with a shy smile, hiding his right hand behind his back as Jared did the same. The lieutenant bobbed his head to the count of three, then together they brought out their hands: the boy's flat and Campbell's fisted.

"You win," Jared said, then laughed at the child's shrill

giggle. *Paper covers rock.* It was a hand game called "Jan Ken Po." He'd picked it up watching the kids on the firebreaks. "Ready again? Jan Ken Po . . . you, me show . . ."

Jared's scissors were busted by the boy's rock—his tiny fist looked to be the size of a walnut.

The lieutenant glanced at his wristwatch.

Colonel Bleecher had arrived an hour ago—and immediately closeted himself with Montgomery Lee in Director Wenge's office. At the time, Jared had been with Hank Fukuda, shivering inside the reefer at the MP compound, going over Shido and Wenge's corpses one more time, making sure that in last night's confusion they hadn't overlooked any less apparent signs of trauma. At last, Jared rasped, "Enough's enough." He had snugged a corner of the blanket over Wenge's bare foot, which looked like white marble but for the purple blush of lividity along the Achilles tendon, then led the chief out into the morning dazzle. "Why don't you try to get some shut-eye? Bleecher should be here any minute, and I'll get back to you when he's gone."

Fukuda massaged his swollen eyelids. "If you don't mind—I'll freshen up, then stand by. I don't think I can sleep."

"Sure, I understand." Jared had padlocked the reefer door and pocketed the key. "I'll drive you back to your apartment. Then you can meet me at admin."

"Thanks."

Jared now pretended to be exasperated with the child, who had just beaten him again. *Scissors cut paper.* An instructive game, he thought: the best you come up with can always be beaten by something else. "Dang, but you're just too slick for this old farm boy." He rose as he heard high-heels clipping down the linoleum toward him. Only Morris Wenge's middle-aged secretary wore them; the *nisei* secretaries kept to what Jared's mother called sensible shoes.

"Hi, Hazel." Her eyes were red-rimmed. How much did she really know? Jared, in following the orders Bleecher had given him over the phone, put it out that Wenge had died of a heart attack and that the lock-down had been only a precaution against camp unrest. The lies had apparently worked: Manzanar was quiet this morning. But they were still lies, and the staff would resent them when the truth came to light.

"Good morning, Jared. The colonel will see you now." She started to weep, braced herself against the tears, then crumpled against his shoulder. "I just can't *believe* it."

"I know, darling . . . I know . . ." Jared gave her a hug, then put on his overseas cap. It was indelibly gray with Owens Valley dust, and his black tie was no longer regulation—it was supposed to be khaki. He barely knew Colonel Bleecher, and prayed that the man from the Presidio wasn't a stickler.

♦ ♦ ♦

"Be seated." Returning Jared's salute, the colonel tossed a frown at the lieutenant's tie, but said nothing. Then he opened the file on the desk before him. The only sounds were those of the onionskin pages being turned by his manicured fingers and the purring of the swamp cooler behind him. The folder was too fat to be a service record—probably a File 201, a personnel jacket. Jared couldn't make out the label but suspected it to be his own, although he had no idea how it could have been retrieved from MP headquarters without the company clerk advising him.

From across the office Montgomery Lee smiled at him desolately. He was so bilious-looking—seemingly more so than from his usual morning hangover—Jared surmised that he had been canned at long last. Yet, he had to hide his surprise a moment later when the colonel said, "Mr. Lee is taking over the helm here. His status as director is provisional, of course, but I've assured him he can rely on the Army's full cooperation."

Bleecher paused, and Jared realized it was his cue: "Yes, sir." He also sensed that something ugly had just passed between the men, leaving the associate director with a dazed, meaningless grin and the colonel with a quiet air of domination. Monty's watery gaze drifted out the window toward the Sierra. Jared thought the granite seemed especially ancient and grizzled this morning.

Bleecher said, "And now if Mr. Lee will excuse us . . ."

Monty continued to stare at the mountains.

"Mr. Lee?"

The new acting director startled. "Oh—pardon me. As you were saying?"

"I was saying *you're dismissed.*"

Monty seemed stung by these words, but then smiled. "Of course. Will the colonel be staying for luncheon?"

"No."

Rising, the new acting director nodded—to himself, for the colonel was preoccupied with the file on the desk again. "Good day then, gentlemen."

Bleecher ignored him, his point lost on no one: the Army was now in complete control of Manzanar. Of the legion of bureaucrats in bow ties and pinstripe bustling around the War Relocation Authority's offices inside San Francisco's Whitcomb Hotel not one was present for this morning's hurried changing of the guard.

As soon as the door clicked shut, the colonel steepled his hands together and rested his chin on them. Then he studied Jared, his eyes cold and aloof. "Tell me what the hell happened here last night, Campbell."

Struggling to keep his accent under wraps, the lieutenant began with the report of a dead body in the judo school. It took ten uncomfortable minutes for him to reach the discovery of Wenge's decapitated corpse. The colonel's expression would turn fearsome when something appeared to displease him, so Jared kept his own gaze on the man's eyebrows, which were silvery, like his hair. It was a trick he had developed for coping with courtroom grillings by aggressive lawyers.

"At what point did you decide to arrest Nitta?" Bleecher interrupted for the first time, his accusatory tone reminding Jared that he had been a district attorney someplace.

"Let's see, sir . . ." Jared hesitated. Something, maybe it was the predatory glint in Bleecher's eyes, or the promise he had made last night to Hank Fukuda, kept him from revealing the liver temperature findings. "I don't rightly recall, sir. What

Major Nitta said about Mr. Wenge at his testimonial dinner musta been milling around inside my head."

Bleecher frowned again, but then changed the subject. "Well, it sounds like you and this Japanese chief have put the investigation on a solid footing. You're a real cop. It's one thing to swagger around with an armband and a billy club, quite another to put a case together. That's why General Van Zwartz wants you to ramrod this."

"Excuse me, sir, but what about Captain Snavely?"

"He's on temporary duty. Naturally, you'll continue as acting CO in his absence."

"Any idea how long he'll be on this duty, sir?"

"Until further notice." Then, unexpectedly, the colonel smiled. It was a well-heeled smile. "The important thing is, your backing comes right from the top. So tell me what you need to put this operation into high gear."

"Well, right off, I'd like the bodies postmortemed as quick as possible."

"Truck them over to us, Letterman Hospital morgue."

"Yes, sir—but that don't solve the problem of getting them to a pathologist in the next few hours. The Presidio's a ten-hour drive, probably twice that long for our wreck of a deuce-and-a-half. Can we fly them out with you?"

Bleecher's smile faded. "In the commanding general's transport? What the devil are you asking, Campbell?"

"To get these bodies to a forensic pathologist as soon as possible, Colonel."

"There will be no autopsies."

"Sir?"

"Come on, man—the causes of death are ridiculously evident. Send them by truck—as ordered—and let's get on with it."

Jared leaned back. The slats of the chair creaked loudly, making him ease forward again. *No* cause of death was evident until all the possibilities had been eliminated. To suggest otherwise was absurd, especially for a criminal law attorney. Had this been a council between a cop and the district attorney, he would have been poking his forefinger into Bleecher's chest by this point. But this was the Army. "Yes, sir."

"Anything else?"

"Well, I've come up against this jurisdictional thing . . ."

"How's that?"

When Jared finished telling Bleecher about his confrontation with the sheriff at the blast site, the colonel slowly shook his head. "Who do *you* think has jurisdiction?"

"Well, it's his county, sir. And WRA Instruction Thirty-four says we deliver over felony defendants to local officials for prosecution. Plus I suppose the feds should have a piece of this—on accounta the explosives."

"There's a war on, for godsake! Hasn't anybody told you that?" Laughing, the colonel smacked his palms against the desk blotter that still bore rings from Morris Wenge's coffee cup. "Western Defense Command is a theater of operations!"

Now it was Jared's turn to smile.

"Do you doubt that?"

"I know it's a war zone on paper and all, sir—"

"No, mister, it's a war zone because the secretary of war says it is. And that means the president says it is. That's all you have to tell these local yokels—my authority comes from the man in the White House. And if any reporter tries to get around the news blackout the general has imposed on this thing, toss his ass in your guardhouse. I'll personally send a detail from the Presidio to pick him up."

"What about legal help for Major Nitta, sir?"

"Damn—is somebody from the ACLU already sticking his nose in this?"

"No, sir."

"Then why are you asking?"

Jared didn't know what to say: he'd been thinking of Kimiko.

"Did you tell his family why you nabbed him?"

"No, sir—I said I couldn't reveal that."

Bleecher visibly relaxed. "Good. Tell them counsel will be arranged through our judge advocate."

"What if he wants a civilian lawyer?"

"He doesn't get one. This is a military matter. First, he's a soldier, not an evacuee. Second, he was arrested during an emergency at which time control of this center had reverted to the MP commander. I've read the WRA instructions, too, Lieutenant."

Bleecher bent over for his briefcase, revealing a thin spot at the crown of his head he had meticulously attempted to comb over. "Speaking of military concerns . . ." He tossed a file marked CONFIDENTIAL to Jared, who was caught off-guard and dropped it. Bleecher smirked. "A little something for you to follow up on. May come to nil, but I think we should keep all our options open, including Nitta's innocence. Have a look."

It was an intelligence report dated 5 March 1942. Behind the cover sheet was a letter from Sheriff Bertrand Coy, Jr., to the Wartime Civil Control Administration—the first agency to manage the evacuation—protesting a proposed "Jap labor camp" between Independence and Lone Pine on Highway 395. He cited the threat alien saboteurs might pose to the nearby Los Angeles Aqueduct, whose water was vital to Southern California's war industries: "We have no guarantee one of the Jap prisoners won't stroll out some dark night and dynamite the pipeline. . . ."

Coy may have had a point there, Jared thought to himself. But it was the follow-up report by Bleecher's G-2 agent that made him suddenly glance up and meet the colonel's amused eyes.

"Interesting?"

"I'll say, sir."

Digging into the back issues of the *Inyo Independent*, the agent had uncovered a long-forgotten criminal conviction that the sheriff had obliterated from the records of his own department: In 1921, Bertrand Coy, Sr., an Owens Valley rancher and fruit grower displaced by the City of Los Angeles water project, was sentenced to five years in the state penitentiary "for attempting to injure an aqueduct siphon with explosives." Coy's property had been called Rancho *Manzanar*—Spanish for apple orchard, the thorough agent had added in a footnote.

Bleecher took the report back. "I need a lift to the airstrip."

"I'll drive you myself, sir." And, as Jared followed the crisply attired officer down the corridor, he admitted to himself that he didn't care for Nicholas Bleecher, but that he had known the strange mix in other men he hadn't liked: despite their arrogance, their pomaded hair, they were square shooters. And really, the colonel had said only what every cop wants to hear from his superior—go ahead, bird-dog the truth; do your job, and I'll back you up.

♦ ♦ ♦

Hank Fukuda got a sack full of crushed ice from his mess hall and hurried back to his apartment before it melted through the paper. There, after sliding open his window, he downed two salt tablets with a long draught of ice water then chilled and wrapped a wet towel around his head. Finally he sank into his overstuffed chair. He felt as if a *sumo* wrestler were sitting on him, and wondered if he would be able to rise again in a few minutes, shower, then slog over to the administration building to meet with Campbell. He closed his eyes. They had begun tearing from having been open to the parched air so long.

Filling out a fifty-page interrogatory on the camp jail for the Spanish consul in San Francisco—who looked after the interests of the aliens in lieu of the Japanese government—and then booking a drunk who had overturned eleven trays of seedlings while rampaging through the guayule lath house, had kept him up the night before. Fifty hours without sleep now. Drowsiness started flowing over him like warm honey. He smiled to himself; like most men, he found his contentment in brief, sleepy doses.

"Damnation." Throwing off the towel, he grasped the dusty padded armrests to hurl himself to his feet. But his legs refused to jack him upward, and his arms felt as heavy as the stone lanterns to be found in most Japanese gardens. The spirit is willing, he told himself, but the flesh weak.

Suddenly, the flimsy wooden door was rattled by pounding. "Chief Fukuda!"

He realized that he was standing, seemingly an impossible accomplishment. "Come in . . . come in."

The boy was about twelve. A dollar bill, tightly rolled into a green tube, was clenched in his right fist. "Mr. Momai wants to talk to you right away."

"Where?"

"His place, sir."

Hank thought about swinging by the station first to pick up a couple of officers, but then decided it was time for a showdown with Momai's clique. Bringing along a backup of club-toting cops would weaken the only real power he had—his fearlessness, which was really nothing but an act, a pretense spawned by desperation. Hank Fukuda felt afraid most of his waking hours.

"Tell him I'm on my way," he said, taking out his wallet and giving the kid his second dollar of the morning. A day and a half's wages—but he didn't want to appear less generous than the so-called Black Dragon Society.

◆ ◆ ◆

They went as small boys and girls on slow rusty steamships across the Pacific. At quaysides in Hiroshima, Yamaguchi, Fukuoka, and Kumamoto—the prefectures their parents had abandoned—they were met by grandparents, uncles and aunts, cousins—total strangers to them. The cities into which they were taken were hauntingly reminiscent of the *Nihonmachi*, the Japan towns of Honolulu, Seattle, Walnut Grove, or Sacramento, yet these new cities were also strange and forbidding; and, when the homesickness came, the children were given *jintan*, a panacea for everything except the taint of having no *mana*, the beneficence that came from being born on Japanese soil.

The strictures heaped on them by *sensei* in unheated classrooms were not reserved for them alone as *Nichi Bei*, Japanese of America. Like all children past six years of age, they were done with indulgence and had to habituate themselves to the constraints that came from centuries of hand-to-mouth living in an island nation where only one-fifth of the land was arable. By 1930, they began coming back to their *issei* parents in numbers large enough to make them recognizable as a group, so they were dubbed *kibei*, which means "returned to America." Sent to Japan before they had mastered English, they were returned to America before they had fluency in Japanese. If they had no language to call their own, many saw themselves without a country as well, although a few talked up *Bushido* for the same reason they would have espoused American-style democracy had they found themselves on the other side of the Pacific at the outset of the war: to be *kibei* was to be apart. Some were different from their *nisei* siblings only in that they seemed more aloof, more puritanical, more Japanese—although few had any desire to return to Japan. But others, particularly the males, suffered from a discontent marked by profligacy that kept their grafted-on *mana* from either completely healing or withering and dropping away. These were thought to be *abunai* by the other evacuees—dangerous. And immoral.

In the sweltering bachelors' barrack, six such *kibei* were gathered around a table. Two were playing *shogi*, Japanese checkers, and the others were feigning interest in the game. The scene was so obviously staged Hank Fukuda wondered if he'd made a mistake by coming alone. But it was too late for second thoughts.

A fifty-tin of Lucky Strikes lay open on the table. All six men had a cigarette going, and the pall of smoke was making them squint. This and the fedoras three of them wore low over their eyes made them look like Dutch Schultz's sidekicks. It was almost comical, and Hank might have laughed—except that these men, as best he would ever know, were the last members in Manzanar of a gang calling itself the Black Dragon. The others had tipped their hands in one way or another and been shipped off to segregation at Tule Lake.

Of course, there probably wasn't one true member of the Black Dragon Society in any of the camps—it was a very select fraternity in Japan committed to "enhancing the spirit of Japanese military virtue." Most of these *kibei* who had returned in the late thirties had done so to avoid the Imperial Army draft —something they had conveniently forgotten when they borrowed the formidable name for their own little band of ruffians.

If that august, *samurai*-glorifying society genuinely did not exist on American soil, as Hank believed, what then was the *Black Dragon?* The answer had come to him one night as he lay sweating on his cot with the searchlights casting false dawns against his windows: the Black Dragon was the slithering beast the *hakujin* imagined rooted in the heart of each *nihonjin*. It was nested there deeper than sight; even reason could not illuminate it. However, the beast could never be expunged from the Japanese heart, so the body enclosing that corrupted heart had to be imprisoned behind barbed wire.

Momai stood. He bowed—a sign, perhaps, that the amenities would be respected, although his pronounced upper lip was curled into a sneer. As usual, he was dressed in a manner only someone fresh off the boat from Kyushu would think jaunty: an imperial infantry field cap, a long tan scarf knotted at the throat, forest green riding breeches, and knee-high lace boots with his white stockings neatly rolled down over the tops. "I thank you for coming, Fukuda-*dono*," he said in Japanese, his inflection not quite in agreement with the term of respect he had bestowed on the chief.

"What do you wish?" Hank asked, his own Japanese less fluid than the *kibei*'s.

"A *bushi* of *Dai Nihon* has chosen the way of the warrior."

"A man has died, yes."

"More than a man, Fukuda-*san*." A lesser form of respect.

"None of us is more than a man."

Momai rapped his knuckles on the table. "Masao Shido is a martyr."

"And what did he do to win martyrdom?"

Momai ignored the question. "We would like his ashes for a Shinto service." He sat again, folding his arms over his chest.

What was the purpose of this? Was he trying to prove to Shido's lackeys that he was now their honcho? Hank had no doubt that Momai was testing him—but why? "Anybody here a blood relative to Shido?" he asked in English.

The *kibei* looked askance at one another; a few shrugged.

"You must excuse us," Momai persisted in Japanese, "but we understand only that which is spoken in *Dai Nihon*."

Hank had had enough. "Cut the crap, Momai. Anybody who thinks there's going to be a Great Japan after this war ought to have his head examined." Momai stiffened—a consummately Japanese gesture that caused the chief to smile thinly. "If someone can prove he's Shido's relation, I'll hand over the ashes. But get this straight—it'll be for a Buddhist, not a state Shinto ceremony. That's all, folks."

"We demand the ashes of this noble avenger at once!"

Hank growled, "You *what?*"

"We *demand*—"

Before he realized what he was doing, Hank had rushed across the floor and seized the scowling *kibei* by the scarf, lifted him out of his chair, and slammed him against the wall, bulging the one-inch boards outward. "You . . . !"

But he quickly got a grip on himself. He had nothing on the man, though—for a blinding instant—it had burst into his head that Momai and Shido had slain Morris Wenge and then Momai had acted as Shido's second in the purifying rite of *seppuku*. Now, only seconds later, he wondered how he could have been carried away by a notion so contrary to the physical evidence. Exhaustion, perhaps. Or bewilderment that Momai was pushing him so hard. He would back off—if only to find out why. Even if he had the power to send them all to Tule Lake, the transfer would only keep him from learning the reason behind their impudence.

He let go of Momai.

Then, sensing movement at his back, he spun around, holding his powerful arms out to the sides. One of the *kibei*, clutching a homemade dagger, had risen. His half-parted lips were pulled back against his tobacco-stained teeth.

Hank motioned for him to go ahead. He was aching for the bastard to try. It would be a gratifying moment in which to die—fighting the very thing that he somehow sensed had cost him his job, his freedom, his self-respect. Death was freedom.

Yowling, the *kibei* executed a judo kick in the air, then resumed a defensive stance as he glanced at Momai.

Surprisingly, Momai, still nursing his throat with his fingers, ordered him to back off. The blade clattered on the floor.

"This will never be forgotten, Fukuda," Momai spat.

"Fucking A." The chief confiscated the dagger and strode out, slamming the door behind him.

♦ ♦ ♦

Ten minutes later, still pumped full of adrenaline, he glimpsed Jared Campbell and a full bird colonel strolling down the corridor of the administration building toward him.

"Colonel Bleecher," Campbell drawled, twisting his overseas cap in his hands, "this here is Chief Fukuda."

In addition to his intimidating stare, the head of Fourth Army G-2 had satiny manners that made Hank want to shrink into himself. Bleecher was strikingly handsome, but handsome in the disjointed way a vain man would look if he had the misfortune of being able to order his own features à la carte.

"A pleasure, Chief. The lieutenant's told me what excellent work you've done so. If there's anything you need—" He interrupted himself: "Say, are you set up to do any explosives analysis?"

"To test for type used, sir?" Hank asked.

"That's right—on debris from the blast site, if you can find any. Let's cover all the bases."

"Well, I suppose I could do some acetone work here."

"Do it."

"I just don't have access to any of the stuff—other than nail polish from the beauty school. And it's not pure."

Bleecher regarded the ceiling with distaste; big flies were noisily bumping their way along the rafters. Then he turned to Campbell. "Who stocks chemical supplies in the county?"

"Well, there's an assay office in Lone Pine, sir."

"See that the chief gets what he needs, Lieutenant—for

any test he has in mind. And keep me informed. Other than that, follow the evidence on your own initiative. Both of you."

Reasonable enough, Hank decided as he trailed them out into the heat of noon. Yet, for all his reassuring words, Nicholas Bleecher was the kind of Caucasian who could make you feel *bootchie*—just by smiling at you. And, as he knew all too well, Bleecher had also slapped together the intelligence dossier on American Japanese "espionage" that had convinced Franklin Roosevelt to sign the evacuation order.

"Hank, after I take the colonel out to the strip," Campbell said quietly, "I'm going to grab about four hours' sleep. Then what do you say we go take a look at that aqueduct?"

The chief nodded, his face deceptively placid.

CHAPTER 10

Twilight filtered through the walls of the tent, the canvas now a soft blue instead of the saffron color it had been earlier under the brunt of the desert sun. Outside, familiar voices. Accentless, Oklahoman voices. The crackling of a cooking fire built from snakelike greasewood branches. Then a guitar, strains of a Bob Wills song rising over the liquid murmuring of the Colorado. Jared found himself listening for his father, and when a silhouette flashed against the west wall of the tent he assumed it to be him, probably stripped down to his trousers and suspenders, only his neck and forearms tanned, the rest of him as white as flour. But when one of the flaps was thrown back, it was not Norvil Campbell, but a decapitated body that staggered inside. The thing loomed over Jared's cot, beckoning with its bloody hands for the return of its head.

Gasping for air, Jared sat bolt upright from his sweat-soaked pillow. Only then did he realize that he was in his quarters.

It was almost four, and the afternoon shadow cast by the Sierra was blueing his window shade. As always, he had beaten his alarm clock by ten minutes, which could only mean that some part of him refused to sleep.

And yes, he decided as he swung his legs over the side of the cot, he was back on a homicide. The victim was making his anguish known. The nightmare, a sad tradition, always came during the first exhausted sleep after he'd examined a body. Sometimes a poor crazy man waltzed out of the shades, clasping the muzzle of a revolver to his own baby's head. But usually it was the latest victim, beckoning with his bloodstained hands.

Slowly, as if his fingers had gone numb, Jared dressed.

♦ ♦ ♦

Kimiko checked behind her. The MP sergeant named Osler was slouched over the battered green desk in the guardhouse, reading a comic book. She turned back to Eddie and tried to smile at him through the wire mesh. "I'm putting together something . . ." She lowered her voice, but not all the way to a whisper, which would only arouse Osler's suspicion. "A writ of habeas corpus."

Eddie greeted the news with a half-hearted shrug.

"They've got to show cause for holding you."

"No they don't."

She was speechless for a moment. "They *can't* do this to you."

"They're the Army. They can do whatever they want. What more proof do you need?" The languid roll of his eyes went beyond the guardhouse to include all of Manzanar, their lives in internment. Then he laughed, inconsolably, and it frightened her. "Near Volturano, we came up to this absolute mess of concertina wire. The Krauts had thrown it across a ravine between two pillboxes. We couldn't go around, so I called for some bangalore torpedoes."

"What are—"

"Explosive charges in tube . . ." Irritation pinched his eyes for a moment. "Well, the lieutenant, most of the noncoms in that platoon, had already been hit. In fact, there wasn't much left of my company at that point. So I was really just a glorified corporal instead of a captain. I sent the first kid forward with a torpedo. He got about five feet before a machine-gun round threw him back into our laps—in pieces." The same unsettling laugh. "I tapped another kid on the shoulder, and he started off. He made it halfway to the first coil of wire, then two more died just trying to reach the torpedo he'd dropped. All in all, I think I tapped six kids on the shoulder before we blew a hole through that wire. And we're not talking about those who went down right after we took out the pillboxes. . . ." Eddie scooted back his chair and came to his feet, although Osler had not announced that their time was up. "I was just helping them with their program, Kimi-*chan*."

"What do you mean—*who?*"

Eddie stared right through her. "The *hakujin*. They're making us all disappear. And now it's my turn to be tapped on the shoulder. *Shikata ga nai*." Nothing can be done.

♦ ♦ ♦

Montgomery Lee had thrown open both the front and rear doors of his bungalow, but the warm breeze only added to the sweat streaming down his neck, his arms, and collecting in the clammy small of his back. He stripped down to his skivvies, and the first sensation of coolness pierced like loneliness. Padding to the kitchenette in his moist, bare feet, he poured about six jiggers of bourbon into a tumbler, then added a splash of water from the tap. He drained this first drink at the sink, then refilled the tumbler with straight whiskey and carried it and a cigar that was still cold from the refrigerator into the living room.

Sinking into his sofa, he lit the cigar and, after a few pulls to get it going, savored the smoke. Time began to slow for him, and the ravagement in his eyes dwindled.

An hour and half a bottle of bourbon later, as he was floating toward unconsciousness, he saw a tarantula in the corner. With more coordination than he thought possible, he bolted up off the sofa and looked for something with which to kill it.

Months before, his secretary had found one of the hideous spiders in her bathroom, so it didn't completely surprise him to see one now. He slid the samurai sword out of its scabbard and quietly stole across the room, although he knew them to be sluggish creatures. He was raising the sword over his head when he suddenly eased it down to his side, though the look of revulsion didn't leave his face.

He leaned over and scooped it up: a lock of coarse black hair gathered together at one end by a few loops of thread.

Quickly, he took it to toilet and flushed it away.

◆ ◆ ◆

Jared inched down into the bucket seat. Elwayne, as usual, hadn't parked the jeep in the shade. The steering wheel was impossible to touch even though the sun had dipped behind the Sierra some minutes before, so he finished his mug of coffee before starting the engine. A thunderhead had formed in the northern distance, its powdery canyons shot through with bands of light.

Finally, he wheeled the jeep around and accelerated out the compound gate, the clutch slipping between gears, although motor pool had insisted it was fine. Hell, the Dodge two-and-a-half-ton was fine, too, despite the shot bearing that howled like a banshee.

On the shoulder of the highway a young Japanese woman was walking beside Osler. Kimiko, Jared realized with a start. She was being escorted back to camp after visiting her husband. Pulling alongside, he said, "I'm on my way to pick up Chief Fukuda, Sergeant. I can take Mrs. Nitta back."

"Thank you, sir." Osler saluted, his coarse face revealing nothing. Did he know? Jared put it out of his mind: he could go mad wondering who knew about Kimiko and him.

Wordlessly, she got in and smoothed her skirt over her knees.

"How's the major doing?" he asked, pulling back onto the asphalt.

She didn't answer.

All the explanations he had rehearsed died with her silence. His mouth went dry.

As if suddenly unaware of Jared, she arched her torso into the coolness streaming over the top of the windshield. Her eyes were fixed on the thunderhead, which was now peach-colored on its sunward side. The summer dress made her seem all the more sensual; he yearned to feel her body through the thin, fluttering material.

"I never thought I'd like my country all buckled up like this," he said at last. "No mountains in Oklahoma. Or maybe clouds were our mountains."

The corporal of the guard waved them past the main sentry house, but fifty yards later the Black Maria—the resettlement transportation wagon—was idling beside the police post while a dozen former residents, returning from visits to their relatives back East, stood silent in a rank, opening their cardboard luggage for a contraband inspection by one of Hank Fukuda's men. The cop signaled for Jared to go through the exit lane, but the lieutenant motioned that it was all right—he'd wait.

He glanced over at her. Her jaw was set. Then she shook her head and said, "Please tell me this all has nothing to do with what happened between us."

His eyes started to water, infuriating him. "It doesn't."

"Eddie didn't do anything to the aqueduct."

He examined her face carefully. She didn't know about the two deaths—he was sure of it. But how had she learned of the target of the blast? It was a mystery to him how the rumor mill in camp worked.

"And how often must I remind you . . . ?" She paused, shaking her head, too upset to go on.

"About what?" he asked, crossly now.

"This valley has been in the midst of an ongoing water war for the past thirty years."

He reached down and slipped his cigarettes from the top of his sock, then decided not to smoke. "Are you saying the ranchers blew the pipeline and are trying to throw the blame on the evacuees?"

"Why not? Think of all the other things my people have been accused of."

My people—she'd never used those words before. It made

him feel miles apart from her; all at once, he was her enemy. "Well, I'll look into it."

"When?"

"*Now*, dammit!" Then, his eyes softened by regret, he lowered his voice. "I'm taking Hank Fukuda down to the site with me. We're going to have a good look. And nobody's fixing the blame on the evacuees. Not even the Presidio. Believe me."

"Then why is Eddie locked up in your guardhouse?"

The search completed, the Black Maria lumbered into camp. Jamming the stick into first gear, Jared followed in the wake of the wagon's oily exhaust. His voice when he spoke was suddenly strained. "Do you honestly think I'd try to hurt him?"

She turned her face away from him.

"What kind of man do you take me for, Ki?"

"I don't know—" She flinched as the mess hall bells, old brake drums or iron triangles, were clanged by cooks all over Manzanar. "I'm not sure I understand any of you anymore."

◆ ◆ ◆

The pavement was still buff-colored where the sand deposited by the ruptured aqueduct had been bulldozed off the side into a pile. As Campbell parked the jeep, Hank Fukuda reached into his black bag. He removed a pair of tweezers and two empty Alka-Seltzer bottles, then pocketed them in his trousers. He would come back for the 35mm camera if he needed it.

Campbell got out and stretched. "We got maybe three and a half hours of light. Any suggestions where we start?"

The way to search a large area like the one they were dealing with was to establish a wide perimeter and then start working in concentric circles toward the seat of the explosion. But Hank, not wanting to sound high-handed, said only, "I guess one part of the haystack is as good as another."

"Then, how about if we kick off in a big loop from here—well yonder where the aqueduct was split—and keep going round in smaller circles?"

The chief smiled to himself.

Walking in tandem about ten feet apart, they worked their way up the arroyo created by the torrent. It was already dry, and Hank's cordovan loafers quickly filled with sand, but he wouldn't delay Campbell by stopping to dump them out. "Any snakes around here?"

"Oh, I suppose." Campbell shaded his eyes with his hand. The sun, having declined at a slant behind a pyramid-shaped mountain, now shone again from the vee of a deep glacial valley. "You see that, Hank?"

The chief followed Campbell's finger to a glint of gold on the slope above them. "I think so—twenty feet to the left of the flat-topped boulder?"

"Right, we'll work around to it."

They continued the search, Hank appreciative that Campbell hadn't abandoned the pattern they'd decided on to go chasing after doubloons or whatever it was sparkling up there. Then he noticed something in the sand and prodded it with the toe of his loafer. "Here's a rivet."

"You want to save it?"

"Naw, anything in this wash won't have any residue left on it. Nothing scours like sand and fast water." He gave a fresh-looking animal burrow a wide berth. "What kind of snakes?"

Campbell hiked his shoulders. "Sidewinders, I guess."

Hank halted. "*Rattle*snakes?"

"Hell, man, ain't you ever been out . . . ?" The lieutenant's voice trailed off. He looked a little ashamed until the chief chuckled; then he grinned. "Rattlers are nothing. They won't even come out till dark. Sissy snakes. Now you take the snakes back home in Oklahoma—copperheads, water moccasins. There's some ruthless snakes. They'll come right up and knock on your screen door just to see if you're home and worth biting. . . ."

The aqueduct had already been repaired, the new section in bright contrast to the rest of the oxidized pipe. The line was humming, almost as if it were a living thing. And the iron, which was cool to Hank's touch, gave off a slight vibration—

it was like taking Los Angeles's pulse at its jugular. "Looks like they cleaned up all the debris."

"Didn't take long, did it? And that's what's wrong showing up a day late to a crime scene."

Amen, Hank thought. The damage had been less serious than he had first imagined. The saboteur, whoever he was, had failed to shut down the system for any length of time.

The men rested for a minute, silent before the broad sweep of mountains and desert. The northern end of the valley was dim with a cloudburst.

Then Campbell frowned as he clicked a pebble against the pipe. "Mr. Lee's now acting director," he said. "Announcement'll be made tomorrow."

Hank crawled under the pipeline first, mostly so the lieutenant wouldn't see the expression on his face. Was the WRA run by lunatics? Monty Lee was a drunk with enough complexes for ten mental patients. The chief had sensed it from the beginning—beneath the veneer of Ashley Wilkes gentility and magnolia-blossom eloquence was a man in the throes of *ki-chi-gai,* certifiable crazy behavior. But the evacuees would be the last people in America to be consulted about the selection of their own turnkeys. So, instead of responding, he compressed his lips and looked for debris.

Skirting the base of the flat-topped boulder, they started going over the ground inch by inch. Hank noticed an obsidian arrowhead, a nice one, but didn't pick it up for fear the lieutenant would think his mind wasn't completely on the job. It was silly, this desperation to acquit himself of he knew not what; but there was also no denying it.

"Here it is, Hank. Now you tell me . . ."

"Hmm." The object had plugged in the sand like a golf ball that lands in a bunker from a steep trajectory. It appeared to be a gold sphere about the size of an apricot. A hole had been drilled through its center. Hank slipped the mechanical pencil out of his shirt pocket. "May I?"

"Be my guest."

Brushing away some sand with his fingers, he revealed it

to be a hollow hemisphere and not a ball. He picked it up by inserting the tip of his pencil into the hole. "Brass, I think. And it's been scorched." He looked at Campbell. "Any idea what it is?"

"The bell off an alarm clock?"

Of course—Hank felt stupid for having asked. But this was quickly forgotten in the realization of what a timer meant: the charge could have been set as much as twelve hours prior to the blast, if the hour hand had been used to make the connection. Putting the bell in one of the Alka-Seltzer bottles for safekeeping, he took no satisfaction from their find—it might explain how an evacuee could have caused such widespread devastation in a single night.

"What else do we need, Hank?"

"I'd still like to find a fair-sized chunk of aqueduct pipe. A piece thrown clear of the area the city workers cleaned up."

An hour later, as they were zigzagging down through the scree at the base of a palisade, Campbell said, "Can I ask you something? Just brainstorming, mind you."

"Okay." Hank tried not to sound too pleased.

"Now"—the lieutenant began to count off on his fingers—"Shido's *hara-kiri,* Wenge's murder, the explosion here—what're the chances none're related?"

"Slim. At least two of them are linked, I'd swear to it. I might even wager that they can all be put together—with the right motive."

Campbell nodded.

They began thrashing through chest-high sagebrush. The chief almost cried out as a lizard scurried away from his loafers, and he stumbled backward, thinking for a second that it had been a snake. But he recovered himself before the lieutenant noticed. Perhaps he had given too much credence to the stories of the *rumpen,* the old vagrant laborers, many of whom had laid track for the railroads and claimed to know the desert. Gazing southward from the barbed wire, they would invariably say that these hills were lousy with snakes.

"Me too," Campbell said abruptly.

"Pardon?" They had not spoken for some minutes.

"I agree. At least two of the crimes are connected. Now, let me ask you this—which two can be laid at the feet of local ranchers? You know, because of the water war and all."

The chief considered his answer for a long moment. "Well, certainly the bombing here. And maybe Mr. Wenge's murder."

"As a cover for the blast? To throw the blame on you folks?"

Hank nodded.

"Boy, that hinges on some mad-dog feelings in the hearts of these valley people. I can see them raising hob with the pipeline. But kill an innocent man? I just don't know."

The chief didn't have an answer to that. It wasn't a rancher's style to decapitate his victim, even with a scythe. A blast of double-ought buck in the belly, yes—but not cold steel.

"Just between us and the horny toads, how could a local ever rub elbows with Shido? He didn't work outside the wire on any of the farm plots, did he?"

"No."

"What about his warehouseman duties? He ever go with the trucks down to the railhead at Lone Pine?"

"Never. And I countersign the permits. He didn't come in contact with locals, even under supervision." Whichever way Hank looked at it, the only plausible solution involved an evacuee, if not several of them. The prospect made him want to scream, to turn the investigation away from camp and toward Kimiko's water-war theory. He knew full well that Campbell was only rehashing her ideas. He had seen them together in the lieutenant's jeep this evening; and, earlier, she had collared Hank in his mess hall while he tried to grab a quick cup of tea, insisting that Eddie was innocent of bombing the aqueduct.

Yet, as alluring as the rancher theory was to Hank in light of the alternative, it just didn't work for him. There was something undeniably *Japanese* in what had happened last night.

"This what you're looking for?" Campbell was standing over a curled piece of iron plate.

"That's it." Hank picked it up by the edges, being careful to brush off as little explosive residue as possible. "Good—it shows some radiation pattern. This was close to the charge."

"Can you imagine being hit by something like that?" Campbell asked with a tight grin.

"No . . . I can't."

Neither man said anything more as they hurried back through the deepening twilight. It would be dark in a few minutes.

The chief knew what Campbell was thinking—the same thing he was: lots of kids, both *hakujin* and *nisei*, were being diced up by shrapnel little different from the jagged piece they had found. It was a guilt they took back with them to the jeep: being out of the fight.

They had no sooner gotten in than headlamps glanced around the bend to the south. Hank grasped the top of the windshield frame as he recognized the sheriff's black-and-white Mercury by its squared-off fenders.

But Campbell, lighting two cigarettes, ignored the station wagon until it had pulled alongside and Sheriff Coy was leering at him, his jowls tremulous. "What the hell are you doing here?"

"Evening." He handed Hank a smoke. "Here, Chief. Care for a Lucky, Sheriff?"

"I asked you a question." Unconsciously or not, Coy had fashioned his pudgy hand into the shape of a revolver. "Answer me, goddamnit!"

"Well, before we start hugging in the dirt, let me suggest something. For a goodly number of years I did pretty much what you're doing—except my department wouldn't let us get wider than we was tall. So I got some idea how your chain of command works. You get on the phone to Attorney General Warren. Ask old Earl, if push comes to shove over an issue of national security, who's going to be standing when the dust settles—the high sheriff of Inyo County or the commanding general of Western Defense Command? If the AG says what I'm sure he's going to say, I fully expect to see Sheriff Bertrand

Coy, *Junior*, at my headquarters at ten hundred hours tomorrow to explain why he was the only living soul in this neck of the woods when L.A.'s pipe went to splinters."

Campbell drove forward, but then braked on a thought and backed up. "That's ten A.M., Sheriff."

The Mercury didn't budge for as long as Hank looked back.

"I've got to work on my manners," Campbell said. He sounded serious.

CHAPTER 11

From the quarterdeck of the USS *Nebraska,* Lieutenant Francis Roper tracked the progress of the admiral's launch. Moments before, it had shoved off from the pier at Hunter's Point and was now slicing across a choppy San Francisco Bay toward the battleship, which would be anchored out here in the stream two more weeks before heading into drydock. The small boat left behind a leaden wake the same color as the noon overcast.

Roper eyeballed the sideboys—four enlisted men pressed out in dress blues and forming a gauntlet—a final time. He believed they looked sharp.

But he had been given some idea of how the admiral felt about the approaching dinner guests when the captain ordered that the crew were *not* to man the rail, a courtesy in which the ship's entire company was bugled to attention. And, in the mandarin nuances of Navy ritual, further judgment had been passed on the VIPs by limiting the number of sideboys to four, when six would have been more appropriate for either a congressman or a general.

And one of each was aboard the launch.

Roper could just now make them out: a gaunt lieutenant-general who, even from this distance, looked like he couldn't make it through the day without popping nitroglycerin. Well, his was a backwater command, so what did it really matter if Van Zwartz thought that nine holes of golf made for a full day of war? At his side stood a colonel whose uniform had definitely not come off the rack at the Army-Navy store. Strictly Brooks Brothers, this guy. And lecturing both attentive officers was the Defender of the Republic himself, gesturing toward the *Nebraska* with his silly-looking Texas Ranger hat as a few strands of black hair were whipped across his bald pate by the breeze. The congressman had dragged two civilian photographers along with him, which made Roper glance up at the signal bridge to make sure the radar gear was securely under wraps.

At Columbia University, he had boldly entitled his honors thesis *Maurice Lamb and the House Committee for the Investigation of Un-American Activities: The Formalization of Constitutional Abuse*. But the first thing the war had cost Frank Roper was his outspokenness. And, now, at last coming face-to-face with the Grand Inquisitor from Amarillo, Roper's biggest concern was that one of the sideboys might fuck up. He had no doubt that he himself would be courteous toward Maurice Lamb; anything contrary might result in transfer to a destroyer, and he could personally attest to the expendability of tin cans in modern naval warfare.

The launch laid alongside, and the boatswain waited for Roper to say "Attention to starboard" before blowing the piping-the-side call.

Lamb promptly messed up the timing of the carefully orchestrated detail by halting on the last step of the accommodation ladder and turning aft toward the national ensign with his hat over his heart—while the photographers duckwalked around him, grubbing for the most heroic angles. The sideboys had to continue to salute for as long as this tableau of patriotic fervor blocked the party's egress onto the quarterdeck.

Thankfully, Western Defense Command came aboard with less pomp.

Roper stepped forward and saluted. "General, gentlemen, if you will follow me please—"

"Just a minute there, young man," Lamb said with a grin Roper instantly detested. "Or should I say *captain?*"

"Lieutenant, sir."

The congressman chuckled. "Then what you got two bars for?"

"This, sir, is Navy insignia for lieutenant."

Lamb winked at the general and the colonel, who were smiling at his antics. "Then what the hell does the captain wear, son?"

"An eagle pin-on device, sir."

The pride with which this man flaunted his ignorance was impossible to fathom. "You mean you ain't the boss of this tub?"

"No, sir, I'm the public affairs officer. Now, if you'll please—"

"I'd like to see the guns first."

Roper had to think fast: this had not been anticipated. After dinner, he had captain's orders to personally give them a tour of the ship with each department head standing by to explain his bailiwick. However, the *Nebraska* wouldn't be rigged for visitors until that time—a detail was still squilgeeing the wash water off the port side main deck. But the congressman, despite his unawareness of naval protocol, was still a congressman, and he didn't look like he'd be put off by a polite explanation.

"This way then, sir." Roper walked on General Van Zwartz's left, a half pace behind him.

"Jesus, will you look at these bastards! I bet you're glad these are on your side, aren't you, Lieutenant?"

Roper didn't know what to say without insulting the fool. Lamb was exclaiming over the secondary battery gun houses. Mere five-inchers. The sixteen-inchers of the main battery turrets were still forward of them. Fortunately, the colonel rescued him. "These, Congressman, are pea-shooters compared to what's ahead."

Lamb widened his eyes at Roper. "You got bigger boys than this?"

"Yes, sir—"

"They can hurl ten tons of steel twenty miles from a single broadside, Maury," the general interrupted.

Roper wanted to groan: the information was classified. If Lamb mentioned it at dinner, would the Big J.G.—the rear admiral—think the public affairs officer had told him?

They were delayed seven and a half minutes more while the photographers kept coaching Lamb to stay in the sunlight and not drift into the three-striped shadow cast by the huge rifles, while the congressman spewed such drivel Roper was astonished not to see the general and his colonel bust a gut laughing. On the contrary, the Army was eating it up. "Boy, I tell you," Lamb went on, "if the Japs aren't one generation out of the trees before these babies open up, they sure as hell will be when they finish!"

Bullshit. Tons and tons of ordnance still couldn't be counted on to neutralize well dug-in Japanese defenders. The frightful Marine casualties attested to that.

Roper spotted one of the Guamanian stewards glowering at him from behind a splinter screen: it was no easy trick keeping beef Wellington at the point of perfection. The man gave a questioning shrug, and Roper returned one of his own.

The photographers, apparently doubling as reporters because of the labor shortage, had cased their cameras and were now scribbling down Lamb's pearls of wisdom. In the span of a minute a startling transformation had taken place: Lamb had ceased to be the show-me country boy and metamorphosed into a glib hard-driving prosecutor of perfidy against America, his eyes fiery, right hand fisted. ". . . And this, the deck of one of our mightiest warships, a sister to the martyred *Arizona*, is a fitting place to announce that, once again, I shall introduce a Japanese deportation bill in the House. It was unfortunate that, due to imperatives of national security, the full story couldn't be revealed when legislation on this issue was considered by the Congress in 1942. But now, thanks to our military intelligence experts, key documents have been declassified and prepared for public scrutiny. It will be revealed once and for all that, due to a corruption of blood that transcends even American citizenship, the repatriation of the 135,000 members of the Japanese race on the United States mainland and 158,923 in Hawaii to their ancestral homeland is not only a necessity, it is an act of Christian charity!"

There were no questions from the press when Lamb eventually ran out of steam. They simply slapped shut their notebooks, then looked inquiringly to Roper as if to ask where and when they could expect to be fed and watered.

He began herding the party toward the admiral's wardroom once again and was almost home free when it was General Van Zwartz's turn to call a halt. He huddled the congressman and the colonel around him at the rail, then made sure that the press was out of earshot—Roper didn't matter; he was apparently a fixture of the ship as far as the general was concerned. "Nick here," he said with almost fatherly affection for the colonel, "has done a splendid job inventorying the property they owned here on the Coast. What was the figure, my boy?"

"Somewhere around four hundred million dollars. Of course, that's not counting what Caucasian shills are holding for them."

"Staggering, isn't it?" Van Zwartz said with a wheezy laugh. "*Four hundred million!*"

The colonel hiked his chin toward Hunter's Point: a yellow toy, a distant Caterpillar tractor, was raising a skein of dust as it harrowed a sloping field. "Jap strawberry farmers, aliens mind you, secretly owned three hundred acres right next to the Navy base there. The usual old trick—they put the title in the names of their American-born children."

"What happens to these properties, Nick?" Lamb asked.

"It's a complicated process involving several agencies."

"Are they resold then?"

"Some of them," the colonel said carefully, but still smiling. He seemed to be sizing up Lamb for the first time during that long pause. "Would the congressman care to become better acquainted with the process?"

"I might. But the important issue is that this real estate—which abuts on the national security—must stay in the right hands."

"Exactly—and in perpetuity," the colonel said.

"It's an issue only we native Californians seem to understand." But then the general quickly added, "Present company excepted, of course. *Who* is going to dominate the entire Pacific Coast—the yellow man or the white? It's that simple. And that perilous for all of us."

The flag lieutenant, a lieutenant-commander in rank, appeared out of nowhere and saluted Van Zwartz. "By your leave, General—the admiral was concerned his distinguished company had gotten lost. This way, please . . ."

Coldly, the admiral's aide glanced over his shoulder at Roper, whose heart sank. He was being relieved of the detail. A little thing like this might prove disastrous to his upcoming fitness report, but how could he have explained to Lamb that punctuality was not optional in the Navy and that resourceful junior officers were expected to deliver even pigheaded congressmen on time?

But then, strangely, an angry kind of satisfaction sifted through him as he trailed the file of VIPs up a ladder: on a tin can, Francis Bacon Roper, Columbia '42, wouldn't have to toady to the likes of Maurice Lamb.

♦ ♦ ♦

"I already been through this with the sheriff," the Water and Power foreman said, displeased at being interrupted in the middle of tearing apart a backhoe engine inside the Independence maintenance yard. "My men saw nothing before she blew. Say—" He shook a big wrench at Jared. "What's this malarkey we're not supposed to talk about this with nobody? Especially the papers."

"National security."

The foreman considered this for a moment, then wiped his sweaty face with a sleeve of his coveralls. "All right . . ."

"I need a list of all your hands who work along this stretch of aqueduct. And where I can find them today."

"Come on . . ." He pitched the wrench into his toolbox and trudged off toward the office. "I can use a look at our dispatcher's knockers anyways." For the first time, he smiled: it was amazing how the mention of "national security" seemed to improve dispositions, although Jared felt like a three-dollar bill using it.

Fifteen minutes later, he ambled out of the office with a roster, a fly-specked map of the water system, and in complete agreement that the dispatcher had good breasts. She'd taken to him too, gone so far as to ask about the hours he worked at the camp, but he'd been unable to rouse any enthusiasm for the redhead. Maybe later, when the change in the seasons came and Kimiko seemed more a part of the past. Fall spread out like a golden salve across this country, gilding the cottonwoods against a raw blue sky, and he expected to feel better if only because of the cooler days and nights. He might want, maybe even need, another woman by then. The hunger would be a fine thing to feel again; it would mark the ebbing of his pain.

He had left Monty in the jeep under a locust tree that seemed to prosper on spilt oil and rusty pipe leachings. The acting director was sprawled across the rear seat, his short legs dangling over the side. At noon, he had shown up at MP headquarters frantic-eyed, and had begged Jared to take him anywhere as long as it was away from Manzanar. "This news blackout is driving me out of my mind . . . the rudeness of these newsmen! And then the prevarications I must invent on the spur of the moment!" He seemed on the verge of tears when his lips suddenly quivered into a smile. "I'm habitually filled with such feelings of loss I find it tedious to lie. Does that make sense to you?"

"Nope, but let's go."

So Jared had brought him along as he began working the already frayed assumption that a rancher had taken out his resentment on the aqueduct. Earlier that morning, Sheriff Coy had left him with the feeling that the man was telling the truth:

not being able to sleep—indigestion—Coy had been out on an early morning patrol and just happened to be in the neighborhood of the bomb when it went off. It was a piss-poor alibi for a cop, so it was probably the truth. And Coy freely admitted that there was no love lost between his family and Water and Power, but Rancho Manzanar was all in the past. He had made his peace with Los Angeles; he even rented pasture for his small herd of Herefords from Water and Power—Jared suspected at bargain rates. The city had shifted tactics from intimidation to co-option since the twenties.

He got behind the wheel, and the rocking of the jeep awoke Monty, who opened a groggy eye. "How long have I been out of it?"

"All your miserable days." Jared turned over the engine, then eased out the balky clutch so the jeep wouldn't crowhop.

Monty lumbered into the front seat, grimacing. "We should do what all civilized men do when the sun's at its zenith."

"Sweat?"

"No, child—adjourn to some roadhouse and await God's great amenity, the best part of the day—twilight."

"Sorry, I got work to do. You settle for a couple cold beers we can take along with us?"

"Settle is the perfect word for it."

Inside a mom-and-pop market with sawdust on the floor, they fished a half-dozen Acmes out of the slurried ice in the red Coca-Cola chest. Monty remembered a church key and a pint of California brandy "to give this plebeian stuff some spine." Out on the covered porch, as they steeled themselves with a few swigs before venturing out into the sun again, Jared suddenly laughed. "You know what we both just done?"

"Never."

"We both said *dozo* instead of please to that fella."

"You're kidding."

"God's truth."

Still, Monty didn't laugh. "One has been a zookeeper too long when he comes to resemble the monkeys."

Jared said nothing.

Heading south through the shimmering heat, he kept to the dirt road that crossed the sloping plain between the base of the Sierra and the main highway. He stopped whenever he spotted a Water and Power truck and questioned the worker, who would either be listlessly chopping weeds on a canal bank or tinkering with the flow over a mossy weir. To a man, nobody had seen anything, although each believed that Manzanar Japanese had been behind the blast.

By five, he was down to two names on the roster: a welder who had left on vacation early that morning, and a laborer who'd been sent up into the mountains for the day to repair snow-depth poles, which a biplane flew over in winter to estimate the snowpack. "Monty, you mind if we run up to Whitney Portal? I want to catch one more man before he scoots to home for the night. The day before the bombing, he was tending that stretch of aqueduct."

"Lovely—I've been meaning to find Bogey's cabin."

"Whose cabin?"

"I'll explain when we get there." Monty chuckled in spite of his exhaustion. Yet, moments later, as the road verged on a cattail-choked pond, he said bitterly, "How I hate reeds . . ."

Jared had heard it once before, whispered in that final incoherence as Monty drifted off—how the stunned and bleeding survivors of the gunboat *Panay* had hidden in a swale of reeds along the Yangtze while the Jap planes roared overhead in the hope of machine-gunning them.

Jared pretended he hadn't heard—and let the moment slide away on the dusty breeze.

◆ ◆ ◆

The worker had not yet come down off the Mount Whitney trail, according to the old man at the pack station, whose neck and face had weathered to alligator skin. "You can see him coming, if you look hard. . . ." And sure enough, far up on a granite bluff, nearly lost in the blue shadows, a human figure could be seen leading a mule down a zigzagging footpath. "Won't take him long," the packer went on. "He's a goat—and flat feets what kept him out of the service!"

Jared offered the man a Lucky, and the packer regarded the tailor-made as if it were a great curiosity; he probably rolled his own. Then, in low drawling voices, the two men began comparing mules to horses, then donkeys to mules, and Monty grew restless. He eventually strolled down the steep road into a forested hollow. The peaks of a number of cabins jutted up through the pines. Jared forgot about him until the packer reluctantly hinted that he had stock to feed.

"If I can squeeze in one more say before chores, hoss . . ."

"Sure."

"Does Bogey's cabin mean anything to you?"

"Them miserable bastards!" The old man did everything but spit.

"Who's that?"

"Picture folks—come up here to make a moving picture few years back."

"Like Humphrey *Bogart?*"

"Oh, he was all right. Kind of a runt. But the rest gone johnrabbit nuts on us. Come up here drunk in the middle of the dark wanting to ride the—" A jenny in the lodgepole corral began braying. "I just got to feed them, pard."

"Understood—thanks."

Leaving the jeep parked at the pack station, Jared started descending the road on foot. The evening was windless, and the sound, far above, of the iron shoes of the mule striking stone rang down through the calm.

Like Monty, he was glad to get away from camp. The unexplained events of the night before had rattled everybody. And, as if the truth wasn't bad enough, grotesque rumors were flourishing among the evacuees despite the information blackout—the MPs had bayoneted Shido to death, then strangled Wenge when he threatened to expose their crime. Still, Jared appreciated the fact that the Presidio wasn't going to release a word until his preliminary investigation was concluded. Chief Fukuda also felt that the hush-up made sense.

Jared wondered how Hank was doing at that moment on the explosive testing.

The road darkened under the shadows of the pines. He found Monty sitting on the porch of a small cabin. The place had been fashioned from square timbers chinked together with mortar, and was boarded up for the duration, posted for No Trespassing.

"Let me guess—Humphrey Bogart's hideout in *High Sierra?"*

Monty nodded, distantly. Nursing the brandy, he looked up as a breeze began fretting the crowns of the Jeffreys.

"You mean Ida Lupino rested her cute little bottom on them boards you're now profaning?"

Monty seemed not to have heard. "I could easily remain here. So inhumanly peaceful. It's *this* the East seeks, not our Christian continuation of deeds and moral choices. There's a melody to nothingness, my friend—and it's sweet . . . so sweet."

Jared eased down and sat on his heels. He picked out a dry pine needle and began chewing on it as his sad eyes rested on Monty's face. "You going to make it in this new job?"

Monty smiled at him, then shook his head no.

"Then what the crap will you do?"

The man's eyes swept dreamily over the cabin, the forest, the backdrop of dusky granite. "What a refuge this must've been for him."

"Who?" Jared blew the pine needle out of the corner of his mouth. He sounded a little exasperated.

"You know."

"No, I don't—Bogey or that con he played in the movie?"

"Oh, Jared, my child, my friend . . . even Mr. Bogart could not truthfully answer that." He came to his feet, dusted off the seat of his trousers with his soft-looking hands. They were no longer shaking as they had been earlier. The brandy was working its transient magic, and once again Montgomery Lee had become his wistful, loving self, although he would soon drown that self like an unwanted kitten in a tub of self-pity.

"Let's go," he said, his voice catching as he inhaled. "I have blundered into paradise for twenty minutes. It will have to do for a lifetime."

◆ ◆ ◆

The laborer arrived at the bottom of the trail with the serene but withdrawn smile of a man who has spent the day alone in high mountains. His mule was loaded down with a shovel, a sixteen-pound maul, and a pair of wicker panniers, from one of which he slipped a denim pouch of chaw as he heard out Jared. He inserted a pinch between his gum and cheek, then spoke for the first time—but hoarsely; he probably hadn't said a word all day. "I told everything to Sheriff Coy."

"Then tell me what you told him," Jared said.

"The boss says we got orders not to say."

"Those orders are from the Army. You can talk to me."

The man didn't look convinced. "I really didn't see much."

"Let me decide that." Jared hardened his tone a bit. It worked.

"I mean I saw nobody that day—except them Catholics in that church bus."

"How'd you know they was Catholics?"

"There was a padre with them."

"Was the name of their church on the bus?"

The worker pondered that for a moment, then spat between his boots. "I don't remember."

"Where was this?"

"Canal bridge three miles south of Manzanar. I was fixing the rock embankment. I do rock and cement work, mostly. Snow poles, too—if they get knocked down by avalanche."

"Why were these church folks there?"

"Lost, the padre said, looking for the road to Shepherd's Creek. They were going to camp up there—him and these boys. Well, we had a foreman what got a little crazy right after Pearl Harbor. He had us take down a lot of signs, figuring Jap secret agents might try to blow up our power stations and all. I guess we forgot to put the Shepherd's Creek sign back up. No tourists lately to squawk about it, on accounta the war."

Jared looked to Monty, who had planted himself cross-legged atop a boulder. The acting director hunched his shoulders as if to say this didn't sound like a promising lead. Jared agreed. He turned back to the worker. "Anybody else come along? Any locals? Even personal friends of yours?"

"Nope."

"Any Manzanar evacuees?"

"No Japs."

"Does the city treat you pretty good?"

The man's eyes clouded momentarily, then temper cleared them again. "Hell, yes—I got me a damn good job!"

"I'm sure you do, hoss. It's just my job to ask."

◆ ◆ ◆

Hank Fukuda sat on a high stool in the darkness.

In 1942, he had partitioned off a corner of the squad room in his station and converted it into a tiny laboratory. Until this week, it had seemed a waste of space: there hadn't been much call for criminalistics at Manzanar. And now, setting down the empty eyedropper to take a long drag off his cigarette, he regretted ever having set up the lab, ever having known how to test explosive residues.

Once again obsessed by the humiliating urge to prove his thoroughness, his worth, as an investigator to Lieutenant Campbell, he had plunged headlong into the string of procedures, thinking only that he would find out if the bomber had used straight, ammonia, gelatin, or even ammonia-gelatin dynamite. Never had he imagined the possibility of discovering something vastly different, something that immediately brought back to mind the carbolic smell still lingering in the air ten minutes after the explosion. Something he hadn't given a second thought until now.

Yet, after going through the procedures the first time, Hank had tried to reassure himself that most everything in the criminalist's world is equivocal. Proof does not come in a godly-clear bolt of lightning: it is always tainted by gradations of doubt.

So, once again, he filled the eyedropper from the beaker of acetone, then waited for his fingers to stop quivering. It was a basic chemical reaction test. Coming in contact with the solvent acetone, the explosive residue on the fragment of aqueduct pipe would either crystallize or dissolve. He squeezed a drop onto the twisted piece of iron and watched the reaction through a magnifying glass.

The faint smear of residue instantly dissolved.

Next, he heated some of the salts in a beaker, and they melted at exactly 252 degrees Fahrenheit. "No way . . . impossible . . ." To his knowledge, only one explosive in the world had that melting point. Laughing feebly to himself, he rose and went to a locked cabinet, opened it, and poured the equivalent of three sake cups of yellow lightning into a clean beaker. He polished it off in a gulp, reminding himself to get some more in the morning from his source, a trustworthy *issei* and former bootlegger with a still hidden beneath his Block 36 barrack.

Then, gingerly, he used tweezers to scrape some untreated residue onto a glass slide, which he clipped under his microscope lens. Slowly, he leaned over the eyepiece. A few lemon-yellow tetragonally pyramidal crystals had survived the detonating temperature.

Hoping against hope, he checked the reference chart and found it was no less true than it had been after the first run-through: trinitrophenol. Also known as picric acid. Formed by the action of nitric acid on carbolic acid. Which accounted for the smell at the scene. *Impossible.* And the somewhat volatile crystals had formed because, at some point, the explosive had been stored outside its non-reactive aluminum artillery projectile—perhaps in a homemade steel pipe bomb.

Finally, he rubbed some of the salts onto his wrist. Then, missing the chain on the first try, he reached up and pulled off the overhead lightbulb. Carelessly, he almost forgot to cover the beaker of acetone before lighting his cigarette. Or maybe he wanted such an accident.

The slights of a lifetime, which he had always been able to fend off with reason, with fond expectations, now crowded in on him from all corners of the blackness: *bucktoothed, bandy-legged, craven, simian, tricky and treacherous, dishonest and debauched, inscrutable and insolent—the jaundiced and devilish Buddhahead mien of the mikado.* All seemingly corroborated now by pretty little crystals he had gathered on a rectangle of glass.

"So solly." Again he laughed to himself, then choked on the taste of vomit. "*Shimose . . . fucking shimose . . .*"

He was still slumped in the stool an hour later when Jared Campbell's voice came through the door. "Chief?"

That which I thought to be trust until this moment was nothing of the sort. Real trust demands that you ante up everything you have and might ever have. . . .

"Come in."

Campbell looked surprised to find him sitting in darkness. "You feeling all right, Hank?"

"Please shut the door." He flicked on the bulb. His wrist was showing the first signs of dermatitis—picric toxicity. The last straw. The last doubt crushed. Yet, he thought he had already come to his decision when, all at once, he hesitated, wondering if greater hope might lie with the man in gabardine who owned his soul. But no, there was something plaintive in Campbell's face, the lines from hard times perhaps, that made him go ahead and say, "The results . . . they're kind of funny."

"How's that?"

"They indicate picric acid."

"You've lost me already."

"Most American explosives are ammonium picrate. This was straight picric." Hank stared down at his folded hands.

"Then who uses this straight picric stuff?"

For an instant, Hank thought he would never get the words out, believing, foolishly, desperately, that if he never got the words out no one would ever know. "Only the Japanese military. They call it *shimose.*"

After a long silence in which Hank kept his eyes on his sallow hands, the lieutenant stirred. His voice had turned raspy. "I got to phone this into the Presidio."

"I know."

His back to the chief, Campbell halted at the door. Briefly, he leaned on his arms against the frame. "You're one helluva a cop, Hank."

Then he went out.

CHAPTER 12

With the tires of his jeep clipping over the tarred joints in the concrete highway, Jared drove down out of the crystalline desert light into a hazy Southern California evening. The chaparral jacketing the hills above the San Fernando Valley was brown, the ordinarily waxy green leaves of the orange groves a dusty tan. Even the sky was rust-colored, no doubt thanks to the smoke from the defense plants that had sprung up between the sea and the San Bernardino Mountains since 1941.

Last night, before phoning in Hank Fukuda's results to the Presidio, he'd had no inkling that the call would result in his being sent to San Pedro this morning. After he had broken the news, Colonel Bleecher sighed. "Terrific—just what I needed to hear right now. Is the chief positive it's this *shimose?*"

"Yes, sir."

"Very well." Bleecher sighed again. "I'm afraid this dovetails all too neatly with other intelligence on Major Nitta."

"Can I ask how, Colonel?"

"Well, through our liaisons, we ran Tadashi Nitta through both the FBI and Office of Naval Intelligence. ONI returned with an unexpected lead. If this doesn't stink of a *nisei* fifth column, I don't know what the hell does. What gets me is their *patience—years* of waiting before striking. How soon can you leave for San Pedro?"

"Morning, sir. Unless it's an emergency, I really need some sleep."

"Understood. No, morning will be fine. . . ."

Yet, instead of heading directly for San Pedro, Jared had worked all of the aqueduct's two hundred and twenty snaking miles from Owens Valley to its terminus at Van Norman Reservoir near San Fernando. He had interviewed more than two dozen Water and Power employees since dawn, dutifully jotting down their names in a spiral notebook and affixing an NFD—No Further Details—to each. And now, as he drove past the pent-up waters that had once flashed down the canyons of the Sierra, he noticed a city truck parked on the asphalted lane atop the dam. He weighed the prospect of one more NFD interview against a shower, hamburger, and cold beer. Then, grumbling at his own diligence, he turned off the highway and sped through the open gate in the cyclone fence that surrounded the lake.

In a shack astride the spillway, the damkeeper was eating what smelled like a liverwurst sandwich. Behind him on the wall were polished brass gauges and a big wheel Jared surmised to be the main valve.

"Hello there, soldier boy." He didn't seem surprised to be interrupted by the Army in the middle of supper. "What can I do for you?"

Jared went through the carefully worded spiel that had become tiresome over the course of his long day.

The damkeeper chewed thoughtfully. "This have something to do with that caper up north we're not supposed to talk about?"

Jared decided to nod yes.

"Well, Lieutenant, I seen nothing suspicious around here. Especially no Japs. Didn't you boys clear them all out of the coastal areas?"

"We think so. But you never know," Jared said without much conviction.

"That's right, you never know. Take half a sandwich?"

Jared waved off the offer. "Tell me something . . ."

"I'll try."

It had bothered him from the moment he had seen how quickly the pipeline had been repaired: the bomber had either botched his job or done it half-heartedly. "What would really shut down the aqueduct?"

"You mean for months and months?"

Jared nodded again.

"Well, certainly not what they done up there near Manzanar. See, pipe gets damaged all the time. Rockslides, you name it. A few hours, maybe longer sometimes, and the system's back on line. But I'll tell you what'd really throw a monkey wrench in the works—collapse one of the water tunnels and it'd take us a year to see that sight again." He gestured out the window at the huge pipe disgorging Owens Valley water into the upper end of the reservoir.

"Then our boy wasn't all that good at his trade?"

"Or serious. Take your pick, soldier."

"What do you mean?"

"Hell, it's happened before—this kind of dynamiting. Just to badger the city. Something to brag about on Saturday night."

"Then you think the ranchers did it?"

"Devil if I know, son." He took another bite of sandwich. "You're the second officer to ask me that."

"Ask what?"

"Ways the aqueduct could be damaged. Same rigamarole as yours, although this kid asked me what would shut it down for just a few hours. That was kind of a screwy question. But I guess he was just covering all the angles."

Jared's thoughts started to gravitate toward a sandwich and a beer again. He was sure this other officer had been assigned to the same temporary duty he'd been stuck with back in 1942—right after being shanghaied out of combat readiness training with his infantry platoon and before being shipped to

Camp Manzanar, the dusty pile of lumber and tar-paper rolls that eventually became the relocation center. Fourth Army had taken stock of everything and anything a Japanese saboteur might hit along the entire Pacific Coast. Jared himself had checked out a dozen reservoirs and twice that many power stations. "Well," he told the damkeeper, "we did that back when it looked like an invasion was on the way."

"No, I'm not talking about the inspection right after the war started. This was just two months ago."

Jared fingered the knot to his black tie for a moment, wondering if the Presidio had ordered another check and he hadn't heard about it. "You remember this fella's rank?"

"Captain."

"And his name?"

"Sorry—but it was Irish, I think."

"You mind describing him to me? Maybe he's in my outfit."

"Well, right off, he had freckles."

"Redheaded then?"

"Don't know. Had a cap on like yours and all the hair showing was clipped down to scalp."

"What about his height and build?"

"Oh, nowheres as big a man as you. Five-foot-nine, tops. And carried himself different than you. Don't take it wrong—but I seen you walking up. You kind of barrel along like you just heard your kid brother's in a donnybrook."

"I been told something like that before. How'd this captain carry himself?"

"Well, quick and nervous-like. Made me nervous just to talk to him. Seemed in a godawful hurry. And he talked with an accent. Not like yours—Eastern or something. Any of this ring a bell?"

"No, it sure don't. He must be one of the new guys."

◆ ◆ ◆

Three miles down the highway from the reservoir was a small diner. Jared had planned to grab a bite at the Hollywood Canteen, which he'd never visited. But the USO didn't serve beer, and he was still forty-five minutes away from Sunset

Boulevard. Besides, he didn't feel like rubbing elbows with a horde of uniforms and hard-pressed victory girls. So he braked for the diner.

But in the time it took him to park the jeep, the waitress flipped the sign from Open to Closed. Through the glass she held up her palms in apology. A pretty face, but a squarish figure—shoulders, waist, and hips all the same width.

He realized he must have looked more than disappointed, for she suddenly frowned and unlatched the door. "You absolutely starving?"

He just smiled.

"Oh, come on in. My cook's gone and the grill's cleaned up, but I can make you something simple. Take that back booth there, honey, so nobody can see you from the front."

"Appreciate this, ma'am."

"Name's Betty, Lieutenant." She tossed a glance over her shoulder, then laughed. "That's your cue to tell me who you are."

"Oh, I'm sorry—Jared Campbell."

She threw together an egg salad sandwich, then had an Acme with him as he ate hungrily. It had been fourteen hours since breakfast at the MP mess hall. "You *like* egg salad?"

"I love anything except dough fried in drippings."

"Why's that?"

"I lived on it for three years."

"You from Oklahoma?"

He nodded as he swallowed. "Originally."

She wound up doing most of the talking, and before long there were six empties on the table and a full ashtray on the dusty windowsill. ". . . So when Walter was killed in North Africa, I really thought about selling out. See, he did all the cooking, and I wasn't sure I was up to running the place myself. I looked into defense work, but you got to sleep with the foreman not to be treated like an animal. And, besides, this is all I got now." Her eyes misted a little. But then she licked her lips, which made them glisten again: between beers two and three, she'd gone to the restroom and put on some lipstick. "Enough about Betty Jean. Let's hear Jared's tale of woe."

He grinned, his beer-drowsy eyes half-closed. "Don't got one."

"Come on . . ."

"Not when I've just had a real nice supper and my pockets are full of Army jack."

Her eyes became business-like again. "You got a meal ticket, honey?"

"No, I'll cash out."

Then he reached over and took her hand, which she'd left at the center of the table after wiping a smudge off the little chrome jukebox selector with a napkin. It was like taking hold of his own loneliness and finding some warmth in it. He really had no thoughts beyond what he had just done, and felt an inkling of regret when she said softly, "How about a mixed drink at my place?"

She lived behind the diner in a travel trailer half-hidden by the drooping boughs of a pepper tree. The pungency given off by the foliage reminded him that he was no longer surrounded by sagebrush, that he was finally away from Manzanar.

Inside, she cracked a two-dollar bottle of rye, one of a half-dozen stowed in the cabinet over the divan, and after three highballs she kissed him, hard, taking his lower lip between her teeth. Her white waitress's dress fell open at the front, but he couldn't recall her having unbuttoned it. Released now, the heat of her body flowed around his face. She began kneading the inside of his thigh with her long fingers. Within a minute, she had showed him how to unfold the divan into a bed. Her dress came off over her head, and she invited him with a doleful smile to help take off her undergarments.

As soon as she was nude, Jared's flushed face went cold with disappointment, although he quickly hid his expression over her shoulder.

For a moment there, he had earnestly wanted her.

But she wasn't Kimiko. Her body was neither shapely nor delicate. Nor was her skin that soft hue that was neither brown nor yellow, but was something else: a tone he hoped would always elude description other than being Kimiko's color.

That he was slow to arouse was not lost on Betty, who knelt before him in the crowded space between the tiny icebox and a closet. She undid the button fly of his trousers.

Closing his eyes, he tried to block Kimiko's face out of his mind's eye. He also tried not to ask himself why he would spend the night here and not in the Bachelor Officers' Quarters at Fort MacArthur. He honestly didn't feel like making love to poor dead Walter's wife, but pressure and warmth were doing their job: he found himself possessed of an erection that didn't seem to be his own. And he feared not being able to come, so vague was his desire.

She never seemed to notice. She rode her waves of passion with Walter in her heart, Jared believed, rode them until he achieved his own release and they finally slept.

◆ ◆ ◆

San Pedro's dawn was foggy.

Shivering in the open jeep, amazed as always by how cold a summer morning in coastal California could feel, he had to flick on the single windshield wiper every few minutes—the moisture refused to accumulate fast enough on the bug-splattered glass for him to leave it on. Off dimly to the side, a pump jack bobbed for oil, looming out of the dripping stillness like a huge grasshopper. And across the black waters of the channel on Terminal Island, a helix of gas was flaming from a pipe, giving the fog a glow like fox fire.

The Presidio had already arranged the interview for this morning, but Colonel Bleecher had warned him that the contact was a tuna fisherman and would shove off at seven on a two-week sail come hell or high water.

Jared checked his wristwatch: almost six. Thirty minutes late because of the fog and he still couldn't find the right mooring. The mist seemed to have dissolved all the street and fish-company signs.

Suddenly, a figure in a yellow slicker materialized alongside the road.

"Pardon, hoss—where's Rocha's outfit?"

The figure remained faceless, a wraith from the waning night. "See this ketch set up on blocks yonder?"

"I think so."

"Rocha ties up on the other side of it."

"Thanks."

Several tuna boats were lashed gunwale to gunwale between two wharves, their engines rumbling. Lightbulbs festered through wheelhouse windows, and darting back and forth across the fuzzy illumination they cast were the silhouettes of fishermen moving purposely but without haste on the fog-slick decks.

The sky had begun to brighten, but uniformly, so Jared couldn't tell east from west. "Which of you is Miguel Rocha?"

"I am," a voice said from the nearest boat. "You're late."

He decided not to apologize as he offered his hand. "I'm Lieutenant Campbell." The skin of Rocha's palm felt like manila rope. "Is there someplace we can talk?"

"Right here—I got to keep an eye on things. Come aboard." Rocha's eyes glowered in his bearded face—clearly, he wasn't looking forward to the interview. "This thing with the Nittas—it happened a long time ago. So maybe I don't remember perfect."

"That's okay."

A priest was sitting on a hatch cover, smiling and holding a mug in his gloved hand.

"This here is Father Joe. You want a coffee, Lieutenant?"

"It's the only reason I get out of bed anymore."

Rocha looked around for a gofer, but saw that all his men were otherwise busy at the moment. He excused himself with a grunt and ducked into the wheelhouse, his rubber boots squeaking.

"Joseph Kerry," the priest said, rising to grasp Jared's hand.

"Proud to meet you, padre."

He had a long face and the tippler's gleam in his eyes, but

the lack of a brogue revealed him to be the homegrown variety of Irish clergy. He also had a fresh sunburn. "I can hear you wondering why I'm here this morning, Lieutenant."

Jared shrugged as if to say it didn't mean anything to him.

"These people are as honest as the day is long. But authority frightens them. Any kind of authority. You'd be surprised how many times I'm dragged along when one of my parishoners tries to secure a bank loan."

"Well, I want the Good Lord in my corner, too, when I wrangle with a loan officer."

Father Kerry laughed quietly, then nodded for Jared to take the mug from an impatient Rocha. The coffee was spiked—Jared only hoped it wasn't with lighter fluid.

"Okay," Rocha said, "let's get this over with. I got things to do. And I told this all to the G-men way back then. So why again now?"

"FBI or Naval Intelligence?"

Rocha glanced at the priest, who reassured him with a nod. "I don't know—guys in suits. G-men."

Jared eased down onto the gunwale. It was damp. "Go on."

"Late spring, 'forty-one—"

"What month, Miguel?" Father Kerry asked, trying to help out.

"June early on, I guess. We was off San Clemente Island, working the handlines on some yellowfin keeping under this big kelp paddy. Fog that day like this, but worse. Nitta and his three boats was over on the other side of the paddy—I seen them once when the fog cleared a little."

"You talking about Toshimichi Nitta?"

"Sure, I guess—the old man." For the first time, Rocha smiled. "You're pretty good with Jap names."

"I've had plenty of practice lately. What about the son, Tadashi?"

"Don't know that one."

"Eddie?"

"Oh—him. The smart one. College. Yeah, he used to come home summers and help out."

"Was he out there that day?"

Rocha looked uncertain for a moment. Then he set his jaw. "Sure—everybody's got to pitch in when the tuna run."

That would never wash in court, Jared told himself. But, again, he decided to back off. Rocha was the kind of guy who would clam up if he sensed that he was being shoehorned into a corner. "Go ahead. I won't butt in again."

"Well . . . after I seen Nitta's outfit, the fog got real bad. Couldn't see my own bow from the wheelhouse—I was on the radio asking if anybody's having better luck than us. One of my hands tells me to come out quick. A noise, he says. And sure enough, it's like the sea's boiling maybe two hundred yards off starboard. Next we hear a hatch come open. A big clang, okay? Then Jap voices calling back and forth to each other. At first I think it's just Nitta's crew. But I know mosta these Terminal Island Japs, and some of these voices is new. Then this loud knock come across the water. You know, like a wooden hull tapping a steel one."

"Could you see anything at this point, Miguel?" Father Kerry asked.

"Not yet. After maybe five, ten minutes, we hear this big diesel fire up."

"One of Nitta's boats, perhaps?"

"No way, Father—this engine had *horses*. And then out of the fog come this submarine, heading south by southeast quick. It damn near clipped my stern!"

"Wait a second," Jared said. "Was there time to offload something from that sub into one of Nitta's boats?"

"Like I said—five, ten minutes. More than enough."

"Any markings on the sub?"

Rocha laughed under his breath. "How about a rising sun on the tower?"

Jared was silent for a moment. "Your crew—the men who were with you that day—any of them aboard right now?"

"Naw, those kids are in the service all over the place. Most these guys here come out of retirement."

"Hey, boss!" A crewman was hollering for Rocha's attention; the boat on which he stood had cast off and was backing around in the channel. "Okay with you if we hit the bait shack first?"

"Go!" Rocha turned back to Jared. "And that's not all—that winter there was funny traffic on the radio. In Jap. When us Americans probably wasn't supposed to be listening in. . . ."

Father Kerry had risen to bless the departing boat.

Jared noticed it on the sternpost: beneath the more recently painted *Rocha III* were the traces of an earlier name. *Umi*—it had once partly read.

"That's about it," Rocha said. "We got to sail now."

Jared continued to stare after the *Rocha III* as it faded into the fog.

◆ ◆ ◆

Hank Fukuda started off from the judo *dojo* at the brisk but unhurried pace of a man who has in the past few minutes nearly severed another man's head—yet is still in control of himself. He made mental notes of what could be observed from the towers along his path. He would ask Jared Campbell, upon his return from San Pedro, to once again question the sentries who had been on topside duty that evening. Perhaps something would surface belatedly, just as he'd learned only last night from the *sensei* that Shido had made it his habit to practice *aikido* for an hour each evening, then meditate in the privacy of the *dojo* office.

The driving rays of the midday sun made Hank wish that he'd remembered his motoring cap. Despite the hundred-degree temperature, three baseball games were in progress and had to be delayed while he tramped across the firebreaks toward the northernmost limit of *Hakujin* Country.

Once there, he stopped and consulted his wristwatch: six minutes, thirty-five seconds—within ten seconds of the first run-through.

Morris Wenge's residence could be seen around the corner

of the administration building. Hank figured that entry into the house and the murder would have required no more than two minutes. From where he now stood on First Street, it was seven minutes to Momai's barrack and ten to Tadashi Nitta's. He had already timed these distances, but would now do so again. Before he could begin, however, he saw an *issei* outside the combination *tofu* and mung factory, struggling to pour the water out of a wooden barrel in which beans were sprouted. "Here," he said in Japanese, "allow me to help you with that."

The little flood of water barked as it splashed against the sandy ground. "*Domo arigato*." The old man hesitated, then offered the chief a handful of blanched sprouts, and he munched on them as he checked his watch and started off toward Momai's block. The mess hall bells began to ring all over camp, confirming it was noon. He tried to keep up the same pace, but ugly thoughts started distracting him. He had seen it flash in the *issei*'s eyes—that *inu* accusation of all who aided the administration. It had come out of the Japanese village, this distaste for informers and collaborators; the overlords had planted both among the common people, who called them dogs and sometimes rose in revolt under the banner of a hanged dog. Even here, centuries later, there was talk of *kyan-kyan*, the barking of small dogs, whenever someone was arrested, no matter how justified the arrest.

But he turned his mind to other things.

From camp to the aqueduct blast site was four and a half miles, a round-trip of nine for an evacuee able to get past the watchtowers. He would add this into his other calculations.

Turning the corner at the outdoor theater, he suddenly shuffled to a halt. By keeping to this direction, he would overtake Kimiko Nitta. She was coming back from visiting the major, her eyes lowered, and he was tempted to cut through Block 21 before she became aware of him. But then shame swept over him—old-country shame, palpable and enervating to the point of submission. "Kimiko!"

She turned her face, but didn't smile when she recognized him.

Hank trotted forward, but slowed to a walk again when a wuffing noise began to follow each breath: cigarettes. "Afternoon."

"Good afternoon, Chief."

"Say"—he thought about gently chucking her under the chin, as he had seen Campbell do so naturally to the other typists, winning their laughter, but knew it would result in an awkward moment for Kimiko and him "—how about lunch at Club Twenty-two?" The new head cook at the Block 22 mess hall was acquiring quite a following.

"Thank you, but no."

"You really mean it—or you just being *bootchie?*"

Caught with her upbringing showing, she smiled: to decline an invitation, particularly the first one, was pure *enryo*, the deference shown to a superior. *I am not worthy of the honor you suggest*. But her restless sigh was strictly American. "Maybe I can use a change."

"You bet you can. How's the major doing?"

"All right." Her eyes said otherwise.

One thing could be said for the heat: it had dulled enough appetites to shorten the line outside the mess hall. In less than five minutes they were sidling past the crockery and utensil counter. Stale food—the odor could never be scrubbed out of these tar-paper barns. Hank gave his U.S. Army plate a swipe with a second handkerchief he kept clean just for that purpose, then peered down the line and scowled.

Canned Vienna sausages—the only meat in two days now. Boiled potatoes. Peaches in syrup. Sliced white bread. *My stomach must be the only part of me that doesn't know I'm an American.* "Where's this new cook?" he asked a pimply kid in dirty mess whites.

Sweat dripped off his chin into the peaches. "*Nani* say?"

"I said, where the hell's this great cook? My stomach's *peko-peko*."

"Ah, he's a *kuichi*." A Jew. "Won't work so much for sixteen *doru*. Quit."

"Swell." Visions of *tori nanban, oyako domburi*, or any number of Japanese dishes died hard, and Hank stopped salivating only when he saw what was being lumped like clay on his plate.

He led Kimiko to a vacant table for eight and checked the metal pitcher to make sure it was filled with hot tea before sitting on the wobbly bench. He tried a bite of sausage, winced, sprinkled it with soy, then made one final attempt before pushing his plate aside.

At first, he thought she was chuckling quietly at his wordless comment on lunch, but when she turned away he realized that she was weeping.

He stared down into his glass of tea and said nothing, feeling inadequate to the moment. He had never learned to talk from the heart, as Jared Campbell seemed to do so effortlessly. The Fukudas had been in California for seventy-five years, but their wives—like his mother—had been mail-ordered by photograph from Honshu. And, somehow, Hank had absorbed the notion from that tiny hunched woman from Aizu Wakamatsu: to express emotions in words is to denigrate them. The paradox born of this sentiment confounded the *hakujin* teachers in L.A.'s integrated schools—Japanese students excelled at everything except letting out their innermost feelings. They lacked spontaneity.

Finally, Hank told Kimiko what he knew to be a lie. "The lieutenant's down south working a couple of leads. I'm sure he'll come up with something that'll clear the major."

He realized from the moist flashing of her eyes that he'd said the wrong thing. Perhaps she felt he was condemning her for what she had undoubtedly done with Campbell. That was the last thing he had intended.

And then he recognized the awkward moment to be one in which he might reveal his own secret. He might comfort Kimiko with it: the five years spent with his both pretty and plain Portuguese lover. Her looks, like water, changed in varying light; and, sometimes, she would seem the most beautiful of women if only because she was not consistently so. In fact, she was so ordinarily plain she attracted far less attention from the cops than the other dispatchers. After their affair collapsed, Hank blamed California's miscegenation laws. Even had they traveled to a state willing to issue them a license, Hank and his new bride would have been fired by any PD for violating their own state's statutes.

Yet, he had admitted to himself—after she had taken a dispatching job all the way across the continent—there was more to it than the laws. Love is no respecter of laws. Like Kimiko, perhaps, he hadn't completely trusted his own motives in taking a Caucasian lover. Was his pretty-plain Portuguese a crutch to use as he climbed the impossible slopes of the American Dream? Or had he been afraid that hidden somewhere deep in her passion—God, she could make him feel like a man with those sliding glances of her dark eyes—lurked the *hakujin* view that Japanese males were timid, shy, garden-loving eunuchs? He prayed not, for he still loved Lucille Dos Santos.

But these remembrances, which might mean much to Kimiko now, refused to thaw into words. He blamed his cowardice on a single phrase that had been drilled into him during an obsequious youth: *ha zu ka shi*—others will laugh at you. And, in moments of stress, he still wore it as tightly as the kimono sash his mother had snugged around him as a child.

"Everything's going to be okay, Kimiko."

She looked up at him, then away again.

"May I suggest something?"

An almost imperceptible nod.

"Why don't you come back to work for me?"

"I don't know . . ."

"Will you at least think about it?"

Another nod.

Then it burst from his mouth, surprising him as much as her: "I approve."

Her face went to stone, marble with an underlying lucency of shame, but then her expression turned neutral, that of a Noh mask which takes on meaning only when the actor tilts it against the glow of a torch. "Approve of what?"

He hesitated, then lied. "Of you . . . your gutsiness."

The lie smarted in his eyes, for she had known precisely what he meant: he approved of Jared Campbell making love to her, seeing her only for herself, wanting her although he had no real place for her, wanting her as his equal—something Eddie Nitta could never do, although the major probably fancied that he was American enough to make her think so. Hank approved because he had failed with his pretty-plain Portuguese, failed to cement the promise even the *issei* resisted: that, unavoidably, true equality would lead to the marriage bed, and it was unrealistic to imagine otherwise.

He knew better than Kimiko that she wasn't faithless. She was *between* faiths. He pitied her for it, as he did himself when he lay alone on his metal cot at night, listening for footfalls on the gravel outside—the Black Dragon coming hooded and armed with clubs to erase the foremost name off their blacklist, that of Henry Yoshio Fukuda.

But he made no further attempt to broach these things. Instead, he poured tea into her glass.

She wiped her eyes with a napkin and smiled.

He asked her to take a sip.

"Thank you," she whispered.

CHAPTER 13

The door boomed against the inside wall.

Eddie Nitta catapulted up and braced his hand on the side of the steel cot.

First Sergeant Osler was filling the doorway, hands on his hips and sleeves folded halfway up his forearms. A cigarette was tucked behind his ear as if he'd been too busy to smoke it, and the flap to his oxblood leather holster was unsnapped so the grip to his .45 showed.

"Come with me."

Outside the cell, Osler ordered him to halt and grab hold of the floor-to-ceiling wire barrier that separated the detention and office sides of the guardhouse. When Eddie rolled his eyes, Osler spun him by his empty undershirt sleeve, then knuckled his face against the mesh. "You're not back in ROTC, Nitta! You do what the fuck I tell you *when* the fuck I tell you!"

For an instant Eddie tensed his arm muscles. Although Osler outweighed him by fifty pounds, he felt he held the advantage: the arena from which he had just returned didn't abide by the Marquis of Queensberry Rules. He would gouge out one of the topkick's eyes with his thumb, rive off an ear, and hand them to him before he knew what had hit him. But then he relaxed, and a corner of his mouth curled with a smile.

Osler was breathing hard. A garrison GI, he wasn't in shape. With his free hand he began to frisk Eddie, roughly sliding his fingers up the crack between the major's buttocks after giving his crotch a vicious squeeze. "Just hand me a reason, Nitta . . . just one little ol' reason." Then his laugh rumbled into a tobacco hack as he shoved Nitta through the door in the wire.

On the desk, the telephone receiver was off the hook.

"Pick it up," Osler said.

Eddie glared at him, his testicles aching dully, then spoke into the phone. "Major Nitta."

"Yes, sir . . ." It was Jared Campbell, almost shouting over the highway traffic in the background. "I got some questions for you."

Eddie said nothing.

"You still there, Major?"

"I'm here."

"I just had me a chat with a fella named Miguel Rocha."

Eddie's eyes hardened, but his voice remained under control. "So, Lieutenant?"

A heavy truck could be heard thundering past. "What was that?"

"I said *so what*."

"Then you know him?"

Eddie hesitated a second. "Yeah, I know him. What the hell is this all about?"

"Hang on and you'll find out." Campbell no longer sounded affable. "I'll tell you exactly what Rocha said. . . ."

For three minutes, Eddie listened with rising incredulity, then could take no more: "Of course there was a goddamned sub out there!"

It was Campbell's turn to fall silent.

"A *United States* submarine, Lieutenant!"

"How do you know that?"

"The officer who hailed my dad's boat identified her as the

Leopard Shark. And the entire conversation was in English, not Japanese."

"But you do speak it?"

"Kind of—my folks made me go to Japanese language school after regular classes. I hated it." Eddie ignored Osler, who, grinning, reached for the smoke behind his ear and lit up.

"And, of course, your daddy speaks Japanese."

"Sure." Eddie felt close to laughing now: it all seemed too absurd to be dangerous, although sweat was twining down his forearm, congesting in a big drop on his elbow.

"Were you out with your daddy that day?"

"Yes."

"What was an American sub doing there?"

"Lost. The officer said their gyrocompass was on the fritz. And the sea floor off San Clemente Island is littered with old wrecks that louse up a magnetic compass. He said his soundman had picked up surf noises—they were worried about running up on the island in the fog."

"How'd this *Leopard Shark* find *you* if everything was so soupy?"

"My guess is the sailor on the hydrophones heard our auxiliary motors going. So my dad gave them a relative bearing—"

"What's that?"

"Like a circle of points drawn around their boat. I forget now, but the island was like three points on their port quarter. San Diego—their home base, the officer told us—was maybe three points forward of their starboard beam." Eddie could tell by Campbell's exhalation that the lieutenant still had no idea what he was talking about. "Anyways, my dad told him to go in such and such a direction and then his compass would clear in a couple of miles. The *Leopard Shark* thanked us and sailed off into the fog." He paused. "Did old Miguel happen to mention that after our boats were seized he bought them for ten cents on the dollar?"

"Were they named *Umi* or something?"

Eddie tried not to betray his surprise—what the devil was Campbell really doing down there? "Yeah—*Umi Baka I, II,* and *III*. It means 'Sea Fool'—my old man says only a fool would try to make a living off tuna."

"Name Joseph Kerry mean anything to you?"

"This is turning into a stroll down memory lane. Sure, Father Joe—living proof that if the meek can't inherit the earth, at least they can confiscate it. Half his parish was deputized by the FBI to rip through our homes on Terminal Island, looking for Jap machine guns and crated Zeros, I suppose. I missed that Mardi Gras."

"Why?"

"I was in college at the time."

"You know if anything was confiscated?"

"Yeah—radios, fowling pieces, and any cash that was laying around."

"No explosives?"

"Jesus." Eddie chuckled, but then just as quickly his voice became raw with anger. "What would I need to take explosives off a Jap sub for, Campbell? And where the shit have I been storing them for the past three years? In the Block Twenty-eight men's latrine?"

"Easy, Major—"

"I've got everything I need right here in camp! Ammonium nitrate fertilizer from the farm warehouse, fuel oil from motor pool, and a rifle cartridge dropped by one of your overweight sad sacks—put them all together and I'd have a dandy bomb guaranteed to blow up any aqueduct you got! *Capische?*"

"And I still got Rocha, who'll swear in a court of law your folks met with a Japanese sub in June of 'forty-one."

"He's a liar! Do you hear me? A liar like all you *hakujin* sons of bitches!"

Then Osler ripped the receiver out of his fist.

◆ ◆ ◆

Jared sat hunched over the steering wheel, waiting for the swing-arm traffic signal to change. The sun had burned off most of the mist before noon, and now an onshore breeze was clearing the view all the way to the burly, tan hills that passed for mountains in Southern California. The go-arm swept up with a clang, but he remained idling at the intersection with Pacific Coast Highway, gazing at the sign that summed up his two choices.

He could continue up Western Avenue into Los Angeles, and there join the highway back to Manzanar. That would be a vote for Miguel Rocha's story. But if federal investigators had known about this since 1941, as Rocha claimed, why had there been no follow-up until now? Colonel Bleecher said the Office of Naval Intelligence had passed on the lead to him, but why would ONI hand an obvious naval matter over to Fourth Army G-2? Weren't they the least bit possessive about reports of Jap subs plying the California coast at will? Hell, in 1942, one of them had actually surfaced and shelled an oil field near Santa Barbara.

Or, instead of heading up Western Avenue, he could turn right—and drive down to San Diego. That was a vote for Tadashi Nitta's innocence. Yet Nitta had revealed a hint of criminal gloating in telling how easily he could have put together a bomb with stuff just laying around Manzanar. And maybe he had, except that he had used *shimose* instead of ammonium nitrate. The cleverer the crook the more he itches to take a bow; by pretending admiration, Jared had let more than one con fit himself for prison denim.

But there was another reason he wasn't eager to clear Nitta of any wrongdoing. And it filled him with shame, a mean satisfaction he couldn't deny. If the major were proven to be a Jap agent, Kimiko would divorce him.

Because of this—to save himself from the meanness of his own lust—he was afraid the spirit would turn him south, toward San Diego and the echoes of a towheaded boy brought up strict and Christian. But hell, he'd sinned so much since those days, what did the spirit matter anymore? A glance at his wristwatch told him that, if he did indeed go to San Diego, he would have to spend the night in a hotel, out of pocket—his orders teletyped from the Presidio specified his business only to be in San Pedro and "involving minimum travel distance." One hundred miles south of San Pedro would be stretching it a bit. And any ranking submariner who might help him locate the USS *Leopard Shark* would be calling it quits for the day and trotting over to the officers' club within the hour. Jared guessed it to be a three-hour drive down the coast, and he didn't have a clue where submarine headquarters might be found. Plus he didn't like being away with Osler in charge of the company, even if Bleecher had okayed it.

Horns blared at him from behind.

Resolutely, he pressed down on the accelerator pedal and headed north for Los Angeles and the high desert beyond.

This, he told himself, fighting down a hair ball of Baptist guilt that was worming its way up his throat, was the sensible way to go. He could be asleep in his own cot by midnight. Tomorrow morning, he would phone Colonel Bleecher, and they could discuss how to proceed on Rocha's information. Most likely, an inquiry regarding the *Leopard Shark* would have to be made through channels—it might even take General Van Zwartz's muscle to get an answer from the Navy sometime before the end of the war.

It was the smart thing to do. And it was about time Jared Campbell started doing the smart thing.

Yet, as he sped up Western Avenue past truck farms in the otherwise worthless land beneath the high-tension lines, the once tidy fields gone ragged with wild mustard, an image kept dogging him: that of *Rocha III* half-painted over *Umi Baka* on the stern of a tuna boat that, perhaps altogether too conveniently, was miles and miles out in the Pacific now glittering at his back.

Then, without signaling, he whipped a U-turn to another trumpeting of irate horns.

Damn the spirit.

♦ ♦ ♦

"Kazuo Hamada. Block Four. Barrack Four. Apartment Four. Must be your lucky number, eh?" Hank Fukuda asked. The question served as a little test: the number four, pronounced in Japanese like the word for death, is considered unlucky. He was plumbing the man's Japaneseness: no *issei* or *kibei* would accept an assignment number like that.

Kazuo smiled unknowingly from beneath the pith helmet that had become an inseparable part of his camp persona, then tugged at the sweat-faded chin strap to swallow. Early in his stay at Manzanar, he had been assigned to the farm plots outside the wire—not that he knew anything about agriculture. It had simply been a means of keeping him away from any unattended apartments during the day.

"Kazuo Hamada," Hank went on. "Also known as Kazuo Hara, Kazuo Hirada, Kazuo Hiroe."

The smile began to jerk at the corners of his mouth.

"And here's my favorite—Kazuo *Hirohito*."

"Hey, Chief—no disrespect intended. I was scared because the booking sergeant tap-danced on me a little. It was the first name what popped into my head."

"Say no more—I understand . . ." Yes, Kazuo Hamada looked like a man who'd gone through life bleeding from one nostril. Hank skipped ahead to page five of the rap sheet. "Also known as Kenneth Loo, Ken Lum—oh, what the hell, let's forget the Chinese and go on to the Filipino. How'd you ever come up with Milton Macadangdang?"

He shrugged. "I shacked with a hooker named that."

"Her name was *Milton*."

"You know what I mean, Chief."

Hank leaned back in his chair and yawned. "Yeah, I suppose I do . . ." The *hakujin* tended to pigeonhole Japanese as being either inhumanly good or bad, a view that didn't take into account the likes of Kazuo Hamada, an inept burglar and sometime grifter whose rap sheet would have been ten times longer than it was had his *issei* victims been willing to press charges. But they seemed as deluded as the white judges that Little Tokyo was a crime-free oasis inhabited by docile, overly polite men and graceful, servile women. Perhaps it was feared that by admitting the existence of *yogore* thugs, of the tonglike gangs that shook down shopkeepers with impunity, of the opium smugglers haunting the waterfront, they would only be giving ammunition to William Randolph Hearst and the exclusion societies his newspapers ballyhooed as the salvation of the white race. Perhaps there was little crime in the *issei*-dominated plantation camps of Hawaii; but Los Angeles's *Nihonmachi* had spawned more than its share of delinquents like Kazuo Hara-Hirada-Hiroe-Hirohito-Macadangdang-Hamada. And it was time to make him squirm. Under sufficient pressure, Kazuo was always good for something. "They're drafting a new list for Tule Lake," Hank said casually.

"So what?"

"Just thought you might be interested."

"I'm not on it . . . am I?"

Hank took a stapled sheaf of papers out of his top drawer and riffled through it. "I'm not allowed to say at this point." He put away the list, last year's budget for his department. "It's still privileged information."

"I answered yes-yes . . ." Kazuo was referring to Questions 27 and 28 of Selective Service Form 304A, asking if he would serve in the U.S. Armed Forces, swear unqualified allegiance to America, and forswear any obedience to the Japanese emperor—issues that had bitterly fractured the camp along a dozen different lines the year before. "I'd go to war for this country in a minute if it wasn't for my bronchitis—"

Hank stopped him short with two words: "Masao Shido."

Kazuo gazed stupidly into the chief's face, then began chewing on his thumbnail. A toll was exacted each time he passed through this station, and he was trying to figure out how little he could pay and still get out. "I hear he's dead."

"And I hear you're on your way to Tule."

His eyes tapered shut for a few seconds. They were watery when he opened them again. "Okay, this is secondhand. I'm party to none of this, right?"

"Go ahead."

"Shido was working the black market with some *keto* staffer."

Hank shot to his feet. "You're going in the cage! That story's older than last week's *sashimi!*"

"No, Chief—please! It's true, God's my witness!"

Hank moved to drag him down the hall. But as terrified as the man seemed, he refused to budge from his chair. Kazuo Hamada would never stand his ground unless he was completely bankrupt in the lies department. "It's the *truth,*" he whined.

"You pass me a crock, Kaz, and it won't be Tule you'll have to worry about. I'll make sure you get a berth on the next repatriation boat. Do we have an understanding?"

"But I'm a *citizen.*"

"Tell that to the *hakujin.*"

"All right . . . okay . . . but you got to realize I don't have a name for the staffer. I just heard about the deal. That's all I know. And it came to me secondhand, like I said."

The chief lit a Chesterfield and passed it to him. "Then tell me who has the story firsthand."

The cigarette trembled out of Kazuo's grasp. "Oh, Jesus—I-I can't do that."

"Why not?"

"I just *can't.* Don't even ask me. For your sake, too. We'll both wind up on the blacklist."

"I've been first on that list for years."

"They'll know it was me. Even though I'm not connected. Please, Chief!"

Hank glowered at the man. "Tell me—*now.*"

Kazuo began to lean over to pick up the cigarette, but suddenly dove for the door, springing the latch with his elbow and then clawing the jamb with both hands to turn the corner.

Hank, reaching for the Chesterfield, let him go. He tapped the ash off the coal and took a quiet puff.

Moments later, grunting sounds echoed down the corridor. Then Wada appeared clutching a bug-eyed Kazuo by the collar and the seat of his trousers. He swung the small man around and planted him firmly back in the chair before righting his helmet and patting his cheek almost tenderly. "He go stay now."

"Thank you, Officer Wada."

◆ ◆ ◆

The commander at submarine headquarters looked like a rich man's son who'd balked at going to medical school. His dress khakis were affected with just enough wrinkles to make him appear casual but not sloppy, and he had planted his shoes on his desk with a wide yawn. Yet, as the man absently stroked his thin, elegant nose with a finger, it occurred to Jared that the gesture was a feint to show off his Annapolis ring, which caught the morning light banding in through the venetian blinds. The scintillations came like Morse Code: *Who the hell are you to bother me in the middle of a goddamned war?* Not only was Jared being reminded that he lacked an equally august talisman from West Point, he was now made to feel like the busboy for a fraternity dining table—all the more so because the commander had been uncommonly congenial toward the enlisted man who had just ushered Jared in. "Then you're not with intelligence?"

"No sir, not directly."

A wispish smile. "I don't understand."

Jared didn't want to bring the Presidio into this, but now realized that he would get nothing from the Navy unless he did. "I'm with the 319th MP Company at Manzanar War Relocation Center. But in this matter I'm taking my orders from Fourth Army G-2."

"But who's your superior officer?"

"Colonel Nicholas Bleecher."

"At the center, you mean?"

"No, Colonel Bleecher's the chief of intelligence at the Presidio."

The commander slowly swiveled around in his chair to gaze out the window. Mid-harbor, torpedoes were being hoisted out of the bowels of a tender and into a submarine tied alongside. He softly clicked his ring against his front teeth, apparently deep in thought. Jared soon realized that it was a calculated delay. An inferior officer from another branch was asking for what was probably troublesome information to dig up: the location of a navigationally blind sub back in June of 1941—and that Army officer was offering nothing in return.

"Well," he said just when Jared had begun to wonder if he'd dozed off with his eyes open, "I'll have to secure my own clearances . . ."

And that, no doubt, would involve a call to the Presidio. The rear admiral to lieutenant general variety. "Understood, sir," Jared said, hoping his unease wasn't obvious.

"It'll take some time. Where are you billeted?"

"Hotel in town last night."

"You're welcome to check into our BOQ for tonight."

"Thank you, sir, but I was hoping to return to Manzanar this evening."

"Hmm."

"Would it be all right if I came back this afternoon?"

"Well, call before you come. Say, fourteen hundred hours. My yeoman will give you the number. Would you care to go through one of the attack boats? He can take you out."

"Thank you again, sir, but no. I got business downtown." Jared was dying to see the inside of a submarine. But he was unwilling to give this country club bohemian the satisfaction of fobbing him off on some bored lackey.

"Very well." The commander picked up a file and started reading—a signal that the interview was concluded.

"Thanks for your time, sir." Jared saluted, but it wasn't returned.

"Hmm." The commander waited until Jared had a hand on the doorknob before murmuring, "By the way, I suppose it's okay to divulge this. It was in the papers. The *Leopard Shark* was presumed sunk on a long range patrol in January of 1943. No reported survivors, I'm afraid."

♦ ♦ ♦

While Jared looped around the train station parking lot searching for an empty space among the logjam of military vehicles, a locomotive huffed up to the platform with brakes skirling and finally stopped in a pall of its own steam. The passenger cars then began disgorging what seemed to be all the sailors and Marines America had at its command; many were siphoned off into waiting buses, but others shouldered their overseas bags and formed a stream that wound through the lot toward Broadway, the main thoroughfare. At last, Jared found a slot being vacated by a Marine Corps staff car and, hiding his only luggage—a canvas furlough satchel—under the front seat, joined the pilgrimage toward the dives and amusement arcades one block distant.

"Lieutenant!" a bald cabbie cried as if delighted to see him. "Let me run you up to a real gentlemen's club!"

"No thanks, but can you tell me where the submariners hang out?"

"You're saying it wrong."

"Pardon?"

"It's pronounced like the poem."

"What poem?"

"You know—*The Rime of the Ancient Mariner*. Sub-*mariners*." Having finished with Jared, he turned away and tried his pitch on a trio of seamen.

Jared strolled on, amazed once again that even a cab driver in California knew more than he did.

He had seen twin dolphins glinting on the commander's chest and now kept an eye out for this insignia as he wound his way into a shooting gallery raucous with *pfft-plink* noises and boyish war whoops. The front of the place was open to the boulevard and a sea breeze was flowing in off the bay—yet, a lance corporal whose fruit salad included the Guadalcanal combat ribbon was bathed in sweat as he unerringly downed little tin silhouettes of bison and antelope. He glanced aside at Jared's uniform, and his eyes filled with a look close to hatred before he went back to decimating the Great Plains.

On the street again, Jared took the crossed pistols insignias that marked him as an MP off the lapels of his tropical worsted blouse and replaced them with his old infantry clip-ons, which he had saved for occasions like this. Nobody likes a cop.

After an hour of elbowing through a dozen arcades and twice that many beer bars, he finally spotted what he hoped was a real-life sub-*mariner*, except that this man's breast insignia showed the profile of a submarine, not twin dolphins. "Pardon, hoss—"

"Sir?" Warily, the sailor set down his glass mug.

Jared pointed. "Does this mean you're in subs?"

"Yes, Lieutenant—it's for a combat patrol." He also had a dolphin cloth patch on his right sleeve.

"You heard of a ship called the *Leopard Shark?*"

"Boats, sir. Submarines are boats."

"Oh. I thought I finally had that straight—" His chuckle was cut short: without taking his leave, the submariner had turned and walked out. Jared bit his lip, then ordered a draft.

An adolescent seaman was staring at him from the adjoining stool, his face broad, homely, and trusting. "Pardon, Lieutenant, sir . . ."

"Well, I'll be damned. Somebody without an accent." Jared offered his hand. "Shawnee—Dust Bowl Class of 'thirty-four."

"McAlester." Hesitantly, he accepted Jared's hand, then grinned when it turned out to be human. "We stuck it out."

"Good for you. I sometimes wish we had, too."

"'Course, Daddy got a job with the prison after the bank tractored down our place."

"Hell, that's okay. Least he didn't take up the tractor himself, like some did." Jared put away his beer in four swallows, then ordered another round for himself and the sailor. "You catch me jollying that sub-*mariner?*"

"Yes, sir." Then the teenager winced a little. "I mean—not on purpose, sir."

"Relax, hoss. What scared him off like that?"

"He thought you was a plant from ONI, trying to get him to talk about his boat. They dress up in all kinds of disguises to catch us blabbing. You know, loose lips sink ships."

"Name's Jared."

"Coxswain Lyle Dobbs—proud to meet you, sir."

"What's a coxswain?"

"I'm steersman on one of the liberty launches in the harbor here." A sudden thought toned down the friendliness in Dobbs's eyes. "You're *not* from ONI, are you?"

Jared watched his beer bubble for a few seconds. "No, Lyle, I'm a military policeman at one of those Jap internment camps."

"You on business down here, sir?"

"Kinda. I need to talk to somebody who served on a sub called the *Leopard Shark*. Ever heard of her?"

Dobbs shook his head. "I been in less than a year," he admitted.

"Well, catch is—the *Leopard Shark* got herself sunk with all hands. So I'm hoping to find somebody who was on her *before* the war. June of 'forty-one to be exact."

"That'll be tough, sir."

"I know." Jared signaled the bartender for two more.

Dobbs's face turned thoughtful, and he didn't touch his fresh set-up. Finally, he glanced over both shoulders before saying quietly, "I got a buddy from Stillwater. We went through boot camp together at Great Lakes. Well, he's on the tender *Nereus*. If anybody can, he'll come up with a name. You want me to try to get hold of him this afternoon?"

◆ ◆ ◆

As a detective, Jared had learned that it's impossible to hang up on a physical presence. So, at two that afternoon, instead of telephoning the commander as instructed, he drove up to the sentry house outside the headquarters building. At the very least he wanted to make it stickier for the Navy to brush him off.

Surprisingly, the Marine guard, after glancing at his ID, scribbled out a pass and said, "The commander's expecting you, sir." Even more surprising was to be met on the front steps by the officer himself, whose smile now looked like it had been scrawled under his nose with a razor blade.

"It's just as well you came directly here," he said, his voice strangely toneless. He sounded like someone who had just received a death threat. "We'll be able to accommodate your request sooner than anticipated. If you'll follow me . . ."

They quick-marched down a maze of passageways that made Manzanar's corridors seem like cow trails in comparison, the white hats leaping out of the way right and left as if Jehovah himself were on the prowl, and eventually arrived in an empty conference room. One wall was given over to a stunning blue panorama of the Pacific, the biggest and prettiest map Campbell had ever seen.

"Very well," the commander said, shutting the door behind them and taking a pointer off the burnished walnut table. "The week of June first, 1941, the *Leopard Shark* was outbound between Wake and Marcus Islands." He swept the slightly shaking tip of the pointer from San Diego to a speck of green that read Marcus. The span was so long he had to take three sidesteps to cover the distance. Then he turned toward Jared, his eyes motionless in his face. "Any questions?"

"One, sir." Perhaps Rocha, like many witnesses years after the fact, had miscalculated the probable dates of the incident off San Clemente Island. "Is there any way that sub coulda been off the California coast a week before or after that spell in early June?"

"Impossible."

"Sir?"

"We're talking about five thousand nautical miles and one of the first fleet boats. For a long patrol, ten knots on the surface, tops. But that's beside the point. The *Leopard Shark* spent all of that May in training maneuvers off the Hawaiian Islands. From mid-June to mid-July she was on station in the Sea of Japan—which is still classified." He brought the pointer down against his leg with a snap that looked as if it had hurt. But nothing showed in his eyes. "Anything else we can help you with?"

Jared stared at the map until it became a turquoise blur. "No, sir."

CHAPTER 14

"I just don't know . . ." Puffing out her cheeks in bewilderment, the *nisei* secretary examined the indefinite leave documents a second time. Hank Fukuda prayed she wouldn't hold them up to the light. If she did, she might notice the smears where the original nigrosine signatures had been chemically effaced. Here it was once again, the dimly recalled Japanese village asserting itself in the California outland: the web of trust no one could violate with impunity. He felt like hell.

The secretary seemed on the verge of voicing her doubts when the *hakujin* supervisor frowned from behind her desk. "What seems to be the problem, Miss Watanabe?"

"Well, ma'am, a special clearance was routed through internal security. And now Chief Fukuda wants us to bump the top applicant on the job-offer list."

"Not me," Hank corrected her, waving a carefully doctored teletype. "Civil Affairs at the *Presidio*."

"Which job is that?" the supervisor asked.

"Greenskeeper at the Shinnecock Country Club, ma'am."

"Oh, no—not the Long Island opportunity," the biddy

said with a grimly defiant smile. "We've exercised great care in selecting someone for that position. He has a degree in horticulture and a pleasing way of dealing with Caucasians. And who better do you offer in his stead, Chief?"

"Kazuo Higashiyama—former greenskeeper for the Beverly Hills Country Club. He has an excellent occupational history." All forged, Hank neglected to add. "And the Presidio wants him out—today."

The supervisor leveled her chrome-blue eyes on Hank—but she obviously knew she was beaten. Leave clearances initiated by San Francisco via Lieutenant Campbell's office were suspected of being for informants who had been compromised or were being rewarded for faithful service. "Tell me something, Chief," she said coldly.

He met her stare. "I'll try."

"How we are expected to build a credible alternative to internment—and find jobs on the East Coast for tens of thousands of you people—when the Army or the FBI barges in and undoes everything we've put together?"

"I don't know, ma'am. I simply have my instructions."

"Why are you handling this and not Lieutenant Campbell?"

"He's down south on temporary duty."

"Then what about the MP travel permit?"

"He filled out Mr. Higashiyama's green slip prior to going." Not wanting the resettlement machinery to bog down in his brief absence, Campbell had signed a dozen blanks, trusting the chief to use them wisely. Hank kept telling himself that this was wise.

The loose skin on the undersides of her arms trembling, she began collecting several forms from a slotted bin, putting them into a manila envelope. "Well, still, it'll take a day to get approval from Records and Statistics, Project Employment, then Mr. Lee—"

"I've already hand-carried these sign-offs through administration—all except Mr. Lee's, which I'll get now. Mr. Higashiyama is to make this morning's escort to Reno."

The supervisor flung the envelope at him, then motioned with her head toward the door for him to leave.

♦ ♦ ♦

The chief's face didn't reveal how upset this confrontation had left him.

Strife with the *hakujin* staff always left him dry-mouthed and a little nauseous. And he had no doubt that within a week of his arrival at Shinnecock, Kazuo Hamada, aka Higashiyama, would be jimmying open lockers at the prestigious club. Within a month he would be in the county clink. And within six months he'd be back in internment, this time at Tule Lake. It was inevitable; even poor Kazuo probably realized this, deep-down. And the resettlement program, the evacuees' only hope of reentering *hakujin* society, would be dealt a black eye; the newspapers, led by the Hearst chain, would crow about how the sneaky Jap truly couldn't be assimilated.

But Hank would gladly loose a hundred Kazuo Hamadas on America in order to find a link between Masao Shido and someone on the Caucasian staff. Such a liaison might have nothing to do with Morris Wenge's murder—but the chief wouldn't bet on it.

Rushing into the station and down the aisle between the desks of the clerk-typists, he paused only long enough to ask Kimiko to retrieve several files for him. She had come back to work that morning, which pleased him.

Then he closeted himself in the lab, unlocked his cabinet, filled a beaker with yellow lightning, and gulped it down. He splayed his fingers in front of his eyes: they seemed steadier than before.

Within a minute, Kimiko was knocking at the door with the files. "Here, Chief."

"Thanks. How you doing today?"

"Better, thanks." She withdrew, smiling as if to convince herself she had told the truth.

Hank sighed, then began leafing through the thick pile of directives for a sample of Montgomery Lee's signature. At last he found the somewhat unsteady specimen, practiced it several times on a piece of scratch paper, then affixed it to Kazuo's visa out of Manzanar. The forgery, he decided with pursed lips, was adequate, and even if the resettlement office became suspicious the acting director would not come dragging into work before ten, by which time Kazuo would be on the road.

Hank had almost forgotten about a loyalty declaration signed in Kazuo's latest alias. He began filling one out, shaking his head at the absurdity of this pledge to the American war effort and denunciation of the emperor. Both Shido and Momai had passed with flying colors, regular yes-yes boys. And why not? To have answered no-no meant a one-way ticket to Tule Lake. Even if a bona fide Nipponese spy were lurking in camp, would he have been so dimwitted as to incriminate himself?

Relax, Hank told himself. Nothing can be done. *Yet.*

◆ ◆ ◆

Forty minutes later Kazuo and he were standing beside the Black Maria while Maggie, the *hakujin* driver, tried to figure out how to squeeze in twelve passengers and their cardboard luggage. None of them looked like people about to be sprung from incarceration, but Hank Fukuda could understand their apprehension: they were preoccupied with the reception awaiting them on the far side of the country. Stories were trickling back of epithets hissed in the darkness of movie theater balconies, of beatings in alleys, of bricks crashing through windows. And everyone recalled that on the night of the attack on Pearl Harbor a *nisei* had been brutally murdered. Uncertainty was taking the desert color out of their faces.

"All right, Kaz . . ." The chief drew the little man aside. "I've come through with my end—give me the name."

The pith helmet bobbed in agreement, but no sound escaped from his lips.

He's *still* scared to death, Hank realized, squeezing the man's shoulders hard. "I swear, if you get cold feet now—"

"Wait." Kazuo looked no less miserable, but he leaned forward, hesitated, then whispered in Hank's ear.

The chief arched an eyebrow: a plausible enough informant. But he refused to let go of Kazuo until he had issued a final threat: "If this is bogus, I'm putting an APB out through the MPs. Consider armed and extremely dangerous, one Kazuo Hamada—"

"Chief, I've never worked with heat on me—"

"Shut up. I'll make it read like you're Tojo's number-one boy in America. Every red-blooded *hakujin* cop in the country will be gunning for you, Kaz. And where can you hide with a face like that? Where can any of us?" He paused, then let his hands fall from Kazuo's shoulders. "Do we have an understanding?"

◆ ◆ ◆

Jared was steering toward the curb to pick up Coxswain Lyle Dobbs when a shore patrolman stepped out into the intersection where Broadway dumped into the naval pier. He halted the lieutenant with two blasts of his whistle, and the Stars and Stripes rippled into view, flanked by a brace of guidons. Jared's right hand snapped to the corner of his eye. His lips thinned over his front teeth as the sound of tramping feet that had been growing over the past few seconds was explained by a long column of leathernecks decked out in the latest-issue jungle fatigues, looking like piebald mules for all the camouflaged combat gear heaped on their backs. Down along the pier, in the shadow of a troopship, a band in dress blues was thumping out the "Marine's Hymn."

Jared watched the ranks flash past in perfect regularity, and finally had to admit to himself that it was time to head back to Manzanar. There was no further reason to remain in San Diego: Tadashi Nitta had lied; and, as unsavory as it would be, Jared would now have to come down hard on him. He trusted that he could get a confession out of the major, but only prayed the shame wouldn't kill Kimiko—she'd wither and die if her husband's treason became widely known. And in Manzanar there was nothing but *widely known*.

"Lord," he muttered, "let me disappear on that ship . . ."

Then the SP roused him with the whistle. The intersection was finally clear, the horde of Marines on the pier unraveling into columns and streaming up gangplanks fore and aft. The band was already packing its instruments into the luggage compartment of a gray bus—another load wrapped up for the islands.

"Just tell me how to get to some quiet joint," Jared said as the young coxswain bounced into the bucket seat and snugged down his white hat against the breeze as the jeep accelerated. "Someplace where we don't have to duck beer bottles."

"What about the *Leopard Shark*, sir?"

"Your buddy didn't know anybody off her, right?"

"Right." Dobbs grinned. "But his CPO knows a motor mac who got kicked outa the Navy even before the war started."

"What's that?"

"Motor mechanic—a real bilge rat."

Palmetto shadows flitted over Jared's eyes, making him blink each time he burst back into sunlight. "This motor mac's here in Dago?"

"As I live and breathe, sir." But then Dobbs sobered. "Only thing is—I don't think he's going to take to you being an MP and all."

♦ ♦ ♦

Squatting on the cement steps of the pink two-story stucco, shaded by an arbor of wilted bougainvillea, was a sailor who looked all of sixteen. The collar to his jumper was nearly ripped off, and he was concentrating on trying to pinch off the flow of blood that was gushing out of his broken nose. When Dobbs asked if he needed some help, he said without looking up, "Shove off."

"Okay, but you can still save them trousers if you soak that bloodstain in cold water 'bout an hour before washing."

Jared's eyes softened: Oklahoma—thanks to dust, depression, and war—had jettisoned her children on a world that didn't know how to take them.

He knocked on the front door, then stood to its side, motioning for Dobbs to do the same. When the coxswain looked confused, Jared gestured that someone inside might chose to answer a with a flurry of bullets. Dobbs seemed genuinely astonished that folks, even in California, would do such a thing.

Then the door cracked open a few inches. The face of a middle-aged Filipina appeared, her eyes clicking to the silver bar on Jared's overseas cap. "Go away. Off-limits. You go now!"

Over her shoulder, Jared could see two Marines, one slouching on the threadbare sofa with a kimono-clad white woman on his lap, and the other kneeling before a floor-model Philco, trying to tune in something worth dancing to.

"Yes, ma'am, I'm sure this ain't what I think it is. I just want to talk to Curly."

"No Curly here."

The door slammed shut, and Jared could hear her fiddling with the mortise lock. Before she could secure it against him, he turned the knob and began pushing the door counter to her bulk, which might have proved enough to bar him had she not started sliding back across the dirty linoleum on her straw thongs.

"Curly!" she shrieked. "Mayday!"

"Ma'am—"

She gave up on the door and began trying to claw Jared's eyes with her carmine fingernails. "Curly, gun!"

Jared grimaced: his own .45 had been left behind at Manzanar. "Why don't we stop this, ma'am"—with his forearm, he deflected another rake at his eyes—"and have us a little chat?"

She bared her teeth at him, hissed like a viper.

"Now this is no way for a lady to act—"

At that moment Curly skidded around the corner on the soles of his feet. In the fleeting instant before the former motor mac third class threw a powerful roundhouse, Jared found himself agreeing with Dobbs's report that here was a rowdy worthy of two years at the Terminal Island Disciplinary Barracks for almost beating a petty officer to death with a wrench. Framed by glossy black hair, his was a ruthless face made only slightly impish by a pug nose and the gap left by a front tooth broken off at the gums.

The blow glanced along Jared's jawline as he turned his head. "Dang you!"

"Like that one? Want another?" Curly cried with a bumptious grin.

Perhaps he expected Jared to wind up for an equally broad swing, or at least back up a step for a quick jab. Whatever he expected, it wasn't the heel of Jared's right hand popping against the base of his nose, momentarily blinding him. He stumbled backward, his eyes quicksilvered by tears.

He had been focusing on the lieutenant's eyes and not his hands—always a mistake when squared off against a street-fighter. "How about you, hoss?" Jared asked. "*You* want one more?"

Curly tried a low blow, but Jared deflected it with his kneecap and then bashed him in the nose again. As the man started sneezing blood, Jared checked on his mama-*san*: she was grappling futilely with Dobbs, who'd apparently bucked some hay in his time. She tried to plant her teeth in his wrist, but he gave a tug on her jet-black braid before she could sink her teeth into his flesh.

The Marine on the sofa pushed the whore off his lap, bloused his shirttail over the erection tenting his trousers, and bailed out the door, his buddy two steps behind him.

"What'd you do that for?" Curly shouted, but his unfisted hands told Jared he had no more fight in him.

"That was for the kid who just got himself a Roman nose in here, hoss. I figured you'd look good with one, too."

Curly laughed between sneezes, then wiped his nose on his arm, leaving a trail of red that he then smeared across his paunch. It had been the desperately friendly laugh with which a bully tries to make peace. "You here to close us down?"

"Not yet."

"That's the only reason brass shows up in a dump like this. Especially *cop* brass."

Jared smiled: he was still wearing infantry insignia—Curly was sharper than he looked. "What makes you think I'm a cop?"

"You was standing sideways to me, so I couldn't kick you

in the balls. Only cops do that." Again, the forced laugh. "Are we out of business, Lieutenant?"

"Depends."

Curly winked at the Filipina. "It's a shakedown, Vina—get the box."

"No shakedown," Jared said. "I just got a few questions. Nothing to incriminate you. In fact, nothing to do with you personally. Answer some things about the *Leopard Shark* and I'll be out of here in ten minutes."

"Level with me, dammit—you're a snow drop, right?"

Jared nodded. It was the usual moniker given to MPs because of their white helmets, gloves, web belts, and leggings, although he'd never heard it used to describe Manzanar's olive-drab detachment.

"What happens if I say nothing?" Curly asked, looking to save face.

"I'll be back with the Shore Patrol in half an hour."

Curly chuckled from the back of his throat—the sound of a dog coughing up a worm. "Lieutenant, I'd like you to meet my wife, Ludivina. . . ."

Simpering now, she did everything but curtsy. "Hi."

And with that, Curly led Jared and Dobbs through the kitchen, swept up a bottle and three shotglasses off a makeshift bar, and jerked his head for them to follow him up a stairway. At the end of the musty second-story hallway he threw open a pair of French windows and invited them to step out onto the flat asphalted roof of the first floor. It was enclosed by a low parapet, against which two whores were propped, their naked bodies glistening with sweat and baby oil, breasts lolling heavily to the sides. Dobbs bumped into Jared's back when the lieutenant slowed to take a deck chair.

"I want to thank you ladies for coming downstairs to help out," Curly said.

"Customers?" one of them murmured drowsily, not bothering to take off the cotton swabs protecting her eyelids.

"I suppose you didn't hear Vina screaming for help." When

they didn't answer, Curly snarled, "Cunts." He handed Jared and Dobbs each a glass and poured them a shot. "So what's so interesting about the USS *Leopard Shit?*"

Jared scooted his chair into the bristly shadow thrown by a date palm. "Were you aboard her in June of 'forty-one?"

"From September of 'thirty-nine till November of 'forty-one. And I picked a damn good time to get off her. Had that skipper been in airplanes he woulda lost a dozen of them. But you only lose a sub once, if you catch my drift."

"You remember having trouble with your compasses off San Clemente Island that June?"

Curly sniffled like his nose still hurt. "No . . ."

That did it. Jared finished the cheap, fiery bourbon in a single swallow. Eddie Nitta's story was as flimsy as a rice-paper house—and it was time to get back and shake it apart.

"That was off Saint Nicholas Island." Curly paused, rubbing the shotglass back and forth across his lower lip. "At least that's what one of the lookouts told me. Hell, I don't know. I spent all my fucking time below the walking decks. Maybe it was San Clemente. All I know is, there was some kind of fog off the south coast that spring."

Jared leaned forward. His jaw was still buzzing from Curly's glancing blow, but he ignored his discomfort. "Weren't you on maneuvers off Hawaii in May?"

Curly fell silent for a moment. "No, that was the year before. And we damn near got rammed by the *Arizona*. See, our bonehead skipper failed to execute—"

"Did you ever surface next to a bunch of tuna boats in the fog?"

Curly stared at Jared briefly, then burst into laughter, freeing a trickle of blood from a nostril, which he then proceeded to lick off his upper lip. "Picture this—the gryo, which had a blown gimbal, was making like a roulette wheel. And I forget exactly why now, but something was wrong with the magnetic compass, too. No echo-ranging on that tub then, either. We was all grinding our teeth thinking we was going to run aground any second. So Carmody picks up some small motor cavitation on the phones, and the skipper takes a peek through the observation periscope. Looks okay, so we breach like a whale. But then he coulda crapped his skivvies!" Curly touched his swollen nose and winced. "You put some English on that fucking jab."

"*Why* did your skipper almost crap?"

"Well, Jesus, we was surrounded by Japs. American Japs, as it turned out. But nobody knew that at first. He thought we was *serious* lost, if you catch my drift."

Jared could feel his pulse hammering out a beat in his neck. He poured himself another shot and downed it.

"Help yourself," Curly said.

"This is important—were you on a long-range cruise the rest of that June?"

"No way. We didn't sail for the Sea of Japan until July seventeenth. God, was that a bitched-up cruise. It was like we was already at war."

"How can you remember that?"

"What?"

"That you went to sea *exactly* on the seventeenth of July?"

"The sixteenth was my twenty-first birthday. And the exec had to get me out of the downtown brig next morning so he'd have enough white niggers for the patrol. Everybody remembers his twenty-first birthday party, don't he?"

CHAPTER 15

The welder's sparks drizzled down the side of the gun turret and across the buckled deck before cascading over the hull into the black water. The outlines of the ship were limned by the last of the sunset, which only made her seem more scorched and forlorn, more of a derelict than the battle-ravaged yet still floating man-of-war she was.

"The *Tacoma,*" Lyle Dobbs said, his voice low.

He brought the liberty launch in closer so Jared could examine the tangle of scrap iron that had once been the light cruiser's bridge. "Her skipper took her damn near up on the beach to help out them Marines landing on Saipan. Jap shore battery clobbered them. Killed the captain, the exec, the—" Dobbs hushed himself with a cough, and the only sound for a few moments was the puttering of the boat's engine. "Well, Japs kilt most everybody on the bridge."

The masthead lighting, the only showing, slanted back across the forward stack, which was riddled like a piece of stovepipe used for a shotgun target. Jared slowly shook his head. "Human courage ain't much of a match for high explosives, is it?"

"I reckon, sir."

"But the captain knew that better than us. And he still took her close to the beach for those Marines."

Dobbs smartly flipped up the throttle and leaned on the tiller with his hip. "Want to see a carrier now, sir?"

"Sure."

With the exception of Dobbs's crew—his boat hooks, he called them: two seamen huddled in the bow, smoking and self-importantly shouldering their gaffs as if they were rifles—they had the forty-foot launch to themselves. Dobbs had arranged for the other boats to cover for him until eleven tonight, when the crews would be swarming onto the Broadway pier to beat the Cinderella liberty deadline. "Was it bad news, sir?" he asked as they slid across the bay toward North Island.

"Pardon?"

"You know—what that fella Curly told you?"

"Oh, I suppose. This whole job's gone cat-wild with bad news." It was so bad, in fact, Jared had shut it out of his mind, like death coming into the house. The night his father passed away he had felt nothing except puzzlement that grief so close could seem so flat, so stale; but the next morning the certainty had hit him with a wallop that made him suddenly fight for breath. He now wondered if this would be the same, although for the moment he felt only weariness. And resentment. He had been lied to, and the lie had gold braid sewn all over it.

Gazing toward North Island, he could make out the spires of a big hotel against the swatch of sky that was still lit rose. Dobbs seemed to read his thoughts: "Hotel Del Coronado, sir."

"The ritz, ain't she?" Jared imagined having dinner there with Kimiko, and in his little dream no one stared at them as they ate. And later they would take a walk on the beach, with no war going on on the far side of the sea that was foaming in the brassy lights of the hotel—although, in reality, the place was blacked out. Converted by the Navy into a convalescent hospital, Dobbs explained from the edges of the lieutenant's dream. And Kimiko looked happy, even when he made love to her on the sand, careful to remain suspended on his arms above her small body so as not to crush her with his weight. Had he ever actually done that—made love to her? A lie made everything, even the good things, seem unreal.

Then a thought glimmered up through the dream and burst it: a flake of inspiration or intuition or whatever. "Dobbs, let's see that carrier later on. The ammunition depot we passed earlier—how about heading back for there?"

The coxswain looked confused, but said, "Aye-aye, sir."

But his confusion was nothing compared to that of the ensign on duty at the floating dock, who ordered his Negro ammunition handlers to get back to work, then—without smiling—invited Jared to have a cup inside his broom closet of an office. "Excuse me, Lieutenant," he said, squelching Benny Goodman with a twirl of a radio knob, "but I still don't get why you need this information *tonight*."

"An investigation into a national security matter."

"Don't you have somebody in ONI working with you on this?"

"Sure do," Jared fibbed—at least Colonel Bleecher had a liaison with Naval Intelligence. "But he was called away this morning on a family emergency. I really didn't figure something like this being top secret."

"Well, the information is certainly restricted."

A colored seaman in sweat-darkened dungarees brought in two mugs. The ensign sighed, took a sip of coffee, then said, "Close the door on your way out, Clinton."

"Aye-aye, Mr. Hughes."

The ensign sighed again—just to let Jared know that he ordinarily didn't do this sort of thing. "Very well. In answer to your question—yes, our forces do capture Jap ordnance from time to time."

"Any of it *shimose?*"

The ensign's eyes widened a little. "Yeah, the bombs and projectiles contain picric. How'd you learn about *shimose?*"

"My ONI friend. What happens to it?"

"Most of it's blown up right there on the islands. But some, the newer stuff, gets shipped home."

"For testing?
"You bet, why else would we bother?"
"You all offload any of that ordnance here?"
The ensign hesitated for a moment. "Some."
"Can't test it at this depot, can you?"
He gave a distracted shake of his head.
"So where's it go from here?"
"Depends on the type. A few months ago, the Seabees got hold of some Jap torpedoes—they went up to Pond Oreille, a sub weapons testing station in Idaho. The bombs go to Jacksonville. But the projectiles are trucked out to China Lake."
Jared's mouth twisted into a smile, but there was no amusement in it. "You mean the base out in the Mojave Desert?"
"Right, the Naval Ordnance Testing Station near Iyokern."
Jared burned his tongue on his first taste of coffee, but scarcely felt it: China Lake was less than seventy miles from Manzanar War Relocation Center.

♦ ♦ ♦

Yuki Ota shuffled out of the co-op store with the graceful unbobbing steps of a geisha—but that was only because she was preoccupied with opening a jar of pickled plums.
She plopped down on the wooden steps, her knees splayed wide beneath her blue plaid skirt—a gift from the Maryknoll nuns, who still had faith in lost sheep.
Yuki devoured the first *umeboshi*, but then paused in the midst of sucking the salty juice off her fingertips: she sensed she was being watched. Her insouciance became more studied, and she buffed the toes of her red patent leather shoes on the backs of her white ankle socks before filling her mouth with another dripping plum. Only then did her eyes sweep across the firebreak in search of her watcher.
Hank Fukuda ducked back behind the edge of the Block 15 men's latrine. Lifting the brim of his motoring cap to wipe the sweat off his brow, he counted to thirty before peering out again.
She wasn't pretty. She had *chocho* lips—butterfly lips—

which he'd never cared for. And the combination of Ike jacket and pigtails made her look raffish. But she had excellent skin. This and her willingness to do anything a man asked, to become any kind of a woman a man desired, had built her a modest clientele in camp.

At that moment, one of her patrons bounded up the steps, for expectation lit up her wide face. But the man ignored her. American behavior, aloofly *nisei*. An *issei* would understand how Yuki's shame might be mitigated by circumstance: in Japan, filial piety could drive a daughter into harlotry to erase family indebtedness. And no one questioned the honorable status of the geisha—except foreigners, who couldn't quite grasp that she was less a prostitute and more an artist, a purveyor of culture. *Gei-sha* was actually a combination of the words for *art* and *person*. And neither common prostitute nor geisha was believed to be a sick person for what she did when her "pillowing price" was met. Her body became a receptacle in which disruptive passions were defused; the harmony of society was preserved by her willingness to endure a stranger on her belly.

However, Hank didn't delude himself about Yuki Ota, who was now doling out pennies to a gaggle of sugar-starved kids. She was a hooker in the grand old American tradition. Her police and probation records forwarded to WRA told it all: an alcoholic stepfather had unknowingly conditioned her to accept the abuses of her trade, and she'd since grown dependent on the easy money.

These facts would make it difficult for Hank to deal with her as he had with Kazuo Hamada. Resettlement was out of the question—the *hakujin* staff knew how she would support herself on the East Coast. Nor could he threaten her with an inter-camp transfer: Tule Lake, twice the size of Manzanar, had more bachelors than any of the camps. In fact, he was surprised she hadn't already finagled a transfer on her own—a couple of *banzai*s during the national anthem at a high school football game would've done the trick.

No, there would be only one chance to turn Yuki Ota.

And as much as everything inside him begged for action, Hank knew he would have to wait a bit longer.

◆ ◆ ◆

The installation at China Lake shimmered through the late afternoon heat: ammunition bunkers heaped in rows across the alkalai sink of an ancient lake, an aircraft hangar with a cluster of hutments nestled in its long shadow, and the black scar of a runway from which Jared had just watched two navy-blue Corsairs lift off, waggle their gull-wings, and drone northeast toward Death Valley.

The wind had been flailing greasewood branches against the sides of his jeep, but now it died away as if the world had suddenly stopped spinning. Silence so oppressed the barren landscape he felt the need to pinch his nostrils shut and blow hard to clear his ears—as if he had descended into the silence from a great altitude. Then he lit a Lucky, his first in hours because of the ferocious wind, and inhaled deeply.

Should he get back to the main highway and continue on his way to Manzanar? He pictured himself doing just that, but it made him feel cowardly. They had lied to him. He wasn't sure who *they* were, but they had already taken shape as a shadow on his self-respect. Since leaving San Diego early this morning, he'd grown more and more angry because of the lie. But something else was hollowing out a hot space inside his guts: an erosive willingness to accept the lie—he just might trade his knowledge about the *Leopard Shark* for a transfer out of the MPs. He kept telling himself that as soon as he had shaken Manzanar's dust off his feet none of this would mean anything to him. After enough time had passed, even Kimiko would mean less to him, becoming only a memory of warmth and golden skin and exotic eyes.

But he knew it wasn't true. A man takes his baggage with him. A man remembers.

He gazed at the tiny humplike ammo bunkers, scores of them sprawled across the sink, then tilted back his head and laughed softly; he laughed at what heartache frees a man to do. "If this ain't fishing, I don't know what the shit is . . ."

Flicking away his cigarette, he retied his shoe laces, then set out for the perimeter fence that lay in the distance like a silver thread across the sagelands.

♦ ♦ ♦

Sunlight slanted in through the open west window of the bunglow and fell across Montgomery Lee's eyes, raising the sensation of a sneeze in his sinuses. He rested his wrist across the bridge of his nose, and the urge receded.

He dozed.

After a while, the shadow of a slender young woman darted back and forth across his partially open eyelids. Furtively, he watched as she feather-dusted his lowermost bookshelves, squatting with her small buttocks toward him. Then, taking a sip of tepid bourbon, he again lowered his head against the sofa armrest, half expecting to feel one of his mother's doilies against the back of his neck like the collar of a hair shirt.

Once more, the warm sunlight seemed to narcotize him. He slept—if only because he did not wish to be aroused, to begin the *sequence*.

Mozart.

From the bedroom came the cranky whine of the Hoover. But before his *nisei* housemaid had fired up her vacuum, he had distinctly heard the Clarinet Concerto in A Major—and in the throes of that plaintive sweetness he almost forgot that the music was coming from the evacuee side of the camp. The Manzanar Community Orchestra. Truly, it didn't seem possible: the expression and phrasing were not Oriental.

"Dear God," he murmured to himself, almost chuckling, "what a genius they have for mimicry."

The vacuum fell silent, and Mozart returned from afar.

The young woman stood in the doorway to his bedroom, a hand poised gracefully on the handle of the vacuum.

She was not as attractive as Kimiko Nitta, who this morning had begged him to furnish her husband with the services of the project attorney. "Dear woman," he had explained, his voice husky from that now familiar mixture of desire and exasperation with himself, "this is a concern of the Army's. Might I suggest you broach the matter with Lieutenant Campbell upon his return?" She had then folded her hands in her lap and looked away with such an arresting delicacy that Monty had come close to striking a bargain with her then and there. Good sense had prevailed, although she was a woman who could levitate good sense completely out of reach with her effortless sensuality—much more so, in fact, than his rather plain housemaid.

Still, this girl had a lissome neck. Two tufts of silky black hair stood out from her nape, one on each side of the vague line of her spine.

She smiled shyly, but stopped when she tracked his gaze to the samurai sword hanging on the wall.

A blush of color came to Monty's pasty face, then vanished as quickly as it had appeared.

"Will there be anything else, Mr. Lee?"

When he tried to command her eyes for a moment, she glanced away. "No, my dear—thank you. I don't know what I'd do without you."

◆ ◆ ◆

Finally, after an hour of sweaty walking, Jared came to the fence. "For crapsake . . ."

It was seven feet high and topped with a coil of barbed wire. He didn't relish the idea of trying to climb over, so he began following it, looking for a way under. Through the rapidly fading light he could make out a sentry house, but it was at least a mile to the east and looked unmanned. He had seen no roving patrols plying the inside of the perimeter since he had left his jeep. Somewhere in the blue stillness to his back, coyotes were bickering. Other than that, the only sound was the soft crunching of his heels on the sand.

He began to wonder why he had bothered to hike down: the closer he got to the bunkers the more endless their rows seemed. And surely their steel doors were securely locked. He carried his pick set wherever he went, but even if he found some *shimose* shells what would that tell him?

Maybe he was looking at the equation wrong, focusing on the factors instead of the solution.

A distant roar stopped him: the two Corsairs, he thought, returning from their afternoon flight. Pivoting around, he scanned the deepening twilight, but couldn't glimpse them. And then —out of nowhere—they were directly overheard, huge and black, their engines deafening.

He threw himself down and scrambled against a clump of desert holly.

The planes dipped behind the fence and then out of sight below the roofline of a bunker. A moment later, their wheels screaked against runway pavement.

Slowly, he got to his feet and beat the dust out of his TW blouse. He realized that his back trouser pocket was empty, and stooped over with a grunt to retrieve his crookneck flashlight from the ground.

Just before the dusk was completely gone he found a spot where a recent cloudburst had gouged a rut under the fence. He was halfway under when he heard a vehicle coming. Lying motionless, he held the side of his face against the warm sand as the grind and thunk of gears being shifted grew louder. Then, as he feared, came the grating of jeep brakes.

Suddenly, a powerful spotlight swept along the fence. Then it froze.

"Eyes!" a youthful male voice cried.

"Where?"

"Right there, Gunny!"

Jared cringed, confused: he was sure he couldn't be seen.

"Have at, kid," an older voice said.

A carbine cracked twice. Jared gritted his teeth, waiting for the bullets to thud around him or clang against the fence. But, instead, a yelp of pain came from a mesquite thicket a hundred yards outside the perimeter.

"I think I got one, Gunny!"

"Keep the light on them! A whole pack of them's running along the fence!"

The jeep sped away, and its engine noise soon faded into the distance.

Jared let out a breath.

Then, as he lay sprawled there on his back, the stars winking on from east to west, the ridiculousness of what he was doing hit him like a punch line: there was only one thing he needed to find out here, and there was an easier way to learn it than skulking around a mess of locked bunkers, dodging trigger-happy Marine guards in the dark.

He had just come up with a way to tell him who *they* were. The Japs in camp had an expression for what he had in mind: they called it *naki naki corru*, which means being forced to call a bluff in poker.

♦ ♦ ♦

Two hours later he was seated at a table covered with white linen, a glass of bourbon and water sweating coolly in his hand. He leaned back while a Negro messman set before him the last remaining portion of roast pork and potatoes. "Thanks."

"My pleasure, sir."

The Navy brass in their crisp khakis looked contented as they smoked stogies a dental officer just transferred in from Guantánamo claimed to be Havanas. Jared, who didn't care for cigars, said he would save his for later. That earned him a few frowns, although the officers, on their third after-dinner drink, were otherwise jovial.

He had presented himself at the main gate, claiming trouble with his jeep's clutch, which was partially true. He was shown to Bachelor Officers' Quarters by a lieutenant, who then invited him to dinner. After sponging the dust off his uniform with a washcloth, Jared had followed the man to an officers' club that, with nightclub-style booths and carpet instead of linoleum, was decidedly on the posh side. His introduction to the men seated around the long center table interrupted talk about the explosion in July at the Port Chicago Naval Magazine on San Francisco Bay. Without apparent cause, tons of shells had gone up, vaporizing nearly four hundred ammunition handlers, most of them Negroes. Jared had seated himself and listened without comment, measuring his sips of whiskey and reminding himself not to eat with his knife when his food came.

Finally, the base commander, wearing a wry look as if to give notice that nobody was going to pull anything over on him, narrowed his eyes at Jared through the thick smoke. He smiled before he spoke. "What do your troops have to say about those colored handlers?"

"How's that, Captain?"

"Fifty of the bastards won't load another round of ammunition until their safety can be ensured. What do you think of that?"

Jared couldn't help but trade glances with the messman, who was standing in the background, a towel draped over his forearm. Nothing showed in the man's caramel-complected face, although its agreeable roundness seemed to have leaned out a little. "Well . . ." Jared looked down into his glass. He knew he was being singled out because of his accent. ". . . if I'd just been hit by lightning I might feel like laying low in the hollows, too."

There was laughter, but the captain didn't join in. "You mean you'd disobey a direct order?"

"No, sir." A patch of reddish heat showed along Jared's jawline. "I didn't say that."

"Then what *are* you saying?"

The club had gone quiet, waiting for his reply. He felt trapped but could think of no comeback to take the smirks off their faces. He had no intention of championing anybody's cause, particularly the colored cause; yet he knew that no matter what he said it would sound that way. "Well, Captain, say I was a Navy lieutenant—"

"God forbid," someone unseen stage-whispered from the bar around the corner.

"—I might roll up my sleeves and give those men a hand. You know, convince them we're not asking them to commit *seppuku* by—"

"My Lord—*seppuku?* I haven't heard that word since my days with the Asiatic fleet." The captain blew smoke out his nostrils. "You *have* been at that Jap trap too long."

Jared grinned. "I'll drink to that, sir."

This brought a chorus of more relaxed laughter to the table. Yet it proved premature: the cords in Jared's neck were showing; "Captain, can I trouble you with a work question?"

"Sure." The man was smiling as if he thought Jared was leading up to a joke.

"You folks missing any *shimose?*"

The captain's smile slowly faded. The club was even quieter than before.

Jared resisted the urge to scrutinize each face around the table. He didn't need to know *which one*. He was after the king, not the knights and pawns.

He drained his glass and set it down with a knock.

The messman was right there: "Another highball, Lieutenant?"

♦ ♦ ♦

He never got drowsy.

Soon after he crawled into his cot in the BOQ billet, the wind came down off the Sierra. The corrugated tin roof of the building rattled and roared like the roller coaster at the Oklahoma City fairgrounds, and flying grit sizzled against the window in surges that promised to shatter the glass. But they never did, and at four the gale died away, leaving a muffled silence and the taste of dust in the air, which Jared tried to kill with one cigarette after another. Dust brought back rotten memories.

The sun, when it finally cleared the cindery-looking hills east of the base, was blood-red and shot rays of the same color through the flat gray sky.

Shortly after, as he lay smoking and thinking, a buzzing out of the northwest broke the stillness and became stronger as his alarm clock ticked down the seconds from a straightback metal chair that was now coated with what looked like moldy flour.

Then the distinctive Pratt and Whitney rumble of a C-41A passed overhead. Through his window the plane could be seen banking in approach to a landing.

He felt none of the satisfaction of being vindicated. It was time to make his choice: roll over and play dead or push them *naki naki corru* all the way. In either case, there could be a transfer in store for him; he might be able to put Manzanar behind him, forever.

In his bare feet he padded down the hallway to the head, where he lathered and began shaving. It was there the captain's yeoman found him. "Lieutenant Campbell?"

"Yes."

"You're required on the flight line at once, sir."

Jared nodded, then studied his own eyes in the mirror, searching them for fear.

CHAPTER 16

It was his first time ever in an airplane and Jared wanted to look out the window, to see the barns and water tanks and windmills furl past as tiny as toys on the rolling land below.

Instead, he kept his eyes on Colonel Bleecher's hands.

They were clean and soft, the nails manicured. He seemed to grasp the silver-rimmed coffee cup with the absolute confidence that not a drop would be spilled. And, in fact, his thin wrists perfectly compensated for the yawing of Fourth Army's sumptuous C-41A. The hands of a banker, Jared realized. Hands that had never been shined up by manual labor, or thinned down to gristle and bone by hunger. He wanted to reach across the fold-up table and break them. But that wasn't possible. Not in this world. They only appeared to be soft; in fact, they were made of iron.

His face deadpan, the colonel spoke for the first time in minutes. "The investigation has become too expansive for someone in your capacity."

Jared said nothing. Before this, Bleecher had claimed that, according to a Navy mechanic, the lieutenant's jeep was finished, the drivetrain shot. Still, he could see the audaciousness of this new lie in the colonel's eyes. Bleecher felt no need to dress up the bottom line: as punishment for doing the unexpected, Jared was being stripped of his mobility. It was that bald, and behind the colonel's impassive ease loomed the same power generals used to order thousands of men to their deaths. Jared reminded himself that a man had to put himself, his life, under some big wheel's command if there was to be any kind of victory over the Axis—except that now this boundless power was being turned against him, not the enemy. Courts-martial and firing squads were sparking in the depths of Nicholas Bleecher's eyes.

Sipping his coffee, Jared asked himself how he might possibly buck the decision. But he already knew how he would respond to the lies, and it stuck in his throat like a peach pit.

"My boys at G-2 will take over from here," Bleecher went on. "You've given them some solid leads. Ones they can really sink their teeth into."

"Will Chief Fukuda go on with his work?"

"Related to this case, you mean?"

Jared nodded.

"No way. But don't take me wrong—he's done some good lab stuff. Meticulous, aren't they? But G-2 has far more resources at its disposal than that little fellow."

Jared was thinking that he and the chief might quietly continue their own investigation when Bleecher added, "I dropped Captain Snavely off at Manzanar this morning."

Jared swiveled his chair toward the window so the colonel wouldn't see the sudden hardening of his expression. But then Bleecher's chuckle made him glance back at the man.

"You really have a distaste for internment duty, don't you?"

"Yes sir, I do."

"Why? Do you think it's wrong?"

"No sir, not exactly . . ."

"Then tell me exactly what you do believe, Campbell."

"Well, I just figure—what with my experience—I belong in a combat outfit."

"Oh, that's right"—Bleecher eased back in his chair and gazed at Jared with laughing eyes—"as a cop, you gunned down a couple of hardheads."

He ignored the slant the colonel had put on the shootings. He was too ashamed of what he was about to do to be worried about the past. "You see, sir, I was in the middle of combat readiness when I was shanghaied from my infantry unit."

"Have you requested transfer before?"

Bleecher knew damned well he had, but Jared let it pass. "Several times. Captain Snavely said he couldn't do without me." *And then hounded me without mercy.*

"I see. Well, I'm reluctant to intervene in a company matter."

"I understand, sir." Jared almost felt clean again. A denial of transfer would save him somehow, even though he would have to stay at Manzanar. All at once, to feel clean was everything—it surprised him: the strength of this feeling.

"But I think you and I can reach an understanding. Don't you, Campbell?"

Jared hesitated, the guilt pouring into his face again, tightening the muscles around his mouth. "I think so, Colonel."

"Good. Type out another request."

The plane began to bank toward Manzanar's airstrip, and as the downside windows filled with desert Bleecher's steward took away the silver coffee service.

"I'm afraid we'll just have to drop you off at the strip," the colonel said blandly. "I've got an early luncheon appointment on the Coast."

◆ ◆ ◆

Captain Snavely had summoned all the *hakujin* department heads as well as the evacuee chief of police to the conference room in the administration building. That the military commander and not the civilian director of the camp did this prepared Hank Fukuda for the surprise he felt upon seeing Snavely in Morris Wenge's chair at the end of the table. He was flanked by First Sergeant Osler and Montgomery Lee, who rightfully should have presided over the meeting but—already glassy-eyed from his mid-afternoon snort—cheerfully took his place at the captain's elbow.

Jared Campbell sat by himself, his chair tilted back against the wall. Unsmiling, he gave the chief a nod.

Hank took a seat at the far end of the table and folded his hands in front of him. Osler tried to bully him with a long stare across the polished wood, but Hank looked right through him.

"All right, all right," Snavely said, his pencil-thin mustaches flitting with each syllable, "it's obvious I can't leave this goddamned place even for a few weeks without discipline going to hell, but I've come to expect that. . . ." On and on he rambled in the same vein, his smug face rewarding itself with otherwise meaningless flashes of smile. But then he paused suddenly and frowned. "Chief Fukuda—"

Hank felt the blood drain from his face. "Yes, Captain?"

"I need a complete list of all evacuee Premature Anti-Fascists by oh-eight hundred hours, tomorrow."

Hank had no idea what purpose this could serve, although it would be the second time he had been asked to submit an *aka* roster. He hated doing it—a PAF label was a bar to future employment with the government; on the first go-around he had kept to the names of the avowed communists in camp, who'd been kicked out of the party after Pearl Harbor anyways. But how did Snavely's request jibe with the written order he had just received from the Presidio to submit all his findings "regarding the incidents of 22-3 August 1944" to Bleecher's G-2 outfit, and then desist from further investigation of the case on his own?

Then it hit him: this had something to do with Eddie Nitta; they were bolstering their case against the major.

"Chief," Snavely said, "did you just hear me?"

"Yes, very well, Captain."

"Very well *what?*"

"I'll do it by morning." He kept looking to Campbell for a hint on how to deal with Snavely, what to say in the presence of men who didn't even know that Morris Wenge had been murdered, but the lieutenant refused to meet his gaze.

"Captain," Osler said smoothly, making Hank think that the question had been cleared beforehand, "any word how long we got to keep Nitta in our guardhouse?"

"Might be some time. The major, because of his combat experience, is too much an escape risk for transport now."

Hank fully expected Campbell to smirk at the absurdity of this suggestion, but the lieutenant had withdrawn even deeper into himself. *Say something,* Hank silently shouted at the slouching hulk of a soldier.

Snavely hastened through a half dozen matters of minor importance, then smiled again. "For the last item of business on the agenda, the chair will recognize the new director. Mr. Lee."

Montgomery Lee rose and steadied himself by pressing his fingertips against the tabletop. His grin was boozily wistful; he licked his already shiny lips. "I make this announcement with regret for ourselves, but with congratulations to a man we all are proud to call our friend. I begged Captain Snavely for the privilege of breaking this news because I am the only other authentic son of the Confederacy in this nest of rabid Unionists—"

The reports officer, a giddy fool of a failed journalist, interrupted him with a loud raspberry.

"Gentlemen, please—a little decorum for the occasion. . . ." Surprisingly, tears had formed in Lee's eyes, and these were enough to silence the laughter. "You have no idea the grief this news causes me. Jared Campbell is as true a friend as I shall ever have . . . I could die with that statement in my mouth . . ." He struggled to go on, but his voice broke and he tried to wave off the attention transfixed on him.

Campbell seemed unaffected by the mawkish display of affection. He was staring out the window, watching a dust devil swirl old newspapers and shards of tar paper around Watchtower 7.

Snavely promptly took over: "After a well-deserved furlough, Lieutenant Campbell will be abandoning us for the infantry. . . ." Never once did he glance at Campbell or directly address him: it was obvious that the two had said all they would ever have to say to each other. ". . . I know each of you wishes him success with his new assignment."

During the applause, Osler got up and rushed to the door—altogether too gleefully, Hank thought—and motioned in a file of *nisei* secretaries carrying pitchers of coffee and a large cake with *Farewell and Good Luck, Lt.* scrawled on the blue icing in red and white letters.

Slowly, Hank turned in his chair to confront the lieutenant. Campbell stared back at him as if from an enormous distance, his eyes either too exhausted or ashamed to implore forgiveness. Then he was besieged by handshakes and backslaps, and the chief had no chance for a word with him until the celebration had broken up and Campbell was hurrying down the front steps.

"Lieutenant!"

Campbell arched his back and massaged it with a fist before turning. "Chief."

Hank didn't know how to begin, but finally blurted, "What the hell happened down there?"

Campbell shrugged, started to say something, then changed his mind; his face was so deeply lined it seemed cracked and broken.

"I learned something while you were gone," Hank said, filling the silence. "Something significant." His heart sank when Campbell had no reaction. "What should I do?"

"I don't want to say. I *can't*."

"*Why?*"

"You'll only wind up in a mess of trouble." Then, for the first time that afternoon, he smiled—but it was a miserable smile, full of self-loathing. "I got me a ticket out of here, Hank. Can you blame me for grabbing it?"

But before Hank could answer, the lieutenant headed for the main gate. He right-turned the corner at the highway and continued on toward the MP compound at a quick-march. He never looked back.

Hank wandered the streets for a while, his heart palpitating ominously. *This was the betrayal I never saw coming—how stupid of me . . .*

All at once he was tempted to rush the wire, to see if the sentries in the towers would really open fire. It was crazy, this urge to test the tommy guns, because he knew that other evacuees in other camps had been shot and killed. Before it could overwhelm him, he trotted back to his apartment and barred the door with a broom handle from within.

When he stripped off his shirt, he could see his heart jiggling his pectorals. He lit the Coleman oil stove, then sank into his overstuffed chair, letting the match burn down to his fingers before dropping it.

The closed-up room had already been sweltering, but soon it was intolerable. Sweat darkened his trousers, then began pooling on the floor around his bare feet. He had to press his lips together to keep the salty liquid out of his mouth. The seconds stretched into little eternities. He gripped the armrests, clenched his teeth and died by the drop.

Back in '42, when the stunned evacuees were packed to overflowing in the barracks, strangers jammed in with strangers, some saw the faithlessness of America in everything around them: one *issei* accused his wife of pillowing a teenage boy assigned to their apartment with them. Weeping, pleading, she denied being unfaithful, but he strangled her with a strip of bed sheet, and then, in a frenzy of self-destruction, sliced, stabbed, and finally hanged himself until dead. Hank found his death poem on the apple crate godshelf, his household shrine, the Japanese characters brushed in elegant calligraphy: *I feel as serene as a forest standing before death/I soar above all my worries/Please forgive the one who speeds toward death . . .* What was more amazing than anything was that he had found the privacy in which to end their lives.

The chief cried out as if his body had erupted into flame but forced himself to remain in the chair, although he was now fighting for breath. His lungs refused to admit the searing air, and his nostrils were clogged with the stench of heating oil.

At last, he could take no more.

He turned off the flame, reached for his towel, and staggered outside, leaving the door open to the wind. He paused on the baked and glaring gravel, hyperventilating.

As he had anticipated, Manzanar seemed less of a hell than his kiln of an apartment.

He took a long cool shower in the bathhouse before heading for the station. He would go to work. There was nothing meaningful left to do, but he would go to work. How *bootchie*, he thought.

◆ ◆ ◆

A limousine was waiting at the airfield for Nicholas Bleecher. Unlike the interior of California, the coast was yet green, the gentle hills sponged by fog much of the summer. Simply by landing, the colonel was already on the estate, but it was still some miles of switchbacking road up to the "Ranch," as the hilltop castle was effacingly called by its owner. Bleecher took his place in the rear seat of the car, and the chauffeur set off through an Elysium of grass and evergreen oaks, stopping a minute later to electrically activate a gate. Then the limo passed through the only opening for miles in a ten-foot-high fence.

"Would the colonel care to study the fauna along the way?"

"Not today, thank you. I can stay only for luncheon."

And so they sped past deer, antelope, giraffe, and exotic species Bleecher couldn't name.

The owner had only recently returned to San Simeon from Wyntoon, his lesser estate hidden deep in the forests of northern California. Shortly after Pearl Harbor, he and his mistress had abandoned the Ranch for fear a Jap submarine might lob shells onto the twin spires Bleecher could now glimpse through the overhanging boughs—the old man's distaste for the Nipponese was well known to Tokyo.

After ten minutes the car stopped beside an ancient Egyptian stela, and the chauffeur let the colonel out. Briskly, he crossed the courtyard between the Casa Grande and its slightly less rococo guest house. Smiling, he shook his head at the castle's facade, which had been peeled off a Norman château and reassembled here within sight of the sprawling blue Pacific. Everything in Europe that could be cut up and then hauled by freighter was here at this remote aerie. The place reeked of fenced goods.

A servant conveyed him through the main hall, their footfalls echoing in the catacomb of a fireplace, and into the dining room. The chamber could comfortably hold a hundred diners, but only a handful were sitting at the far end of the longest table Bleecher had ever seen. The aged host, a paunchy man with a long face that sagged down into his silk ascot, rose hunched to greet him. "Nick, how good to see you . . . come, sit down." His was a surprisingly high voice for someone so rotund.

"And how very good to see you, sir."

"Everyone, please—Colonel Nick Bleecher, Jim Van Zwartz's cloak-and-dagger man."

Bleecher had met everyone except the dashingly handsome English actor, who seemed a bit unsettled to learn that the colonel was an intelligencer. Bleecher knew why: the fop, who had just starred in a picture glorifying the exploits of the RAF and was about to embark on a war-bond tour with Marlene Dietrich, had flirted with the British fascists before the war—as if Fourth Army gave a fuck.

"T-tell us, Colonel," the host's mistress asked, her stutter reasonably under control today, "w-what's really going on with the war?"

"The war is won, Miss Davies. It's the coming peace that concerns me."

His host smiled knowingly around a bite of strawberry Jell-O.

Lunch, as usual, was surprisingly prosaic: steak and cottage fries with slices of tomato. And, once again, Bleecher was amused to see in the baronial splendor of the dining hall bottles of catsup and mustard arrayed at handy intervals along the table.

Afterwards, his host politely made sure his other guests were occupied with some form of entertainment or sport, then withdrew with the colonel into the adjoining billiards room. He selected a cue off the wall, although it was obvious from his arthritic hands that he had no intention of playing. "Well, Nick, I didn't ask you to come all this way just for lunch, although I always enjoy your company. What do you say we lay our cards on the table?"

"Always. About what, though?"

"Jim tells me something's cooking at Manzanar."

"I see." Bleecher hadn't known about the general's slip but hid his displeasure.

"The general says we can go ahead and print it, if you'll clear it first." His host winked. "Which makes me ask—who's the general and who's the colonel here?"

"The general's completely in command, sir. It was considerate of him to think of the intelligence ramifications of the story."

"I know. Just joshing you, son." But the flintiness in his eyes said he wasn't kidding. At eighty years of age, he still had a nose for rooting out the lodes of real power no matter where they were buried. "But look here, Nick, Jim just hemmed and hawed when I asked him for specifics. He said only that it's the biggest thing since those pro-Tojo Japs up at Tule Lake were waving the meatball flag for page one."

"It is, sir. But I need a bit more time before release."

"Why?"

"Our investigation got off on a tangent."

"Who dropped the ball?"

"An MP lieutenant."

"I hope you canned him."

"Transferred him—to Tenth Army. They'll be hitting the Japanese archipelago, probably starting with the Ryukyu Islands. Okinawa, just between us. I've seen the casualty estimates." The colonel began to smile, but then thought better of it.

The old man nodded, yet seemed distracted. "Can you give my people anything?"

"I already have—to the *San Francisco Examiner* last night, sir. I said, 'The very fact that no sabotage by persons of Japanese ancestry has taken place to date is a disturbing and confirming indication that such action will be taken. . . .' "

His host slowly grinned. "Are you that sure of this thing, Nick?"

"Yes . . . absolutely, sir."

◆ ◆ ◆

Jared returned to his hutment and changed into a sleeveless GI undershirt, his faded Shawnee High School football trunks, and a pair of canvas sneakers. After doing a few calisthenics in the shade of the motor pool garage, he jogged out of the compound toward the dirt road that skirted the perimeter wire in four one-mile legs. The temperature was still busting a hundred degrees, but he took off at a dead run.

He hadn't gone far when a bugle made him shamble to a halt and salute. A boy scout was blowing retreat as the flag was lowered through the airborne dust. It rippled out of the small lemon-colored hands of two more scouts, but they took hold once more and quickly folded it into a triangle.

Jared picked up his feet again. He wanted to be in shape for combat readiness training. He wanted to be as fit as the men in his new platoon; most would be at least ten years his junior. The sweat started flowing off his forehead and stinging his eyes, but he refused to wipe it away. He wanted to sweat. Sweat got rid of poison, and he was heavy with poison.

Somewhere along the north leg a ranch dog fell in behind him, a shepherd-collie mix, breathing loudly and seemingly dropping more water off his tongue than he could ever drink at one spell.

"You sure you want to do this, boy?" The dog arched his whiskery brows the way the smart ones do when asked a question. "All right—come on."

A hundred yards ahead, a jackrabbit walked—not bounded—out onto the road and recuperated from this effort by holding its big blood-radiators for ears tall to the wind. Then it caught a whiff of the dog and streaked back into the sagebrush on an untapped reserve of terror. The mongrel let it go with a half-hearted growl.

"Know just how you feel," Jared said, his voice coming in short, staccato bursts as his sneakers continued to pound the hot, sandy road. Glancing up, he saw the sun sparkle off the lens of a searchlight. He tried to console himself with the thought that it would be the last time he would look skyward on a run and see a watchtower.

Hank Fukuda would just have to understand.

Someday after the war, after Manzanar, Jared would get ahold of him and explain—nothing could be done. The people behind this had oceans of power. They could shoot anybody who got in their way and chalk it up to military necessity. The war had made them gods, and only peace would humble them again. And by going overseas and fighting for that peace, wouldn't he be bringing on the hour when the clock would strike twelve on those tin gods and they'd be turned back into mere mortals that much sooner?

All at once there was no panting at his side.

Twisting around, Jared saw the dog shoving his nose through the barbed-wire strands, flagging his tail for a small girl on the other side to reach through and pet him. He wondered how she had made it all the way out there without being spotted by one of the towers, but he wasn't worried that his sentries would open fire on a child.

"Hey, boy!" he whistled, but the dog ignored him. Jared trotted back. "Don't pet him, honey, and he'll go his way."

She tried to push the animal away, but even in rejection he found something irresistible about the child. His paws started flailing at the dirt under the fence.

"No!" she scolded him. When that didn't work, she resorted to Japanese, the inflection probably her grandfather's. "*Ie, inu-san!*" No, Mr. Dog!

Jared tried to whistle again but a soft laugh prevented him

from pursing his lips. "This here's an American mutt, honey. He don't understand Japanese."

Then she said, "You can't come in here, doggie. If you do, they won't let you go back to America."

The smile left Jared's face as if it had been slapped off.

After a moment, he had to brace his hands on his knees. His sweat splattered and then soaked into the sand; he watched in a daze as the glittering droplets tumbled from his nose and chin.

A *nihonjin* woman ran from the blocks, but halted yards shy of the fence, her face clenched with fear. Jared hand-signaled the towers that it was all right for her to proceed. She raced out and grabbed the child, called her a *baka*. The dog fled into the brush.

Jared tried to say something in the child's defense, to assure her mother that the almighty *hakujin* wasn't offended. But the first syllable to clear his lips convinced him that his voice couldn't be trusted with his dignity. Turning, he bolted into a headlong stride that soon set his lungs on fire.

Rounding the corner from which Tower 5 jutted, he decided not to veer off on the Bair's Creek footpath for the MP compound, as he usually did. Instead, he went through the south gate and was still running like a man who never intends to stop when he mounted the police station steps.

CHAPTER 17

The desk sergeant rose from his chair as the mess hall bells began clamoring across the evening. "Ah, *mesu beru*." Like the handful of other *kibei* in the police department, he had come back to America at an early age, missing the militarist inculcation of Japanese schools in the thirties, and was a gentle man who seemed not to resent the crack between cultures into which he'd fallen.

"Ah . . ." Stretching a kink out of his back, he began reciting the evening's menu: "*Buroni, buredo and bata, raisu keiko*." He gave Kimiko Nitta a restless grin—as with most everyone in camp, all the expectations of his life had been reduced to meal times, and now Pavlov was ringing for him once again. "You go first?"

"No thanks," Kimiko said, whispering almost, the last clerk to remain at her typewriter. She had no appetite, particularly for bologna sandwiches and rice cake. "Go ahead, I'll come get you if something happens."

"Okay—no prisoner in cage. I go."

"*No isogu*," she muttered. Take your time.

Eddie couldn't have visitors until morning, and she had

only the Nittas ahead of her tonight. Her mother-in-law was reacting to his continued incarceration by becoming even more *yakamashi*, or nagging, than usual, down to tossing her daughter-in-law a brush to scrub the floorboards. Kimiko had refused, sending her father-in-law into a melodramatic *issei* rage, replete with shouted threats that Japan might still do well in the war—and if America could not be vanquished, at least the *nihonjin* in her clutches would be afforded greater respect. All the rancor that had ebbed since the first confused days of internment now gushed from his mouth afresh, yet with a new-sprung obstinacy. He actually took pride in his Tadashi's refusal to defend himself: it was *manly*, he said.

Meanwhile she was going mad trying to figure out how to get around apparently censored mail and acquaint the ACLU with Eddie's arrest. Or had the organization received her letters but was declining to act? The lawyer promised from the judge advocate's office at the Presidio had yet to materialize, and Acting Director Lee had refused to let the project attorney help Eddie. And this evening the rumor was all over camp that Lieutenant Campbell would be transferred soon. She hoped that it was true—for his sake. But for herself there was only a surprisingly bitter premonition of abandonment at this news.

She burrowed back into her pile of paperwork.

The door was propped open to a stale breeze, and soon someone came drumming up the wooden steps, the footfalls so plodding she was surprised an instant later to see Hank Fukuda trudge inside. He ordinarily flew up the steps.

"Chief?"

He had stopped two paces beyond the threshold and was gaping around as if the room were unfamiliar to him. His skin looked sallow, feverish almost, and she thought for a moment he might be ill. But from the dark heaviness around his eyes, she sensed that it was something else, an emotional blow, a death in his family perhaps. Unable to force herself to ask what was wrong, she waited with a listening face.

He smiled at last, thinly. "Where's the sarge?"

"Eating—he'll be back in a minute."

"I see." He took the absent watch commander's desk, which faced the front door, and suddenly seemed relieved to have something to do. He ran his tongue along his teeth distastefully—as if they were coated with grit. She had already rinsed her mouth of the afternoon's windblown dust.

"Kimiko," he said reflectively, just when she had turned back to her work, "may I ask you something?" He appeared to focus on something out the door, something approaching. "You know—personal?"

Warmth came to her face: she was sure he was going to bring up Jared Campbell. Maybe she wanted him to—she wasn't sure. "Okay."

His eyes were still tracking something. "When you were first brought here, what'd you feel?"

"Exhaustion."

He shook his head carefully, as if it ached. "No, beyond that . . ."

"I don't know," she lied.

"Did you feel relieved—even a little?"

When she finally shrugged, he gave a quiet laugh. "Me too. I knew I wouldn't have to fight it anymore."

"Fight what?"

He chilled her with the same lifeless smile, then gazed out the door again, his expression growing puzzled as feet suddenly pounded up the steps.

Jared Campbell took three running strides inside, then came to a stop. His body was terribly flushed; she could feel the heat radiating off him all the way across the room. Glancing around, he asked, "We alone?"

Incredibly, Hank looked as if he detested the man. He refused to speak, his face pecked by little spasms, so that after a few moments she answered for him: "Yes, Lieutenant."

Jared met her eyes—his own bright with agitation—before turning back to the chief. "I can't quit. Sure as hell would like to. But I found out something what oughta go to the Army's top cop—the provost marshal general. So I'm going to keep digging till I got a case. I'll use my furlough if I got to. Are you still with me, Hank?"

Hank spun away so Jared couldn't see his expression—Kimiko believed that he had closed his eyes. Then he nodded fiercely.

Now that he had spoken, Jared looked drained and vaguely annoyed with himself. He walked down the corridor toward his office, leaving a trail of perspiration spatters on the linoleum. Then his door clicked shut.

Kimiko went to Hank and—after a moment's hesitation—rested her fingers against his back. But he raised a hand, and from this she understood that he didn't want to be touched. He was finding his way back from some desolate place. He needed no distractions.

She vacillated again, but finally went down the corridor and knocked on Jared's door.

"Enter," he said.

He was leaning on his arms against the desktop, his sweaty head slumped between his biceps. He didn't look up. "It's a railroading, Ki."

"Against Eddie?"

"Not just him. All you folks, I suppose."

"Then why was he singled out?"

Jared sighed wearily. "I don't think the bastards—"

"*What* bastards?"

"Fourth Army brass—I still don't know how high up this goes. But I figure they didn't have the major in mind until I arrested him." Jared lifted his head, his eyes pleading. "You got to understand—I picked him up because the probable cause was there."

"How?"

"It was *there*."

"Did Eddie ever say he wanted to blow up the aqueduct? And where could he have gotten dynamite?"

Jared stood up and spread apart two venetian slats to look

outside before sitting on a corner of the desk; his careful pause made her feel bitchy—what was he hiding from her? "The aqueduct bombing isn't the half of it, Ki. . . ."

And then he told her how Masao Shido and Morris Wenge had truly died. He spared her nothing.

When he had finished, she sank into a chair as if her legs had suddenly lost the strength to support her, but a realization cut through the buzzing inside her head: it had been perfectly logical for Jared to suspect Eddie after he had rebuked Morris Wenge at the testimonial dinner. "I didn't know . . . I just didn't know."

"No way you coulda. The chief and I were ordered not to say a word. Did the major tell you I phoned him from San Pedro?"

"No, I . . ." She pressed her fingertips to her brow. "Why?"

"G-2 handed me this lead on a silver platter—the Nittas loaded some explosives off a Japanese submarine onto one of their tuna boats before the war."

"That's preposterous!"

He silenced her with a wave of his hand. "I know. I did some checking in San Diego I wasn't supposed to. The long and the short of it is, the major's telling the truth, and this smoothy from G-2, Colonel Bleecher, is crossing his fingers behind his back. Even though Japanese stuff *was* used to blow the pipeline."

She wondered if he said "Jap" instead of "Japanese" among his *hakujin* buddies, but it was a thought tainted by distrust and she tried to dismiss it. Then the bigger implication hit her. "*Who* says the explosives were Japanese?"

"Hank."

Not knowing what to say, she clasped her hand to the back of her neck. Hank Fukuda was the last person she would have thought of.

Then, Jared's face crinkled into a smile. "I did a little checking on that, too. I'd swear this *shimose* was borrowed from a Navy bunker down the road here. Captured stuff they test. But what I got so far won't hold up in court."

"Then how can you be sure it's from there?"

"Because when I started snooping around China Lake, asking questions, Bleecher flew in lickety-split. He took away my jeep, talked me into an early furlough, and greased me a transfer back to the infantry—all on one short airplane ride."

She shot to her feet. "My God—*you're* in danger then."

He laughed and mumbled something about not thinking so, but she saw the truth in his eyes. Never before had she seen him afraid; he seemed a stranger to fear, but now it left him unnaturally shy and remote. She felt the distance between them and wanted to close it. Then, without warning, almost without realizing it, the distance was no more: she had snaked her arms around his damp chest and was clutching him.

But he didn't respond.

After a moment she let go of him and sat on the desk. "I'm sorry."

"I'm not so sure about that."

"Please—"

"And I can't start something up only to call it off. I can't suffer like that again. I'm not built to take suffering the way a woman is."

"What makes you think a woman can?"

"Damn you . . ." His eyes flared at her, then slowly softened with confusion. "I don't know. Yeah, maybe. All I know is, you made up your mind pretty easy."

"I didn't. You know how I felt."

The pleading crept back into his face. "I got kin in Oklahoma."

"Jared . . . Jared . . ."

"You can stay with them till the war's over. On the outside, safe and free."

She wiped her eyes with the heels of her hands—she was weeping and hadn't realized it until she felt the wetness. "And where would you be? Overseas?"

"Hopefully."

"Not again . . ." She cupped her palm over his lips, and he kissed it, hungrily. At that moment, she meant to tell him that she had presumed upon his love and here at last he was returning it—decisively, unstintingly—and now she might not have to go on pretending that it didn't matter if she were loved or not; but instead she said, "Let's not go through this again. We have so little time . . ." Then she took her hand away, and they sat side by side, silent. So little time for what? She felt foolish, yet insistent as well.

The wind began pushing hard against the building, the clapboards snickering on the gusts.

After a while, she whispered, "What will you do now?"

"Go on furlough." He smiled at the way she looked when he said this, at the glimmer of disappointment she couldn't hide. "To Frisco—that's where the answers to this mess are."

"What can we do to help?"

"Lay low—I mean it."

"That may not be so simple."

"Why?"

"Eddie's friends are talking about a general strike until he's released. They're organizing a negotiating committee—"

"No!" His vehemence startled her. "The bastards'll ship him out to Tule if there's a strike. Listen, you can ask the chief—Snavely's already talking up what an escape risk the major is. Don't you see the groundwork they're laying?"

"Do you think they'd go so far as to . . . ?" Instead of finishing, she rubbed the gooseflesh off the backs of her arms.

"I don't know how far they'll go. I'll sure as hell find out in Frisco."

He looked so boyish slumped there, starting at the linoleum and into the future. Once again, she needed to hold him. He was going to San Francisco for *her*—she was sure of it—and he was frightened.

He wasn't going because of the injustice against Eddie, although she would think well of him if he did. Still, that reason for going wouldn't liberate her like the one she now clung to: he was expressing his love without asking for her body, without calling into play her "seductive eyes," the lesser parts of the self she wished to become; because of this she felt a momentary respite from being *hinekureta,* warped and frustrated by the need of the everlasting child in her to be loved—only the Japanese would have a word for it. And it was *bootchie* as well for her to be so moved by his gesture, which months ago she might have dismissed as being sentimental. Nevertheless, she felt a strange and exhilarating completeness, and now she wanted to gratify him as well. Shame seemed a small price to pay in order to gratify him.

But it was nearly impossible for her to form the words. "Do you still want me?"

He laughed grimly. That was all.

"I need to please you, Jared." She struggled not to cry; she sounded like such a fool to her own ears. What was pressing her to do this?

"Why'd it have to be *you?* I'm a simple man—"

"No, you're not . . . you're not." She was weeping again, for herself more than him. "You're a tender man. Men like you have tangled feelings."

"—and I don't go looking for this kind of punishment. But, damn you, I need a tomorrow for my love. And you don't."

The bitchiness came back, hard and sudden. "Then damn you—because you don't spend every minute of every day tormented by not knowing what's going to happen next!"

"Who says—"

Her mouth covered his. He pulled away a few inches, his breath seething against her cheek, cooling her tears. *"Why?"*

"Because it makes me brave for a little while." She began pulling him down by the neck, and his hands let go of her long enough to push file folders and reports off the desk onto the floor. "Hurry," she whispered sadly, already regretting what they were about to do.

But he froze, watching her, his lips tightened as if against some kind of pain. "We got all the time we need. If we're brave like you want, we got the time . . ."

"No, no, no."

"Promise we'll make another time. The whole night. And then another."

"Yes, my darling—hurry."

He gave a soft groan, and then shivered as her warmth enveloped him. "You lie, Kimiko . . . you lie with your pity . . ."

But eventually, he closed his eyes.

♦ ♦ ♦

It came unexpectedly in March of 1941, a venture into his own ethical wilderness. Uncharted moral territory. And he immediately did what most men would have: equivocated, tried to stall for time. He told himself that if he didn't do it others would, others out for personal gain, for vengeance. Others less understanding of the dilemma faced by the *issei* than himself.

In a driving spring rain, the deputy chief of the special investigations division climbed the exposed stairs of the granite block building to the third-floor crime lab—and asked for Henry Yoshio Fukuda. Hank was invited to lunch, which was surprising. But more surprising was that the deputy chief had no driver that day. Thankfully, he got right to the point as he darted impatiently through the noon traffic on the slick, blue streets; even after all these years, Hank found small talk with his *hakujin* superiors to be painful.

"There's a war coming, Fukuda."

Hank didn't have to ask with whom.

"What do you think about that?"

"Sir?"

"You got any personal problems with America fighting the Japanese?"

"No sir."

"Terrific . . . I figured as much. I've heard some good things about you. Got somebody I want you to meet."

They drove west on Wilshire for ten minutes, then parked under the dripping porte cochere of an Italian restaurant. It seemed warm and cheery inside, maybe because of the rain outside. But the place was swanky enough to make him think that he might not be served. It happened from time to time, even in Los Angeles. When the maitre d' began fawning over the deputy chief, however, addressing him by rank, Hank knew there would be no problem.

The first thing that struck him about the man waiting in the private dining room was his neck. He wasn't a particularly heavy man, but he had a very fat neck. Also, there was a straw boater, fifteen years out of fashion, topping the coatrack behind him, and from this he guessed that the stranger was a G-man.

They had the room to themselves, except for a waiter who respected their privacy, so little time was wasted spinning chit-chat for the benefit of eavesdroppers. The man was indeed an FBI agent; he even flashed his ID, perhaps out of habit. "Here's the thing, Fukuda—the day's coming quick when we're going to have to separate the wheat from the chaff as far as you people are concerned. I don't have time to beat around the bush, so I'll ask you straight—are you a loyal American?"

He said that he was, feeling humiliated by how defensive he sounded, how anxious to please.

"Your father's people have been over here quite a while, right?"

"Since 1869."

"What about your mother's folks?"

He had a strong inkling the agent already knew this. "She was a picture bride. Arrived in this country in 1904."

"You speak Japanese?"

"Yes, passably."

"That means you went to Japanese school, right?"

He nodded: a room above a shop on East First Street that sold Japanese books, kimono cloth, and cooking utensils. Ironwood benches and a *sensei* who despised his young charges for their boredom. The kids called him Mr. Bootchie behind his back.

But Hank volunteered none of this.

And then the questions came like machine-gun fire: "Can you read *katakana? Hiragana?* Ever heard of a nationalist society called *Budokai?* One called *Heimushakai?* You know any of the *kaisha-in*—company people—with Sumitomo Bank? Would you raise some eyebrows if you attended a state Shinto ceremony in the next couple days . . . ?" The man with the fat neck had his Japanese culture down pat, but it was just his job—he sure as hell wasn't a Nipponphile.

And that's how it had begun—over lasagna and red wine.

A number of times he had nearly landed himself in hot water by trying to warn *issei* not to tout the Japanese war effort in China, or to frequent the Olympic Hotel, where genuine spies from Japan were under FBI and ONI surveillance. The Japan they remembered from their youth was not the militarist power of the present; but it did no good—they continued to boast and gloat.

And then, suddenly, he was fighting for his own freedom.

He had assumed all along that when the wheat was separated from the chaff he would be counted as a kernel. But that had never been intended, for the mayor later testified before the Lamb Committee: "I may say that I was quite active in getting the Japanese out of Los Angeles and its environs. . . . I hope we were somewhat helpful in General Van Zwartz making his decision for complete evacuation. . . ." So the city fired Henry Yoshio Fukuda in March, one year after he had agreed to work for the FBI. The Bureau, however, would never let him go.

Hank now stepped off the police station steps into the fragile coolness of the desert dawn.

From the direction of the main gate, through the morning twilight, came a large silhouette that began to define itself as Jared Campbell. Dressed in his olive-drab uniform instead of his suntans—perhaps for San Francisco's chilly fog, the chief thought—he was bouncing a duck canvas grip against the side of his leg like a schoolboy with a book satchel. He waved with two fingers as he drew near. "Morning, Chief." An earlobe was still smeared with shaving cream.

"Good morning, Lieutenant." Hank resisted the urge to clasp both of Campbell's hands when they shook.

"Gonna be as hot as sin today, Hank."

"Always is when it starts sweet and cool like this."

Campbell lowered his voice. "Keep going after the white fella tied up with Shido, but be dang careful."

"You think we're being watched?"

"Me more than you. They probably figure they already got you under wraps. But take it slow and easy, Hank."

They fell silent as a pair of teenage sisters, thin and pretty in the dresses they had sewn for their resettlement east, set down their luggage some distance from the men.

"Where you all headed?" Campbell asked.

"Missouri," one of them said quietly. They were afraid of going, afraid of the uncertainty. The chief wasn't sure he himself would have the courage to return to the *hakujin* world.

"Your folks already back there?" Campbell went on.

"Yes . . . our brother."

"It's nice. Green. You'll like Missouri."

"Thank you."

"Don't thank me, honey, I don't own the state." Then he dropped his voice again. "Wish to hell I had some way of getting ahold of you without going through the switchboard."

Hank knew that the moment had finally come. Campbell was risking much. And for what? There was nothing he could hope to gain from this, unless it was Kimiko. And how was that purpose served by clearing her husband? Still, whatever his reasons, Jared Campbell deserved the truth. "There's a way."

Campbell laughed. "You ain't been holding out a shortwave radio on me, have you now?"

"Just about. I've got a way to telephone you. It won't be charged to a camp phone."

The lieutenant nodded—he knew at once what the chief was talking about. Then he stared off at the Sierra: the snow in the higher elevations was beginning to pinken. Behind him, two more evacuees lined up, yawning as they opened the wire-handled shopping sacks that served as their luggage to one of the chief's patrolmen, who was searching for WRA property. Because of troop movements through Reno, the train schedules had been fouled up, and the camp transport had to leave four hours earlier than usual. Campbell finally turned back to Hank: "How long this been going on?"

"Since before the war." For a few seconds, Hank felt as if he were going to throw up.

"The Bureau?"

"Yes."

"They know what I've been doing?"

"No, I haven't reported in since we started the investigation."

"You mind holding off a bit longer?"

"As long as you say." Hank tried not to show his relief: Campbell had taken the news much better than he had expected. "Where do you plan to stay?"

"I don't know—what's a decent place on a soldier's jack?"

"Try the Hotel Cathay, Sacramento and Powell." Hank had stayed there with his Portuguese lover on several occasions and found a Chinese staff that looked the other way on miscegenation matters.

"Will do. When can you phone—whenever you want?"

"No, we have to pick a time each evening."

"Eleven too late?"

"No, fine."

More and more evacuees were streaming in from the blocks, their aged parents in tow, scuffling the ground with their wooden *getas*. The ride would be crowded. There came murmurings from the small throng, last-minute pleas, the *issei* begging their *nisei* children not to go. Hank couldn't bear to listen; he kept hearing his dead mother's voice.

All at once, Campbell's face looked drawn. "If something happens to me, get in touch with the provost marshal general. Send him everything we got so far."

"But if he won't listen?"

"Hell, I don't know." Campbell frowned. "Write General Stilwell in Burma—or maybe it's China now. He's supposed to be a good man. Commanded Third Corps in Monterey when the war broke out. He might already have Bleecher's number."

"Maybe they're friends."

"Maybe, but I doubt it. Vinegar Joe's a *soldier*."

The Black Maria finally came creeping down the street from the motor pool, its blue-gray exhaust rising behind it in the shape of a horsetail.

"Well, here goes, hoss."

When Campbell reached out to shake hands again, Hank pressed four fifty-dollar bills into his palm.

"What's this?"

"Something for expenses."

"Come on, I don't want your money."

The chief's face was adamant. "Keep it."

Campbell nodded thoughtfully, then pocketed the wad. He leaned over and squeezed into the Black Maria.

It soon became evident that there was scarcely room for all twelve passengers and their belongings. Campbell volunteered to take toddler twins from their mother, who could then balance her suitcase on her lap. Within seconds, the tiny boys were busy picking the clip-on insignias off his blouse. Hank strained to take a mental snapshot of the scene as the vehicle pulled away.

He believed that he would never see the man alive again.

He wanted to remember how Campbell had grinned at what the twins were doing to his uniform. It would be a good thing to recall if everything else went sour.

CHAPTER 18

The gong had been secreted away the night in December of 1941 that the *Nishi Hongwanji* Temple was raided and closed by a joint force of FBI agents, MPs, and Los Angeles police officers. Only later, through the intervention of Morris Wenge, was it recovered from a Little Tokyo basement and brought to Manzanar. It now began tolling from the stage of the outdoor theater, slowly at first, but with mounting emphasis. On a folding table set before the makeshift altar was the framed photograph of a GI, snapped before the homely young *nisei* could think to smile, freezing him for all eternity with the expression of someone who has just been tongue-lashed. Self-deprecation even in *absentia*.

Hank Fukuda, in the last row of benches, was already bored. He hated Buddhist funerals nearly as much as Shinto weddings, yet the almost incidental atmosphere of death lent a meditative quality to the moment, and he found himself thinking of Jared Campbell, of reasons and possibilities:

The old folks—the wrinkled, dying *issei*—were always griping about the lack of *mana* in their offspring: the spirit of the homeland imbued in those born on its soil, the wellspring of the willingness to sacrifice oneself to the common good. Perhaps there was such a thing as an American *mana*. And if so, maybe it had been instilled in Campbell by the wronged red and gray earth of Oklahoma, and then by the migrant camps that awaited his people wherever night found them on the rich but forbidden soil of California. For why else should a man love justice more than his own safety, unless he knew down to the last mote of him that the two were one and the same?

The gong's last reverberation warbled to silence in the hot crystalline air. A horsefly sortied back and forth above the mourners.

Or perhaps as in a *koan*, a Zen riddle, there was no one solution to why the lieutenant had changed his mind about going on with the investigation. Hank had only been terrified the whole of the sleepless night that the man might come to his senses and change his mind.

Yet, enlightenment works in mysterious ways—the chief chuckled quietly to himself.

The robed priest, looking rather like a Ku Klux Klan imperial wizard in his peaked headdress, knelt at the low reading desk and began intoning in Sanskrit. Small children started running up and down the aisles. No one scolded them: a Buddhist funeral, unlike a Christian, was not held to be a departure, a grim farewell mitigated by "sure and certain" hopes, as if such hopes could exist in a world where tons upon tons of sparrows fell unnoticed each day. The deceased, who had fallen near a village called San Columbano—unpronounceable for *issei* tongues—was not imagined to be somewhere in Italy, nor even filing through immigration at heaven's gate. His *kami*, or the indefinable holiness within him—which the Anglo-Saxon mistook for that paragon of private property, the soul—was now woven into his family's lineage. And it was this web of spirits, this perpetuity of relationships, that was now being celebrated by whispering among brothers and sisters, aunts and uncles, nieces and nephews, whispers about mundane things the *hakujin* would have thought unseemly on so grave an occasion. Whispers about food, about the weather, about the chrysanthemums already turning blowsy under the desert sun. Reckonings of life, Hank supposed. He had long since given up trying to decide who was right about death, these Shinto-Buddhists or the Catholics across the firebreak at St. Francis Xavier's. The grisly ambience of forensic medicine made him believe only in postponement.

Patrolman Wada's sweaty bulk slid in beside him on the sun-chapped bench. At that moment the deceased's father hobbled forward on legs bandied by stoop labor to light the incense burner.

"Where's she now?" Hank asked in a hushed voice.

"Her apartment. Sleeping, I betcha."

"And you're sure you saw her get inside the camouflage net factory last night?"

"Yeh, and I figure how she slip inside—towers gotta blind spot on that side building. She go crawl in a window. Latch bust, I go see this morning."

Hank's gaze bleared as he watched the rest of the family file up to the altar. He ran Wada's information through his mind again: Yuki Ota had made it her habit to work out of her apartment, coupling only with *nihonjin* patrons—until late last night that is, when Wada had tailed her and seen her slip inside the factory. Who had she intended to meet there? Hank was sure he was *hakujin*: Why else would she forsake the privacy of her own place? Before Wada could learn the identity of her customer, he himself had been rousted by First Sergeant Osler, apparently making his rounds. Not wanting to alert Yuki to the fact that her every move was being watched, the patrolman had wisely withdrawn.

"Tell me again what Osler did as you walked away. Did he approach the factory?"

"Nah."

"You absolutely sure?"

"He no look. Last I see of damn buggah he turn into some headlamp and wave."

Hank frowned. "Whose headlamps? You didn't mention this before."

"Nah? Eh, wastetime."

"Let me decide what's a waste of time. Who did Osler talk to?"

"Just Montgom'ry Lee make one drive round camp. He show up station later when all *pau*. Ask me how things mo' better. Nice guy—no jam me up all time like that buggah Osler."

"Has Lee ever dropped by the station before?"

Wada steepled his huge shoulders—no.

"How'd he explain himself?"

"He leave off letter."

"For me? I saw no letter this morning."

"Nah, for *wahine*."

"Which woman?"

Wada grinned. "Pretty one . . . Kimiko."

Both men jumped as a squad of *hakujin* soldiers who had been standing in the background, looking jaded and out of their element until that moment, loosed a volley into the parrot-blue sky. Two more followed, and then a bugler started playing taps.

◆ ◆ ◆

Small-arms fire. It didn't sound Kraut, but Eddie Nitta fumbled for the field telephone to raise battalion. This could be the counterattack they'd been expecting. He was lying on his right arm, so he reached out for the phone with his left. Except that the nerve impulses controlling his left hand had no paths to follow, and the message withered in thin air.

He opened his eyes on the cell.

Taps.

The notes were drifting in through the wooden walls of the MP guardhouse. He wondered who had been killed now, and from which battalion. His? He waited for the feeling of loss, but nothing came, even after several minutes. And then he recalled how spent Kimiko's early morning visit had left him. She had looked band-box neat, and more cheerful than he'd seen her since his return—desperately cheerful.

"I've decided to take a new work assignment, Eddie."

"Yeah—what?"

"Secretary to the acting director, Mr. Lee."

"What happened to his *hakujin obasan?*"

"She was Mr. Wenge's choice. And you know how the two men never saw eye-to-eye. So, she's taken a transfer to Minidoka. And now Mr. Lee wants me." She started to help him light his cigarette, then caught herself.

"How'd this come about?"

"Well, he wrote me a very nice letter—"

"No, I mean who recommended you?"

"Chief Fukuda, I guess."

"A Jap recommendation wouldn't wash with Lee. Not Lee."

She shrank into herself almost imperceptibly. But he had noticed. "Well, Lieutenant Campbell has always seemed pleased with my work. He must have mentioned something to Mr. Lee—"

Eddie cut her short with an unexpected grin. "Why are you doing this?"

She stopped breathing for a few seconds. "Because we need Lee's help."

"For what?"

"Legal help if things don't work out."

"Yeah—what things?"

She had covered her eyes with a hand as she took a few deep breaths to recover herself. "The chief's working like crazy to clear you. People *care,* Eddie. More people than you know. And I think Mr. Lee can be persuaded to help us. . ."

The bugler continued to play. He could really blow taps. It was probably all he did in the Army: taps for funerals with some service command unit. Cushy.

Growling, Eddie swung his legs over the edge of the cot and sat up. He listened. They were creeping back: the feelings of that morning along the Volturno River. He resisted them by dredging every indignity he could recall: How in November 1942 a detachment from the 100th Battalion was sent to Cat Island at the mouth of the Mississippi to assist with the training of sentry and attack canines. The Army wanted to familiarize the dogs with the smell of Jap blood before shipping them out to the Pacific. How some of Eddie's men had been detailed to mow the lawn around headquarters to within twenty feet of the building, the distance at which it was believed a man could no longer read a classified document on a desk inside. Then *hakujin* GIs were brought in to finish the job. How one afternoon his company was suddenly restricted to quarters—and machine guns were then trained on the barracks, front and rear. Only later did Eddie learn that FDR had visited the post.

And still, the bugler—by being so goddamned good—was bringing back the feelings of Volturno, and Eddie rose to slam the wall with his fist, nearly throwing himself off balance.

"Knock it the fuck off!" came an MP's muffled shout from the guardhouse office.

The Volturno and Tanaka: the two were one memory now, a piddling river north of Naples and the only sky pilot Eddie could ever stomach. A Presbyterian from Honolulu who packed a Buddhist rosary tassel in case one of the boys asked for one. Later KIA at a village called Belvedere while holding up the front end of a litter. Before the battalion kicked off to cross the river in its first clash with German troops, Tanaka had said, "We're not here to prove that we're loyal Americans. We can't use you if that's your reason for fighting. That just means you have a chip on your shoulder. And we're not here only to kill the guys on the other bank, guys who at this minute are saying their own *Unser Vater der im Himmel ist*. We're here for one reason—to help bring about the eventual equality and brotherhood of man. Now let's get it done. Amen." That was it. A sermon all of thirty seconds. A pep talk, sure—although there had never been any doubt that the troops would fight. They'd do it for the same reason men have always fought: they were more afraid of letting down their buddies than facing the enemy. Country had little to do with it. And Tanaka had rightfully sensed that if some must die that morning it had to be for something more than the reality of the country that was "mollycoddling" their families behind barbed wire. So he had reminded them of the dream—no, the mirage—of the *Bei Bijin* their parents had glimpsed across the Pacific. The Beautiful Country. Something to sleep on, forever.

At 0400 hours, the battalion had clicked on bayonets and begun wading across the frigid Volturno. When the Germans opened up with flares and machine guns, the entire first line of *nisei* cried, "*Banzai!*"

The Krauts had quit firing. They couldn't believe it: Tojo had fucking double-crossed them.

Giggling, Eddie again smacked the wall. His fist split along the knuckles. "*Banzai!*"

Yet he knew that he would go back if the Army asked him—that was the funniest fucking thing of all.

♦ ♦ ♦

Jared found her among the slots. The fingers of her right hand were smudged black from nickels. She stopped mid-pull on the handle when she noticed him smiling at her from the next row over. She leaned a little to the side so his view of her powdered cleavage wouldn't be obstructed by the machines. "How's it going?"

"Could be better. This here Reno's a lonely old town, ain't it?"

She laughed. "Buy me a drink?"

"God Almighty—a mind reader."

She laughed again, then again and again through three casino bars and six gin fizzes—until Jared was infected by her hilarity. Still, as they chortled across Virginia Street and into the lobby of his hotel, his eyes were sober as he sneaked a glance over his shoulder. All afternoon, he had felt a faint ticklishness on the back of his neck.

"Listen, hoss," he explained to the clerk, "this here's my sister—"

She snorted behind fingers that were still coin-smirched.

"We was twins separated at birth," Jared went on, "and didn't even know it till we got talking just now. Got us a lot to catch up on. So I don't want any of our family reunions interrupted by your house dick. Hell," he wheezed, slamming the counter, "by *anybody's* dick for that matter!" He had to support her to keep her from slumping to the worn paisley carpet; she finally managed to wipe away her tears and with them half her mascara.

Jared then winked at the clerk. "This little lady's to be given all the access to me she needs over the next ten days. Do I make myself clear?"

Turning away, the clerk mumbled something to the bell captain, who was shaking his head.

Jared loaded her into the elevator by her elbows. The doors no sooner rumbled shut than his ear was filled with a wet tongue, which he pretended to enjoy. Then her hand began kneading his crotch, which wasn't unpleasant. But gently, he disengaged himself from her practiced grasp. "Easy—my mama don't know I like girls yet." He peeked at his watch. Twenty minutes.

Arriving in his room, he headed for the bottle in the bottom dresser drawer while she shucked off her dress, brassiere, and corset, revealing good breasts but a tummy cratered by the stretching of at least a couple of babies. "That's okay, honey," he said, his speech unslurred all at once. "I don't got the spirit."

She glanced up at him from inspecting her legs. In lieu of nylons, she had painted them with liquid makeup, which had run here and there. "The booze?"

"Never put out the fire yet." He downed a slug.

"Then what, for chrissake?"

"Let's talk." He had picked her because, pushing forty, she looked like she had to hardscrabble to make a living at it. A woman in her prime might have laughed at his offer.

"That's all you want to do—*talk?*" She sounded hurt and kept her distance when he took a step toward her.

"No, that ain't all."

She watched as he laid five tens and his room key on the pilling cotton of the bedspread, her eyes still more suspicious than greedy.

"I know the cops and the MPs shut down the Stockade District, putting you all out of your houses. So you got to give some hotel a cut for using their room hourly?"

Her silence answered his question.

"Want to save that much for the next ten days?"

She hooked her bra together over her belly, then shifted it around and slipped her arms through the frayed straps. "How?"

"I want this room to look lived-in. Bed mussed for the maid and all that. I'll be leaving some stuff on the bathroom sink. A couple shirts in the closet. Make sure your male friends come up from the lobby a minute or two after you—that's so the house detective don't get wise."

"Why you doing this?"

He crooked his thumb at the cash. "I figure this ought to cover any questions like that. Say somebody asks about me—it'd be nice if you told them I'm sure making a party here in town. Can't hardly keep up with me."

"When d'you plan to be back?"

"End of the ten days. And there could be another fifty if I find out you did me a nice job."

"You AWOL or something?" A regular victory girl.

"Nothing like that. Personal affair."

At last she shrugged. "What the hell."

Five minutes later Jared was down the back stairs and across the street, waiting on the crowded platform for the Union Pacific locomotive to come to rest.

His coach car, it turned out, was so antique that the guttering light was issued by bracketed gas lamps, but he felt lucky to find an empty seat. He refused to store his furlough satchel overhead. Instead, he snugged it between his ankles. Through the canvas he could feel the hard edges of his .45.

The train lurched and started west, climbing toward Donner Pass. Soon Reno sank behind them, dimming like a flashlight tossed into a lake.

♦ ♦ ♦

Hank Fukuda chose Wada to muscle down Yuki Ota's bolted door.

The hinges groaned under the pressure of the cop's shoulder, then suddenly separated from the jamb with a loud *screak*. The door slammed flat against the floor with the former *sumo* wrestler riding it all the way to the linoleum. He raised his head to get his bearings, and Hank followed the man's gaze across the *chochin*-lighted room to Yuki's apple-shaped buttocks, which were uplifted. Stupefied by the vision of a fat cop wallowing on her door and two more scrambling through the rectangle its collapse had left in her wall, she froze in a tableau as instantly recognizable as Washington crossing the Delaware: hunkered down on her knees, she was reaching back between her plump thighs to guide her block manager's already flagging penis into her.

"Hi, boys," she said.

"Get dressed," Hank snapped, resisting the temptation to smirk.

Offering no resistance, Yuki put on her Ike jacket, then politely asked the chief's men to help her hunt for her skirt, which was finally located dangling from one of the rafters. Her degree of feigned abandon was matched perfectly with each customer's frenzy, or lack of it. A real professional.

The block manager, meanwhile, looked like he wanted to borrow a dagger. The chief knew him well from Los Angeles —a latter-day *issei* and big shot in the Young Men's Buddhist Association who'd once chastised Hank for being a fair-weather Son of Nippon for showing up at the temple just for the big festivals, and then only for the girls and free food.

Hank began whistling the tune to "Jesus Loves Me," except he had other lyrics in mind, as would any *nihonjin* who'd been raised a Buddhist. The irony of these unspoken words was not lost on the block manager, who scowled as he felt the bite of the handcuffs around his wrists:

Buddha loves me, that I know,
For the Sutra tells me so . . .

CHAPTER 19

As soon as the ferryboat had glided out of its slip at the clock-towered Ferry Building, the stocky man strolled forward. Carrying his straw boater in his hand, he made his way to the greasy cable at the limit of the lower deck. There he spat into the curl of foam heaped around the pig-nosed bow, then squinted up into a whorl of seagulls, the roll of fat on the back of his neck bulging even more as he craned skyward.

From a window in the deckhouse, Jared watched him for a few minutes, then quick-stepped down the stairs to what had been the automobile level prior to the completion of the Bay Bridge—now the boat ferried only pedestrian traffic back and forth from the transcontinental trains in Oakland. He made sure that the man had no backup hiding behind a newspaper on the deck. Only then did he approach him.

"I thought you'd be blitzing through France or liberating the Philippines by now," the man said, keeping his eyes on the water. "Still baby-sitting the Yellow Peril?"

"Wish I could say otherwise."

"Things been pretty quiet at Manzanar?"

Jared said nothing for a moment. The ferry was now out

far enough for the oily-looking surface of the water to be riffled by the wind. He swept his overseas cap off his head and folded it over the cloth belt of his blouse. "Been anything *but* quiet, Bob."

"How's that?"

"We may have us some fifth column stuff going on. . . ." Jared paused, dangling the bait.

Robert Cade hesitated before biting. But Jared could see in his eyes the disbelief that *anything* could happen at Manzanar without his knowing. And the FBI, Jared knew all too well, would barter only when assured of getting better goods than those it was holding. "You talking *Jap* unrest?"

Jared took an already mashed toothpick from his shirt pocket and began chewing on it. "Maybe."

Cade chuckled low in his throat without smiling. "Who's putting you up to this? And what the hell does he want?"

"You remember that night after Pearl Harbor?"

"Sure. Why?"

"Just remembering, that's all. We sure broke us down some doors, didn't we?"

Cade finally grinned. "And scared the holy shit out of some aliens. That's why I asked Berdoo PD for the biggest, dumbest flatfoot they had—the chief gave me you. But if you're looking to dig up an old debt, Campbell, forget it. I don't think your heart was in rounding those bastards up. I had to shout at your ass to get you to knock down a couple of those doors."

"Well, I'd've felt better if we'd found some guns or short-wave radios or something. Most of those folks didn't open up because they figured it was a lynch mob. But no, Bob, I'm not looking for a favor." Jared tossed the toothpick into the bay. "I'm looking for Hoover's ramrod on Jap espionage cases. And I figure that's you."

Cade looked amused. "Why?"

"Well, most agents die or retire out of South California. But you got promoted to Frisco—right after you hauled in more Group A aliens than any ten agents. I also recall hearing you'd built yourself quite a trapline of *nisei* stoolies. And two years ago or so when I phoned just to say howdy, your secretary said you was on assignment in Hawaii—"

"She said I was on *assignment?*"

"Well, no—but I figured Hoover couldn't afford to give any of his hired help time to vacation. They might unwind a twist and come to a mind they hate his guts."

Cade didn't smile. "All right, Campbell, why all the black-bag crap? Asking to meet me on the goddamned Oakland ferry in the middle of my workday?"

"Well, I'm sure Colonel Bleecher's filled you in—even if you're going to pretend he ain't."

"About what?" Cade asked carefully.

Jared almost got cold feet. He was relying on his gut-feeling that a certain amount of animosity between two intelligence gathering units—like the FBI and Fourth Army G-2—was to be expected. But what if Cade and Bleecher were in bed with each other? Given their respective personalities, a friendship between the men seemed unlikely, but Jared had to rule out the possibility for sure before divulging anything more. Whatever happened, he would never reveal that it was Hank Fukuda who had confirmed his longtime suspicion that Cade headed the Justice Department's counterintelligence effort west of the Mississippi. "Well, Bob," he lied, "the colonel promised me he'd fill you in on my investigation."

"Bleecher's a liar and a nut case. Just like his boss, Van Zwartz."

"Then he didn't tell you about the aqueduct bombing?"

Cade's face flushed, and Jared's faith in Hank Fukuda was reaffirmed: the agent knew nothing. "When was this?"

"About a week ago now."

"Dynamite?"

"Residue came back picric acid."

"*Shimose?*"

"Damn, but you know your stuff."

"That sneaky son of a bitch," Cade hissed.

Jared felt sure he didn't mean Bleecher. Since Pearl Harbor, the word *sneaky* had invariably been linked with *Jap*. Cade was referring to Hank Fukuda, and Jared would now have to try to get the chief out of hot water for not reporting in to his control. "Yeah, this case's got the whole place in a flip-flop. Bleecher put me and the camp chief of police on it full-time. And then the captain glued my dogrobber on the chief—just in case he ain't as loyal as he seems."

"What do you mean?"

"My corporal keeps a twenty-four watch on this Fukuda fella. Even sleeps in the Jap barrack with him. I understand the reason for security where evacuees are concerned, but hell if I know why the colonel didn't fill you folks in."

"It adds up. Believe me." Cade clamped his lips together for a moment. "I'm being paid back . . . you bet I am . . ." Then his anger surged out of him, and it was obvious from the livid glaze that came to his eyes he didn't care where the chips fell. Jared figured he was probably hoping every word would be reported back to the Presidio, verbatim. "Oh, it's been a Chinese fire drill these past three years, running down shadows for Lieutenant General Fruitcake and his fancy-pants colonel. See, when Van Zwartz started gearing up to exclude all the Nips from the coast, Mr. Hoover made me a liaison to the Presidio. It was my job to hold up the Justice Department's end. And make damn sure we didn't get screwed by Fourth Army."

"Why was Hoover worried about getting screwed?"

"This war isn't going to last forever. And believe me, these internment camps are going to wind up being egg on somebody's face. The civil liberties crowd'll make sure of that. The Director just didn't want it to be us—not with a liberal in power like FDR, who'll forget as soon as the peace is signed that it was *him* who signed the exclusion order. So in early 'forty-two I found myself having to bunk right on the fort. That way Bleecher could summon me day and night about some new Jap plot I was then supposed to get the Bureau cracking on."

"Like what?"

"Oh, like a Jap spy ring in place at Douglas and Boeing plants. We found a grand total of four *nisei* working in aircraft production. Three of them were already informants for Naval Intelligence, and the last one, it turns out, was working for our Seattle office. Your colonel ran our asses ragged up and down the coast after that kind of crap. Jap flower growers shining car lights out into Santa Barbara Channel to signal subs. That one turned out to be white kids violating the blackout and parking on the beach to make whoopee. And then there was a report of San Diego Japs hauling asphalt down to Baja California to build an airstrip for Zeros—"

"You remember a case in San Pedro—a tuna fisherman named Nitta supposedly making a rendezvous with a Japanese sub?"

"No, but only because it sounds like the ten thousand other screwball leads the Presidio passed on to us."

"But how many panned out?"

Cade smirked. "Guess."

"Well, at least a couple."

"Zip, farm boy."

"But what about the military necessity? There was supposed to be a military necessity to evacuate these people."

"There wasn't one."

Jared looked stunned. "Jesus . . . you sure?"

"What the fuck? You think you're doing something useful out there in cactus-land?"

"I figured the president had a *reason* for signing the order. He wouldn't do something like this just for ducks. He had to have a good reason."

"Yeah, and it was based on some horseshit intelligence from Bleecher's unit—fucking amateurs is what Joe Stilwell called them. That's what prompted FDR to go with evacuation. And that's what made the Director cool about internment. Fourth Army *lied*. You may lie to FDR, but you don't lie to Mr. Hoover and get away with it. He finally blew up at Van Zwartz and told him to quit wasting our time—"

"Wait," Jared said, "I thought Hoover was all for evacuation."

"Bullshit. Not that he likes Japs any more than the next

guy. He just had to bite his tongue when the War Department carried the day with Roosevelt. That's all. His agents—we told him a mass roundup would kill our *nisei* network. We'd spent one hell of a lot of time and bucks before the war grooming these kids. How do you think we got the information we needed to draw up the subversives lists? That scoop came right out of the Little Tokyos—the Japanese American Citizens League, mostly." He laughed sarcastically. "And then our JACL informants, the poor bastards, got hauled off in the same busses with the jerks they'd squealed on."

"If Hoover thought it was wrong—"

"Hold it, Campbell—he thought it was *unnecessary*. There's a big difference."

"Whatever you say—but why didn't he dig in his heels?"

"What? And go to bat for some zipper-lids right when it looked like Tojo just might win this war? Not even the ACLU was eager to square off against the most liberal administration in this country's history—not over a few Japs, Campbell. Just count the Jews in government and then the Hebes on the ACLU's board of muckamucks—you'll get the picture. Nobody wanted to buck FDR. Not in the middle of a war. And don't forget that my boss serves at his pleasure."

Cade checked his wristwatch, then glanced over his shoulder toward the San Francisco waterfront. "I'm not saying it wasn't a pickle for everybody involved. It was. For everybody except Van Zwartz and Bleecher—they fancied the idea of getting rid of the Japs even *before* the war."

"How do you know that?"

Cade ignored the question. "It all boils down to this—the Director's too smart to be the fall guy when Van Zwartz and company overstep themselves. And that's coming." He smiled, but there was bitterness in his eyes. "Early on, I handed Bleecher our detention index. All the juiciest subversives—Shinto priests, Jap language teachers, editors of J-town papers who followed Tokyo's line on the war in China. Mr. Hoover, in personally clearing this, told me to give Bleecher *very specific recommendations* about each person on that list. Needless to say, I did.

But the colonel and his junior detectives went right out and scooped up whole families—everybody in the house over the age of fourteen wound up behind barbed wire."

"What'd Hoover do about it?" Jared asked.

"Had a stroke. When I relayed his displeasure directly to Van Zwartz at his digs on the fort grounds—have you seen how the other half lives in this war?" Cade didn't wait for Jared's shrug. "The general went ape on me. He dragged me upstairs into his study, took one of what looked like a dozen diaries out of his safe, and read me his version of a phone conversation he'd had with the Director. The guy's a nut about writing things down. Goes through life thinking he's being misquoted. He read where Mr. Hoover had promised him his 'unequivocal cooperation.' Can you believe it? The old fart thought he had a contract." Cade's anger had finally run down, and he seemed to realize that he'd said too much.

"What'd the Bureau eventually do?"

"We backed off."

"Why—especially if the Army was getting outa hand over this thing?"

"Listen, plowboy, what kind of name is Van Zwartz?"

"I don't know. German?"

"It'd be *von Schwarz* in that case. It's Dutch—just like Mr. Rosefield of Pennsylvania Avenue. Bleecher's Dutch, too. Do I have to draw a picture for you?"

The ferry slowed, then churned out a quarter turn to clear the Oakland mole, a long breakwater edged by boulders. "I just can't believe FDR's cut of the same cloth," Jared said.

Cade's chuckle was now contemptuous. "Any of your folks land jobs with the WPA?"

"Yeah, my daddy helped build a post office or two. But that ain't the point. FDR's money, but he ain't *that* kind of money."

"Look who's splitting hairs like a college brat. Is this Jared Campbell talking? The same flatfoot who dragged a dead horse one block from Muscupiabe Avenue to Third Street because he'd didn't know how to spell Muscupiabe for the report?"

Jared's face darkened. "That's a mean-spirited lie told by a sergeant who figured his kin shared California with Adam and Eve—"

"Easy, pardner." It took several seconds for the agent to stop laughing. "Now it's your turn—why you are gunning for Van Zwartz and Bleecher?"

"What makes you think—"

"Come on—you're not here on Presidio business. If Bleecher wanted to rattle my cage, he'd send Dunnigan around."

"Who's he?"

"Some mouthy little Mick. It takes no genius to see you don't want a certain somebody to know you're here. I'm betting that somebody's Nick Bleecher. Right?"

Jared gazed down again: rainbows of oil and bits of flotsam were sliding past the bow. "This case went bad on me, Bob. And I think Hoover should know what these fools've been up to." Then, wearily, he rubbed his face with his hands. "Damn, but I can't sleep sitting up on a train. Can you?"

"Cut the chitchat. How's Mr. Hoover going to know this big secret unless you tell me?"

"In a few days—I promise. Everything I know. And you're right—it can't be known I'm here in Frisco. If it gets out, your boss gets nothing on Van Zwartz and Bleecher. Oh, is that Hudson DeLuxe you left on the Embarcadero your private car?"

"No, my wife has ours. And stop saying *Frisco*—people here don't like it."

"Dang, I hate to inconvenience her, but can I borrow it a couple days? What if you all got some ration coupons to spare?"

The agent formed a fist as he studied Jared's smiling face, then slowly shook it out. "You rotten Okie prick."

♦ ♦ ♦

Hank Fukuda stared at her over the glass top of his desk. The reflection distorted his face, magnifying his chin and making him appear intensely powerful.

He wasn't like other men. She waited for his glower to be softened by the hint of a smile. But none came.

She herself betrayed no reaction—other than to continue

to chew her bubblegum. Outside his open window, a midday stillness lay over the camp as if the heat had pulled the sky down to the desert floor. A raven passed over the station, wings beating heavily.

Perhaps he seemed different because there were so few men his age in camp. The *issei* had scrimped for decades before being able to send back to their home prefectures for picture brides. Like most *nisei*, Yuki had been forty years younger than her father, who died of natural causes when she was nine. The wide gulf in camp between the young and the old was bridged by only a few men in their late thirties and early forties. Here sat such a man—neither a boy nor a dotard but a full-blown man. She liked the ripe but clean smell of his body, the traceries of the years in his face and hands.

"You know who First Sergeant Osler is?" he finally asked.

The question made her lean her head to the side. She had expected him to zero in on her client, the block manager. She had felt sure she was incidental to this affair: Fukuda, for whatever reasons, wanted to get at the block manager. Why else had she been busted after three years of hands-off by his cops? "Sure, I know Osler. He should bathe more often in this heat."

Fukuda raised an eyebrow.

She shifted her buttocks on the straight-backed chair, crossed and then recrossed her legs. She had not put on her panties when arrested last night, and was now gratified to catch a sudden warmth in his face. "What's going to happen to my friend, Chief?"

"He's already been released on his own recognizance."

From this Yuki realized that she, not the block manager, had been singled out. She spat out her gum. "What's going on here? You know what I do. You've never messed with me before!"

He was looking directly at the dark crease between her thighs. "Close your legs," he said quietly. "If you need more clothes, I'll send for them."

"Why? We could have ourselves a party right here."

"I don't have parties."

Something in his tone of voice made her press her knees together. Unconsciously, she closed her Ike jacket collar around her throat. He had just told her what he really thought of her, and the hurt that winced through her caught her by surprise. She now told herself she didn't like the man. He seemed different only because he was prudish, a mothball.

He lit a cigarette but didn't pass it to her as she'd hoped. "Why were you inside the net factory the night before last?"

"I wasn't."

He took a manila folder out of his top drawer and let it drop from a height of two feet onto the glass desktop. It lay there for several long moments before he sighed and unwound the twine fastener. Then he took out a yellowed card. "Know what this is?"

She squinched her eyes at the ten black smudges. She was nearsighted but refused to wear glasses. "Fingerprints?"

"Yours, from when you went through camp intake." He then held up a half dozen note cards with cellophane tape stuck to them. "These were lifted from *inside* the window on the east wall of the factory, which can't be secured. Any idea whose they match?"

When she said nothing he reached into his bottom drawer for what appeared to be a kindergartner's clay model of a pair of sandals. "From the ground below the window—plaster-of-paris impressions of the soles of these . . ." And with that the chief dumped her red patent leather shoes on his desk beside the castings. "Who were you going to meet there?"

The look in his eyes left her feeling panicky, but she managed a grin. "This seems like a lot of trouble just to collar me."

"Yes, it would be. Who was coming to see you?"

Yuki looked down at her thumbnails, the chewed ends of which she began clicking together.

"Wada!"

The chief's bellow startled her. The mammoth cop who had caved in her door now stepped inside. "Boss?"

"Throw her back in the cage."

"You betcha."

♦ ♦ ♦

The last thing in the world Jared needed was to have his name recorded on an MP's clipboard at the Presidio's main sentry house. So the morning after meeting Cade aboard the ferry, he parked Mrs. Cade's De Soto on a residential side street two blocks from the post and approached the gate on foot. There, sheltered from the bay breeze by a bus kiosk plastered with war-bond ads, he smoked a cigarette and tried to look as if he were keeping watch for a buddy who might appear at any moment in the rush of soldiers and civilian employees flowing past the MPs toward work. Now and again the guards quit yawning long enough to nod at one of the blue ID buttons being turned out for their inspection.

Jared shook a second Lucky out of the pack as soon as he spied a shavetail lieutenant waiting to be waved through and asked the officer for a light.

"Sure." A Zippo came out of his pocket.

"Damn, ain't this wind mean?" Steadying the man's hand with his own, Jared kept the young second john between the MPs and himself as they sauntered past the sentry house. "Thanks, hoss."

"You bet."

Once inside the post he resisted the urge to glance back and see if the MPs had taken note of him. He doubted that they would have even noticed Hermann Goering waddling through this morning; besides, only one man out of the thousands garrisoned here knew him by sight, and he intended to give Colonel Bleecher a wide berth.

Backdropped by the Golden Gate Bridge—towering and rusty-looking from this angle—a buck private was watching some sycamore leaves being blown from the big pile he had just raked up, the brim to his fatigue hat flapping in the breeze.

"Where's General Van Zwartz's residence, soldier?"

He saluted, then leaned on the rake handle. "Keep on going up like you are, sir. General's place is on the very top."

"Thanks."

James Van Zwartz was fighting his war from a two-story Victorian from whose portico Jared expected Ulysses Grant to swagger at any moment, a train of cockaded adjutants in tow. Colored troops were clipping the privet and mowing the carpet of velvety rye grass, which was shaded by a dense stand of eucalyptus and coastal pines. He tried to figure out the floor plan from the placement of the windows: chemise curtains in an upstairs opening suggested the location of the master bedroom, and this half convinced him that the adjoining dormer with wooden shutter panels inside the glass, was to the general's study.

He was wondering if, as in most old houses, the stairs would creak underfoot when the cat-wild madness of it hit him. *You just don't go and burglarize the house occupied by the commanding general of Western Defense Command, not without winding up in Leavenworth for a whole lot of years.* Cade had tempted him with talk about those diaries squirreled away in a safe, but getting caught with his hand on the dial could be dicey, particularly if Van Zwartz had nothing to do with Bleecher's high-jinks.

No, it wouldn't be a good idea to violate the old man's nest.

Putting the notion out of his head, he hiked down the wooded ridge to the military intelligence headquarters, which he didn't enter. Instead, he ambled through the parking lot behind the building until he found the placard emblazoned with a silver eagle. In the reserved space was a 1941 Plymouth sedan, painted olive-drab and identical to all the other staff cars in sight—none had bumper markings. He memorized the serial number stenciled in white on the engine cowling, then drew his hand out of his trouser pocket, spilling loose change onto the concrete.

Stooping to recover the coins, he casually took a roll of electrical tape out of his coat pocket and looped it twice around the rear bumper of Colonel Bleecher's car. Then he ripped the piece of black tape from the roll and continued on his leisurely way toward the main gate, whistling what only remotely sounded like "San Antonio Rose."

◆ ◆ ◆

He had rolled his swivel chair over to the window, which was open to an afternoon cloudburst. The rain was sheeting off the eaves and forming a necklace of silvery puddles on the ground, and he was listening to the liquid noises as if they were music. Yuki felt as if she were intruding, but the chief silently motioned for her to step inside and help herself to the tea service on his desk. Wada let go of her arm and quietly shut the door behind her.

She filled a cup for herself, then sat, pulling the hem of her skirt down over her knees. She waited for the leaves to settle to the bottom of the cup before taking a sip. Her nails shone with fresh crimson; her cosmetics and toiletries had been fetched from her apartment.

He seemed more sad than intimidating today, but still very much in control of things. When he finally looked at her it was with neither contempt nor approval; and when thunder sounded nearby, he didn't flinch, as she did.

"You lived on Bainbridge Island, didn't you?"

"Yeah—for a while."

He suddenly smiled—a shy and self-conscious but utterly appealing smile. "Did you like it?"

"Kinda. I had a lot of friends."

"*Hakujin?*"

"Yeah, mostly. I didn't have much to do with the *bootchies* there." She crinkled her squat nose. "Real mothballs."

The chief offered her a cigarette, which she accepted with slightly agitated fingers. "Thanks."

"What do you think, Yukiko?"

She became even more sloe-eyed as she inhaled deeply. "About what?"

"After the war—will they take us all back?"

She let the smoke out slowly. "I suppose . . . everybody except the people at Tule. They're goners."

He nodded, then gazed out the window again. The western sky was beginning to clear, and a mountain was taking shape among the clouds like a dream unfolding. In camp, the rain was now barely dimpling the small ponds it had just created. "But you have some doubts the *hakujin* will want us back?"

"Sure. They dumped us here, didn't they?"

"True, they dumped us here . . ." Then he said nothing for a while, instead just sitting and watching as the thunderheads broke apart into shreds of mist. He smoked. He drank tea. He glanced in her direction now and again.

"Don't you have some questions . . . or something?" she asked at last.

"No, not this afternoon. I'll see you back to your cell if you like."

◆ ◆ ◆

After five hours of waiting on a side street a block east of the Presidio's main gate, five hours during which he listened to the radio and smoked his throat raw, he almost missed Bleecher's car. Just as the Plymouth sedan stenciled with the long-awaited serial number sped eastbound on Lombard Street and Jared fired up Mrs. Cade's De Soto to give chase, a squad car materialized in his rearview mirror. The cop crept past, carefully eyeing the parked De Soto. Jared waved, but the patrolman didn't wave back—he was probably deciding whether or not the lieutenant was worth rousting.

Meanwhile, Bleecher's Plymouth continued downtown.

Jared gave an inward groan.

Finally, the cop turned left at the intersection with Lombard, and Jared pulled out from the curb. Within seconds, the squad car was locked in the traffic piling up outside the gate. Jared gave a whoop and spun the steering wheel to the right, pressing the accelerator to the firewall as he barreled after Bleecher.

He was glad he had taped the rear bumper: the city was lousy with 1941 Plymouth staff cars, each indistinguishable from behind, and all of them seemed to be on the road as the clock ticked down to the cocktail hour.

Following a pitch for Victory Gardens, the radio announcer cued in the number-eight tune on the Hit Parade:

"He's just a fellow on a furlough,
out looking for a dream,
the one who's in his dreams every night;
a lonesome fellow on a furlough,
in search of company,
somebody who will be his guiding light . . ."

Jared smiled to himself, but then leaned forward: suddenly, giddily, Lombard Street plunged down a steep hill in a tight coil of S-curves. With no other vehicles available to him, he prayed that Bleecher, the only occupant in the Plymouth, wouldn't glance back just then and get a broadside look at the De Soto.

Seven blocks later, when the sedan pulled up in front of a Chinese laundry on the corner of Grant Avenue, it wasn't the colonel who got out, but a captain of medium height who left his service cap in the car. He had close-cropped red hair.

Hurrying, he went inside without a laundry sack under his arm, which didn't click in Jared's mind until, two or three minutes later, the captain emerged empty-handed as well. Maybe his clothes hadn't been ready for pickup, although Jared didn't think that was the case: the officer had the nervous, hustling stride of a numbers runner—he was making the rounds. He was also freckled, as had been the captain who had called on the damkeeper at the Van Norman Reservoir. Dunnigan—Bob Cade had mentioned that Bleecher had a Mick errand boy named Dunnigan. "Proud to meet you," Jared muttered, shifting his toothpick to the other side of his mouth.

The captain restarted the Plymouth and nudged it into the southbound traffic on Grant, which was slowed by Chinatown jaywalkers and the chockablock narrowness of the street. Jared let a few cars pass to shield him from the sedan, then followed.

Bleecher's man gave no sign that he thought he was being tailed.

The Kraft Music Hall had come on the radio, and a new announcer was jabbering about ration points and fluffy macaroni. Then Bing Crosby joshed with a convalescing sergeant before singing:

> *"I'm a cranky old Yank in a clanky old tank,*
> *and I'm heading for a hullabaloo.*
> *I'll be riding my tank through a Tokyo bank,*
> *sure as I'm an Army buckaroo . . ."*

The Plymouth stayed on Grant until it angled into Market Street, then the captain turned toward the domed tower of city hall a mile to the west.

> *"When I set my khaki down in old Nagasaki,*
> *I'll be singing like a wacky jackaroo,*
> *And you can bet by cracky, every sukiyaki lackey,*
> *will be looking mighty tacky when I do—"*

He flicked off the radio as the captain parked in a loading zone outside a side door to the federal building, and was looking for his own space when an office boy trotted down the granite steps and slipped the captain a big manila envelope through a crack in the passenger window of the Plymouth. An instant later, the captain drove away and the boy raced back up the steps. In gold letters on the glass door he went through were the words FARM SECURITY ADMINISTRATION ENTRANCE.

The signal at Hyde Street was against Jared, and he slapped the metal dashboard in frustration as the Plymouth pulled away and took the next left. He would have run the intersection, but the cross traffic prevented it. In the time it took him to round the corner the staff car had vanished. He turned right thinking the captain had taken the next side street, and was turning right again when he glimpsed brakelights winking off in the gloom of a Van Ness Avenue alley. The Plymouth. And the captain, still seated behind the wheel, was talking to a potbellied security guard who had taken the envelope from him.

Before he could be noticed, Jared drove down to the next block.

Waiting for the Plymouth to reappear, he spread a city map across his lap and quickly determined the building in whose shadow the alley lay to be the assessor's annex to city hall.

Then he lit a smoke and waited.

Four minutes later the Plymouth reappeared. It joined Bayshore Boulevard and headed south at a speed well above the wartime limit.

◆ ◆ ◆

Hank Fukuda motioned for Yuki to take a stool in the tiny laboratory.

The odors in the cubicle reminded her of high school, but she felt no nostalgia. She had gotten a B in chemistry, the last decent grade she'd earned before running away from home. She waited for the chief to speak again, but he was absorbed with a pair of tweezers, removing specks of something from the coarse weave of a *tatami*. The cut-out section of mat on which he worked was bloodstained, but she decided not to ask him about it; she had begun to like his thoughtful silences, the way his breath whistled softly in his nose.

"My great-grandfather," he said in a measured voice as he tried to pinch something minuscule with the tweezers, "left Honshu for California in 1869."

"Why—he get kicked out of Japan?"

"In a way. He was samurai. There'd been a civil war, and the lords—the guys who hired the samurai—were overthrown. So he sailed east with twenty-six others. You heard of the Lost Colony of Wakamatsu?"

"Nope."

He frowned, and she found herself wishing she had said otherwise. "Well, that's what old Sentaro helped found—a Japanese colony east of Sacramento."

"What happened to it?"

"Drought ruined their tea and mulberry seedlings, and the colony disbanded. Most went back to Japan. Sentaro stayed on."

"Why?" Yuki helped herself to a stick from a pack of Wrigley's on the workbench. "He'd gone bust here, right?"

"Sure, but he knew something the others didn't." All at once he became annoyed with the tweezers and reached for the roll of cellophane tape. Deftly, he formed a loop with the sticky side out and began dabbing the *tatami* with it.

"What'd this Sentaro know?"

"Only that Japan's a jealous mother. She doesn't welcome home her prodigal children." Grunting softly, Hank sat up and began massaging a cramp in the small of his back.

Without thinking, she brushed his hand aside and began kneading the spot.

"Over a little . . . there . . . good." He paused. "Ever wonder why only fifteen hundred people went back on the repatriation ship in 'forty-three? I mean, most of the *issei* are still Japanese citizens. Of course, America never gave them the chance to become Americans—but still, why didn't more of them apply to go back?"

"Their kids?"

"Maybe so. Splitting up families had to be a part of it. But I think the *issei* were really afraid of the reception they'd get back in good old Nippon."

"Why?"

"We come from a prejudiced people, you and I."

She looked at him questioningly.

"See, Yukiko, my great-grandfather cut off his topknot and threw it in the American River. He wasn't any simple peasant, old Sentaro. He knew that, in the eyes of his people, to leave Japan was to betray her. And no matter how much money he brought back from America, that money would be unclean because it had come from the *gaijin*, and he himself would be unclean because he had lived with the foreigner, eaten his food, and shared his thoughts. There would have been only one greater shame for Sentaro to have committed . . ." He bent over the square of *tatami* again.

She withdrew her hand from his surprisingly sinewy back muscles. "What shame?"

"To have coupled with the *gaijin*."

◆ ◆ ◆

South of the Navy base at Hunter's Point the brakelamps of the staff car flashed once, twice, and then held red through the twilight as the captain veered off onto a dirt road that ran parallel to Bayshore Boulevard for a quarter mile before dropping out of sight over the side of a bluff.

Jared idled at the turnoff, watching the dust raised by the Plymouth settle again on the freshly bulldozed road. Glancing north and south, he saw that there was no other way for the car to rejoin the boulevard. Then he backed up—jerkily, thanks to a clutch Mrs. Cade probably rode only slightly less than she did Cade himself—and pulled behind the latticework below a billboard that read:

IT TAKES 8 TONS OF FREIGHT TO K.O. 1 JAP
SOUTHERN PACIFIC

He left the De Soto without shutting the door.

Behind him a fog bank was humped grayly over the peninsula, waiting for an onshore breeze to push it all the way over into the bay. He moved quietly through the brush, although a diesel engine was grumbling unseen at the foot of the bluff. Crouching as he came to the overlook, he sat on his hams in a thicket of wild mustard. Then he fumbled in his shirt pocket for a toothpick, keeping his eyes fastened to the scene below.

The captain had parked alongside a crawler tractor and was talking to the operator, who remained perched on his iron seat. Jared couldn't make out their words over the Caterpillar's engine, but the operator had pulled his goggles up into his dusty hair and his rubber mask down around his throat and was listening to the officer keenly. As he spoke, the captain pointed across the contours of the harrowed, hilly ground to a small frame house that had been knocked off its pier-and-post foundation—the handiwork of a bigger Cat, no doubt—and seemed to be sinking into the sea of dirt clods surrounding it.

After a few minutes the captain got back into the Plymouth, gunned his own engine and made a slapdash turn across the plowed earth, and started up toward the boulevard. Jared let him go. The operator readjusted his goggles and dust mask, then throttled forward, easing his batteries of gleaming discs back into the ground.

A battlewagon was tied to a buoy off the point. While Jared sat on the bluff wondering why a G-2 officer was carrying on like a right-of-way agent, a bosun's whistle shrilled across the waters. Five minutes later, a bugle sounded retreat and the flag on the fantail was struck, but then the fog descended and muffled all sound except the insect drone of the Cat, which began probing the mists with its headlamp.

Eventually, he figured it was gloomy enough to have a look at the house.

The fog half-turned to rain and began prattling on the clawed earth around him. These had once been strawberry fields, and in some places the runners, stunted by neglect, were writhing out of the soil, trying to reestablish their colonies.

Tacked on the wall of the house was a sign barely readable in the dimness:

POSTED

NO TRESPASSING

Violators will be prosecuted according to
Section 602 of the Calif. Penal Code

NATIVE SON MANAGEMENT CORP.

And within those cracked walls, across a capsizing floor, were glimpses reminiscent of what he had seen years before in that foreclosed wasteland outside Shawnee—rooms empty except for the detritus of a forced and hasty abandonment: a broken lacquered tray tossing back the orange flicker of his Zippo lighter from the sideboard; a teapot lid, its varnished bamboo wickers unraveling from the handle; a cotton rice sack in the pantry nesting a litter of pink, squirming mice; Japanese language newspapers scrunched up as if to be used for packing material; and on the godshelf, stripped now of its wooden tablets bearing the names of the dead, only a stand-up calendar advertising Nihonwashi Pharmacy. All the months but December had been torn away. December 1941.

Jared clicked shut his lighter.

He stood in the darkness and felt the fog press against the shattered house.

CHAPTER 20

"You must forgive me the hour, Mrs. Nitta." Montgomery Lee shaded his eyes with a hand as if the flat rays of dawn coming in through his office window were giving him a headache. "But during normal hours I'm beset with a string of such things—why, they'd befuddle Solomon. . . ." He paused to examine the contents of a file, then frowned and dropped it to the floor, where Kimiko was stooped, gathering the culls of Morris Wenge's administration into a pasteboard box. "And I must admit that I've put off this unhappy chore too long now. . . ."

She glanced at the papers he had just discarded: letters by Wenge protesting the draft classification of *nisei* as 4-C, enemy aliens.

"Nor have I been able to bring myself to move into the director's residence. . . ." His thin, almost pretty lips drew back over his teeth, which were beginning to show a patina of neglect. "Another man would be impervious to such things—or at least would appear to be. Wouldn't you say?"

She was trying to say whatever he wanted to hear, but it wasn't easy. His ramblings jumped back and forth between extremes, a collection of non sequiturs she could no more pin down than live butterflies. Yet, once again thinking of Eddie, hoping that Lee could be persuaded to let the project attorney help him, she struggled to sound sympathetic—though she couldn't bring herself to meet the man's gaze. She was not sure how far she would go to please him and was afraid that he might glimpse the degrading vacillation in her eyes. Either way, Eddie would die in the end; she had to keep swallowing around this fear. "I can understand why you might not be comfortable in Mr. Wenge's house."

He crouched beside her, and her heart tripped over several beats before picking up its rhythm again. His body smelled musty from last night's whiskey, and his eyes were like those of a consumptive child. They danced around her throat, making her want to hide it with her hand. "Why, my dear, do you think I'd be uncomfortable there?"

"Well, Mr. Wenge died in the bedroom, didn't he?" Then the color drained from her face. "Of a heart attack?" she quickly amended, believing for an instant that she'd somehow betrayed Jared Campbell's confidence.

But Lee only went on smiling. "You'll understand me better as we work together. You'd understand, perfectly, in a blink if you could look into my heart and see my *oya-on*."

It surprised her to hear him speak of the ascribed loyalty, indebtedness even, a proper *nihonjin* should feel toward his progenitors. "And what would I see, Mr. Lee?"

He laughed softly, but his eyes grew moist at the same time. "The promise that they would love me if only I would remain miserable in that love." Then, laughing again, he came to his feet. "A crinoline hell, Mrs. Nitta—I was reared in a crinoline hell. Shall we empty the desk now? Oh, and may I rely on you to help me one or two evenings later in the week?"

◆ ◆ ◆

The morning fog was being driven by the wind, but it never seemed to clear. Jared slouched behind the wheel of Mrs. Cade's De Soto, drowsily keeping an eye out for headlamps on Lombard Street. A half dozen Plymouth staff cars had crept past, beetle-like, since first light, but none was stenciled with the serial number that had run through his sleep all night. He was half tempted to go downtown and do some snooping at the Farm Security Administration and then city hall before knocking off for an early lunch. What the hell was Dunnigan—if it had indeed been Bleecher's errand boy—doing playing bagman between the FSA and the city-county assessor? He would give himself another ten minutes before heading downtown to find out.

Hank Fukuda had not phoned for the second night in a row. Jared hoped that meant all was well at camp. Without knowing why, he kept having a vision of Kimiko screaming silently—and he was gripped by the sensation he was falling, as in a nightmare, each time it suddenly happened. Maybe he shouldn't have told her so much. He had come close to asking that both the chief and she do nothing in his absence. If somebody on staff had been plugged into Masao Shido's black market shenanigans, he wouldn't take kindly to evacuees rattling the skeletons in his closet. But Jared had held his tongue, maybe because he still couldn't believe that Shido had ever come to terms with a *hakujin*.

A squeal of brakes from behind made him sit upright—and grimace. A squad car had pulled up bumper to bumper, its lights on high beam.

The cop lumbered out, spit sideways, then sauntered forward—the same patrolman who had given Jared the once-over the day before. "What are you up to, soldier?" Not *lieutenant* but *soldier*.

Jared pasted on a grin. "Waiting for a buddy."

"Two fucking days now? Must be some buddy."

Jared let his grin fade as he propped a knee against the dash. "Well, it's a long story . . ."

"I'm nuts about long stories."

So, smiling wistfully, Jared told him that his wife, a Presidio secretary, had tumbled for her major. He was trying to win her back, but she wanted none of it. She'd moved since the separation—maybe off-post with her major—and he was hoping to catch her walking to work. She liked to walk to work—when she could—being on the hefty side.

"What you gonna do if you find them together?"

"Nothing—just talk."

"What do you mean by 'just talk'?"

"Strictly tee-hee and giggle. He may be a son of a bitch, but he's still a major."

The cop asked for Jared's ID, then copied the information into a spiral notebook he had been keeping dry from the fog in his slicker pocket. "Says here you're an MP."

"That's right."

Fortunately, he didn't ask to see the car registration, which would have really complicated Jared's morning.

"All right, soldier—I got you cold if one of the post secretaries or a major gets bashed. We got us an understanding?"

"I just want to talk to her, honest."

"You posted in the area?"

"No, on furlough." Jared quickly volunteered his leave orders, but—as he'd hoped—the cop declined to examine them.

"That's okay—just stay out of trouble." On the way back to his cruiser, he tossed over his shoulder, "This town's lousy with women. Hell if I'd waste my furlough chasing one that don't want me."

"Ain't that love though?" Jared laughed.

The cruiser made a U-turn, one wheel bouncing over the curb, and melted back into the fog. Jared was wondering how far the scribbling in the cop's notebook might possibly go when the serial number flashed across his mind's eye. "God Almighty!"

He had almost missed Bleecher's Plymouth.

◆ ◆ ◆

After leaving the bus station parking lot, the staff car seemed to follow the downtown streets pell-mell. Yet, when Bleecher emerged onto Lombard Street above the curves, Jared realized that he hadn't been trying to shake a tail—which he inadvertently had, several times, owing to patches of dense fog—but simply knew shortcuts involving less traffic. Like Dunnigan yesterday, the colonel, to all appearances, drove without a hint that somebody might have the piss and vinegar to shadow him. In that sense, Jared told himself, these guys were rank amateurs. But amateurs could be dangerous: they didn't know the limits.

He had been surprised to see the colonel himself behind the wheel, but it was nothing compared to his shock a few minutes later when Bleecher stopped for a man waiting in front of the bus station—a lean middle-aged man with a long face and lively eyes. Today he was wearing a double-breasted jacket, bow tie, and fedora, but Jared had last seen him in a cassock aboard the *Rocha III*.

Bleecher and Joseph Kerry shook hands, then the colonel took the padre's suitcase and loaded it in the trunk—a bit of candying that led Jared to suspect that the man who had called himself Kerry was indeed a priest. Bleecher wouldn't redcap for one of his lackey operators.

From that moment on, Jared leaned forward and clenched the shift knob whitely, afraid he might lose the Plymouth along the way, although he expected it to ultimately vanish through the Presidio's main gate, where he wouldn't be able to follow. But instead of staying on Lombard all the way to the sentry house, the colonel veered off onto Richardson Avenue—Highway 101—and cut across the post through a fenced corridor toward Fort Point.

Through the fog-jeweled cyclone wire, Jared could glimpse a column of troops, some men dissolving into pockets of mist, others seeming to materialize out of them. On the other side of the highway was Crissy Field, a shopworn P-40 parked on its apron. And then the base of one of the Golden Gate's towers loomed out of the low woolly ceiling, and he realized that Bleecher was going to cross the bridge. He lifted his right hip off the seat so he could dig into his front trouser pocket and was bringing out a handful of silver when he saw that, instead of continuing up to the toll booth, the Plymouth was exiting onto a lane marked BRIDGE VIEW PARKING.

Waiting for Bleecher to park and do whatever it was he

was going to do, Jared was forced by the lack of a roadside shoulder to pull up to the far right booth. There was little traffic and no one directly behind him.

The attendant held out his hand, but Jared said, "I just really want to walk out and have me a gander."

"Then back up and take the view exit. Five cents for a ped crossing—you can pay me now."

Jared flipped him a nickel. "How high's this bastard?"

"The concrete road is two hundred and twenty feet above the water. Tops of the towers are seven hundred and forty-six feet. Now back up before somebody blocks the way—or I'll have to send you over to the Marin side."

Jared whistled softly as he craned his neck out the car window, eyes tracing the huge cables where they arched up into the fog. They seemed to be anchoring down heaven.

At that moment Bleecher and the priest paid their toll at the far left booth and strolled out onto the sea-facing sidewalk, apparently so wrapped up in their conversation that they didn't look over the railing, which was the first thing Jared would have done. There was nothing so high in Oklahoma, not even the tallest water tank. The colonel glanced over his shoulder once, and Jared sank down in his seat, but Bleecher seemed to take no notice of him—he was more concerned about foot traffic, and there wasn't any on his side of the bridge.

Jared backed up and parked, waiting in the De Soto until the two men were midway between the toll plaza and the southern tower, obscured every few seconds by plumes of fog that rolled across the six-lane road like prairie-fire smoke. Then he got out of the car and trotted over to the footpath on the bay side, opposite the colonel and the priest, wishing he had brought along his three-quarter-length wool coat. It was cold, ungodly cold for summer, and the bridge was a mass of clammy, dripping steel.

To the north, a fog horn gave out two sharp blasts every forty seconds.

He kept his head down as he walked; there was no view for the first hundred yards anyway. But then the wind shredded apart the fog, and in the momentary clearing he could see the gray waters of the channel mussed by whitecaps. He had no sense of great height until he spotted a flight of sea gulls, as tiny as grains of salt, skimming the surface. This made him halt and grasp the rail, and he closed his eyes for a few seconds before going on.

He had not expected to experience dizziness, but it felt strange to be so far above the sea. He liked bridges and, as a kid, had pored over diagrams of graceful suspension jobs like this by the hour—but never had he associated them with such chilling altitude.

Meanwhile, Bleecher and Kerry were well past the first tower and nearly halfway to Marin County. Over the next several minutes Jared closed the distance until he was directly across from them, but he had no chance of catching their conversation over the wind, which was howling there at mid-channel, strumming the steel-wire suspender ropes like harp strings. When the two men drew to a stop at the gently crowning center of the span and leaned on their forearms against the rail to talk, Jared muttered, "Shit." Then he backtracked a short ways, counting his steps.

What he did next he would have put out of his head entirely had it not been his only hope to learn what Bleecher and Kerry had to say to each other.

He pocketed his overseas cap and spit into his pale hands. Checking one last time that neither the colonel nor the priest had taken notice of him, and that no cars were coming, he swung his legs over the rail and eased onto the two-foot ledge beyond it. Grasping one of the suspender ropes, he dangled his lower body over the side, trying to jam the toes of his shoes into the crosshatches of the slanting truss below him.

Cursing himself at once for doing it, he glanced down between his heels—and felt his testicles creep up into his pelvis. "God Almighty!" Closing his eyes as his feet fumbled for the truss, he whispered in a voice of praising he hadn't used since boyhood, "Lord Almighty . . ."

He knew that sometime before his crooked fingers grew

too numb to clasp the wire rope he would have to let go and grab the lower lip of the beam that supported the sidewalk—a reach of only five feet, but seemingly impossible with the bay and the Pacific curdling each other more than two hundred feet below.

Breathing as if he'd been gut-shot, he willed his hands off the suspender rope. In the split second before he scrabbled for a new hold his scalp bunched up in a wad of gooseflesh and he saw himself—from on high—tumbling down, then hitting the water with a splash no bigger than a thimble.

But his hands held fast to their new purchase.

From there, the twenty-foot descent along the angled truss to the undergirding wasn't so awful—he told himself he was just going down a ladder into an empty silo. Keeping his eyes level, he began. Halfway down he paused to wipe his hands, one at a time, on the front of his blouse—the steel straps of the truss were wet with dew.

Beneath the road deck a network of crossbeams formed something like an arbor, and the huge eyebar on his side of the span was comfortably wide. Counting the steps back to the crown of the bridge where the two men hopefully yet remained, he kept denying the truth until he had counted out the last pace and stood gaping westward, his hand riveted to an upright support.

Then it could no longer be denied—the only way to cross to the other side was on one of the naked trusses.

Perhaps there were traverse catwalks at the towers, but it was a sure bet the two men would no longer be standing there by the time he stutter-stepped along a quarter-mile of eyebars back to the same point on the opposite side of the understructure.

Cupping a hand behind his ear, he listened.

Not a syllable floated his way.

He hadn't really thought it possible—not across six lanes and down twenty feet from two men who were probably keeping their voices low. And then there was the fog horn, whose twin blasts suddenly seemed close by.

The beam was twelve inches wide, but looked as skinny as a two-by-four set on end.

Ninety feet from side to side—that's all the bridge looked to be. The distance across his daddy's dooryard from the veranda to the equipment shed. The distance from bag to bag on a baseball diamond. Three first downs for Shawnee High. He just had to think of something other than how small those gulls had looked against the water.

He pressed his toe against the beam as if testing it for solidity, then started taking six-inch steps toward the west.

The wind now hit him full in the chest. His tie wriggled out of his shirt front and began fluttering over his shoulder, but he kept his eyes straight ahead, doing his best to ignore the bird droppings splattered atop the beam.

Suddenly he sensed that something was moving beneath him, something enormous. He froze before he could take another step, then peered down.

It looked like a parking lot gliding out to sea, and he had no real idea of what it was until the top of the superstructure floated by what seemed only fifty feet beneath him. Two sailors were sprawled on a high lookout deck; they began rippling crazily in the heat and sulfurous fumes that boiled up from the smokestack. Jared's mouth filled with an ammonia taste, and he buried his burning eyes in the crook of his arm. When he opened them again, the aircraft carrier was gone into the fog—and his head was spinning. Vertigo. It came to him not in a lurch but as a slow, inexorable sensation that he was capsizing. He started to crouch but stopped when it only intensified the sensation.

A little voice—his own he supposed, although it was calmer than he expected—told him that he would survive the fall. He was even thinking ahead to the cold, turbulent water and how he would shuck off his blouse and shoes as soon as he broke to the surface.

He had been resisting the dizzy tilt to the left when it came to him with a jolt that he was overcompensating to the right. He spread his legs and dived for the beam, thudding against it with his rib cage and chin, and instantly wrapped his arms around its damp rust-colored steel.

He started to slide off.

Groaning through bloodied teeth, he braced his hands together and hooked a shoe around the opposite ankle. He stopped slipping, then slowly righted himself on the truss.

Five minutes later he felt strong enough to go on, although no longer did he try to walk upright. Straddling the beam with both arms and legs, he inched forward on his belly the remaining seventy feet to the eyebar on the seaward side of the bridge, where he lay on his back, fighting for breath and warding off the urge to retch.

Voices.

Exhausted now, he was almost indifferent to them. His only thought was that he would never do that again. He would use the eyebar he was on all the way back to the toll plaza if need be.

Between gusts, cigarette ashes fell past his eyes like snowflakes.

". . . We've got to make the best of it, Joe," Bleecher said.

The priest mumbled something, but Jared couldn't make it out.

"The general doesn't like it either . . . as a Christian, I mean. But we've got to make the best of it . . . for our sake."

"Ours personally, Nick?"

"No, no—the country, I mean."

"Good, these rumors distress me no end—"

"Ignore them. I'm talking about the things we Sons have fought so long for. We both know damned well 1924 was only a partial victory."

"Maybe a Pyrrhic victory . . ."

"No, no, no . . ."

And then nothing more could be heard. Jared listened for retreating footfalls, but there was only the barely perceptible sizzle of the fog being driven against the bridge.

He lay there for a long time before getting up.

CHAPTER 21

"Archdiocese of San Francisco," a woman's voice answered on the first ring.

"Yes, ma'am, I wonder if I can ask a question or two about your religion. See, I'm a Baptist myself . . ."

"I'll try, sir," she said noncommittally after a moment.

"Thanks so much—I didn't know where else to turn." Jared switched hands on the receiver so he could write. "You all got any societies in your church with 'Sons' in it?"

"I beg your pardon?"

"You know, like Sons of the Saints or something?"

Her laugh was short. "I'm afraid not—for obvious reasons of propriety."

"How's that?"

"Well, saints shouldn't beget any sons. Although, come to think of it, there are the Sons of Saint George."

"There you go!"

"But I'm afraid that's an Episcopal society—of which I know nothing. Are you sure the order you have in mind is Roman Catholic?"

"I figured it might be, but I musta got something mixed up."

"Sorry I couldn't help you, good day."

"Yes, ma'am, 'bye." Jared replaced the receiver in its cradle and switched off the rattling little fan in the booth, then sidled his tall frame out into the lobby of the Hotel Cathay.

He was beginning to think he had heard Bleecher wrong on the bridge earlier that morning. Or then again, had the colonel been referring to the Native Son Management Corporation, whose sign was tacked to the ruined farmhouse near Hunter's Point? Still, Jared would swear that Bleecher had said to Father Kerry, *"I'm talking about the things we Sons have fought so long for."* And real estate development in North California just didn't seem like the kind of thing a padre from a poor parish in the Southland would go to bat for.

Jared returned his empty beer bottle to the hotel bar, and downed a double shot of sour mash. "Thanks for the hospitality, hoss," he said to the bartender, who was wearing a lapel button that read I AM CHINESE AMERICAN. "Now, how's a poor lost soul get to the Hearst building from here?"

Following the man's directions, he set off from the hotel on foot. The ocean had finally run out of fog to send ashore, and the bay—where it showed between the buildings—was all bright and sparkly. He felt spent, but invigorated, too. Catching his breath on a hilltop and unconsciously trying to smooth the wrinkles out of his hand-cleaned ODs, he glimpsed the bridge that had almost claimed his life that morning. It occurred to him then that he had felt just like this as he'd walked away from the weedy irrigation ditch in which he'd been baptized, dripping dissolved sins into the parched earth. Once again, he had gone through something frightening and mysterious, and once again the world seemed cleaner and prettier than he had ever remembered it.

The clerk in the library-like "morgue" of the *San Francisco Examiner* was a weaselly young man harboring some kind of anger or shame that made his eyes too sharp for his small face. Right off, Jared thought he was a 4-F, something not to be envied in a town where it was suspect for a man between the ages of eighteen and forty to be out of uniform.

"It's been a while," the clerk said while trying to sip root beer through a collapsed straw. "What do you need now?"

On a hunch, Jared decided not to mention that he had never set foot in the building before in his life. Still, as a homicide dick, he had haunted newspaper morgues a thousand times, so he felt he knew the ropes. "Well, how about a gander at your index of religious and fraternal organizations?"

"No can do. Just tell me what you need and I'll dig it out."

He'd been afraid of that. "All right—let's start with the Sons of the American Legion, then the Sons of the American Revolution—"

"Then how about the Sons of Bitches, Lieutenant?" Jared knew the type: a cocky guy who'd had the amazing fortune of never having his lips banged by a fist. He tilted his little head to the side disdainfully. "You guys from G-2 get me, you really get me. Just tell me *who* the fuck you're after this time and I'll yank his folder. Okay?"

Seeing the chance for a draw play, Jared hid his surprise. "The colonel wants me to go through his file."

"Why? Nothing but bouquets for Nick Bleecher. Mr. Hearst loves General Van Zwartz and everybody on his team. You too, probably. Want to go down to San Simeon for the weekend?"

"Stow it."

"Oh, Army lingo—or isn't that Navy?"

The clerk returned from the back shelves with a thick untidy file of newspaper clippings. Jared adjourned to a table scarred with cigarette burns and began adding his own when the man refused him an ashtray.

Nicholas Bleecher's file began in 1921 with his graduating from USC Law School and passing of the California bar, apparently on the first try. The son of Alameda County aristocrats, financiers—as Jared had figured—with a silver taproot going back to the Bank of California's operations in Nevada's Comstock. Married Miss Gracious Houghton, equally blue-blooded but less good-looking than himself, the same year. A Congregationalist, *not* a Catholic wedding, Jared noted. Hired as a San Mateo County deputy district attorney in '22 after a world-cruise honeymoon. Appointed Berkeley city attorney in January '23 and then assistant DA for Alameda County six months later. A Duesenberg engine of a young man, blasting away at the world with all thirty-two valves. His election as DA came in '28. Served in that capacity until Pearl Harbor, when he made a to-do about cashing in his colonelcy in the California Guard for a lieutenant colonel's slot with Fourth Army, and was promoted back to full bird within two months.

"Closing in ten minutes," the clerk said.

Jared laid a five-spot on a corner of the table. When he glanced up half an hour later, it was gone and the clerk was strolling up and down the aisles between the shelves, his hands bulging his pockets.

Stuffed behind the obligatory biographical material was a clump of incidental stuff—community service and society shindigs mostly—held together with mummified rubber bands. It was in no logical sequence, and Jared had to keep flipping through it, developing a dislike for Mrs. Gracious Bleecher as he plowed ahead from party to party. The price of one of the socialite's evening gowns could have grubstaked a family of ten for a year back in '35, her jewelry an entire Hooverville; but the same getup never covered her gradually ballooning shape twice. "A couple more years, honey," he mumbled, "and the colonel won't know whether to slop you or sleep with you."

Then the word *Sons* leapt at him from a photograph caption: "A state-wide delegation of Sons of the Forty-Niners expresses appreciation to U.S. Rep. Gerald Callahan for his support that led to congressional passage of the Immigration Restriction Act."

The clerk rapped the table with his knuckles. "I got to eat."

"Go on ahead, I'll lock her up."

"The hell you say."

Jared brought out another fiver.

"That's good for just ten more minutes. I mean it."

Jared waved him off impatiently.

Twenty years of good living had filled out their faces, but, even had he been unable to recognize the colonel and the priest at first glance, the story beneath the caption confirmed their presence at the nativistic love feast: "Nicholas Bleecher, the organization's volunteer legal counsel, said, 'I hope this legislation will plug those loopholes in the immigration laws used so cunningly by the Japanese race to establish an emperor-worshiping colony on this side of the Pacific. . . .' " And so on. Jared's eyes skipped down a few paragraphs: "Sons Chaplain Joseph Kerry, in his blessing at the Capitol Hill luncheon, invoked the memory of his famous granduncle, Denis Kearney, whose Workingmen's Party contributed to passage of the Chinese Exclusion Act in 1882 and formation of the Oriental Exclusion League in 1905. Father Kerry was also chaplain to the First Battalion of Engineers, California National Guard, which saw service in France during the Great War. . . ."

Jared shut the folder on the clippings—all but one.

This he slipped into a blouse side pocket.

♦ ♦ ♦

The recent downpour had settled the dust, and the only signs of the usual evening windstorm were the groaning of the station roof joists and the flapping of a torn piece of tar paper against the window glass.

"I can't wait any longer, Yukiko."

She said nothing. Her jaws were slowly working on a wad of bubble gum.

"You see," Hank went on, "I didn't report your detention to the administration."

"You mean I'm not really under arrest?"

"Perhaps."

"What's that mean?"

He began to fidget with his fountain pen. "I'm not sure myself." All he knew was that he had to telephone Jared Campbell tonight, if only to touch bases. Desperately, he wanted something positive to report, something that would link Shido to a member of the *hakujin* staff. "I'm kind of winging it right now."

"What happens if they find out I'm being kept here—you know, *chokku chee kind?*" Underhanded.

"I'll be dismissed."

"Could you wind up at Tule?"

"Yes, I think so. What I'm doing is a violation."

"Then why're you doing it?"

He was silent for a moment. "You ever hear our Hawaiians say 'jam me up.' "

"Sure, all the time."

"Well, someone on the *hakujin* staff is trying to jam us up. All of us, Yukiko."

She began clicking her thumbnails together—this evening they were plum-colored. "What am *I* supposed to do about that?"

"You can tell me who he is."

Her jaws stopped working the gum and she glanced up at him. "I don't know what you're talking about."

"Yes, you do. You told others you know who this man is."

Her eyes flitted back to her nails. "Who said?"

"I promised not to say. Just as I'll keep quiet about what you now tell me."

"Why do you need me then? Your stoolie musta told you who this guy's supposed to be."

"No, he didn't. He was too afraid. He only said that you knew."

She settled a little lower in the chair. "You going to punish me if I keep quiet? Send me away?"

"No. I like you. I care what happens to you."

Suddenly, she scratched her cheek as if an insect had stung her. A few moments passed before Hank realized her eyes had moistened. Her nostrils grew wide as she sniffled, then she tightened her broad face so as to keep herself from sobbing. "He can be so *rough*."

"Who?" Wada had seen two *hakujin* come together outside the net factory—First Sergeant Osler on foot, and Montgomery

Lee in his jeep. Her suggestion of a rough man now made Hank ask, "Was it Osler?"

She stared at him, her face as smooth as porcelain. At last, she nodded yes.

"And he met you there—to have sex with you?"

Another slight nod, although now she wore an obstinate little smile.

"When did this start?"

"Two years ago, maybe."

"How? Did he catch you with someone else at the factory?"

"Yeah, sure—how else?"

Hank didn't like the way she brushed her lips with a hand after saying this. He reminded himself to slow down. "Tell me how you and Osler started getting together—your own words, Yukiko."

"Well, we did it that first time and I guess he liked it. So we arranged another night. And then another . . ."

"It became a regular appointment?"

"Sorta—at least once every two weeks."

"How'd Osler let you know he was ready again?"

She paused. "He'd set his coffee cup on the windowsill."

"To his office window?"

"Yeah . . . it was like a signal."

"You walked all the way through *Hakujin* Country to the fence to see this?"

"When I could."

"You must have excellent eyes."

"They're okay."

"How far would you say the MP compound is outside the perimeter? Two hundred yards?"

"I don't know. I don't know distances."

"Which building is Osler's office in?"

She started clicking her thumbnails together again. "You know, headquarters."

"MP headquarters can't be seen from the fence. The mess hall, guardhouse, and enlisted men's barracks all stand in the way."

"Then maybe it's the guardhouse. I always thought it was the headquarters."

Hank opened his top desk drawer and tossed his pen inside, exasperated. "I'll forgive you this first lie, Yukiko. You're afraid, and I know what it is to be afraid." He slammed shut the drawer. "But now I want to know the truth. As your friend, I'm relying on you to tell me the truth. . . ."

Her eyes slowly flooded with tears. Then she reached across the desk and seized his hands. What she did was more frantic than sensual, yet he felt a little chill up his neck. She was the first woman to touch him in years, and this was the second time within days.

♦ ♦ ♦

An hour later the chief stepped out of the station into a withering south wind off the lower deserts. He gazed around for a moment, the peaks of the Sierra like shark's teeth against the paler band of night sky just above the horizon. At 10:45 each night he hand-carried an envelope across First Street to the administration building. In it was the department's daily report. His officer manning the small rock-and-mortar police post saw him coming and trotted down to the larger MP sentry house to get the key from the corporal of the guard.

"Here, Chief," he said, returning out of breath and handing it to Hank. "How's things going tonight?"

"Quiet."

"Yeah, quiet here, too."

The chief then continued on his way to the darkened administration building and let himself in the front door. As soon as he was inside, he dropped his envelope in the slotted wooden box stenciled PROJECT DIRECTOR, then rushed to the switchboard, uncovered it, and turned it on. The PBX operator locked away her headset for the night, but Hank now brought another out of his coat pocket and quickly connected with the long-distance operator, who was instructed to bill to a number in Daly City, although the number he wanted was in San Francisco.

Waiting for his call to be relayed by a string of operators, he glanced at the phosphorescent dial of his watch: he had but a few minutes before the corporal of the guard would grow antsy. The MP might even come looking for his key, as he had one night, forcing Hank to lie that he'd been in the latrine with a case of the skitters.

It was not the kind of excuse that would work twice.

♦ ♦ ♦

Jared was sprawled on his hotel bed when a police cruiser wailed past eight stories below, its siren echoing hollowly in the silence of the room. Listening to that sound in the dimout, he suddenly realized he missed it—the Saturday-night hustle of city streets, working those streets in whipcorded wool and Sam Browne leather. At least in those days he'd only been up against some fool with a gun or a knife and a crazy lust for vengeance—not something as massive as Fourth Army.

The telephone rang, and he fumbled for it on the nightstand. The hotel operator asked him to stand by for long distance.

It was immediately apparent—the strain in Hank Fukuda's voice: "Jared?"

"How's things, hoss?"

"I only have a minute."

"Understood."

"Kimiko's working for Montgomery Lee now." The chief said this as if it were the worst possible news in the world.

"I'm surprised you let him steal her away from you."

"I had no choice. She wanted to go."

"Why?"

"She thinks it'll help Eddie's situation."

"Well, maybe it will. Monty's really not a bad sort."

"That's the thing—he *is* a bad sort."

Jared's throat was teased by a chuckle, but he also felt confused and uneasy—what was Hank driving at? "How's that?"

"He had a black-market deal going with Shido. I think he's our man."

"How'd Monty and Shido ever get together, Hank? It makes no sense."

"Believe me—they did. Summer of 'forty-two, maybe even earlier, Lee stumbled across Shido stealing from the warehouses. Instead of turning him in to you, Monty started running the operation—"

"But why? His kin are worth more than all the stuff that could be trucked into those warehouses for a hundred years."

"Here's my idea—it served both their ends. These guys *wanted* things in a ruckus. Remember what the rumors of staff theft of sugar did to this camp two years ago? And Monty could always betray Shido to the Black Dragon. I'm sure he was holding an *inu* rap over Shido's head. Oh, and as far as old Masao's past, he was a crook from the word go, like you always thought. He was part of the Japanese gambling crowd that muscled the Chinese out of the West Coast opium trade in 'thirty-six. I just don't have time to go into all of this, but it holds water."

"All right, but can you place Monty and Shido together?"

"I have an informant who swears to it. They met in the net factory after hours. My informant and Lee were there one night when Shido came in. Shido was madder than hell that she was there, but Lee threatened her life if she ever talked. That's what scares me, Jared. Kimiko's tied up in this now, and I don't know what to tell her. Look at what Lee did to Mr. Wenge—"

"Whoa, hoss, you're jumping too fast—"

"Jared, I'm out of time. I've got to go. Trust me. You just have to trust me."

"I do, but tell me this—what was your informant doing in the factory with Monty?"

"She serviced him on a regular basis."

At last Jared had to laugh. "No, no—I'm sorry, friend, but all this *don't* hold water."

The chief's anxious breathing sounded like surf through the receiver. "Why do you say that?"

"Poor old Monty can't have sex."

"Are you sure?"

"Positive. I've seen the injury with my own eyes." The

silence stretched on for so long Jared finally said, "Maybe we should say good night."

"I feel so stupid."

"Don't . . . you didn't know. And without knowing, it'd all seem to fit together neat as a pin."

"Should I mention anything to Kimiko?"

"No, she's okay. I'd bank on it. Things are going good on this end. Get some rest."

"Yes, I need a clear head. Good night, Jared."

◆ ◆ ◆

It was noon, and his apartment was an oven.

His first thought after twelve hours of dreamless sleep was that he had failed the lieutenant by passing on Yuki Ota's nonsense. In the midst of his self-loathing he came close to swearing off any further work on his end. He was only chasing shadows and might well tip off Wenge's murderer that Campbell was doing something other than drinking away his furlough in Reno.

Following a meatless lunch, still not having checked in on the department, he took a long soak in the *ofuro* before the bathhouse got crowded with laborers coming in from the farm plots. Cleansed after two hours, his pores fully opened to catch the slightest breeze off the sage, he finally walked over to the station, intending to release Yuki.

But she refused to leave his office.

"I don't blame you for lying," Hank said wearily. "Life here is a lie. But I have no further use for what you tell me."

Fear—at least it seemed like fear—knotted her face, but he no longer believed in any of her expressions, even when she began crying.

"I can't go . . . not now . . . he'll know I talked to you."

"Mr. Lee?" he almost scoffed.

"Yes."

"Yukiko, I know about his *condition*."

Surprisingly, Hank thought, she didn't seem taken aback. Instead, she simply went on crying, her mascara running down her cheeks like ink.

"So he didn't meet you there—especially for sex."

"What do you mean?"

Hank came to his feet. "Enough. You're free to go."

"I don't understand. What do you mean?"

"The man can't have intercourse, for chrissake!"

Her shoulders jerked at his unexpected shout. "I know. But I could make him happy with the *harigata*."

Hank's eyes floated roundabout, dazed, before finally fixing on the wall clock: it would be several hours before he could contact Jared Campbell.

♦ ♦ ♦

The boy could have been no older than eleven, but he expertly laid the bowl of egg flour soup on the table in front of Jared, then withdrew through a curtain of red glass beads into a kitchen filled with the clattering of crockery and brassy Cantonese voices. Before Manzanar, Jared had thought Chinese and Japanese food to be one and the same. Now that he knew the difference, he prefered Chinese—it was greasier and spicier, and he'd been suckled on lard and Tabasco.

On the bench seat beside him was his canvas satchel. It had been a fruitful day, although he'd made no attempt to tail Colonel Bleecher's Plymouth.

Instead, he had dropped by city hall. It had taken only a few minutes to discover that the first vice president of Native Son Management Corporation was one G. Houghton of Berkeley—Gracious Houghton-Bleecher, no doubt. Interesting, but one stroke didn't paint an entire picture. For that he decided to beat Captain Dunnigan to his daily swing by the Farm Security Administration—a gamble, but he figured the chances of the Presidio connecting him to this brief appearance would be slim. He was in Reno, after all.

At 4:30, he strolled into the federal building with his hands in his pockets and a smoke hanging out of the corner of his mouth. He immediately noticed the office boy who had shagged the envelope down to Dunnigan at curbside. Smiling, he hooked a finger for him to approach.

"Yes, sir?"

"Captain Dunnigan's on sick call today." Jared struggled to mask his accent. "I'm supposed to pick up the traffic."

Without batting an eye, the kid said sure and ducked into a glass-enclosed office in which sat a duffer who actually wore garters around his sleeves. He handed the envelope to the kid, but then followed him out to the service counter. "The colonel's set of copies is inside. Only one this time. We've got orders to cut back."

"Fine," Jared said, and turned to go.

"Lieutenant . . ."

"Yes?"

"Your name, please?"

Jared tossed off the name of his old chief of police, and an hour later he dumped the contents of the envelope onto the table of a Chinatown restaurant around the corner from his hotel. In the flickering light of a candle lantern, he studied the legal forms, downing cup after cup of green tea.

He had known that the Farm Security Administration was entrusted with the rural property of the evacuees, but he hadn't realized that Western Defense Command—the Presidio, in short—had issued loans in behalf of Japanese farmers to large corporations that were to manage these properties while the owners were in the camps. But something was going wrong. These firms, run by men whose surnames Jared recognized as those of some of the most powerful agricultural families in the state, were showing horrendous operating losses, and for some reason the loans were being called in—full payment within a year. Naturally, with the average evacuee making sixteen bucks a month, the Japanese farmers couldn't hope to make the balloon payments *and* keep up with the taxes to save their land. So Dunnigan had been trotting over to the hall of records to expedite the double-edged foreclosure proceedings, probably in behalf of Native Son Management Corporation, which then scooped up the land at what Jared strongly suspected were bargain rates. And this was just San Francisco County, which was virtually all city. What was happening in the rest of the state?

The long and short of it was: Nick Bleecher was making a killing off the evacuation. Jared laughed bitterly under his breath, remembering Shawnee, remembering the tractors. It never ended—greed. It just never ended.

Tomorrow morning, he promised himself, he would see what had intrigued Captain Dunnigan about a Chinese laundry down the street.

Turning around in the booth, he looked for the boy. His pork chow mein hadn't arrived in over twenty minutes, and two sailors across from him were singing out for another round of beers.

Ripping the paper covering off his chopsticks, he separated them and began rubbing them together to get the splinters off, as he'd seen the evacuees do. He wondered why Hank Fukuda had fallen so hard for the cock-and-bull that Monty Lee had had a deal going with Shido. The story tied together some ragged ends, but then again it unraveled some news ones: like how had Monty gotten to the judo *dojo* without half the evacuees in camp seeing him? Maybe the chief, like himself, was just dog-tired, and that explained his faith in the word of some two-dollar geisha.

No, Monty was the not the inside man on this job. In fact, on the evening before his departure, he had spent a few hours with the new director in his bungalow, and Monty, clearly in anguish, had said, "I don't know if I can stand the violence of this place anymore. I've just got to get out of here. But before I leave, I must do something for you. . . ."

"All the good's been done—I'm leaving this hellhole."

"No, you'll see . . . and you'll thank me one day."

If Jared had to guess who was Bleecher's man inside Manzanar, it would be Snavely or Osler, not poor old Monty Lee, who fancied that he could grant wishes like some kind of soused genie.

A shadow passed over Jared's table. He nudged the teapot, which had been emptied to its leafy dregs, to the edge of the table, but no hand took it away to be refilled.

Then Jared glanced up into the face of a Chinese.

He was wearing a pin-striped zoot suit, and his grin was nearly lost in the shadow thrown by his floppy hat. Languidly, he began to reach inside his wide-lapeled coat, his right hand moving as serenely as a cloud.

Jared saw the scarred wooden grips of the revolver in the same split second he realized that he would never have time to go for his own handgun, which was crammed in the back of his waistband.

The Chinese slid the revolver out of his shoulder holster, and Jared made his move. He didn't grab for the gun or try to deflect it. Instead, with startling swiftness, he plunged one of the chopsticks into the man's eye, driving it until the tip rammed up against the back of the skull.

The revolver bounced across the grimy tile floor, but Jared never heard it hit, so intently was he watching the man's hands shrivel into bony fists. There was no cry, no grimace of pain —only the forming of those bloodless fists as he tumbled across the table between the two sailors, spraying their jerseys with vegetables, Chinese noodles, and his own blood.

Someone screamed, and Jared seemed to awaken out of a trance. His lips parted, and he slowly rubbed a hand along the side of his face as if it had gone numb.

Then he started to walk out—walking, not running.

Suddenly, he halted, about-faced, and went back to the booth for his satchel. Then he broke into a trot toward the front door, his face bilious at the thought he could do such things so well.

More than anything else, his expression was one of amazement.

CHAPTER 22

By seven o'clock Hank Fukuda could wait no longer.

He scribbled out the daily report, even though swing shift had another five hours to go, then personally hurried to the corporal of the guard for the key.

The MP was standing outside the sentry house, smoking a cigarette as if it tasted sour. His khakis were an umber color where his sweat had soaked through. "Ahead of schedule, aren't you, Chief?"

"I'm not feeling well tonight—want to turn in early."

"Aren't you dying in that coat?"

"No . . . feeling a chill, actually."

Yawning, the corporal reached behind him for the key. "Whatever."

When Hank got there, the front door to the administration building was unlocked.

Puzzled, he tread lightly into the foyer and listened. Susurrations were echoing down the corridor, hushed voices, one male and one female. He glanced at the covered switchboard, but then decided to investigate first.

Montgomery Lee's door was ajar, and light spilled out in a triangle across the linoleum.

Hank thought twice about interrupting, started to turn, but finally knocked quietly.

"Enter," Lee said, his tone of voice brittle.

He looked small behind Morris Wenge's big desk. Across the room, Kimiko Nitta was reorganizing a file cabinet. Both their faces were flushed, yet the chief could hear the swamp cooler murmuring. Lee didn't smile, as he habitually did in greeting, and Hank was gripped by an unreasonable fear that the man knew he was being stalked.

Kimiko seemed unusually distant as well, but then she tried to smile. Perhaps she still felt awkward about quitting, even though the chief had assured her that he understood why she might want to work for the director. Now, however, he had to get her away from him as swiftly as possible—without alarming him.

"Here's the daily report, sir."

"Please put it on the desk—anywhere there, Chief." Lee went back to thumbing through cardboard folders, but then muttered offhandedly, without meeting the chief's eyes, "I do sincerely hope there's mention of a female detainee on today's jail checkoff." When Hank didn't answer, Lee glanced up. "Is there, Chief?"

"No, sir." He could feel the blood start to swish through his temples.

"May I ask why not?"

"The subject isn't under arrest."

"Is she being held in the cage?"

"Yes."

Lee grinned, and Hank felt a trickle of sweat go down his spine. "Well, if that's not being under arrest, I have no idea what is."

"The subject—"

"Who are we talking about?"

"Yukiko Ota, sir." Hank noted that Lee's eyes didn't react

to this news—but then again, he obviously already knew she was being held. "Miss Ota has consented to remain under our protective custody."

"For what purpose?"

"Questioning—a prostitution operation in camp."

"Is she involved?"

"I believe so, sir. But I've granted her immunity—if she truthfully answers our questions."

"And what makes you think you have the power to grant such immunity?"

The chief remained silent.

"Well," Lee went on, "bring Miss Ota around in the morning. I'd like to question her myself."

"Very good." Hank looked to Kimiko, hoping he could warn her with his eyes, but she would not meet them with her own. "Will that be all, Mr. Lee?"

"Yes, thank you, Chief."

As soon as he started down the corridor he made up his mind to go ahead and risk phoning Campbell, even with Lee in the building. The game was up—someone, perhaps one of his own men jockeying for *hakujin* favor, had informed on him. He had to come up with a way to protect Yuki; her peril was even more immediate than Kimiko's, as Lee would certainly find some way to silence the only witness to his trysts with Masao Shido.

His fingers trembling, the chief uncovered and flicked on the switchboard, then plugged in his headset. He wrestled out of his coat and held it against the lower half of his face, hoping the material would keep his voice from carrying. The few minutes it took to make the connection to San Francisco dragged on forever, and more than once he imagined footfalls clipping down the corridor.

At last the receiver on the other end of the line was picked up.

"Jared?"

"Who's this?"

"Sorry," Hank said warily, "must have the wrong number."

"You want Jared Campbell?"

He hesitated. Jared hadn't mentioned meeting anyone in San Francisco. And there was a hint of menace in the Boston-accented voice that made the chief want to hang up. Still, he found himself asking, "Is he there?"

"Just stepped out for a minute. May I take a message?"

"No . . . that's fine."

"May I say who called?"

He yanked out the headset, then rushed from the administration building, forgetting to return the key to the sentry house and failing to greet his on-duty sergeant as he strode toward his laboratory. There, still hyperventilating, he pocketed a half-pint tube of benzidine solution and an atomizer, then broke out the last of his yellow lightning. He polished off most of a beaker as he slumped on his stool and waited for the twilight to fade to darkness.

◆ ◆ ◆

From the crest of Hyde Street he gazed back down the steep hill toward Alcatraz. The soft gray sky seemed to be rusting over as the sun finished its decline, but still shining whitely across the bay was the big cell block. The Army had originally built it, he reminded himself, to hold soldier-prisoners before the Justice Department took over the island in 1933. Jared started walking again.

He spotted a candy store on the next corner. Sneaking a glance over his shoulder, he stepped inside, the bell on the door tinkling. "Public phone, ma'am?"

"All the way in the back."

He got an idea of how agitated he still looked by the way the woman stared at him. He turned and smiled at her, but knew it probably looked more like a grimace.

There was a slot machine beside the telephone, and he absentmindedly fed it a couple of nickels while waiting for the unlisted number in Daly City to ring.

"Hello?" The special agent sounded like he was still chewing on dinner.

"Cade?"

"Campbell? Where are you?"

"Listen hard—they know I'm here."

"How?"

"I don't know—maybe a cop who field-interrogated me, or this 4-F at the *Examiner* office, or, hell, maybe even you—"

"Bullshit. You been back to your hotel? I left a message."

"No, I've been walking the past hour. Thinking." And dodging cruisers that were probably already looking for him, he told himself. Fortunately, the city was teeming with GIs—an entire infantry division was set to shove off for the Pacific and was out on the town tonight. Pausing to strain the breathy pleading out of his voice, Jared dropped another nickel in the slot and gave the handle a frantic pull. The reels blurred, then thudded to a stop on a mix of nothing. "I need the car one more day—just one more day, Bob. But I can't go back to—"

"Sorry, that's what the message was about. I already picked it up at the hotel lot."

Heat flushed the sides of Jared's neck. "I got the goods on them!"

"You got nothing but trouble, kid. Believe me. And don't call me again."

"Your boss can have them for breakfast! What the hell about our—"

But Cade had hung up.

"Lord Almighty," Jared whispered, using the receiver to massage his forehead. *Even Hoover's spooked.*

The smell of chocolate was making him ill; it seemed sweet with decay—like death.

He asked to use the lavatory, and slid his satchel under the basin and splashed his face with cold water after locking the door behind him. He was amazed at how pale he looked. Deathbed pale. And then he saw that his black tie was flecked with blood. He wanted to rip it off, throw it away. But it was his only one, and he dabbed the spots with a moistened paper towel, which he then flushed down the john.

He hadn't completely squared with Cade. He had *some* of the goods. But the capstone to the materials he had lifted from the *Examiner* morgue and the Farm Security Administration was still locked away in a safe on the heavily guarded grounds of the Presidio. Only James Van Zwartz's diaries would contain what the provost marshal general, or even the inspector general—the ombudsman of the U.S. Army—needed to see, the very thing that had been suggested by Colonel Bleecher himself. *"The general doesn't like it either . . ."* he had said to Father Kerry on the bridge, *"as a Christian, I mean. . . ."*

Jared knew he had no place left to run—except straight at the bastards. Even going back to his hotel was now out of the question.

First things first. The cops and the MPs would be hunting for a lieutenant.

He plucked the silver bars off his shoulder straps and overseas cap and dumped them in the wastebasket. Then, with his pocket knife, he skinned the officer's braid off his sleeves, leaving shadowy curlicues he hoped would be visible only in strong light, and lastly cut away his cloth belt because an enlisted man's blouse had none. "Done." His voice sounded thin and scared to his own ears.

Having busted himself to buck private, he went back out into the hallway and cracked open the commercial pages of the phone book to machine shops.

♦ ♦ ♦

Somehow, Hank Fukuda had known that Montgomery Lee would leave his bungalow locked tighter than a drum. And lacking a set of picks, he knew of only one other way to get inside.

Wrapping his handkerchief around his fist, he punched out a pane in the kitchenette window, cringing as the broken glass tinkled into the sink.

It really hadn't been much of a sound, he told himself. It was his nervousness that had made it seem like a loud crash.

Still, he didn't budge for several seconds, waiting for a cry of alarm to be raised from the white clapboard *hakujin* barrack across the street. The glow of the searchlights was dimming the stars, and a fine mist had spread over the valley in the last hour, the fumy advance of a summer storm perhaps.

He glanced back at the only light burning in the administration building.

Now that he thought about it, he was glad he had come unexpectedly upon Lee with Kimiko. It was a form of insurance: the director—whatever he was capable of—had been seen alone with her, and Hank was counting on this to discourage him from harming her. Of course, this hope did nothing to ease his dread that Lee *wanted* to harm her; the director's rapacious desires had buzzed and crackled around that office like electricity. Why had Kimiko seemed so oblivious to them? Tomorrow, he would see her on the sly and explain why she must get out of camp, whatever the pretext. Lee was focusing his attention on her, and the chief was willing to bet his own life that Lee had focused that same grim attention on Masao Shido and Morris Wenge.

He reached through the broken pane then and bent his arm torturously in an effort to grasp the doorknob. His fingers kept slipping off the smooth brass, however, and he realized that his arm was too short. Grunting, he stood on his toes. Finally, his hand closed around the knob.

The interior of the bungalow was fetid. It smelled vaguely of Lee himself, but with a faint reek of corruption Hank found unpleasant. On the sinkboard, among the splinters of glass, was a bottle of bourbon, half empty. He was tempted to take a swig, but instead slid his flashlight from his trouser pocket and muted the beam by holding two fingers over the lens.

There was no cutlery in the kitchenette, not even a paring knife. Lee apparently took his meals in the *hakujin* mess hall, if he bothered to eat at all.

Hank crept into the small living room, first making sure that the drapes were drawn, and shone the beam over the sofa, a Japanese tea table, and then a showy folding fan in a stand on a bookshelf. He hadn't expected Lee to have Oriental tastes, but the discovery seemed more ominous than reassuring, as if Lee had surrounded himself with such objects to keep his hate fresh.

Then the cone of orangish light froze on the sword hung on the wall, not the *katana*, but the shorter *wakizashi*, which samurai could wear indoors—and someone more contemporary could readily conceal under a jacket. He stared at it, momentarily numbed by the prospect of what it might mean. Hadn't Jared Campbell ever seen it? he wondered.

Then he took the atomizer from his coat pocket and quickly filled it from the tube of benzidine. Sliding the blade out of its scabbard, he sprayed the steel all the way down to the hilt guard. After that, he counted to ten, trying hard not to grin. To grin might tempt bad luck.

Benzidine, a white crystalline powder, is mixed with alcohol to form a solution that can be swabbed or sprayed on most anything; mystically almost, it turns a vivid aqua-blue color if it comes into contact with a trace of blood as insubstantial as one part per 300,000 parts of water.

But Lee's sword had not been blooded in a long time, if ever.

Disappointment caused Hank to squeeze shut his eyes.

Then he took a deep breath and refilled the atomizer.

◆ ◆ ◆

"You think you can turn out something like this in an hour?"

The aged toolmaker bent over Jared's sketch once again, his face thoughtful. "It's well after five-thirty now. It'll cost you overtime."

"That's all right. That's fair."

"What is it—some kind of jig?"

Jared kept his eyes level on the man's. "Bracket for a mortar base plate. Busted ours while loading it aboard the ship this afternoon."

"When you headed out?"

"Less than six hours. And my topkick wants a new one before we sail."

Shaking his head, the toolmaker shuffled over to a wooden crib filled with sheet metal and angle iron. "Okeydoke—but dang if I can picture what your widget does."

◆ ◆ ◆

"Did you wear traditional attire at your wedding, Mrs. Nitta?"

Kimiko was startled when she saw Montgomery Lee's expression: it was so sympathetic she immediately thought of the *hakujin* friends she had once imagined having for herself, young men and women of intellect, of culture, who would come to her bookish apartment in a city like New York after a concert or a play and ask barbless questions that served as her only reminder that she was, after all, remotely *nihonjin*. Yet this warmth had come so abruptly on the coattails of the severity he had shown toward her all evening that she felt uneasy. "I'm sorry, I'm not sure I understand your question, Mr. Lee."

"What's to understand, my dear? Did you wear that glorious headdress?" His soft-looking hand slowly drew a circle around his head.

"No."

"Then what of your *uchikake?*" He was referring to the heavy outer wedding gown.

"I wore a white dress."

"Oh, you mean the snowy kimono worn beneath the *uchikake?*"

"No, Mr. Lee—a simple white dress." Her hands became busy with files again, and she hoped that her anxiety wasn't evident in her face. He was scrutinizing her body boldly, almost without pause now. She could feel his dark, moist eyes as keenly as if they were hands—sticky hands. She wanted to tell him that he was scaring her but couldn't find the words.

"I too wore white on my wedding day." And then he laughed.

She stared back at him, unable to think of a single thing to say. Finally, she lowered her eyes.

♦ ♦ ♦

The atomizer hissing rhythmically in his hand, Hank Fukuda doused the bathtub. Somehow it seemed the reaction was taking longer than usual—unless the tub, like the *wakizashi* in the living room, was free of blood residue.

"Damn," he whispered, "come on, give me some—"

And then aqua-blue tints began radiating out across the

porcelain from the drain grate. The chief nodded with satisfaction, then flipped on the taps and washed away the benzidine.

The positive reaction might mean only that Lee had cut his foot on a dropped bottle of shampoo. But he didn't believe so—the finding smacked of presumptive coincidence, the gossamer tissue that begins to bind a case together.

Quickly, he went to the kitchenette window. The air flowing in through the broken pane was sweet and cool, though unexpectedly humid. He had to mop his sweat-bleared eyes on his sleeve before he could see that the light was still burning across *Hakujin* Country from Lee's office.

He turned and continued his search.

Buried in Lee's sock drawer was a shoe box overflowing with old photographs. He was about to leave it alone, so strong was his distaste for prying, but then began leafing through a few of the snapshots if only to form some idea of Lee's past. One, in particular, gave him pause: a boyish-looking Lee, in Navy dress whites, happily flinching under a squall of rice; hiking up her layers of crinoline so she might keep up with him, was an equally young blonde, clutching Lee's arm with one gloved hand and fending off rice with the other. Despite her laughing mouth, she had the invasive gaze of a chick sexer—he knew the look well: determining the sex of baby chickens had been one of the few jobs open to *issei* in the twenties.

He had never heard Lee mention her, so the marriage must not have lasted.

It was then that Hank noticed how Lee's fellow ensigns had formed an arch by crossing their swords over the couple's heads.

"*Baka!*" He slapped his forehead, then ran for the bedroom closet.

However, it contained nothing out of the ordinary—just Lee's pungent summer suits and unpolished oxfords. He was ready to shut the door when he noticed a scuff on the sidewall at about shoulder height. Black neoprene, he thought, after it refused to smear even under the vigorous rubbing of his fingers.

He looked up. "Maybe . . . maybe . . ."

Turning around, he scanned the ceiling. There was no molding anywhere else, yet at the top of the closet were strips of cavetto painted a shade darker than the room itself.

He went for the step stool he had seen in the pantry.

His years in a crime lab had conditioned him to look for the anomaly, even if it appeared inconsequential—*particularly* if it appeared inconsequential.

"Maybe now . . ."

Standing on the stool, he shone the flashlight beam obliquely across the closet ceiling and saw faint grease smudges about two feet apart—the kind a man would leave if he reached up to push, which he now did, gingerly. The ceiling gave: it was nothing more than a square of plasterboard. He nudged the panel all the way upright, then let it topple back into the darkness. Dust sifted down into the closet, and he stifled a sneeze as he pocketed his flashlight.

Grasping the exposed joists, he muscled himself up into the attic with his arms and folded himself over the edge. He crawled into the blackness over a carpet of dust, then braced his knees and loafers on a pair of crossbeams so he could sit up. Although bent low, his head still bumped against the tarpaper roof, which was yet warm with the day's heat. In fact, the breathless space was like an oven.

He switched on his flashlight, and a big moth pinwheeled out of hiding and headed directly for the lens. Hank caught it in his hand and tossed it through the hole into the bungalow, where it could be heard a moment later popping madly against a lampshade and then the refrigerator.

Tucked back against the slope of the roof was an orange crate, one of thousands that had arrived in camp filled with culls from the packing houses down south. It was covered with a bed sheet that was not very dusty.

He duckwalked down two joists as far as he could before the pitch of the roof halted him, then started to drag the crate toward him. But it was so heavily laden the flimsy wood threatened to crack if he moved it any farther. Instead, he raised a corner of the sheet and reached inside blindly.

The first object he took out was a bundled gown, bright red, which he then unfurled. It had a stiff roll at the hem—a Japanese garment with a singular purpose. Hank smiled quizzically: Why would Lee keep a *bootchie* wedding gown? Had it belonged to the blonde in the photograph? A souvenir of a Far Eastern tour with the Navy? That made as much sense as anything else he could come up with. But the material still smelled of perspiration. It had been worn recently.

He reached inside the crate again and his hand recoiled.

"*Jesus!*"—the rigored face of a corpse.

It had to be an absurd fiction of his strained imagination, but it was several moments before he could make himself put his hand under the sheet again.

When he finally did, the corpse's face proved to be a Noh mask, beautifully crafted and feather-light. He ran the beam over the gilded eyes and teeth, the flesh-colored horns jutting out of the wispy black hair. Hannya, perhaps the most famous tragic mask, that of a once-beautiful woman turned hideous by the poison of revenge. Thirty years before, she had ravaged his sleep for weeks after his grandparents had made him suffer through a performance of the play *Dojoji*. Her scowl still had the power to send a flutter through his guts.

Why does Lee keep something so exquisitely alien to him?

Beneath the mask was another object that suggested the phantasm of a corpse: hair, coarsely textured, like Japanese hair. He seized the heavy wig and brought it out. The *katsura*, which was donned by male actors when they played female roles.

Then he found the headdress—his *issei* mother had worn one like it on her wedding day. In the old tradition, women were held to be devils, and it was the purpose of this strip of white gauze over pink silk, the *tsunokakushi*—the hornhider—to symbolically conceal the bride's intrinsic evil from her betrothed's sight—at least until the binding sips of sake could be exchanged.

Bewildered, Hank clutched the hornhider. *Why?*

Then, suddenly, he stretched the gauze between his hands until it was as thin as a membrane. "No . . . no . . . no . . ."

The evening of the *obon* festival, the evening both Shido and Wenge had been butchered, he had glimpsed an actor in Hannya mask, hornhider, and red gown crossing the firebreak west of the warehouses. A curious hodgepodge of a costume, particularly in combination with the bamboo sword the actor was holding; but at the time Hank, no aficionado of Noh and Kabuki, thought little more than there was going to be a wedding play, although he understood the lithe performer—mincing in the general direction of the judo *dojo*—to be male, for men portray both sexes in Japanese drama.

"*Baka . . . baka . . .*"

Only now did it occur to him that the play at the *obon* had not called for an appearance by vengeful Hannya. And this actor, whoever he was, had failed to show up at the outdoor theater, for in an unmindful way Hank had been keeping an eye out for him—until the report of a suicide inside the *dojo* office had overshadowed everything else.

And now, even before he tilted the nearly empty box, he knew what things remained inside: a *takemi* and a pair of black cotton gloves. The gloves he stuffed into his pocket, the weave to be compared later with the pattern moistly imprinted by skin excretions onto the rice-paper screen in the *dojo* office. But he paused to examine the replica of a sword. That a real one would never be used had as much to do with camp regulations as a centuries-old Japanese edict: bamboo had replaced steel after a famous Kabuki actor was accidentally slain during a performance.

No seams were visible in the wood. But, giving in to a hunch, Hank clamped the flashlight in his armpit, then grasped the *takemi* at both ends and pulled. Slowly, the bamboo sheath slid away from a hidden joint at the hilt, revealing an embossed blade of gleaming steel.

He had to rest the sword against his knees, his hands were shaking so violently. "Jesus . . . Jesus Christ . . ."

Etched among the scrollwork on its flat were the letters

United Sta. It had been broken cleanly in two at some time, as if a man had snapped it over his leg, and the break had been honed into a new point. He remembered then that several blows had been required to sever Morris Wenge's head—and the cut-down length of this blade explained why.

Careful not to disturb any possible latent fingerprints, he squirted only the tip with benzidine. Later, he hoped to flake what appeared to be a trace of dried blood off the hilt. Perhaps some bloodstains would show up on the gown as well. And with luck, a good serologist might be able to get a match with Shido's or Wenge's blood phenotype, although it was beyond science to link a stain to a specific person. Still, it might be one more strand of gossamer tissue.

The tattletale tinge of aqua-blue swirled in a drop that hung off the point of the sword, then fell into the dust.

An exultant sound, something like a chuckle catching halfway up his throat, escaped him but he gently laid the United States Navy officer's sword on two joists, afraid he might drop it. Think, *baka* . . . think! he chastised himself.

Lee had indeed enforced Shido's *seppuku*. But how had he compelled the *issei* to submit? What power did the frail acting director have over the robust old *issei?* Hank wondered if something in his own way of looking at the world was keeping him from understanding what had passed between the two men. And how then had Lee crossed back into *Hakujin* Country—flamboyantly costumed as a Japanese bride—in order to murder the man who had coddled his bitterest enemies?

"The net factory," he finally whispered.

It was only a block off First Street, the racial line that divided the camp. Lee had done his changing in the factory.

Joy seized him, electrified his senses, made him want to shout like a schoolboy as he bundled up the sword and gloves in the heavy gown and clambered back down into the closet. He knew now that an evacuee had not killed Director Wenge.

But his wild joy dissolved the instant he peered out the kitchenette window and saw that the light in the administration building was no longer shining.

CHAPTER 23

"Sure you can't remember the address?" the cabbie asked.

"I'll know it when I see it."

"Oh—one of them nights. You may not find her alone this time, Private."

Jared chuckled quietly from the back seat, then lapsed into silence again. Had he really been looking for a half-recalled house, he would never have found it—the dimmed-out neighborhoods south of the Presidio consisted of nearly identical two-storied jobs, flat-faced, crammed shoulder to shoulder as if the big earthquake had shook them all together. The front lawns were no bigger and no more distinctive than doormats. From the intersection, he glanced up Presidio Street: a light, its top shielded to the sky as a precaution against enemy bombers, was shining palely over the East Cantonment gate, and an MP was standing outside the sentry house on the concrete island between the traffic lanes, hands clasped behind his back in a bored semblance of parade rest.

Jared tapped his cigarette ash out his open window. It was a warm night, the first that actually felt dry and summery. "Try a right turn here, hoss."

"She lives on Cherry Street then?"

"Not this old gal." While the man laughed, Jared scanned the low hills to the immediate north, dark and shaggy with the outlines of eucalyptus and the broad-topped coastal pines. "Left now at the next corner."

"That's Washington Street. And it turns into Presidio Terrace, which circles back on itself."

"Good, that's where she lives—on a loop."

"Why didn't you tell me that in the first place?"

"Sorry, didn't remember till now." Jared picked out a house, any house. "By golly, here she is!"

"Thank God."

He thrust a two-dollar bill at the cabbie and bailed out. "Keep the change." A modest tip to keep himself a blur in the man's memory.

He waited until the cab turned the corner, then strolled up the sidewalk, bouncing his furlough satchel against his thigh, careful not to look like he was in a hurry.

A covered walkway between two houses, its arbor fragrant with honeysuckle, connected to an alley. A dog barked, but it was at least a block away. He became conscious of the .45 chafing against the sweaty small of his back.

In the alley, he upturned a garbage can and climbed over a stone retaining wall, then scrambled up an ivy-clad slope to the Presidio's cyclone fence. His hand went to the wire cutters in his blouse pocket. He had bought them off the toolmaker, explaining that they'd sure be handy on Jap barbed wire.

"Of all the pig luck . . ."

The fence was eight feet high, its top laced with corkscrews of concertina. The foliage inside had been trimmed back three yards, enough for a road to have been bladed out of the hillside, so there was little hope of finding a tree limb hanging over the wire. And the jeep tracks on the road looked fresh. A roving motor patrol, probably on the hour. Which made the cutters useless: snipped strands of wire sparkle like diamonds—it was something sentries were trained to look for.

He tested the tautness of the fence by pulling on it, and

discovered that it was well-made, not a jerry-built job like Manzanar's. Crouching in the darkness, he felt for how it was fastened to its posts: ties of galvanized wire an eighth of an inch thick—at least the cutters would be good for something.

Heaving a sigh, he trotted back down the slope to the alley. He prowled the narrow lane all the way around the loop, his stride quick with impatience now, and finally saw where a sliver of light fell across the pavement, slipping from the crack between the double doors of a garage.

Inside was a resiny smell of pine shavings he found pleasant, but the white-haired man looked angry at being surprised. His lips hitched at the corners as he ran his eyes up and down Jared's uniform. After a moment, he shut down the whirring lathe on which he'd been turning a table leg. "Who are you?"

"Sorry I startled you. My car's around the corner a piece, and I got a flat clear off the rim. Wonder if I can borrow a jack?"

"Don't know you from Adam, do I?"

"Well, how much is a jack worth? Two, three dollars?"

"Oh, no, it's worth way more than that." He threw a glance toward the trunk of his dusty Nash. "It come with the car, that jack."

"Tell you what I'm going to do—I'll leave a deposit."

"How much?"

"Ten dollars?"

A wind had risen by the time Jared crept back up to the fence, a warm and arid flux out of the south. He kept checking for the glow of paint-reduced headlamps on the dirt road as he wedged the point of the jack handle inside the lowermost tie, then pried up a little slack so he could sever the wire with the cutters.

He thought he heard a jeep in the distance as he clipped off the next tie up the pole. Quickly, he used the lug wrench end of the handle to gouge out a slanted place in the hard ground. This was to hold the jack base at an angle to the fence. Then, fitting the lift bracket to the bottom row of chainlinks, he began pumping the handle, gritting his teeth against the loud snicking of the ratchet.

The fence slowly bulged outward, until there was enough clearance for him to squirm under. He disconnected the handle and tossed it and his satchel onto the road. Fumbling in the darkness, he released the pawl toggle, and the fence sank back into place. He didn't think it had been bent too badly, but he couldn't be sure—not without using his flashlight.

It was then that faint headlights brought the leaves behind him into trembling definition.

Scooping up the jack with one hand and his satchel with the other, he pitched himself across the road and tumbled down a small embankment covered with wild mustard. The headlamps grew brighter, and he prayed that they wouldn't reveal his footprints in the dirt.

The wire cutters. He couldn't recall if he'd picked them up but resisted looking, for at that instant the jeep jounced into view. The windshield was folded down over the hood, and the light reflected off the fence back into the listless eyes of the two MPs. They seemed to be hypnotized by tedium, but the soldier in the rear was manning a Browning .30-caliber machine gun, his right hand clasping the trigger grip, his forefinger within an inch of opening fire.

Jared lay motionless in the mustard long after the jeep had rumbled past. Rifles he had expected, but not machine guns. How many more Brownings lay between him and General Van Zwartz's house?

The first thing he did after dusting himself off was to find the wire cutters—left at the base of the pole, as he'd feared—and hurl them deep into the brush. The fewer burglary tools found on his person the better it would look at his general court-martial. *Christ, what confidence, I'm already doping out my defense.*

Then he loaded the jack into his satchel and set out toward the northwest, orienting himself by the towers of the Golden Gate and making sure to keep to the woodlands and off the exposed fairways of a golf course.

Through the years, the eucalytpus had shed tons of bark off their massive blond trunks, and the wind now rattled through these papery heaps, sounding in Jared's mind like searchers crashing through the undergrowth. Once, he stopped dead in his tracks when he thought he heard whispering, but it was only the wind being sliced by the knifelike leaves.

He zigzagged up a weedy ravine and halted at the top of a ridge, the old brick complexes and the more recent cantonments of the Presidio spread out before him in the darkness. As he watched from above, catching his breath, runway lights winked on at Crissy Field and a fighter skimmed in low over the metallic-looking surface of the bay. Its snout was like a shark's: a P-40, he realized, moving on again as soon as it bounced to a landing.

Gradually, he worked his way down through woods cleared of their debris—upper-class woods. Rooflines began to be visible through the trunks and foliage—married officers' housing. The largest and handsomest was occupied by Lieutenant General James Van Zwartz, and on both floors lights were still leaking around the blackout shades.

Jared slumped behind a masonry wall, then dug his thumb into the notch between his brow and the bridge of his nose—and pressed until he felt pain. He was afraid to get comfortable, afraid it would make him think twice about going ahead when Van Zwartz's windows eventually went dark. But he was out of choices. It was a lousy thing to kill a man. He knew that already from three acquaintances with killing men, from the sleepless nights afterward, his soft woman of a heart wondering why even while his brain kept shouting like a fed-up daddy, *There was good reason—now go to sleep and quit fretting about it, dammit!* This time, however, with the young Chinese, it would appear to others that he had killed *outside* the law. That was called murder. But what the hell was the law anyways if men like Bleecher could raddle it with lies, then use it to round up harmless working people, steal their property, and maybe even kick them out of the country? Nothing seemed to make sense anymore, not even the things he believed in. So maybe it was best to stop thinking.

He took the pistol from his waistband and zipped it inside

the satchel, which he would leave outside. Breaking in unarmed might mean a shorter sentence. As if it mattered. As if anything mattered in this lost cause.

But maybe his anger counted, and maybe that would be enough to see him through this night. He would go down angry.

He bowed his head and rested, becoming aware of the cadence of crickets for the first time. Then shoes could be heard scuffling along the sidewalk—a sentry was ambling past the house, bayonet fixed to his rifle.

Lonely is the burglar, Jared thought, his shadowy face seemingly all bone and gristle as he watched Van Zwartz's house.

◆ ◆ ◆

It was getting late, ten almost, yet Montgomery Lee showed no intention of letting her go back to her in-laws' apartment.

"A pity, Mrs. Nitta . . ."

"Mr. Lee?"

"I was just thinking—a pity you couldn't have a traditional wedding."

"Well, it was here in the camp and—"

"I gathered it was." He spun away from her and faced into the artificial breeze gushing out of the swamp cooler. It lifted the dark locks off his forehead, twirled them into little spikes. "Is your father in the system somewhere?"

"No, deceased."

"What was his vocation, if I might ask?"

"A pharmacist . . . to a Japanese clientele in Walnut Grove."

"Oh!" Lee turned back to her, his eyes suddenly bright. "What a grand affair it could have been!"

She resisted shaking her head. "He was a man of modest—"

"I've been to a Shinto wedding, you know. Please sit down—you've been working like an *inu*."

She sat on the edge of the chair.

"Yes, it was in Tokyo, Mrs. Nitta." His voice was deep and soft and courtly, but his eyes were adamantly cruel, those of a small boy caught mistreating a defenseless animal, she thought. "You look surprised."

She smiled, but only because for an instant she'd been afraid her mouth was too dry to form words. "I'm sorry?"

"You seemed taken aback when I said I'd been to a Shinto wedding." His face flushed momentarily. She believed it had been in anger, and had no idea why.

"I . . . I don't know what to say, Mr. Lee."

Then, bewilderingly, he laughed in a warm, easy way. "Say what is in your heart, Kimiko-*san*," he said in Japanese. From these few words she decided that his mastery was better than her own, which had been acquired at language school after her regular classes. But before she could confirm this, he switched back to English. "Oh, it was quite an honor, I'm sure. An imperial naval officer. And his bride was a dream. A butterfly who floated into the shrine like . . . like . . ." His gaze drifted toward the ceiling. ". . . you, Mrs. Nitta, gliding into my office for the first time." He laughed again. "And her little maidens, her *miko* . . . with soft white throats, listening like little birds to the vows of harmony and respect unto death. And the drinking that night! My God, but you people can drink when the mood strikes! *Banzai!*"

She tried to stop knitting her fingers together. He was watching her hands.

"What's wrong, Mrs. Nitta?"

"I'm very tired."

"Of course you are." But, again, he gave no sign of dismissal. "You must forgive me for keeping you over like this. But I've been lonelier than usual."

She tried to look sympathetic. If only she could please him, even briefly, he would let her go and this excruciating evening would come to a close.

"You see . . . I recently lost my best friend."

"I'm sorry, Mr. Lee. I didn't know."

"Of course you knew." He laughed again, but more wearily this time.

Her smile vanished and was replaced by bafflement.

He studied her as if he were considering something flagrant and unmentionable, something that would repel her beyond measure. It was the calculation of his risk that was glazing his eyes—she was sure of it. "Come here, please."

She hesitated.

"Come now, Mrs. Nitta. I won't bite."

He was her employer. She must do what he requested, even if it seemed odd. His ways would seem less threatening when she became better acquainted with them, she told herself as she rounded his desk.

"Am I upsetting you?"

She shook her head, although what she really meant was *Yes, but I'll endure it.* She detested her own submissiveness, detested it because she knew it ran deeper than her hope that Lee might help Eddie.

"Good, Mrs. Nitta." He opened his top drawer and brought out a book.

She gasped as soon as he turned the buckram cover to the first page.

"Oh, yes," he murmured, obviously taken with the picture, "it amazes me as well . . . amazes me you people would codify your arts of seduction."

It was a Brides' Book, an heirloom now, but years before a *nihonjin* mother would have presented it to her daughter before her wedding. It contained twelve drawings, one for each month of the year, and each showing a different attitude of love-making. Suddenly, she felt more revulsion than fear. There was something diseased within this man, something unhealthy struggling for release. She must go before it wormed free. She must put aside her feelings of obligation, feelings that had been deeply ingrained in her by parents who had grown up in a village where for centuries even the most unreasonable lord could do whatsoever he pleased. This antiquated sense of submission was now endangering her, and she had to get out.

"I'll see you in the morning, Mr. Lee," she said evenly, turning to leave.

But he reached out and seized her by the wrist. The power

in the grasp of his slight hand shocked her more than the brazenness of the act itself.

"Before you do, Mrs. Nitta," he said, his voice still low but seething now, "you must tell me which of these you used to seduce Jared Campbell."

There it was. The condemnation she had been dreading. It really didn't matter who now delivered it. It had come at last, and she felt a curious relief that came close to enervating her. She stopped straining against his grip, although her eyes remained wide with fright. "Please . . ."

"Please *what?*"

"I mean you no harm . . . I mean no harm . . ."

But he seemed momentarily distracted, as if he had come to a decision. His moist, boyish eyes were no longer busy calculating risks. He was beyond comprehending risk.

"You mean *me* no harm?" he cried, his lips pulling back from his yellowed teeth.

"Please, Mr. Lee—"

"Well, that," he said with abrupt reasonableness, "is probably factual. . . ." He loosened his grip for an instant, but then quickly took both her wrists in his hands. She decided not to struggle for the moment: at least he was talking. "But the *truth* of the matter is that you mean me immeasurable harm. There is an enormity to the harm you intend me." She cringed as he lightly kissed all ten knuckles of her hands, which were growing purple in his grasp. "Oh, you wrap it in grace and femininity, a cloying femininity. But the scales have fallen away from my eyes, and I see the truth of the matter. But poor Jared, our mutually beloved Jared, is not so immune. You sent him to San Francisco, didn't you?"

She glared at him, more out of fear for Jared than contempt.

Then, without warning, he backhanded her.

"So I must liberate him from your deception!"

Instead of slapping her again, he cupped her chin in his palm and stroked her lips with his thumb. "Dear sweet angel . . . don't make me do this . . . stop me while there's still time . . . stop me . . ."

She was too sickened to feel rage; what she did next she had to force herself to do with all the courage she could muster.

Whimpering softly, making him think perhaps that she was returning his caress, she softly closed her teeth around his thumb. Shutting her eyes against the sight of his smooth, hairless hand, she bit down until the taste of blood drew a rush of saliva to the front of her mouth.

He yowled, the plaintive cry of a hurt child, and through her terror she felt a pang of regret.

But then he struck her hard across the side of the head, his fingers entangling in the fall of her hair. He yanked his hand free, tearing away long strands of black hair.

"Bitch!" He grabbed her by the shoulders and slammed her against the wall. "Yellow bitch! See what you're doing to me!"

She wanted to cry out, but her face was completely numb. And when he drove his fist into her chest, she sagged to the floor without uttering a sound.

Her field of vision had gone gray, and she found it impossible to take the deep breath she so desperately needed. Even if she screamed, she wondered if she would be heard over the cooler. Besides, the adjoining window opened on *Hakujin* Country—she could not imagine help coming from that side of camp.

Lee was rummaging noisily through his desk drawers.

She toppled over to the side as if she'd fainted. But then, keeping low to the floor, she began slinking toward the door.

"Stay where you are," he hissed, still going through drawers.

She kept crawling, pulling herself along the linoleum by the palms of her hands.

"I'm quite serious, Mrs. Nitta."

Something in his voice made her stop and look back: he was grasping a short dagger. The diamond pattern on its hilt seemed Japanese.

"You," she whispered, paralyzed by his approach and the numbing realization that he had killed Shido and Wenge. His

movements were measured—but only because he didn't want his quarry to bolt, she thought, hating him for the first time. Still, she had no legs on which to run; fear had atrophied them. No matter how fast she ran in her mind's eye, she could still feel the plunging fire of the dagger in her back. "You did those things. And you're going to let Eddie take the blame."

He gave no indication that he understood her words. Instead, his eyes were consumed with expectation as he knelt about six feet from her. The sweat on his forehead looked clammy, and he held the blade flush against his thigh. "I want you to know I find you lovely . . ."

For a terrifying split second, she felt herself begin to black out, and then—as the blood slowly seeped again into her brain—she found herself back in her barrack-stall at Tanforan Race Track, watching manure dust swirl in a slant of sunlight, listening to a boy who knew *aikido* tell everyone what to do if assaulted by the *hakujin*. Another student had suggested a swift kick to the privates; however, after the laughter had died, the boy who knew *aikido* said that a blow to the testicles was a low order of pain—it was the eyes that were crammed with nerve endings, it was the nerve-rich jelly of the eyes one should attack.

Kimiko now remained still, unbreathing, as Lee crept forward on his knees.

"Thank you . . . thank you for not running. For *him*, I thank you."

It was nearly impossible to keep herself from scrambling back toward even a temporary moment of safety. She was facing violation beyond reckoning, perhaps beyond pain as well, although the humiliation would be every bit as keen as pain. Any second now, she would be opened by this man. She imagined the gush of her own body's heat curling up around her face as he withdrew the knife. But she did not budge.

He kept the dagger clamped to his thigh, and with his free hand reached out, trembling, for the hem of her skirt. Without benefit of nylons, she felt his fingers advance up between her legs, acutely.

She waited until he touched her, began kneading her with a cunning tenderness, letting him come to the threshold of his foul rapture, before she raked her fingernails across his eyes as savagely as she could.

As he recoiled against his desk screaming, she sprang up and lunged through the door, slapping off the light button as she ran out into the corridor.

Yet, unbelievably, within seconds, he was right behind her. He caught her shoulder and spun her to the floor. But she rolled away from him and into the darkness.

When nothing happened after a few seconds, she slipped out of her shoes.

"Mrs. Nitta," he said in a whisper, "there can be an aesthetic to this . . . please do not deny us the aesthetics of this."

She heard the rustle of clothing, then something tapped loudly against the linoleum. The dagger. He was driving it overhand at her, blind.

She screamed.

"Don't do that!" he bellowed. "Don't, you bitch!"

She shrank against the wall—and felt a door jiggle in its frame against her back. Reaching up, she turned the knob and tumbled inside the room, rising again to find the lock.

His weight began pressing against the door, but there was no lock to be found. She gave up and stumbled backward into the center of the room.

He burst inside, his breath exploding from his throat. "If . . . if you truly loved him . . . you would submit!"

A searchlight flickered across the windows, creating shadows that reeled off the desks and chairs at crazy angles, making the entire room seem to spin. She was in the resettlement office, she realized. Then she recalled that it was connected to a string of offices, perhaps as many as three, by interior doors.

As she started for the first door, her bare feet padding quietly on the linoleum, his face swung toward her, hawklike. From this she realized he was still having difficulty seeing. Still, he followed, the dagger jutting out of his fist.

She slammed the door on him, but it bounced back immediately and he barreled into the second office, pausing to listen, waiting for the searchlight to sweep this way again.

Partially hidden by a file cabinet in the corner, she, too, waited for the light.

His footfalls started across the floor toward her, then stopped. From the vague outline of his silhouette, she saw that he had positioned himself so she would have to run within the radius of his dagger arm on her way toward any of the three doors in the room.

At that moment the windows were lit up again.

Atop the cabinet, almost touching her elbow, was a china sake bottle filled with straw flowers. She grasped it as he started for her and heaved it at him in the same instant the light flashed past.

There was a dull knocking sound in the darkness, then the tinkle of shattered glass. But he didn't cry out, and she braced herself for his next onslaught, believing she'd missed her mark.

Yet, when the searchbeam came back after a deep, awful silence, he was standing with his arms spread wide and his spine arched like a man who has just been doused with cold water. In the harsh light, the blood sheeting down the side of his face and onto his white shirt looked like tar.

"Well," he said, weeping now, "I expected no less. I honestly expected no less."

She turned for the window and was able to lift the lower sash a few inches before his arm shot out and held it fast.

"No!" she screamed.

"Yes, Mrs. Nitta . . ."

Collapsing, she cowered in the corner. She had failed in all things, and this was somehow fitting—penultimately, she was being laughed at, and now only the swift climax to her shame remained. She listened to the laughter of hell, which sounded much like a man sobbing pathetically.

From afar, someone called out her name. It could have been Peter, or Eddie, or Jared, or even her father. It could have been anyone.

CHAPTER 24

Jared stood at the darkened foot of James Van Zwartz's stairs asking himself if the general's diaries were all that Bob Cade had cracked them up to be. They might not even be incriminating. The thought instantly chilled the sweat on his face.

The house was silent but for the ticking of a mantle clock in the parlor. Still, he wanted some sense of who might be in the place before he went upstairs. There was either a need to rush or there wasn't—burglary called for that kind of decision.

From the second floor came the clacking of bedsprings as someone murmured and rolled over. A woman's voice. The *Mrs*. General, probably—unless the old boy was younger than he looked in his official photograph.

He wondered if an orderly or a servant might be posted in one of the downstairs bedrooms, but the only sound on the ground floor came from the clock.

He had shucked his shoes at the wall outside, leaving them inside his satchel, and now wore his socks over his hands, having put them on as soon as he had picked the brass mortise lock on the back door, which was prettier than it was intricate.

The most useful things he knew about burglary hadn't come from investigations, or even from jawing with old salts in the dick division. His knowledge had come from a raw-boned colored man with a natty smile who realized at once why a cop—particularly a rookie detective—would find it handy to get into places he wasn't invited. Earl had been one hell of a commercial burglar in his day, but the bottle had snatched him in middle age and he'd gotten nabbed for breaking the cardinal rule of his trade: fence everything, keep nothing. Figuring himself too old for banks and payroll offices, he had hit a retired admiral's mansion on the heights above San Bernardino and among the loot was a silver platter engraved with a four-stacker and the admonition *Don't give up the ship!* Having been a steward on an Asiatic Fleet destroyer in his youth, he just couldn't part with the prize; and, following wide publicizing of the crime in the papers, a Delilah of a snitch had brought Earl's proud new possession to the attention of the burglary dicks.

Pending trial, he was kept in the city jail, where Detective Campbell brought him tailor-mades and asked him questions about better days. Earl took a liking to the young detective, and soon the cell looked like the University of Burglary, with disassembled locks strewn across the cot and an old safe Jared had hauled out of evidence standing next to the toilet. "But just remembers, Mr. Campbell," Earl would say miserably after each lesson, "you ain't learning from the best. The best don't get hisself caught. . . ." He had died in San Quentin, denied a proud death by a silver platter.

Jared finally started up the stairs. They were carpeted with a runner, but he kept to the bare wood on the wall side of each step, where the aged oak was least likely to creak. He never put his weight entirely on one foot. In this way it took him over five minutes to reach the landing above. And then he almost overturned a tripod table, catching it at the last second.

The master bedroom door was ajar a few inches.

From within came the swelling and ebbing rasps of deep sleep. But he knew that old folks didn't sleep that well for long.

The study door was shut, and he said a little prayer to himself that the bolt wouldn't click when he rotated the knob.

It didn't.

The first thing he did after gingerly shutting the study door behind him was to pull back the wooden shutter panels and open the window, which looked onto the street. He would have to time his exit from the house between the rounds of the sentry and perhaps a motorized patrol as well.

There was a boxlike silhouette in the far corner.

Taking his flashlight out of his blouse pocket, he gave the safe a quick scan, then turned off the light: a vintage Monitor built by American Safe Company—heavy but not formidable. Still, he had no illusions about the difficulty of cracking it under these conditions. He couldn't exactly whiz up an electric drill or peel off the face plate with sledgehammer and prybar.

He had been mulling over his options ever since he had surprised himself by deciding to do this. Maybe William Powell would hold his ear to the dial and listen for the tumblers to fall into place. But Jared had tried the manipulation method under Earl's tutelage, learning only that it could take from two to three hours to discern even the simplest combination in the chatter of the lock mechanism—and by then he'd been so frustrated all he had wanted was to have a go at the dial with a hatchet. No serious safe burglar used manipulation, and he now hoped that he wouldn't be reduced to that nerve-jangling technique.

He had also considered a punch job: knocking off the dial with a quick hammer blow followed by center-punching the spindles back into the vault space; a kind of smash, grab, and run plan he had dismissed in short order. Acquainted with the natural obstinacy of mechanical things, he had little doubt that the spindles would refuse to budge, and he would still be center-punching like a madman when the MPs barged up the stairs in company strength.

In the end, he decided to go with a bridge, which the toolmaker had unknowingly fashioned for him. Earl had used nothing but.

Jared took a rolled-up undershirt out of his front trouser pocket and slowly unfurled it so the tools within wouldn't clink. Working in darkness, he attached the bridge to the door frame of the safe, then threaded the lag bolts by hand into the holes of the device as far as they would go. Never once did he remove the socks, although they encumbered his grasp. He would leave no fingerprints.

The approach of a jeep at idle speed made him freeze with the half-inch wrench in hand. Light splashed across the window, then whisked away. The jeep continued down the street. He started breathing again, and his pulse gradually returned to normal.

He began turning down the bolts. Slowly. A quarter-twist every thirty seconds, which he counted out *one-one thousand, two-one thousand*. He wanted them to gradually back the door out of its frame without snapping the lock bar. When Earl and he had done this successfully, the resultant noise had been no more than a soft groan—not unlike that an old house is apt to make of its own accord in the middle of the night.

The bolts began to resist the torque of the wrench, but still the door refused to give. His fingers were shaking a little now; he blew on them even though they weren't cold.

Then, faintly, he smelled it—tobacco smoke.

He put down the wrench to listen, and a few minutes later a rumbling cough came from the direction of the master bedroom. The old bastard had awakened for a cigarette.

Jared rose on his arms, taking much of the weight off his legs so his knee joints wouldn't crack. The pain of stooping on his haunches over the past half hour had become excruciating. Stiffly, he crept across the room to a wing chair, then sat down and watched the door.

He remained there for nearly an hour, waiting for the smell of smoke to thin out of the air, letting him know that the general had gone back to sleep. He tried to keep his mind empty during that time, and refused to admit to himself that he was sitting in a lieutenant general's reading chair.

At last he returned to the safe. And, with a few more turns

of the wrench, the door yielded, making a shuddery noise louder than he'd expected. Still, he didn't believe it had been enough to wake the old man, and he swung the door open the rest of the way with one hand while reaching for his flashlight with the other.

The cash caught his eye first—hundred-dollar notes still in their bank bands, at least fifty thousand dollars. Maybe a slush fund this big came with three stars, but he doubted it, having already gotten some idea of Nick Bleecher's financial savvy.

He ignored the bills and reached for the four slender volumes on the bottom shelf. They had leather covers and marbling around the edges of the pages.

He opened the first diary.

Most of the entries were in plaintext, innocent-enough notes about meetings, phone calls, personal triumphs, and setbacks. But here and there Van Zwartz had reverted to military cipher. Early on, Snavely had sent Jared to a bonehead cipher course so someone on staff could "intercept coded Jap messages coming in and out of Manzanar," although it had never occurred to the captain that a Jap agent would write in Japanese, of which Jared couldn't fathom a single character. But he had learned enough to recognize that Van Zwartz's shaky capital letters were arranged in transposition cipher, something like a picture puzzle—the parts were all present but would have to be jiggled into the right pattern. However, this wasn't the time or place to fiddle with it; he would have to trust that Van Zwartz wouldn't use a cipher in the first place unless he had something to hide.

Laying the flashlight on the floor, he stuffed the diaries inside both side pockets of his blouse. Then he began unscrewing the bolts so he could take the bridge device with him. He would leave nothing behind but a sprung safe full of cash.

It was then that he noticed the file jacket still inside. Had there been a half dozen of them, he might have ignored it. But there was only one.

"Pinkerton," he whispered, testing the code name on his tongue.

He went through the intelligence report twice, his eyes blearing with denial and disbelief until anger finally clarified them—another lie at his expense, although the wrong done ran deeper than that, ran much deeper than his own pride.

He failed to notice the slice of light appear on the wall, then quietly expand to a rectangle of amber the size of a door. He was thinking of Kimiko, who had gone to work for Monty, and how he had sloughed off Hank's warning. He folded the file in half and, unknotting his tie, slipped the dossier down the front of his shirt, his satisfaction at having the goods on Bleecher spoiled by his fear for Kimiko and his own amazement that he had never seen past his affection for Montgomery Robert Lee.

"Hold it right there," a grating voice as full of fright as menace said.

Jared heard the hammer of a revolver being cocked for single-action fire. He knew that he could not let himself be taken. Bleecher would have him in front of a firing squad within the week, and no one would be the wiser. He tensed the muscles in his legs, coiling them like springs.

Then, without turning, he hurled the flashlight over his shoulder. As the beam jinked wildly around the room, he dove headlong through the window screen, taking it with him out onto the roof of the portico, where he spread-eagled to keep from reeling over the edge.

The revolver exploded from inside the room, once and then again.

Pushing off the shingles with his hands, Jared scuttled backward, away from the window. Yet when he tried to stop himself by bracing his knees against the roof, there was only air beneath his legs. Arms flailing for a purchase on something, anything, he tumbled over, seemingly in slow motion, as the third report came from Van Zwartz's revolver.

"Christ!" He clawed for the rain gutter and just when he thought he could hang on, his fall beginning to slow, an entire length of guttering pulled out of the eaves with a wrenching screak and he was pitched down, face-first, into the hedges below.

He sprawled motionless there for an instant, deep scratches burning his face, then cartwheeled off the sagging branches onto the lawn and sprinted for the low wall. His legs went rubbery when he heard the acceleration of a jeep, closely followed by the squeal of brakes in front of the house.

"There!" the general shouted down to the MPs. "Fire on him!"

Jared stayed in a tuck as he somersaulted over the wall.

A clack echoed from up the street: the Browning machine gun being charged. He reached into his satchel for his shoes, the taste of bile clinging to the back of his throat. Somewhere along the way, the socks had come off his hands. His fingers were too agitated to untie his laces, and he crammed his bare feet into the scuffed shoes, mashing the backs with his heels, before starting up the wooded slope.

"Shoot the son of a bitch!" Van Zwartz hollered.

White flashes lit up the pale eucalyptus bark all around him. The long burst, bullets knocking against the trees like woodpecker bills, made him belly flop onto the ground, his chin skidding in the dirt, which tasted medicinal, like the smell of the leaves. "God Almighty . . ." He spat, and crawled behind a stout trunk. He saw himself sprawled there with his butt higher than his head, saw himself as if he were outside his body. The brief vision made him want to laugh, although he knew it was no time for laughter. Then, grittily, he smiled in spite of his terror. "Time for a little of that psychological warfare . . ."

The beam of a spotlight swooped back and forth overhead like some predatory night bird. He dug inside the satchel for his automatic. Thumbing off the safety, he peered around the base of the tree, showing no more than an inch of his face. One MP was manning the machine gun while his partner worked the spot in a series of nervous arcs.

"Yah-yah-yah-yah!" Giving out with an ear-splitting rebel

yell, Jared fired three times into the earth a few yards in front of him.

The light winked out, but in the split second before everything went dark he glimpsed both soldiers scrambling for cover behind the jeep.

Rising, he dashed for the top of the ridge, smacking branches aside with the satchel as he went.

It was only a few pounding heartbeats before another burst erupted at his back. Some of the rounds thwacked hollowly against tree trunks, others whistled overhead and away into the night.

♦ ♦ ♦

Hank Fukuda heard the scream and then Montgomery Lee shouting, "Don't do that! Don't, you bitch!"

Whirling around in the middle of First Street, his face grizzled by fatigue and shock, he started back, uncertainly, for the darkened administration building he had just skirted on his way to his apartment. He had been trying to avoid Lee, thinking the director had finally knocked off for the night and would be staggering home to his bungalow.

Still clutching the bundled-up wedding gown, the chief shook himself out of his daze and sprinted around the end of the building for Lee's office. When he got there, it was blacked-out and silent but for the whirring and dripping noises from the swamp cooler. And the window beside the cooler was latched.

Then Lee's voice drifted toward him from somewhere down the corridor, on the far side of the building now. His words were too garbled by rage to be understood.

Hank was rushing along a bank of office windows when he heard a door within boom against a plasterboard wall. Cupping his hands around his eyes to block out the glare of a searchlight on the glass, he tried to peer inside. Shadows spun and mingled in the room for an instant, but the darkness returned before he could make sense of them.

Then he heard shoes drumming the floor in the adjoining office, followed by a quiet so fragile, he opened the gown across the ground and fumbled for the *takemi*. He flung the bamboo sheath aside and hefted the broken sword with both hands.

At that instant another door slammed against a wall, this one in the next office down the line.

The watchtower light in this sector was being operated manually by the sentry tonight, so it was hard for the chief to predict its next pass. He sidestepped frantically, trying to position himself so the approaching reflection of the searchbeam wouldn't blot out his view of the interior. He thought of his flashlight, but when he patted his coat pockets he found them empty—running had jostled everything out of them.

Inside, something shattered and tinkled against the linoleum.

He thought he would go mad waiting for Lee to show himself or pass by the front door, which he would then stave in with his shoulder. He ached to cry out to Kimiko, to assure her that he was close by, but was afraid she might stop trying to elude the lunatic the instant she heard a friendly voice. Lee would need only a blink of an eye to murder her.

Then he had it: a strobelike glimpse of the director. His face and shirt were bloodied. Kimiko had drawn blood, stunning him perhaps, and now she was tugging at the lower sash, trying to escape through the window.

In the next fleeting pass of the searchlight, he could see Lee's fist pinning down the sash. It was as bony and unforgiving as a talon. Protruding from it was a dagger—an *aikuchi* not unlike the one he had plucked from Masao Shido's belly.

"No!" Kimiko screamed, her voice, loud and panic-stricken, coming through the crack in the window.

"Kimiko, drop!" Hank bellowed. "Drop to the floor!"

Then he heaved the sword down through the window, the shards of glass exploding around him. He wasn't sure if he had caught Lee's forearm with the blow, but the dagger was no longer in sight.

He used the blade to ream the jagged remnants of glass out of the wooden frame, then clambered over the sill, past

Kimiko, who was still screaming, and rolled onto his back, holding the sword before him in blind defense until the return of the searchlight.

"I'll kill you! All of you! To the last one!" The voice was no longer Lee's: it welled up out of a demon's gorge, slathered with fury. He was about ten feet across the office, which gave Hank enough time to reach back and dig his fingers into Kimiko's shoulder. The pain quieted her.

"When I move, go for the lights," he whispered. "Do you understand?

"Yes . . . yes," she sobbed.

Hank scrambled to his feet and advanced, whooshing the sword before him as he'd been taught in the kendo classes of his youth. His advantage was marginal: the broken blade was scarcely longer than Lee's dagger, and the director was now probably too far gone to be afraid of the searing pain of cold steel.

Blade rang against blade in the darkness. Instinctively, Hank backed off a pace before widening his stance and going on guard once again.

Lee must have withdrawn as well, for nothing happened until the searchlight pulsed against the windows. Then, both men attacked, blade sliding over blade. Hank felt Lee's dagger skid along his upper arm, but didn't believe he had been cut until he felt an unctuous warmth twine down around his wrist.

"Lights, Kimiko!"

They flickered on, slowly, unevenly, a neon ceiling fixture, and Hank was confronted by Lee's ghastly leer.

From outside came the sounds of a jeep pulling up.

Hank began to feel pain from his wound, but still had control of his arm muscles when he tested them with a flex. Despite the pain and his hyperventilating, he forced himself to sound calm. "It's finished, Monty."

All at once, Lee seemed more bewildered than enraged. The blood was trickling from the laceration on his brow, and he tried to blink it out of his left eye, which was already bright pink and swollen. "Go away, both of you." His voice was flat.

"Do so, and we'll say nothing more of this." He tossed off a shooing gesture with his free hand. "Lieutenant Campbell doesn't have to know about this . . . if you both go now."

"It's over, Monty. Drop the dagger."

Boots were pounding down the corridor toward them. Hank allowed himself a colorless smile: the MPs were coming.

"The dagger, Monty—you don't need it anymore."

His expression reflective, Lee smeared blood into his hair with a swipe of his forearm. Then he laughed softly as Osler and Elwayne threw back the door and stepped inside cautiously.

The first sergeant took in the scene over the sights of his .45.

"Thank God," Lee said pathetically, lowering his dagger as he slumped against the wall.

"You're hurt, Mr. Lee," Osler said, shifting his aim onto Hank's back.

"These . . . these *people* tried to assassinate me!"

"Drop it!" Osler barked at the chief.

Incredulous, Hank glanced to Elwayne: confusion was twisting the corporal's face.

"Drop it or I shoot!"

Kimiko started to say something, but the first sergeant shouted for her to keep her mouth shut.

Hank let the broken sword fall.

Osler advanced three strides and kicked it into the farthest corner. His body smelled of something, nothing like cologne, but something common and familiar.

Then, pressing the muzzle of the pistol into the chief's flank, he used his left hand to pat down the chief from armpits to crotch. He finished the search by pulling Hank's coat off his shoulders and down around his elbows, denying the chief the use his arms. There was a large bloodstain on his shirt from his wound, but the flow from the cut already appeared to be congealing.

"They conspired to kill me," Lee went on, his voice breaking. "The two of them, Sergeant."

"I'm aware of that, Mr. Lee."

"You are?"

"Earlier, Fukuda went to the sentry house for the key to this building. He never brought it back, and the corporal of the guard called me. I was looking for him when I saw the light on in here."

"Thank God . . . there is indeed a God."

"Take possession of the evidence, Corporal."

"Top?" Elwayne asked.

"The key, man—take the key off him."

Elwayne approached, his hands on his hips as if he had no idea what to do. "Where is it, Chief?"

"Right front pocket."

"Thanks."

"Don't thank the son of a bitch!" Osler shouted, then—for some reason—motioned for Kimiko to stand out of the way. After Elwayne handed him the key, he gave the corporal his pistol. Then he interlaced his fingers and stretched them outward. "Cover the prisoners—but don't train the fucking thing on me."

Elwayne nodded unhappily. Hank had always sensed that the corporal liked him, perhaps respected him. *There are good men everywhere; even in a stinkhole like this there are good men . . .*

"Mr. Lee, take that chair there," Osler said. "You look like you're going to faint."

"Yes, thank you . . . the shock . . . the *enormity*."

The chief immediately recognized the object Osler slipped out of his rear trouser pocket: the spring-loaded sap Jared Campbell had forbidden him to carry after the last beating of an evacuee.

Kimiko gasped, and Hank turned toward her with a gaunt smile. "*Ga-man,*" he said. Stick it out.

"*Hai,*" she whispered. "*Hai.*"

Waiting, meeting Osler's gaze, he realized that it was citronella. The first sergeant was wearing it as a mosquito repellent. Never again would Hank be able to smell citronella without associating it with bone-shattering pain.

The first blow landed a few inches above his right ear. It jarred his vision into a screen of bright orange pearls, which faded to a sickly pink color before kaleidoscoping into a washed-out semblance of Osler's gratified face.

The chief commended himself: he was still on his feet.

The next blow, as if simply for the sake of variety, was not to the head. It thudded against his upper chest. He knew at once that his clavicle had been broken. It only took twelve pounds of pressure to snap the collarbone, yet Osler was grinning as if he had ruptured a steel beam with his bare hands.

Hank realized that he was down on one knee. The pain must have made him black out briefly. He rose to his feet again and tried to say *ga-man* once more—for his own sake as much as Kimiko's—but his lungs were on fire; he could scarcely breathe.

Nevertheless, his quiet will to endure infuriated Osler, who now began flailing him without pause, beating him around the face, the shoulders, the knees, the shins—and finally the feet when he could no longer stand.

The light was fading inside Hank's cranium, but still the merciful and all-encompassing blackness he hoped for refused to come.

From afar, roaring oceans afar, Elwayne cried, "He ain't resisting, Top!"

"Shut the fuck up!"

Osler sapped Hank so relentlessly that the sweat-weakened threads binding the leather together eventually gave, and hundreds of tiny balls of lead shot danced like quicksilver on the floor. The sound was like rain on a pond. Hank thought that it was raining on his father's carp pond in the backyard. There were sleek orange shadows moving in the depths.

♦ ♦ ♦

As soon as Snavely turned the lock, Lee elbowed past him into Jared Campbell's sweltering quarters, hurled the books off the table, and overturned the metal cot with a growl.

"What are you looking for?"

Lee ignored the captain and yanked open the doors to the wall locker. He began dumping uniforms onto the floor.

"I think we should wait and have a transportation detail from Tule Lake take them." The captain smoothed down his thin mustaches with a knuckle.

Lee turned and glared at him.

"At any rate, I don't think I should go," Snavely went on. "One of us should stay here."

Grinning contemptuously now, Lee turned his attention back to the locker. "Whatever, Captain." On the shelf he found a snub-nosed .38 special, Campbell's revolver from his detective days, wrapped in a swatch of oily felt. He studied the piece for a long moment, then tucked it in his pants pocket. "Osler and I can handle this—and the sooner the better."

"I have every confidence . . ." Snavely's voice trailed off; eventually, he wiped his mouth on his sleeve.

Lee took FDR's portrait off the wall and smashed the glass against the back of a chair. Nothing was concealed inside the frame.

Then he saw the red ribbon among the books on the floor, scooped it up, and examined the black printing. His face slowly darkened.

"What is it?" Snavely asked.

Lee touched a match to the ribbon, then ground the ashes into a black smear on the linoleum. "Nothing."

It had been the second-place prize for the 1928 State of Oklahoma High School Mathematics Competition.

♦ ♦ ♦

On a dock behind the produce market in which his father had a stall, a glittering mountain of ice stood waiting to be tonged apart and hand-trucked inside the huge, noisy building. And for some reason, a reason too childish, too American, to be dignified as *Bushido*, Hank Fukuda and his cousin would strip off their shirts and each lie on a cake, staring at each other to see who would be first to jump off his bed of fiery cold.

Hank groaned.

His forehead was going to shatter from the cold. A lethal ice cream headache.

But then the *hakujin* iceman appeared and demanded to

know what he and his cousin were doing. And when they had no excuse, as all good little *nisei* have no excuse, he demanded to see their fingers. He said he was checking for class rings from McKinley High School in Honolulu. He said some of the Jap fliers shot down over Pearl Harbor had been found with McKinley High School rings on their dead fingers. Hank tried to argue that this wasn't possible. He was only nine years old, and there would be no attack for years and years and years . . . and, besides, the ring story was a lie . . . all these stories were lies. But the iceman pressed him down against the cake, held him to the awful coldness even when he begged to be let up.

"Chief?"

He opened his eyes, then pushed away the damp handkerchief Kimiko was holding to his forehead. He had to vomit.

Someone else cupped a towel around his mouth, and he closed his eyes in humiliation as he emptied himself.

Lips pressed against his temple, even as he was still retching. As soon as he could, he craned his neck to see who had kissed him so tenderly.

It was Yuki Ota, in whose lap his head was cradled. She had been crying.

"Where are we?" he croaked.

"MP guardhouse," Eddie Nitta said from across the floor. The major was prepared to say more, but Hank waved him off.

It was impossible to hold back the void.

CHAPTER 25

Jared hunkered over the pile he had formed by shredding eucalyptus bark and blank pages torn from the back of General Van Zwartz's most recent diary. Taking one last glance around the ridge lines, he thumbed open his Zippo and ran the wavery blue flame along the edge of a crumpled sheet of paper. A yellow tongue of fire danced up a few inches and flattened out on the wind before forking brightly into the heap. Thick, acrid smoke began seeping out of the far side of the pile. He threw on green branches, and their sizzling juices turned into more smoke. Within minutes, long palls were being whirled along by the gusts, ravished through the trees like fog.

Picking up his satchel, he trotted down to the next pile he had built—and touched it off as well.

Soon, the stars faded and the distinctions they had tossed across the land melded into a uniform darkness.

Before making the piles, he had found a windfall in a thicket of dead branches and set it aside. Now he clamped one end under his arm and dragged the limb up a slope until he was overlooking the perimeter fence. He couldn't see them, but he knew soldiers were down there, strung out along the dirt road, one every hundred yards and at closer intervals wherever the track curved sharply around the hills. Their flashlights had twinkled like fireflies when he had come upon them an hour before; most were out now.

Crouching in the brush, he waited for the smoke to do its work. The dimmed-out city sprawled below him, sleeping. It was almost four, the patrolman's witching hour, when the exhausted calm of the streets tries to sew his eyelids together and he fancies working eight-to-five in some factory or even going on the bum—but Jared wasn't sleepy.

He had to get in touch with Hank, warn the chief to hide somewhere in camp until he could get back to Manzanar and get him out. By now, Bleecher would know Jared was going for the jugular, and he was sure to get even by scooping up Hank and making him disappear, permanently. But if he could slip the chief out of Western Defense Command, maybe get him to some fort back East, they could then sing their stories to the provost marshal general or even the inspector general—they could get somebody to listen, once they were outside California.

Preventing this at the moment was Fourth Army, whose commanding general had clamped down the Presidio tighter than a head gasket. The post roads were being coursed by jeep patrols, their spotlights fanning the brush, and the stands of eucalyptus and pine swept by entire companies of infantry. When Jared had seen the ring of troops just inside the fence, he had been tempted to head west to Bakers Beach and try to swim around the cordon. But he had figured his canvas satchel wouldn't keep out the seawater, and he wasn't about to have his only hard evidence reduced to mush. Besides, he was a pond swimmer, not an ocean swimmer.

He had realized then that he would have to deal with the wire—but without the cutters, which he regretted having thrown away. Jacking another bulge under the fence was out of the question, too: the clicking of the ratchet would draw every bayonet within a mile. So he'd chucked the jack and begun thinking about a diversion. He recalled hearing about a con who'd gotten over the wall at McAlester by lighting a trash fire in the exercise yard. And it had seemed a better idea than anything else he could come up with—including trying to bluff his way through one of the gates, which had to be bristling with MPs and Bleecher's G-2 boys.

A dogface somewhere along the fence shouted, "Fire!"

Somebody else took up the cry.

"Well," Jared muttered, making sure his pistol was snug in his waistband, "dying can't be much tougher than living."

Grabbing the limb and his satchel, he started down the dark hillside, trying to move quietly through the brush. But branches entangled the limb, and twice he had to pull it free with all his strength, his shoes thrashing the undergrowth as he stumbled backward.

Fortunately, noise was no longer a problem: The men were hollering and waving their flashlights at one another like Boy Scouts on a jamboree. He had just crept into the thick of the smoke when a soldier ran ten feet in front of him, oblivious to everything except the handkerchief he was clasping to his nostrils and mouth. Before the man could be ordered back to his post, Jared hoisted the limb and leaned it against the top of the fence, where it bent a vee into the concertina. Next he flung his satchel over—it was a desperate feeling to let go of it, even briefly.

"All right . . ." He spit into his hands.

But it was harder to shimmy up the smooth limb than he had guessed. And the smoke began smarting his eyes, burning deep in his throat even though he was holding his breath. He kept slipping, the wood gliding helplessly between his thighs. Finally, he had to grasp the fence itself and pull himself up by his arms, using his legs only as a brake to keep him from losing what his upper body had gained.

He knew that the barbs would feel like fishhooks even before he threw his forearms across the wire, but there was no choice. Still, he groaned as the spikes penetrated his woolen sleeves and bit into his flesh. Hooking the toe of his left shoe in one of the diamond-shaped meshes, he swung his right leg over the top—but didn't quite make it. His trouser cuff was snagged. "Son of a bitch . . ."

He started to cough, which only made him suck in more of the suffocating air.

He was forced to close his hands around the wire in order to lift his left leg up onto the springy bed of coils. The needle-sharp prongs sank into his fingers and palms, and then his calf and ankle, resisted only by underlying bone. "Sweet Jesus . . . oh, sweet Jesus . . ."

Panic began to well up in him, the fear that he would be impaled here forever—Van Zwartz and Bleecher would let him rot atop the fence, rot down to a skeleton in tatters of olive-drab.

Then he heard boots stamping along the road.

Gnashing his teeth and seething in a breath, he opened his fists and rolled outward. For an instant, nothing happened, but then he heard the sound of wool ripping, and he plummeted like a sack of coal, somehow managing to get his legs under himself in the instant before he struck ground.

It felt like a blindside tackle, except that he kept rolling and rolling . . .

♦ ♦ ♦

First light, just a streak of mother-of-pearl below the clouds banked in the east, found him behind what looked to be a college dormitory. There were a half dozen unlocked cars in the parking lot, but only one whose youthful owner had neglected to take his ration coupons out of the glovebox. It was hard to believe: all these kids having cars. A car was a family machine, a tool owned in common, used to transport five or six or even seven pairs of callused hands from picking job to picking job on bald tires and a frayed fan belt. But then he realized he was just trying to make himself feel better about stealing it.

He checked the dormitory windows. Most of the shades were still pulled down. Wincing, his hands raw and swollen, he unlatched the hood of the yellow 1939 Ford coupe.

So far, since leaving the Presidio, he had noted no unusual

activity on the part of San Francisco PD. This made him suspect that Van Zwartz and Bleecher were holding their cards close to their vests; until they could get the diaries and Pinkerton file back, they wanted no police reporter latching onto the story.

Behind him, the fires on the post were still smoldering, but they didn't look as bad as they had an hour before when the wind was nursing tall flames up out of the trees.

"Well," he said, surveying the V-8 engine, his exhaustion making things look slightly smaller than they actually were, "here's what comes of a misspent youth. . . ."

He took the chewing gum wrapper he had fished out of the ashtray and twisted it endwise with the foil facing out. After glancing over his shoulder again, he was thinking to gap the distance between the positive post of the battery and the terminal on the ignition coil when he swore to himself, realizing that the distributor was buried low in front of the block on a '39 Ford. He tossed away the gum wrapper and fumbled for his pocket knife, checking the lot and the dormitory once more. He had to spend five tense minutes wriggling off a steel conduit before he could cut the wire to the coil and crimp its end around the battery terminal. At last, he hurried behind the wheel and pressed the starter button on the firewall with his toe, having bypassed the key-operated ignition switch. The engine grumbled to life. He pampered it with a few choke adjustments before quietly putting down the hood.

Driving south on Masonic Avenue, he kept within the posted speed limits. To avoid the bridges, whose toll collectors might have been alerted to watch for him, he would skirt the bay and head east from San Jose toward the Sierra Nevada. As much as he wanted to phone Hank Fukuda right away, he wouldn't stop until he was completely out of the Bay Region. A Be-on-Lookout would soon be broadcast on the peninsula for the Ford, but its license number wouldn't show up on the state-wide hot sheets for another week.

He found himself wishing there was more traffic. The morning streets were like the rows of a fallow field.

Shifting gears, he suddenly listened with a keener ear to the sounds coming from under the hood. "Whoa . . ."

He backed off on the pedal, made sure the choke knob was all the way in, then tried upshifting again.

"You itty-bitty pistoned son of a bitch!"

He had stolen one of Ford's gutless wonders, nearly identical to the L-head V-8 except that it was somewhat reduced in size and threw only sixty horsepower.

"I hope to hell I don't need a gallop out of you!"

Realizing that hot-wiring two cars in the same hour would be pushing his luck, he sat back and wondered how long it would be before his adrenaline wore off and fatigue set in. He rested his hand atop his satchel. He kept an eye on the cross streets.

◆ ◆ ◆

Hank Fukuda awoke to waves of pain so dazzling, so breathtaking, they nearly washed him back into unconsciousness. There seemed to be no one single source to them; they flooded his being as a whole. Even the lulls between the undulations were filled with nausea and torment. At times, he could not even recall the thing, the experience, that had left him so shattered. And he had difficulty focusing any farther than an arm's length—had he been able to extend his arms. Eventually, he realized he was belted across the chest, waist, and legs to a litter. Overhead, a vault of olive-drab canvas was fluttering.

He was supine in the bed of a truck; the MP deuce-and-a-half, he believed—for First Sergeant Osler was sitting at the tailgate, his tired face in need of a shave, his left hand holding open one of the rear flaps. Through this Hank could see a moist, somber sky. It was September now, he reminded himself, and the last time it had socked in like this in September more rain had fallen over three days than in the entire previous year: a tropical disturbance funneling up the valley from the Gulf of California, its great barges of clouds tottering under their loads of moisture. There was a velveteen feel of rain in the air now;

ordinarily it felt as sere as dust. Telephone poles, in bleared multiples of two, crept past. Their insulators of dark green glass had once sparkled like emeralds—at least they had on the poles lining his youth. Now they seemed as opaque as avocados.

A faint howling from the engine made him think that a bearing was going bad, but then he dozed off as the truck began inching up a grade.

When he drifted up out of the blackness again, it was much hotter under the canopy, although the sliver of sky showing between the flaps was darker than before. The truck had stopped, but on a slant; they were still on the grade, then. The gurgling of the radiator was blended with a drone of *hakujin* voices.

It would take forever, pecking away like this at the four hundred and fifty miles to Tule Lake. He wasn't sure when or how he had come to the conclusion, other than from the northerly direction in which he sensed the Dodge to be headed, but he now accepted the fact that he and the others were bound for the segregation camp on the Oregon border.

He found it hard to think beyond that.

Yuki Ota was sitting above him, her right wrist cuffed to a bench bracket. With her free hand, she pressed the neck of a GI canteen to Hank's lips. He took two sips of tepid water, but no more, although he was still thirsty. He didn't think he could endure the racking pain if he vomited again.

Kimiko, her face drawn even in sleep, was nestled under her husband's remaining arm, which was manacled and bent uncomfortably around her shoulders. He had an odd, pensive look in his eyes. Perhaps he sensed that the decisive moment in his life was coming and foresaw liberation in it, while Hank could envision nothing but ruin and more pain. However fanciful, this expectation was putting an edge on his handsomeness, honing it with a vibrancy that had been lacking since his return from Europe. He was soldiering again, and his eyes were sharp as he calculated the odds.

Hank had given up on the odds.

Osler had propped his legs up on the opposing bench, eyelids sagging over his pupils. An M3 submachine gun was dangling from a shoulder strap across his slightly bulging gut as he dozed, unaware that Eddie Nitta was studying him. But then he stirred. One of the cab doors had opened and shut; someone was walking around to the back of the truck.

It proved to be Montgomery Lee. His neck was shiny with sweat, and a bandage was pasted to his forehead. "How are they?"

"Bellyaching for a potty stop," Osler said, a yawn warping his mouth to the side.

"Absolutely not. We'll get a can or something. But they don't leave the truck."

"This piece of crap cooled down yet?"

"Your driver thinks a few minutes more."

An MP driver plus Osler and Lee—that made three of them, although the chief had no idea what he could do with this information.

"When do we get something to eat?" Yuki demanded.

There was a low chuckle, but it wasn't from either of the Caucasians. An evacuee sat up at the cab end of the bed, where he had been sprawling unnoticed by Hank. He regarded evacuee and *hakujin* alike with a triumphant insolence, then said to Yuki in Japanese, "You must pillow him for your bread."

There was something disturbing about Momai being along, something even more so in how Lee stared him down. The *kibei* fell silent. But Hank suffered a lapse in concentration before he could decide why.

Only when the truck started moving again did the reason occur to him: he had been deluding himself about Tule Lake.

They would never live to see the main gate there.

Lee was going to wipe the slate clean, and Momai's sullen presence somehow confirmed this. Yet, before Hank could speculate on the hint of a connection he had just observed between the two men, the light faded around him.

◆ ◆ ◆

The grass had been scorched golden by the summer sun. The rolling rangeland slipped past as if in a dream, the fat and promised land of California. And the blowsy forenoon might have entranced Jared entirely, had not a big bug or two popped wetly against the windshield every few minutes, shaking him out of his stupor.

He was thirty miles east of San Jose, coasting down into the San Joaquin Valley on a county road too untraveled to warrant a white stripe. Clouds lay over the Sierra far ahead, but here all was sunlit, hot even.

He had half expected them, but there had been no roadblocks to impede him on his way through the Bay Region. The Presidio was going to rely on its own resources.

It was time to telephone Hank Fukuda. It would be a hard thing to broach, especially over the phone, but he would ask the chief to make sure Kimiko was all right.

Then he shook his head violently, reminding himself that he had come to a decision while threading the backstreets of Palo Alto. He was still hundreds of miles from Manzanar. He needed to enlist forces larger than himself to save Hank—and possibly Kimiko as well. His stomach lurched sickeningly as he thought of the Pinkerton file inside his grip and Kimiko.

No, his first call would be to the Army's top cop. And if the provost marshal general refused to help, he would go straight to the inspector general and lay the whole ball of wax at his exalted feet. Only then would he try to get in touch with Hank.

A half hour later, sunk even deeper in his languor, he drove past the faded words GROCERIES and GAS and had to back up to turn into the crossroads market. It had been a long time since he had scattered chickens with the front bumper of a Ford, and he laughed softly, wearily.

Galen's Shade Tree Market had a gasoline pump out front and a kid in patched coveralls watching the world go by from the shadow of a huge walnut tree that was already jettisoning its green fruit. Across the dirt road was a boarded-up garage with the words GONE TO WAR painted on it.

"You Galen hisself?" he asked the kid, almost too tired to joke as he lifted the hood and disconnected the hot-wire to let the engine die.

"Junior."

"All right, Galen Junior, fill 'er up to the top—and I mean the *very* top—and you got yourself a quarter tip. Coupon holder's in the glovebox." Then, hanging on to his satchel, he went through the screen door, setting off a clapper bell rigged to the jamb. The one-room grocery brought back cold memories: three cents a box and a family of seven picking all day for a pound of flour and some baking soda but no side-meat that night. Galen himself looked like the kind of flinty-eyed man who gave no credit.

"Got a phone?"

"Yes, but it ain't public." He gave Jared's disheveled uniform the once-over.

"Met up with some Marines last night, they said my daddy shoulda stood in bed." He tried to smile, but couldn't. It took a moment for his quaking fingers to pinch a twenty out of his billfold—he was thinking about what he would say to the provost marshal general. "This ought to cover it. And if it don't, my wallet's busting with jack."

Galen accepted the bill with a frown. "Anything else?"

"Yeah, I can use a little privacy—and a cold Acme if you got one."

Five minutes later, Jared was talking to a whiny-sounding light colonel somewhere deep within the bowels of the War Department. He claimed to be an aide to the PMG, so Jared took a swig of beer, then told him his name, rank, unit, and that he had a murder implicating Fourth Army personnel to report. He also said that he believed his life was in danger.

The lieutenant colonel asked him for his number, which Jared read off the dial, and promised to phone back shortly.

He hung up wondering if he'd been brushed off as some kind of crank. Then he sat on the counter and glanced around the the store, nursing his beer. The sugar safeguarded behind glass caught his eye. Sacks of it. It was precious enough these days, but time was when ten cents' worth was too much. As impossible to buy as caviar. He hated Galen, and that was probably silly. Times change. But time was—

He jumped as the phone rang. "Campbell here."

The caller identified himself as the provost marshal general of the United States Army and ordered Jared to start from the beginning, to tell everything he knew.

"Yes, General . . ." He fought down a swelling in his throat, then spent the next ten minutes saying things that sounded incredible even to his own ears. He could only pray that he was being believed. At one point he had to wave Galen back out the screen door—the PMG was making him go into that much detail. Finally, he was finished, and the general asked, "Where are you now?"

"Don't exactly know, sir. Some little speck between San Jose and Patterson. A store and garage on a county road."

"The automobile you took—describe it."

"A 'thirty-nine Ford coupe, yellow."

"Very well, Lieutenant, stay where you are. Help is on the way."

"Sir, about Chief Fukuda—"

"We'll see to him as well. Through channels."

After hanging up, Jared strolled the narrow dusty aisles still clutching his furlough satchel. Galen came back in, slamming the door behind him and not bothering to be coy about taking inventory after his brief absence. "You get a statement of charges?"

"Forgot. Just keep the twenty."

"If you say so."

Jared realized that he was hungry. He broke open a tin of butter cookies and then a quart of milk from the musty-smelling refrigerator case. Then he sat down to wait, telling himself that he felt relieved. The wheels had been set into motion.

But those wheels seldom moved with any speed, and it worried him what the PMG had said about seeing to the chief's safety through channels. Manzanar was a long ways from "channels."

Hurriedly brushing the crumbs off his sore, puffy hands, he sent Galen out the screen door with another Jackson portrait, then dialed the operator.

He lied to Bob Cade's secretary, saying he was from Naval

Intelligence. The agent came on the line sounding a bit wary. "How can I help you, Commander?"

"By not hanging up."

"*Campbell?*"

"Don't hang up. Please, Bob. I got them. I got the bastards cold."

A long pause that was sandpapery with static, then, "You talking about the Dutch boys?"

"Yes . . . yes. Diaries and then some."

"How'd you accomplish that?"

"I hit somebody's safe last night."

The agent whistled. "Shit, no wonder the Presidio's locked down today. You behind the fire, too?"

"Give me a minute—I'll tell all. But first you got to help Hank Fukuda."

"Who's he?"

"Listen, save the bullshit. And get on the phone to your L.A. office—hustle a couple of agents up to camp. Have them isolate Hank and somebody else, too . . . jot this down—Kimiko Nitta, Block Twenty-eight—"

Cade gave out with an acidulous laugh. "I don't have a clue what you're carrying on about, plowboy."

"Stop it!" Jared shouted. "You've used Hank all these years—now help save his life, for chrissake!"

After a moment, Cade exhaled. "I'll see what I can do. Where are you now?"

"Outside San Jose," he answered, his voice under control again. "Halfways to Patterson."

"On a beeline back to Manzanar?"

"I was. But I decided to get ahold of the PMG before an accident might come my way. I'm ready to go to the inspector general, too."

"*The* provost marshal?"

The way that Cade had said it made Jared clench the greasy receiver tighter. "What's wrong?"

"Oh, Okie boy—you shouldn't have done that."

"What the hell are you talking about?"

"The PMG, the IG, Van Zwartz—they all tumbled out of the same pod. The same fucking West Point class. Those are the three musketeers who ran roughshod over any objections to the evacuation in the first place. Oh, yeah—you did swell by phoning the PMG."

Jared squeezed his eyes shut. "Thanks for warning me."

"Hey, cowboy, you weren't dealing face up to me either. At least not until now, when your own teat's in the wringer."

"And who the hell left me out in the cold yesterday?"

"Easy, friend—that was before you got your hands on something *useful*."

"Well, I'm hanging on to my goods," Jared said, stubbornly.

"What do you mean?"

"I mean I ain't relying on anybody but me from now on."

"Still thinking of going back to camp?"

"Hell yes. I know you wouldn't understand, Bob, but I figure I owe some people."

"Don't bother. They're not there."

"How's *that?*"

The agent hesitated briefly. "I phoned your captain this morning . . . something happened last night . . ."

Jared thought he was going to be sick. He was afraid he was about to hear something that might end the promise of joy in his life. He didn't want to hear another word and had to steel himself to say, "Go on."

"What do I get in return?"

"Damn you, Cade—"

"Hey, I need *something*. You know that. You know the game."

Jared sank his teeth into his upper arm for a moment. "All right . . . first gander at what I got."

"Good, thanks. Fukuda's been arrested—"

"No, no. . ."

"Some other Japs, too. I'd have to check to see if this Nitta woman was included. But four or five of them are on their way to Tule."

"When'd they leave camp?"

"About five this morning. The director even went along."

"Monty Lee himself?"

"That's what I hear."

Jared checked his watch. "Damn, they're to Reno by now."

"Not by a longshot. Snavely says the truck broke down about a hundred miles north of Manzanar. The MPs supposedly threw a new water pump in a jeep to take up to them."

"Can somebody from your Reno office stop them?"

"The U.S. Army? Stop them from doing what? Transferring some evacuees from one camp to another? No way—not without seeing what's in those diaries first. Why don't you drive on back as far as San Jose? I can leave right now and pick you up in, say, an hour. The train station parking lot. It's a piece of cake to find—"

"Thanks for shit, Bob." Jared hung up and started for the yellow Ford at a run.

CHAPTER 26

At least the truck had broken down in a forest of pines; the scent of their sweet resins was mixed in with that of the rain.

After a while, an hour perhaps, someone came along in a Model A. She knew the tintinnabulation of one by heart. Her frugal father, whose outlook had gradually become as small as the prescription bottles he filled, had owned nothing but rattly used Model As. The man told Montgomery Lee that he would be glad to help the war effort by telephoning the MP garrison from the next town. Lee Vining, he called it. Three hours later—hours of silence between Eddie and herself—a jeep arrived bearing an Army mechanic with a Brooklyn accent who griped that it had taken him all this time to scrounge up a rebuilt water pump that would fit the military Dodge.

Eddie smiled scornfully. Of the five evacuees in the bed of the truck, only he seemed not to accept.

She didn't expect him to beg help off the mechanic; the man was an MP after all and would do nothing. But she sensed that her husband was going to do something. And this frightened her more than it gave her hope—for resisting, he would only be murdered first.

As to the others, they were content to act out their little scenarios of acceptance: the prostitute Yuki, in the attentions she was showering on the chief, whom she loved perhaps; the chief, in his quiet submission to pain; even the sneering *kibei*, who was being vindicated by each new insult to his dignity—he had just been compelled to pee into a lard can that the driver had dug out of a roadside trash can. All had refused Osler's offer of combat rations. And as to herself, she was still weaving the fabric of her own acceptance.

She knew that she was going to die soon.

She had known from the moment that the chief was refused medical attention.

Now, finally, she must become *someone*, she who had been neither Japanese nor American, she who had been so eager to please, so easily slighted, so repressed and marginal a woman.

Eddie, the night he made love to her in such haste and confusion, had offered her the avenue of shrinking back into the kimono. But the roots of her desire didn't lead back into Meiji Nippon—and therein lay the absurdity, the gross insensitivity, of the evacuation! Those roots were in the Renaissance, in the Enlightenment, in Spinoza and Freud, Bach and Gershwin, Rousseau and Darrow—in the intoxication with God called *reason* that was so hopelessly muddled now by the Kingdom of Dogs, the name her *issei* father-in-law so aptly pinned on Manzanar.

Still, as big drops began prattling on the canopy of the truck that would convey her to death, she couldn't drag herself across the ruthless distance to honesty. Not even now, with her right hand chained to a bench.

In her third year of Latin at Stanford, she was reading Juvenal when the line jumped out at her: *Honesty is praised and starves*. And she cried in silence to herself, How *bootchie* a sentiment for a Roman! A Japanese believes that honesty is always at odds with survival.

But survival was no longer the issue, she realized with a frail smile.

Eddie must have noticed the smile and taken his own meaning from it, for he suddenly brushed the side of her face with his lips. It was unusual for him to do this—particularly in the presence of others, but she found herself wishing that she might draw warmth and solace from the dry feel of his mouth on her skin.

But she couldn't, even as she returned his kiss.

Still, he would know the tenderness she now felt for what it truly was. Where were the words? Where?

Outside, tools could be heard being tossed into a metal box: soon the truck would be on the road again.

"Here we go," Eddie said, clearly trying to comfort her, "setting up in another barrack." His soft laugh was less than convincing, and for the first time his eyes betrayed that he too suspected they would never arrive at Tule Lake.

On the other side of the canvas, the *hakujin* were saying good-bye to one another; Montgomery Lee sounded especially affable. It terrified her all over again, his affability.

Then her eyes flooded with tears, but they had nothing to do with Lee. She had just glimpsed how to spin the truth, her personal truth, from all the lies and delusions, the only materials of her life. "Eddie?"

"Yeah?"

"I don't think we should live together when we get there."

He looked hard for the fugitive reasons in her face, then turned away. "I guess," he said at last.

◆ ◆ ◆

"Well, honey, you're gutless—but you're reliable." Affectionately, Jared stroked the dash as the Ford putted past the boundary sign for Yosemite National Park.

The radiator water hadn't come close to boiling. And after one more mountain pass he would be across the Sierra and in Lee Vining, a village straddling the highway to Reno and Tule Lake beyond. Some yokel was bound to have noticed the Dodge deuce-and-a-half, if it had even rolled through yet.

After leaving Galen's Shade Tree Market, he had been

tempted to trade the coupe for something with more power. But the small towns along the way had been no place for auto theft; cars were as familiar as faces. And, besides, just outside a bulge in the road called Chinese Camp he had passed a county cop going the opposite direction, convincing him that Fourth Army was broadcasting nothing at this point. He would keep the Ford, at least until Reno.

The firs and pines were throwing long stripes of shadow across the road. It was going on five o'clock. "Making good time," he kept telling himself. He was reaching inside his pocket for a cigarette when a strange sound made him hold his breath to listen.

"Dang!" He was sure the Ford had thrown its muffler.

But the thunderous roar continued to swell, and then he realized it was coming out of the sky.

A cross-shaped shadow flitted across the road and up into the conifers.

Leaning his head over the steering wheel, he had a glimpse of the aircraft as it pulled out of a steep dive. A P-40—was it the same one he had seen at Crissy Field at the Presidio? No, he told himself, it wasn't likely.

The plane banked to avoid a granite dome, and he could see the flashing of the cylinders out the black exhaust tubes. "God Almighty." He wondered what it would feel like to fly a machine like that. Thrilling, he supposed.

He reached for his pack again and shook up a cigarette. An instant later, it tumbled out of his lips. The roar had swelled again. But this time twin trails of machine gun fire were sparking diagonally across the road in front of him.

"Jesus!" He started to hit the brakes, but then made up his mind to jam down on the accelerator instead. The pilot was warning him to stop. That meant somebody was following by car. The P-40 for damn sure couldn't land on the road and take him into custody. And the somebody in that car had to be Nicholas Bleecher. But how was it possible?

"Think, man, think!" he cried. Then he cranked down his side window and scanned the crowns of the trees.

The Presidio was two hundred miles behind him to the west. Even had Bleecher set off from San Francisco as soon as the provost marshal general briefed him as to where the renegade lieutenant was, the colonel still couldn't have caught up in such a short time.

"*Unless* the prick flew ahead to that airbase near Merced," Jared said, exasperated with himself for not taking the possibility into account. He had circumvented the installation by twenty miles in case the MPs had been ordered to keep an eye out for a yellow 1939 Ford coupe. And it made sense that, while Bleecher hopped into a vehicle commandeered from Army Air Corps and gave chase, the Presidio's P-40 would be busy combing Highway 120, the only trans-Sierra road in these parts, for the Ford. "Dang me! I shoulda wired another car!"

He had no idea how long he'd been under aerial observation. Bleecher must only be minutes behind; the pilot wouldn't have closed in unless the colonel was in position.

Ahead, darkening the crest of the range, was the big storm he had watched from afar all day. A shred of the huge gray mass was being uplifted into an anvil shape. He told himself that no pilot in his right mind would fly into weather like that, and decided to chance the twin .50 calibers. He could be under the clouds in fifteen minutes. Besides, the flyboy probably only had orders to scare the Nazi spy—or whatever it was Van Zwartz was telling his people—into a ditch.

But Jared had no intention of pulling over. Not with Nick Bleecher behind him.

On its next approach the P-40 came straight at him as low as the trees would permit. The circular blur of its propeller blades reflected the red of the setting sun, but the machine gun ports in the wings spit no sparks, and Campbell passed it off as a dry run until the pilot suddenly throttled back and a fat pod plummeted from the undercarriage, glimmering silver as it fell past the wall of clouds.

Christ, Jared thought, grinning with shock, too taken aback to feel anything other than a gallows curiosity, *the bastard has gone and dropped a bomb on me.* Abstractly almost, he watched the plane lumber straight up into the sky, then he faced forward again to see where the bomb would hit. He didn't wonder what the blast would feel like; he only knew it was imminent and didn't bother speculating.

Yet, time slowed as he waited for the flash, the heat, the blackness; and then the bomb struck the pavement ahead of him.

But it failed to disintegrate into orange flame, and instead came skipping toward the windshield, bouncing erratically like an onside kick. He instinctively ducked, but it spun over the top of the Ford and clanged against the asphalt fifty yards behind the coupe before finally veering off into the forest and snapping a young fir in two.

Fuel tank. The bastard had dropped his empty belly tank.

Jared laughed, then wiped his dripping face on his sleeve. The interior of the Ford stank of his fear.

Nothing happened for several minutes. He finally lowered the passenger side window, too, listening for the P-40's next approach.

When it appeared again it came out of the north and lazily executed a banking maneuver. The pilot probably wanted to see what damage he had done. The plane's arc across the sky was so slow that Jared could make out the expression on the man's face. He looked smug. "Hey, hotshot!" Jared slipped his pistol from under the seat and brandished it out the window. "I got one too!" He had no intention of squeezing off a round—God knew it was dicey enough to hit a moving automobile, let alone a machine that could move in three dimensions at once. But he wanted to give the pilot one more thing to think about—he wanted to buy time. Overhead, thin clouds were riffling westward like a flannel sheet.

The pilot rocked his wings, then turned for his next go-around. He had seen the pistol.

The road became a corridor through gigantic trees, redwoods maybe, and Jared hoped their two-hundred-foot height would fend off the P-40. He was halfway down the straight stretch when something drew his eyes to the rearview mirror.

At first he thought it was the sun flickering through the branches. But then the daub of bright red fire unraveled into specks that waffled toward him like the fireballs of a Roman candle.

At last he realized—and began jerking the wheel back and forth, nearly overturning the car as he zigzagged down the road: tracer rounds. Then for a split second, cringing with his eyes half-closed, he imagined himself inside a fifty-gallon drum being beaten with a hammer. His nostrils filled with the stench of scorched upholstery, and he had the feeling that something hot had just whisked past his ear. He glanced up: the felt headliner was hanging down in tatters, smoldering, and in the dashboard was a jagged hole the size of a quarter. He traced the trajectory of the bullet and saw that it slanted directly into the engine block.

"Shit!" Oil vapor, white and pungent, began pouring from the grill and fanning out across the hood.

Meanwhile, the pilot veered sharply against the face of the great anvil-shaped thunderhead, took three victory rolls, and droned off to the west.

Jared watched the oil pressure needle fall as he vainly pumped the gas pedal. Nearly blinded by the smoke, he coasted off the road and onto the mat of dead pine needles, hoping to hide the Ford in the trees. Within spitting distance of the asphalt, however, the tires sank into the soft duff and the coupe came to an abrupt stop.

He listened to the last of the oil dribble out onto the ground. Then he heard a car engine in approach—at top revolutions.

Seizing the canvas satchel in one hand and his .45 in the other, he bailed out of the coupe and strode into the middle of the road.

The staff car barreled out of the shadows, then reduced its speed, finally halting about a hundred feet from where Jared stood waiting. He could see two men in the Plymouth. Bleecher was sitting in the front passenger seat. His driver reached around for something in the back seat, then stepped out.

The driver was Captain Dunnigan, and he was hefting a Thompson submachine gun.

◆ ◆ ◆

Eddie Nitta peered out the slit between the flaps. He had read about Mono Lake, but never seen it.

The bus ride past its salt-encrusted shores with Kimiko beside him on their way to Manzanar had been at night. It was almost night now, and what little light that remained was being blurred by a hard rain. The two volcanic islands out in the middle of the lake were scarcely visible behind the watery curtain. Still, he could discern how barren, how desolate, they were. California's Dead Sea, he remembered it being called in the travel article he had read so long ago.

Finally, he forced himself to look at his wife.

She seemed miserable but also obstinate. The tears probably meant nothing. And he sensed that she might flush with rage should he reveal his own. Still, he felt his rage, rancorously. It fed on the sight of her weary beauty. But he didn't make a show of straining against his handcuff. He would never strike her, and she knew it.

He glanced around the bed of the truck: the others must have overheard, even though the rain was loud against the canvas.

Why did she have to tell him *now?* Or at all, for that matter? Of course, he had suspected something for a long time, but had chalked it up to Dear John paranoia. More recently, he had felt the distance, been galled by it. Only *issei* could ignore emotional distance in marriage. Still, what good was this admission of hers? He cleared the rawness out of his throat and asked her forthrightly, taking pains to suppress the accusatory tone that threatened the civility in his voice.

"I'm not sure, Eddie . . ." Then her expression went blank. It was ghastly. For an instant, he was afraid that she had wanted only pleasure. The notion made him want to cry out like an animal, wordlessly. He was a man and felt he had little control over a woman's pleasure.

But then she whispered, "I needed someone, Eddie."

"*Anyone?*" he demanded, turning to glare at Momai until the *kibei* looked away.

"No," she went on with an infuriating evenness, "someone who could make me see myself *differently* . . . someone to make me less suspicious of myself. . . ." She ran out of words, and the odd mixture of humiliation and resolve came to her eyes again.

"This is all a crock." He choked, then nearly sobbed, but caught himself in time. More than ever, he felt the presence of the others. Of Osler, buffing the moisture off his greasegun with his sleeve. Of Hank Fukuda, floundering in and out of consciousness. Even of the whore, mooning over Hank. Yet their presence also compelled him to make some kind of accommodation with Kimiko. Damn his ingrained *bootchiness*, but he was powerless to resist such an accommodation. The world could blow to pieces, but still the illusion of harmony must be preserved. He wasn't even a man, then; he was a walking calcification of secondhand traditions.

"I suppose I understand." He paused, eyes smarting, but she said nothing—only stared back at him, unblinking. "I failed you . . ."

"No, Eddie—"

He cut her short with a fierce snap of his head. ". . . as a bridge."

"I'm sorry . . . I don't understand."

"Yes, you do. Hell, even with a doctorate, I'd be lucky to land a drafting table someplace. No engineering firm in the country will hire a Jap. We both know that." Then his eyes went cold as they fell on Osler. "But I won't let you down again."

He leaned back against the damp canvas and pretended to sleep.

♦ ♦ ♦

At first Jared thought Dunnigan was going to say something. But then the captain snugged the tommy gun's stock into the crook of his shoulder and squinted down the barrel.

Jared was already diving for the side of the road when the first burst chattered over the sound of the wind. He scrambled against the base of a redwood and returned one shot blindly before picking himself and moving again. As he sprinted into the woods, he could hear a handgun crack twice. Bleecher's.

He thrashed across a swift waist-deep creek, its snow-fed waters burning his flesh with their iciness, and stumbled up the far bank into a copse of willows. He turned, his lungs heaving, and glimpsed Dunnigan in pursuit.

The captain reached into the haversack he had slung over his shoulder for a fresh box magazine, which he then slapped into the Thompson as he ran.

Jared had only one extra clip, and it was tucked away in the satchel. He decided to stay alongside the creek. The din of the flowing waters would help mask the noise of his flight. Maybe if he circled around, leading Dunnigan on a wild-goose chase, he could take Bleecher unawares—and the staff car to boot.

But then the creek meandered out of the trees and across a wide meadow. He hesitated a few seconds, then saw that his only chance to elude the captain was to cross the grassland to the wall of pines on its south side. The ground was spongy and tufted with a wild plant that looked like cabbage. The mud in the low spots almost sucked the shoes off his feet, and his trot was soon reduced to a slog.

Thunder sounded in the distance, and the next gust of wind swirled rain past his eyes.

"Halt!" came a shout from behind, unexpectedly close.

Jared shambled to a stop, dropped the satchel, and raised his left hand as if he'd had enough.

"That's it, peckerwood," the captain said.

"Don't shoot."

"Then ditch that .45."

"You got it." But instead, Jared flopped down in the ooze, twisting as he fell, and fired twice, quickly, without taking aim.

Dunnigan stood his ground and let fly with a long burst.

Jared rolled to the side and laid his dominant right eye over his sights. He could hear Dunnigan's rounds whistling overhead as he drew in a breath and held it. He told himself to take his time, to go at it as if he had all the time in the world.

Long bursts of automatic fire pull the muzzle of a submachine gun high. He could afford to squeeze off careful fire. It was the only way to even the odds.

His first shot did nothing.

Neither did his second, third, or fourth—all high and wide, he guessed, the fear beginning to ice up his guts. He heard frantic wheezing, and was surprised when he realized it was his own.

Again, he rolled a few yards to the side.

Dunnigan dropped a spent magazine out of the Thompson and smartly jammed in another.

Geysers of muddy water sprouted in front of Jared. He ignored them and concentrated only on the black dot he was visualizing in the center of the captain's sand-colored field jacket.

On the second pull of the trigger, Dunnigan vanished.

Thunder crackled in the distance.

He raised up for a quick look and saw Dunnigan's chin, as white as bone china, showing like a little pyramid between the man's yawning knees. His arms were outflung.

Joy twisted Jared's mouth into the semblance of a grin, the savage joy of having won his life back just when he had figured it lost.

But then, through the slanting rain, a crouched figure raced over to Dunnigan's body. Jared hesitated, wondering how many rounds he had left, and in those few seconds Bleecher recovered the Thompson and the haversack, then started walking backward toward the trees.

"Let's talk about this, Colonel!" Jared cried. Nevertheless, his hand tensed around his pistol grip.

Bleecher answered with a short burst, mostly to cover his retreat.

Jared fired only once before the slide snapped back. The pistol was empty. He rushed over to where he had dropped the satchel and, with hands shaking wildly, reloaded with his spare clip.

Bleecher, meanwhile, had withdrawn to a cluster of boulders, from which the muzzle of his Thompson flashed now and again out of the rainy twilight. The colonel had learned something from Dunnigan's death: he was resorting to aimed fire.

Jared could only keep running in a southerly direction, hoping to ambush Bleecher in the forest someplace, or eventually circle back to the staff car, as he had first planned. But he had only taken a few strides when his ankle folded under him. And then more bullets sizzled close by, hissing through the rain. He didn't look down at his leg, but instead kept moving, hobbling until he had reached the line of trees.

Blood was seeping from his left shin. When he wiped it away with his handkerchief, he could see the veiny blue of the exposed bone. The graze was painful, but he didn't figure the bone itself was cracked. Chipped, maybe. "Dang!"

He kept trotting, favoring his left leg.

♦ ♦ ♦

As the sun met the horizon, its rays suddenly pried under the hood of the storm and dazzled through the firs. Jared raised his gun hand to shield his eyes. Raindrops sparkled like gems around him.

The forest floor was falling away—gently in some places, over plunging granite terraces in others.

He was limping heavily now, his shin swollen into the comical shape of one of Popeye's biceps; but the throbbing ache was sickening. He feared resting for even a few minutes. He might not be able to stand up again.

Bleecher had pressed him harder than he'd expected for a man almost fifty, forcing him to trade shots simply to keep the colonel's head down while he limped for the next bit of cover. Maybe the chase, the trail of blood drops, had brought out the predator in Bleecher, helping him overreach himself in canniness and ferocity; or maybe he, too, was scared to death of losing. Whatever—as soon as Jared got a few more yards on him, he intended to circle back and hot-wire the staff car, stranding him.

The setting sun continued to fester in his eyes. And then

a low rumble too drawn out to be thunder reached his ears. It sounded like corrugated tin being rattled by the wind. Then the sun was gone, and an amethyst gulf opened up below him.

"Jesus!"

He halted and clutched himself with his arms—another few feet and he would have stumbled blindly over the 3,000-foot precipice into Yosemite Valley. Nightmarishly far below, a snaking river gleamed like oil in the twilight, and a speck—a touring car, he finally realized—was creeping along a thread of road, its headlights scarcely pinpricks in the gloaming. Turning in the direction of the rumbling noise, he saw where the creek he had been following plunged off the forested plateau, the sheets of water making a tinny sound as they capered over one another down the dizzying distance.

I'm sitting on top of Yosemite Falls, he realized, feeling the mist on his cheek for the first time.

Quickly, before Bleecher could trap him out on the promontory, he clambered up the slope again, looking for a place to cross the creek.

He found it in a fallen lodgepole, stripped of its bark by time. The log straddled a deep whirlpool where the creek—after malingering there in a languid spin, a dollop of foam at its center—seemed to gather speed before racing down a granite chute and finally out over the brink.

Jared kicked the muck off his shoes, then took the rain-slick log a half-step at a time. The water looked cold and troubled as it blurred past his shoes.

He was almost across when he heard twigs crackling behind him, and then the Thompson barked three times.

He dove for the bank, somersaulted, and fired twice at Bleecher's shadow. But the slide clicked open for the last time: he was completely out of cartridges.

He could hear the colonel chuckling. And why not? Bleecher had him cornered in a nest of boulders, with bare ground on three sides of the rocky outcrop and a whirlpool on the fourth.

Jared crawled into a brushy clump of mountain mahogany,

the deadwood snapping loudly as he burrowed down to await Bleecher's inevitable advance.

"Campbell?"

"Evening, Colonel."

"I can't see you."

Now it was Jared's turn to chuckle. But the chuckle died in his throat as an idea came to him. He hurled the satchel out into the open, where the colonel would be sure to see it.

"Why'd you do that?" Bleecher called out.

"I'm finished. Goods are yours again."

"Bullshit. You expect me to stroll out there and pick it?"

"After siccing that kid on me in Chinatown I don't know what to expect from you, sir. All I know is, I'm finished. Even if you don't do me in here, I'll need piped-in sunshine where you're going to squirrel me away."

Bleecher sounded amused. "That's true enough."

"How about a taste of the truth from you, too?"

The colonel was silent for a few moments. "You mean you want to *know?*"

"Hell, who wouldn't? Tell me how this all came about and I'll toss over my piece."

"Come on, Campbell—why would you want to do that?"

"Like I said—I'm finished. You hit me in the leg back there."

"Prove it—stand up."

"Well, I ain't ready to do that. But have yourself a look at this . . ." Jared tied a stone in his bloodied handkerchief and threw it across the creek in the direction of Bleecher's voice.

The colonel laughed gleefully. "I *thought* I got you!"

"You sure did, sir."

"Break the bone?"

"Don't rightly know. Hurts enough to be broke. Whatever, I'll need help back to your car."

"All right, we'll talk. But first, let's up the ante on this little quid pro quo."

"How's that, Colonel?"

"Level with me—what possessed you to take the Jap side in this?"

"That's easy. You lied to me. Used me. Kinda agitated me, and I don't take to being agitated."

"Is that all it takes with you people?"

"Us people?" Jared began sifting through the dead limbs, looking for one that hadn't been riddled by carpenter ants. Mountain mahogany was a heavy wood; it wouldn't even float. "You mean cops?"

"I mean *Okies*. That's what got me when you started overstepping your bounds in San Diego—the evacuation of Jap farm labor has done nothing but open up jobs for you Dust Bowl trash."

Jared smiled. "Guess I never looked at it that way."

"Well, don't bother now. What do you want to know?"

"Why in God's name did you give Monty Lee a job, knowing what you did about his past?"

"You've just answered your own question. I hired him *because* of his past."

"I see." Jared tested a five-foot branch by tapping it against rock. The wood, although silvered with age, sounded solid. "Meaning, you wanted to stir up things at Manzanar, not tone them down. Just like Shido and his Black Dragon boys wanted to keep things in a tizzy for their own reasons. Monty and Shido—it don't figure. And, then again, it figures perfect."

"You're smarter than you look, Campbell. That's been the real revelation in this thing. And it's too bad. I could use a man like you. You have a certain hillbilly cunning I admire."

"Thank you, sir, but there ain't many hills where I come from. This all makes me think you folks had something to do with the riot back in 'forty-two."

"Yes, but that's another story. And I'm not going to wait for it to get dark so you can slip away."

"Then I'll stick to the point. What was the plan before I stepped in and bitched it up?"

"Simple. Masao Shido would have appeared to have blown

the aqueduct, then killed himself to swallow the blame. Japs finally commit sabotage, and Congress makes sure Japs get repatriated after this war. But then Lee went wild, opening up all kinds of possibilities. You opened others. We improvised."

"But how'd Monty get Shido to do himself?" Jared asked.

"He cut a separate deal with Shido's sidekick in the Black Dragon. Some yahoo named Momai. Know of him?"

"Sure do—nasty little monkey."

"Well, he stood to take over Shido's slice of the black-market pie. So he drummed poor old Masao out of what was left of the gang on some trumped-up violation of *Bushido*. Disgraced him—you know how their minds work. And then Lee put the icing on the cake by threatening to expose old Masao to the whole camp as the thief who'd been stealing sugar out of babies' formula."

"But didn't Shido have the goods on Monty, too?"

"Sure, but who the hell was going to take an evacuee's word over the associate director's? Shido knew he'd been had."

"Got a point there, sir. But here's the nut I haven't been able to crack—how'd Monty get inside the judo *dojo* with nobody seeing him?"

"In some kind of Jap costume—at least that's what he told me."

"I'll be damned." Thoughts swarmed Jared's mind as it all promised to mesh together, but he forced them aside. "You mean to kill those evacuees you're trucking up to Tule right now?"

"I have no idea what Mr. Lee intends—we're out of touch. But I wouldn't preclude an accident along the way. Even an attempted escape. These are some pretty dangerous people. As we might reconstruct from your preliminary report, Shido blew up the aqueduct, then his partner, Major Nitta, helped him commit *seppuku* before calling it a night by lopping off poor old Morris Wenge's noggin. Rabid, fanatical Japs."

"*Why*, Colonel?"

"The big reason, I'm sure you mean."

"You bet . . . that's what I'm trying to get a handle on."

"Well, you might find it hard to understand, given your proclivity for yellow flesh . . ."

Jared's jaws tightened: they knew about Kimiko and him. He found this more unsettling than anything Bleecher had yet revealed.

". . . nevertheless, Campbell, we are now concluding a war between the white man and the colored man. And the entire issue of this struggle has been: Which shall predominate?"

"At OCS, they told me it was between democracy and fascism. Between law and no kind of law at all."

The colonel laughed. "I'm sure they did."

"And I believed them. Millions of guys like me believed them."

"I commend each one of you."

"And we piss on you, Colonel. Every last damned one of us pisses on you—for trying to twist the truth into a lie."

Bleecher said nothing for a moment. Then: "You changing your mind about going easy?"

"No, I just had to speak my piece. I'm finished and know it."

"Then get up so I can see you."

"Can't."

"The hell you say, Campbell."

"My leg's so swelled now the skin's shiny. I shouldn't a sat down. But I'll chuck over my .45 like I promised."

"Do it."

Jared regarded his pistol with a frown, then hurled it in Bleecher's direction. "So how you going to explain whatever happens to me?"

"There'll be no need. That's the beauty of an emergency like a war—you don't need to explain anything."

"Certainly some four-star over Van Zwartz's head will have a question or two."

"Then you were an accessory to the crimes committed by Shido and Major Nitta."

"Wouldn't that be a tight stretch?"

"Not when it's revealed that you were fucking Nitta's wife, apparently with his approval."

Jared fought his anger, then smiled coldly to himself. "Ain't a thing you can't make seem ugly and mean."

"It's a talent. I was one hell of a prosecutor. And after the war I'll make one hell of an attorney general. And then governor. You have any other weapons? A knife?"

"Yeah, I got me a pocket knife."

"Throw it in the drink."

He did so.

"All right, Campbell, I'm coming across. From now on, stay down until I order otherwise. If I see you move, I'll kill you."

"I understand."

He lay flat with his cheek against the dead limb. For the first time he realized that he was soaked and chilled to the bone. Whatever happened, this man could not be allowed to survive, to go back to the Presidio and take up where he had left off. He had to die so others might live.

Then he heard the hollow thudding of shoes on the fallen log.

Jared bolted up and flung the limb at Bleecher.

The colonel batted the deadwood aside with the Thompson, but the maneuver cost him his balance. Letting go of the submachine gun, he landed athwart the slippery log on his midriff—his body folded there for a split second, his eyes enraged—before he slid into the pool, vanishing briefly.

Bursting to the surface, gasping from the cold, he began treading water. "You fucking Okie! What was that supposed to prove?"

Jared stared down at him blankly.

Without realizing it, Bleecher had been caught by the slow spinning of the vortex. He dug a hand into his inner coat pocket and brought out a revolver, which he tried to level on Jared.

But he never got to discharge it.

The current buffeted him completely around, then impelled him into the mouth of the chute. After that, for a hundred cascading yards, the creek was hemmed in by granite parapets that steadily rose higher and higher over his head. Dropping the revolver, the colonel clawed at cracks in the stone, even at hanging clumps of wildflowers, as the roar of the falls swelled.

Jared hobbled along the shelf above, watching as Bleecher began to swim, holding his own against the swift current for a few seconds. Then, utterly exhausted, he gave up and was driven downstream again.

"Save me!" he screamed, his face seemed to be all eyes.

"I can't," Jared said, although he doubted the man could hear him. "You'd only kill me." He glanced ahead and could now see where the creek surged out into the stormy sky.

Bleecher tried scissors-kicking, and managed to get half his torso out of the water by the sheer hysteria of his efforts just as the crystal flow bent downward and disintegrated into curtains of foam.

He thrashed around one last time before he slipped over the edge and was gone.

CHAPTER 27

He had fallen asleep in an ocean of wheat, his hand cramped around his Colt Detective Special. A combine was working its way toward him, slash by voracious slash. He could hear the cutter bars clattering. He rose—and then saw at his feet the dead baby wrapped in the arms of her dead fool daddy, shot through the head, both of them, sprawling in the ripe wheat, turning black under the harvest sun. He tried to run, but had no legs. Besides, there was no possibility of joy after seeing this, and that possibility was what made it worth strapping a body to your soul for seventy years. You gagged on reality, but kept tasting the possibility—that was fucking life, wasn't it? So he turned willingly into the blades, and the machine roared down on him like a tornado, swept him up in its gleaming arms, and threshed him to pieces. He felt himself shaking apart into pieces.

"Ah!" Jared's eyes clicked open.

Crying out again, he spun the steering wheel hard to the left, and then right just as sharply when he sensed he had gone too far left. The brakes screamed as the Plymouth broadsided out into the sage, the headlamps skimming over the tops of brushy hummocks.

The staff car drifted to a stop without overturning. But his hot-wire had jarred loose, and the engine died.

He sat nursing a crick in his neck for a moment, then slowly shut his eyelids—they felt like welts, like shiners from a tavern brawl.

He listened, not sure if the sound he heard was the ticking of the overheated engine as it started to cool or the storm pelting the roof.

Finally, he got out and unlatched the hood, his hands still aching from the punctures caused by the Presidio's concertina. The rain spit and hissed on the exhaust manifold as he reattached the wire to the battery terminal. Then, bracing himself against the pain that dogged his slightest movement, he shuffled back inside the Plymouth and lifted his wounded leg to let in the clutch. The swelling on his shin was deep purple and feverish to the touch. He groaned helplessly, then stubbed the starter button and pulled back onto the highway.

North of Carson City but still south of Reno, he reminded himself. A few minutes later a mileage sign slipped past in a blur. Only when its silvery backing was shining in his brakelamps did he realize what it had been. "Dang . . . let's pay attention here."

It was half past one. Earlier, he had sensed empty periods of time between checks of his watch that might well have been sleep. Now he knew.

He rolled down his window to the humid coolness and damned the wiper blades for trying to kill him with their mesmerizing rhythm. But the rain was too heavy to turn them off.

"God Almighty, I can use a cup," he said, his voice an ugly rasp. But he couldn't force himself to stop, not even for a minute to run inside an all-night diner. He feared that he'd wind up regretting those sixty seconds for the rest of his life. He tried not to think about Kimiko and the chief. It did no good to think about them.

Time. Figure the time again. Juggle it in your head, boy, and see if there's still time. . . .

♦ ♦ ♦

At nine o'clock earlier that evening, in darkness and a ripping downpour, he had arrived back at the Plymouth staff car Bleecher had indeed borrowed from the Army Air Corps at Merced. He rummaged inside the glovebox by the flickering glow of his Zippo and was gratified to find a flashlight. The colonel and his captain had set out fully expecting trouble: a combat medical bag lay on the floorboards. Jared took out the sulfa and dusted his foreleg and his hands, but didn't touch the Syrettes—he had no use for a morphine jag. Then, with what was left of his waning strength, he pushed the disabled Ford farther into the trees and kicked pine needles over the tire tracks, hoping neither would be noticed by the party that would soon be sent out to search for the colonel. He staggered back to the Plymouth and sat behind the wheel, only to grope for a key that wasn't in the ignition. That meant Bleecher had thought to remove it, for Jared had frisked Dunnigan's body, finding only a loaded .45 in a shoulder holster, which he saved. Using wire torn from the Ford, he hot-wired the staff car and was squatting with jack handle in hand, preparing to deal with the accelerator governor, when a cackle welled up from the back seat.

He jumped away, stumbling to regain his balance as he whipped the .45 out of his waistband.

Silence.

He approached the rear door and threw it open, then stared a few moments before letting go of the breath he'd pent up. He would have sworn that he had seen Bleecher back there for a second, raging whitely at him with the same expression he had worn as he went over the falls. He knew then that if he survived he would see that face for years—it would ruin his sleep for years.

But finding a radio in the back seat brought on such a tangle of speculation that he soon forgot about Bleecher's ghost.

At best, the Signal Corps Radio 300 handset had a range of a few miles. The colonel had probably been using it to communicate with the P-40. But what if, by some fluke, he'd been able to raise Merced and give his location before Dunnigan and he had bailed out to give chase? As the crow flies, Merced was maybe sixty miles from Yosemite Creek here, but there was also nothing in between except mountain air. And then there was the pilot to think about. Surely, on his return to the Presidio, he had briefed Van Zwartz. And just as surely, after hours dragged past with no word from the colonel, the general had ordered somebody to investigate the area where the pilot claimed to have forced the Ford coupe off the road.

Quickly, he aimed the flashlight on the post-type governor beneath the accelerator pedal. Dunnigan had already bent it over. Jared was about to mutter something about the captain not being half-bad after all, when it suddenly struck him as not being funny, even to his own ears.

Three men. He had killed three in the last twenty-four hours. It didn't seem possible.

By ten o'clock, he was speeding down the far side of Tioga Pass and into an electrical storm so frenetic he might have imagined himself back in Oklahoma, except that he was winding through a series of switchbacks blasted out of a sheer mountainside. He had to lean close to the windshield and then keep wiping the steamy glass with his sleeve to see anything. Each hairpin was a blind curve, a paved ramp to oblivion, and on the straightaways he had to dodge rockfalls. On bends and straight sections alike, he had to guess where the center of the road lay, for the asphalt was black and ripply from the inch of runoff sheeting across it, and the night seemed to suck the brightness out of his headlamps, leaving them as faint as candle lanterns.

When he finally reached Lee Vining at eleven, he found nothing open and had to climb a flight of exterior stairs to the darkened apartment over a small grocery. After listening to the old bugaboo about "a matter of national security," the owner threw on a slicker and trooped down with him to the gasoline pump, where he dispensed ten gallons in violation of the godly power of the local rationing board. "I'll tell you the truth, soldier—I don't like this."

Jared gave him five extra bucks to sweeten his disposition, then asked, "You see an Army two-and-a-half-ton go through today? Northbound?"

"Not today."

He felt a crush of disappointment. Maybe Bleecher had found a way to warn Lee that Jared was looking for him, and the truck had returned to camp. At that point, he didn't know what to think or do.

"But a big Dodge come through about six this evening," the grocer went on, "headed north."

Jared almost allowed himself a smile: that put them about four hours ahead of him. It would be close. Then again, maybe there was no hope and he was only kidding himself. He tried to do some calculations of time and distance in his head, but a wave of dizziness wiped them out. "You see anybody in the back?"

"Don't recall. Flaps was down, I think."

And off he accelerated into the night once again, the lightning seeming to follow him as it twitched in reflection on the surface of Mono Lake. Drenched pinion pine and sage smells came rushing in through the windwing along with glancing raindrops that stung his face, a good feeling. But eventually he stopped believing he could stay awake. He felt his spirit slowly fading; it was like dying, this gradual dimming of his spirit. Over a hundred miles of mesmerizing roads, crossing the Nevada line, through darkened ranch towns, and then into that small township of a state capital, Carson City, his exhaustion set up like concrete. At times he could barely stir his leaden limbs to shift gears.

The only thing to pierce his washed-out consciousness was the fear that a roadblock would be awaiting him around the next bend. He began to brake for each curve, and once he'd hollered as if from a nightmare when he saw shifting lights and imagined in them the silhouettes of a dozen MPs. But they had turned out to be a couple of bomb-shaped signal pots laid out by the highway department to mark a flooded spot.

The prospect of being arrested didn't unnerve him. It was bound to happen; he had resigned himself to a spell in a stockade. But what if the evidence in his satchel were destroyed? Then he would have nothing to save him from the gallows, nothing to explain why he'd had to kill Bleecher and Dunnigan and the Chinese zoot suiter. And Van Zwartz could hang anybody he wanted with no one becoming the wiser. There were stories, mostly out of some military prison in England, of GIs being court-martialed and hanged all within the same day.

No, the evidence was his lifeblood, Kimiko and the chief's, too, and he had to make sure it didn't fall into the hands of Fourth Army.

But who could he turn to outside Western Defense Command? Not the PMG, not even the IG—if Cade's information could be trusted. He needed a friend in a high place, and he'd never had such a friend in all his life.

These had been his thoughts as he'd drifted off into the dream of the dead baby and her dead fool daddy, only to startle awake to the staff car plowing sideways through the brush.

◆ ◆ ◆

Now, with Reno's lights in the distance, made bleary by the rain, he came up with somebody he might be able to trust, a man already familiar with James Van Zwartz and Nicholas Bleecher. A man in a high place, but not a lordly man. An unassuming man in a high place, then.

He massaged his fiery eyes with his fingers.

There was just one fly in the ointment: the man was in China.

Still, he would try. He just needed a little local help. He thought of the hooker he had hired to tend his Reno hotel room, but she had probably taken his money and run.

Still, he would try.

Flicking on the flashlight and propping it under his thigh, he dug in the satchel for his fountain pen and the Pinkerton file. Between glances up at the roadway, he began scribbling out his letter on the front of the folder. For once in his life, he didn't stew over his spelling and grammar. The words poured out of him and onto the folder.

♦ ♦ ♦

South from the hotel, Virginia Street was so straight she almost thought she could see Los Angeles, five hundred miles away. She kept watch in that direction for the two o'clock bus, the last of the night. It would take her home, where first thing she would fix herself a bourbon and milk, then open the letter from her son in the Quartermaster Corps. She had been hoarding it all swing shift, imagining as she wiped the greasy smudges off the slot machines and vacuumed the green carpet under the blackjack tables what he would have to say about France. They were supposed to have different ideas about race, the French.

Her nose was running a little—from the cold mist following the rain, she thought. She dabbed it with her fingers. As always, they smelled of ammonia; she didn't like it, but had gotten used to it.

Headlights glimmered a far ways down Virginia. For a moment she thought it might be her bus, but then she saw that the lights were spaced too close together for a bus, and that this vehicle was coming like a cannonball, stopping for nobody.

The rain started up again suddenly, as if somebody in the sky had dumped a big pail on Reno. The drops drummed overhead on the copper awning, and she burrowed deeper into the mauve woolen coat she had brought out of mothballs early this year.

The speeding vehicle was a brown Army car, and she immediately thought of her son. He drove a truck. In France.

All at once, the driver braked as if he had run over a dog and pulled to the curb beside a wire trash basket. The soldier, a big ofay with *shoulders*, got out and limped around the front of the car to the basket. He began tearing through the rubbish, looking for something, looking over the bigger pieces of paper, even the newspapers, then growling and throwing them aside.

"My, my," she chuckled to herself, the steam running away from her mouth.

He hurried back into the car and drove another half-block before braking again in front of the post office. There, he hobbled up the stone steps with some kind of traveling bag in tow and disappeared inside for a few minutes. He came back down looking twice as out of sorts as before, and sat behind the wheel for a minute or so, before inching across the Truckee bridge to her side of the river. His eyes fastened on her.

Then he veered right and parked in front of the hotel.

She clutched her purse tighter.

Slowly, he opened his door and climbed out, then rested his elbows on the roof of the car. He didn't seem to realize it was raining. There were scratches on his face, and his uniform was all a mess, wet and torn. He had been in a fight, sure to say, though it was hard to believe he had come out on the short end of it, seeing how burly he was.

"I need help . . ."

"I don't know you," she said defensively. But she also recognized his to be a nice face. There was no anger deep in it, just a lot of pain on the surface right now. His voice was soft and tired. But she heard herself saying, "I got no money. You know I'm poor. You know that, soldier."

His nod was in the nature of an apology: he didn't like doing whatever it was he was doing. "I know. That's why I'm asking you this favor. You can trust the poor. They'll help you out. The rich sure as hell won't."

She found herself laughing. He had an easy sincerity, a way of keeping his slow-moving body in tune with his words. "You drunked up?"

"No, Auntie." He grinned a little.

"Name's Evelyn."

"Proud to meet you, Evelyn. Mine's Jared."

"What you need so awful bad tonight?"

"Well . . ." His eyes drifted north along Virginia. "I got to be on my way. But I need something mailed first thing in the morning."

"Is that all?"

"I got no pasteboard box, no wrapping paper, nothing. How's the road north?"

"Bad—flooded, truckers say. But truckers say everything's bad." She scrutinized him for a few more seconds. "Give me your mail. Write out the address."

He ducked back inside the car and penned something on the back page of a little book before ripping it out and gathering up more of the books and a folder, which he then shielded from the downpour with his body as he brought them over to her.

She glanced at the stack of materials, then into his pale eyes. "Law after you?"

"Yeah." He surprised her. "But not the law the way it oughta be. Something's wrong and I got stuck trying to put it right. God knows I wasn't looking for a quarrel. I never liked a quarrel." His head lolled to the side for a moment, like he was dizzy. "And now I'm afraid they'll get me before I can put it right. They already come close to getting me. They'll be trying again up the line, sure as hell. So I got to make sure the truth survives, even if I don't. Can you understand what I'm saying, Evelyn?"

Her reply was a sad, throaty laugh. Then she took the stack from him. "And I suppose you don't want me looking at none of this stuff."

"I wouldn't—for your sake. It's just pure devilry. But I'm leaving that up to you."

Ignoring the green wad he was slipping into her coat pocket, she read the address out loud: "APO . . . San Francisco . . . China-Burma-India Theater of Operations." She looked up and smirked. "You kin to this General Stilwell?"

"No."

"Then why you having me put the name Stilwell on the return address, too?"

"So nobody'll open it along the way."

"You sure keep to the sly side of goodness!"

He gave her arm a squeeze, then limped back to the driver's

door. There was blood around a tear in his trouser leg; she hadn't noticed it before. He paused before getting back inside. "You got a boy in uniform, don't you?"

"Now how'd you know that?"

"God love ya, Evelyn." Then he sped off just as the driver of her bus, the rain sparking down past the big headlights, tapped his horn for him to clear the space.

God love ya. The way he had said it made her wish she had argued a little about the money. She felt even worse when she saw it was a fifty-dollar bill. No—two of them.

"Damn you, ofay . . . ain't nothing free with you."

CHAPTER 28

Hank Fukuda awoke to the tires sizzling through deeper and deeper water. Then the wheelwells were filled with sloshing noises, and the truck churned to a stop. Its engine continued to rumble for a few minutes, then died, leaving a quiet in which rain could no longer be heard pattering against the canopy. A thin light was filtering through the canvas. Too early for dawn, so he decided it was the moon. This would mean that the storm was clearing and the Dodge would make better time—toward what, he tried not to think about.

He felt little pain now and could almost imagine that he was floating a foot or two above his stretcher, hovering on his palpable hatred for the *hakujin*.

The moonlight gave his fellow evacuees nimbuses like icons, although their faces were yet in shadow. Only Osler, slumped closest to the light at the parting in the flaps, had features—sleep had erased his habitual scowl; his lips had flews like a dog's, the chief noticed for the first time.

In the cab, Montgomery Lee mumbled something to the driver, but Hank couldn't make out the words. He sounded cross. After a night of soggy mountain roads, he was exhausted.

Everyone was stuporous; even Momai was giving out a steady, cottony snore.

Fingers brushed the fringe of Hank's hair, and he looked up.

Yuki.

She was lying on the bench above him, her face dangling over the edge. It was too dark for him to glimpse her expression, but he could feel her smile as if it were an ember. And when her fingertips trickled across his lips, he surprised himself and kissed them.

She reached down for his hand, desperate with affection. But there was something else in the soft pressure of her grasp.

He squeezed back, hard, although the mere use of his arm muscles triggered spasms in his head and stomach.

"Yes . . . thank you," he whispered, for he suddenly found himself desiring the thing she was offering in the gloom of the truck. It wasn't her body. She had a stubby shape, almost comically so. Nor was it her butterfly lips, which might have been sensual had they appeared more pouting. And, in truth, the chief knew that he couldn't be gratified in the midst of such bodily torment. No, it was something else entirely he needed.

Yuki Ota knew how to restore a man's balance. Sometimes, she would siphon off his lust so he might go calmly among other men again. She would swallow his spite whole, for cash, and by this reckoning she was a whore. But that reckoning was too severe, too unkind, for in everything she did Yuki seemed selflessly mindful of the harm even one unbalanced man can inflict on the world. And now she was reminding him to forget everything except the warmth of her hand.

Soon, he stopped hating Lee and Osler and all the others, the bastards who sold mock Jap-hunting licenses, the American Legionnaires who would revel in the newspaper reports of his destruction. And when he stopped hating, he began to feel safe. Inordinately safe.

The truck wasn't moving, although water was chortling

around the tires. He didn't know what to make of that. Trying not to think, he clasped Yuki's hand.

And finally slept. He dreamed of his mother.

◆ ◆ ◆

"Why have we stopped?" Kimiko asked Eddie quietly. After endless miles of silence, she wanted to hear him talk.

"Sounds like a flash flood. It'll go down in a while." He said nothing more, the molten forces within him continuing to build beneath his brittle exterior. Niggardly—his refusal to show his rage was niggardly; but she found herself too weary to goad it out of him. She no longer felt the need to be punished. Dying would be punishment enough.

An hour passed, and the waters didn't recede. On the contrary, the driver had to start the engine and back up a short distance when rocks driven along by the swelling flood could be heard tumbling across the asphalt.

Osler stirred once, massaged his chin where it had been resting against the greasegun on his chest, then dozed off again. His forefinger never left the trigger.

Kimiko could tell that Eddie was watching the sergeant.

Hank appeared to be sleeping once again. Minutes before, she had seen Yuki reach down and touch his face, then take his hand. In profile now, the young woman could be seen fixating on him as if he were an object of meditation. It all seemed exquisitely appropriate; that these were their final hours made anything seem appropriate, Kimiko realized with a sudden flux of terror.

With her free hand she reached for Eddie's.

Violently, he shook off her searching fingers.

But she tried again.

This time he hesitated before freeing himself, and from that she took hope. He could not forgive her—his was too rigid a nature for that. But he might sense that he had not failed her—at least, not in any way she would ever rebuke him for it. She was extravagantly fond of Tadashi Nitta; after all, she had consented to become his wife without being in love with him. Clumsily, her hand tried to say this for her in the predawn darkness.

Then the engine fired and the truck rolled forward again, the tires picking up the silt laid down by the flash flood and hurling it against the splash guards.

◆ ◆ ◆

The insides of Hank Fukuda's eyelids were a translucent orange. He opened them on strong morning light.

Osler had finally tied up the flaps, and over the lip of the tailgate the chief could see a reddish hillside pocked with green smudges that became junipers when he strained to focus his double vision. He had heard that the hills around Tule Lake were clad with junipers, and there was now a faint gin smell to the calm air.

Yuki was asleep with one side of her face flattened by the bench. A bead of spittle had collected in the corner of her mouth.

Osler was wide-awake, watching the terrain slip past in eroded undulations. His hands were clutching the greasegun by both pistol grip and magazine, but then he wiped his eyes with his forearm, almost as if he felt an urgency to keep them clear.

All at once, the driver backed off the accelerator, and the truck began to glide. The brake shoes grated against their worn, glazed linings, sending a shudder up Hank's spine.

Yuki yawned and sat up as the driver turned off the paved road. The risen sun poured into the back of the truck, and her skin was suffused with a rich honey color. She would never look prettier, Hank realized sadly. The front wheels thudded across a shallow ditch and then, rocking from side to side, the truck climbed a gentle incline for about half a minute. Where Lee told the driver to park, the Dodge was partially hidden from the highway by a cone of black sand the road department had piled up for winter use.

Osler let the tailgate drop with a crash, and Hank almost cried out: it had been like a grenade going off inside his skull.

Both doors to the cab groaned open, then slammed shut.

Footfalls crunched across the moist, gritty soil to the back of the truck, and Lee's face floated into view, his forehead no longer bandaged. Although Hank couldn't quite squint the man's expression into focus, he could see the jagged line of crusted blood on his brow. The MP driver was resting the butt of a carbine on his hip.

"*Benjo*-break," Lee said tonelessly to the first sergeant. "Uncuff them."

"You sure?"

Lee paused. "I'm sure."

Hank caught a glimmer of something from the exchange: Osler wasn't fully won over to whatever Lee had in mind. Was there reason for hope in this?

"Why don't we cuff them in pairs before letting them out, sir?" Osler asked, a hint of pleading in his voice. Yes, the chief told himself, it was all great fun in the planning, jawing about annihilating some Japs; but now that Osler had had time and several hundred miles to think about it, he'd gotten cold feet. For good reason. It's hard to orchestrate a massacre. And then the killing itself requires either insane rage or inhuman calculation—a lummox like Osler could muster neither at a moment's notice.

And then the moment had arrived.

Hank wanted it to be over, the anxiety to be blotted out. He prayed for oblivion. A flight of ravens rustled overhead—how far would they wing by nightfall?

"Kindly do as I say, Sergeant," Lee went on, his tone of voice so reasonable it sounded utterly demented under the circumstances. "Uncuff the prisoners so they can relieve themselves. I don't want them fouling themselves."

Osler had to clear his throat to speak. "Yes, sir."

"Mr. Momai and the private here will carry down Chief Fukuda's stretcher and set it on the ground. Release his belts so he might relieve himself as well—if he wishes."

Osler questioned this, too, but Hank found himself more interested by the familiar way in which Monty had addressed Momai—the two men shared a past; it was obvious in the slack way Lee had used Momai's name. Still, he knew he would die without knowing the full truth. Death makes the truth irrelevant, he reminded himself, unless you believe in God or Buddha or something. This year was the 2,510th birthday of Lord Buddha—an observation without special meaning; it had simply occurred to him. He tried to swallow.

The driver shouldered his carbine so he could help Momai pick up the stretcher. Attentively, Lee watched them. He held a .45 in his left hand, but he also had a revolver tucked in his waistband. Why two handguns, when Osler and the driver were more than adequately armed for the coming business?

Strangely then, Lee looked up as if he expected something dreadful to come out of the sky.

Hank's vision exploded into a blinding field of white as he was hoisted and jostled out of the truck. This bright agony faded only when his stretcher was rested on the ground.

He stared out across the rain-washed sagelands, the slopes still in shadow looking dusty, but those lit by the sun glittering, alive with a temporal beauty he ached to freeze in his mind's eye. He had wasted a lifetime by not being constantly engrossed by the beauty of the world. He wanted the driver to hurry and loosen his restraints so he could rub his hands together, then clap them once, sharply, as his grandfather had done a thousand times to summon a certain *kami*, the compelling spirit of the present. *Naka-ima*, the middle present, the moment of complete now, the most cherished of all conceivable times. It made sense now. A vivid present banishes an intolerable future—his grandfather had known . . . the old man had known.

"I don't think Fukuda has to go, Mr. Lee," Osler said with a joking lilt to his voice, which otherwise had turned tremulous. "He already got the shit beat out of him."

"Unbind him!" Lee shouted, his eyes blazing. "Do as I order, sailor!"

The sergeant stood gaping at Lee. "I'm not—"

"Do you understand what an order is, sailor?"

Hank had to close his eyes, so piercing was this last cry.

When he opened them, they were filled with Yuki, who was massaging the wrist Osler had just uncuffed.

Eddie Nitta and Momai were standing at the foot of the sand pile, their backs to the women. The major was issuing a steaming arc of urine into the black sand; but the *kibei* only sighed—after miles and miles of sitting on his kidneys, he was having trouble getting started.

Buttoning up his fly, Eddie glanced over his shoulder and gave Hank a slight nod. It was conspiratorial, and the chief wanted to return one of his own, but he had no idea how he could help the major overpower the three well-armed *hakujin*. He didn't even think he could sit up.

Unexpectedly, Lee knelt beside him and said so the others couldn't hear, "Can you speak?"

Hank shook his head no.

"No matter." Lee brought the revolver out of his waistband and held it in his right hand. "Know what this is?"

He shrugged as if to say, So what—a snub-nosed .38 special.

"Jared's." Lee smirked, and the skin over the bridge of his nose thinned whitely. "The one he slipped to you before he went on furlough . . . the one you hid on your person until now. . . ."

Hank turned his face away angrily—this was how Lee intended to justify the murders to the country: he would plant a throwaway gun on the chief's corpse.

When he rolled his head back toward the man, Lee had risen and was saying to Kimiko, "You and Miss Ota may retire to the brush out there to attend to your needs." Kimiko looked cold and ill; she was clutching herself with her arms. "The others and I shall avert our eyes—"

"No," Hank croaked.

Lee spun around, his eyes strangely exultant. "What was that, Chief?"

Hank said to the two women, "Don't go. He wants us to spread out. Make it look like we ran . . ." He had to pause for breath. "Stand pat. Make them drag our . . . bodies . . . leave bloodstains . . ."

He struggled to explain that only in this way might Lee's falsification of the scene be betrayed by some physical evidence. An investigator, perhaps even Jared, might then salvage the truth from the carnage. But the effort to speak was too taxing, and the breathless daze in which he found himself was only a shade of gray lighter than semi-consciousness. His restraints had been removed, but still his arms felt like lead ingots.

"Come on, Mr. Lee," Osler nearly whined, "let's load them up and get on into Tule."

For several moments there was only the sound of Lee inhaling and exhaling, huffing as if he were hiking up a mountain. Again, he glanced skyward. "Riffraff," he said at last.

Then a shot cracked the quiet and echoed into the hills.

It begins. Straining, Hank lifted his head a few inches off the stretcher. But what he saw confused him: none of the evacuees was down.

Then he noticed that Momai was perched on the balls of his feet as if he were about to leap into the air. He had finally been able to urinate, and his stream was still curving down into the sand when, in an instant, its color went from yellow to a cloudy red. Slowly, he sank to his knees, his fist yet holding his penis as he collapsed. A crescent of blood appeared on the lower back of his shirt.

"Top!" the driver cried, stumbling backward and seizing Osler by sleeve. The first sergeant was too stunned to push away the private's clinging hand. "Jesus!"

His eyes open wide in amazement, Momai twisted his upper body around. A gush of blood from his belly revealed a ghastly exit wound—an artery had been clipped, and he was flagging fast. His head began to bob drunkenly, but he continued to stare at Lee, who was brandishing both the pistol and the revolver, though the chief believed from the sound of the report that Momai had been shot with the snub-nosed.

"Domo arigato," Momai thanked him, then went on in Japanese, "You have vindicated me."

Lee shook his sweaty head. He too resorted to Japanese, surprising Hank with his proficiency. "I have simply made an end of you."

He fired again, driving Momai spread-eagled against the sand. Hearing boots thumping the ground in retreat, he spun around and growled when he saw Osler running for the road. "Where do you think you're going, Gunner's Mate?"

"Let's get outa here!" the sergeant shouted, shading his eyes as he peered down the highway. "A fucking car's coming!"

"I told you this would happen," Lee said derisively, but with a rapt smile pasted to his face. "And I told you not to lock the ready boxes. But you perceived no threat—you and the goddamned captain said we'll have no trouble upriver from Nanking! And now look what's happened!" He laughed, dangling both handguns at his side. "Well, you're committed now, aren't you?"

At that instant Eddie Nitta lunged for him, wrapping his arm around Lee's legs and dragging him to the ground. Shrieking, Lee dropped the .45 but with his right hand hung on to the revolver, which he would have turned into Eddie's face but for a blow the major delivered to his ear. By the time Lee recovered, Eddie also had a hand on the snub-nosed and they began grappling for it.

"Shoot him!" Lee cried at the driver, who stood with his back against the side of the truck, sweeping the muzzle of his carbine in confused arcs. "Kill him, sailor!"

Hank clawed his fingers into the muddy soil and began pulling himself toward the .45, which lay ignored in a small puddle. Taking a second to recover his breath, he became aware of the women, who were hovering close by, desperately looking for some way to help Eddie. Yuki was scuffing the earth with the heel of her shoe, trying to kick up a rock.

The chief filled his lungs. "Run!"

They gaped at him, frozen with fear.

"Run, you stupid women!" he cried in the most adamant *issei* voice he could muster. "Or we die for nothing!"

Yuki moved first. She grabbed Kimiko by the skirt, tugged

her toward the brush. Then, after an agonized moment, they both started running up the slope, reminding him of deer in the way they kept interrupting their flight to glance back.

It worked, Hank realized. He tried to rise on all fours, but crumpled again, his head hammered by a fiery pain.

"Get out of the way!" the MP was hollering at Lee, who suddenly kneed Eddie in the groin and scrambled free, taking the revolver with him.

Eddie was making another dive for Lee's legs when there was an explosion from the carbine. The major was spun around in midair as if he had been swatted by a wrecking ball. He landed hard on his armless shoulder, bellowing in pain. Immediately, he began pressing his hand against the fleshy part of his left thigh, but the flow of blood was so insistent it trickled through his fingers. He vomited, then tried to rise but couldn't. It was all he could do to keep from bleeding to death.

Hank expected Lee to dispatch Eddie with the revolver, but instead the director was gazing out across the sagelands at Yuki, who, incredibly, had stopped fleeing and was coming back at a run. Chuckling, Lee said to the MP, "Fire when ready—God knows they strafed us when we were in the reeds!"

The carbine clattered against the ground.

Lee whirled in time to see the soldier leap behind the wheel. His entire body was convulsed by outrage as he trained his revolver on the man. "Are you jumping ship, you bastard?"

The soldier ducked as he gunned the engine, and the Dodge lurched forward, skirting the sand pile. Osler, who had been lumbering back from the highway as the olive-drab sedan grew ever closer, jumped on the running board and shouted for the driver to keep going. He brandished his greasegun to discourage Lee, who suddenly chortled and lowered the revolver. "I have no need of ninnies! None!"

Then, executing a smart about-face, he raised the handgun once more—this time at Yuki, who was now only thirty yards away.

She halted and wiped her palms on her hips. "Let me take the chief, Monty, and I won't say nothing . . . ever."

Lee showed no reaction, but kept the handgun at eye level.

"No . . . no . . . no," Hank moaned, rising on arms of gelatin. "Go!" he rasped at her.

She smiled pathetically. "I can't go without you."

Hank steeled his heart against her smile. "Get out of here, *imbaifu!*"

She flinched; he had called her a whore.

Then Lee squeezed the trigger again and again, and by the time the revolver snicked hollowly on a spent primer, Yuki had vanished. Then he began hunting around for the pistol he'd dropped.

"Dear God, no!" Hank looked down and realized that he was on his feet. He took a faltering step toward where she had last been, then another, although the sky was spinning.

He could hear a car pull up behind him, but didn't turn around. It only meant *hakujin* reinforcements. He wanted to die walking toward Yuki. It was the final meaning he could give to his life. His wobbly legs were measuring out his last truth.

But then Lee raced past him, nearly bowling him over, the man's crazed eyes more distressed than triumphant. This so confounded Hank that he had to stop and brace his hands on his knees.

What the hell was going on? Was Yuki still alive?

Then he saw that Kimiko, too, had decided to double back.

Lee was running toward her, trying to wipe the mud off the .45 with his shirttail. Her body tensed as she saw him coming, but then she leaned over and ripped out the side seams of her skirt before starting to flee up the slope again.

Then the chief blacked out for several seconds.

"Hank!" someone shouted from behind.

Reeling, almost losing his balance, he struggled to bring the Army Plymouth into focus. The driver's door was ajar, but no one was inside. Then movement near the sand pile drew his eye to a soldier in ODs, crouching over Eddie. The soldier stripped off the major's web waist belt and cinched this makeshift tourniquet around Eddie's bleeding thigh. He murmured a few words, and Eddie nodded drowsily. Then the GI picked up the pistol he had laid on the ground while attending to the major, and limped directly for Hank.

Carefully, he scanned the brush as he came.

Hank seized Jared Campbell by the shoulder straps. "Yukiko might be hit out there . . . help me walk . . . she might be hit . . ."

Campbell looked in bad shape himself, but he supported Hank with an arm. "Where's Kimiko?"

"Ran away."

"And Monty?"

"After her . . . went after her." When Campbell started to let go of him, Hank said, "Just help me out to Yukiko . . . please . . . for the love of God, please . . . she's right here someplace."

Twenty yards later they came upon her.

She lay curled around a gnarled trunk of sage. Campbell saw everything he needed to know in an instant and kept moving, following the tracks across the rain-softened earth.

Hank fell heavily beside the young woman.

It was some time before he found the strength to brush the grit and broken twigs out of her hair. Traceries of leaf shadow fell across her face like a lace mantilla. She didn't look as if she were sleeping. Death is seldom becoming: her lower jaw was dangling, her half-closed eyes milky.

But he lied to himself. She was sleeping. He told himself she was sleeping as he wrapped his arms around her.

♦ ♦ ♦

"Oh, piss!"

The highway kept bifurcating into two asphalt streamers that shot off from the hood ornament toward infinity. It was becoming nearly impossible to draw them back together into the one road that was cutting through the hills south of Tule Lake. Jared figured he was less than thirty miles from the segregation camp. This meant something. But his mind meandered from one thing to another, bumping off problems like a beach ball.

"Concentrate, boy . . ." He was dying for a cigarette, but had smoked his last one an hour before when the silken dawn air had suddenly turned to chloroform and the countryside flashed white, as if the film had snapped in a projector.

He would have to sleep. Soon.

He turned his thoughts away from sleep and tried to focus them on Kimiko. He didn't think she was dead. He could still infer her presence in the world; he trusted the feeling, and it sustained him through the agony of not being able to sleep.

Last night's rain had done him a favor: all the old tracks on the dirt side roads had been erased. And nowhere had the dual tires of a deuce-and-a-half sheared the fresh mud. Which probably meant the truck had gone on into Tule Lake, the decision had been made not to murder the evacuees—thank God.

And Jared didn't believe Monty would try to kill them inside the camp. Too many witnesses. No, the Manzanar evacuees would be isolated in Tule Lake's stockade till Monty could contact Van Zwartz for his next move. That would take time; the general was probably still stewing over what had befallen his fair-haired colonel. He probably wouldn't let anything happen to the evacuees until assured that Lieutenant Campbell was out of the picture, for good.

Meanwhile, Jared would turn off the highway and nudge the Plymouth deep into the brushy cedars, or whatever these stunted trees were, and sleep until nightfall. All the internment camps were built pretty much on the same model, and he was sure that he could find the stockade, even in the dark.

Then, out of his stupor, he glimpsed a truck pulling away from a heap of sand, lumbering toward the highway. A man was standing on the running board, grasping the door handle to keep from being bounced off.

Jared had been searching so long for a two-and-a-half-ton Dodge it didn't seem possible to suddenly come across one. Still, from under the seat, he took Dunnigan's .45 and laid it beside him.

The man on the running board was Osler, and he was

armed with a submachine gun. *God forbid,* it hit Jared, *they've just finished—I missed my chance by minutes! By fucking minutes!*

He pushed the accelerator pedal to the firewall. Osler hoisted the greasegun as if to spray the Plymouth, but at that instant Jared spun the steering wheel hard to the left and sideslipped off the pavement in the direction of the truck, showering Osler with mud before the tires found traction and he sped forward again.

The first sergeant never opened fire. Instead, he jumped inside the cab beside his driver, and they continued on toward Tule Lake. The tailgate was down, and no one was in the bed.

Jared decided to let them go, two fewer armed men to deal with.

Then his heart sank. One body was sprawled against the sand pile. And Tadashi Nitta was apparently dead a few yards away, his trouser leg awash with blood.

But staggering out in the brush was the unmistakable figure of Hank Fukuda. His face was horribly bruised, swollen almost beyond recognition, and he failed to respond when Jared shouted his name.

Nitta groaned, and Jared saw that blood was still flowing from the man's left thigh. Had he had two hands, the major probably could have stemmed the flow himself, but he needed a tourniquet. Using the man's belt, Jared tied off the femoral artery. "Loosen this in a couple minutes."

Nitta's eyes were cold on his.

"You going to make it, Major?"

He nodded tersely.

"Where's Kimiko?"

"Don't know—find her."

Jared shouted for Hank's attention once more, and the chief slowly turned and stared, dazed, as the lieutenant walked up to him. Jared kept an eye on the waist-high brush, expecting Monty to pop up at any turn.

For a moment, the chief gaped as if he didn't know him, then muttered something about Yukiko being out there somewhere, that she had been shot. He also said that Monty was chasing after Kimiko. They found the other woman's body a short distance away. She had died instantly, a bullet between the blades of her back had apparently smashed through the heart, for there wasn't enough blood showing to fill an eye-dropper.

He let go of Hank, who crumpled beside her.

Then he began following Kimiko's tracks, which were deeper at the toes than the heels—she was running hard. He fell into a shuffling jog, gritting his teeth against the lancinating pains he felt each time his left foot struck the ground. After a hundred yards, another set of tracks joined Kimiko's. Monty's. He, too, was running all out.

The ridge line above was unbroken by human silhouette, but then a flock of nutcrackers flew up from the woods. "There," he said to himself.

Hobbling now, he worked his way up to the crown of the hill and scanned the tree-studded plateau beyond. The terrain was flat, but this only improved the concealment offered by the cedars by putting them all on the same plane. All he could see was a wall of green branches.

His leg felt like it was going to shatter. Nausea began to rob him of his wind.

Then, after zigzagging through the trees, the tracks grew muddled, showing the streaks and divots from a tussle.

"Sweet Lord . . . no . . . no . . ."

Monty had overtaken Kimiko, forced her to the ground. Yet there was no sign of a shot having been fired, no blood spilled onto the soil or flecked across the nearby sage. And, after twenty feet, the tracks resumed, although along a straighter line now. Monty had taken control of her. Every other step her ankle appeared to be turning. He was probably wrenching her arm behind her back to make her go the way he wanted.

A bloodlust suddenly came over Jared. He wanted to feel the man's spindly neck in his hands; he hated with the viciousness a man can only have for one he once loved as a brother. Still running as best he could, he cracked the pistol's slide an inch to make sure a live round was seated, although he had already done this twice in the car. It had become a passion, this yearning to shoot Montgomery Lee.

"We're over here, Jared . . ."

He stopped and turned in the direction of Monty's voice. The pounding of his heart took away his breath, and he started to hyperventilate. He made sure the thumb safety was off, but kept the pistol at his side.

They were standing in a little cove among the trees. Monty was holding her before him, restraining her with his left arm wrapped across her chest. The muzzle of his .45 was denting the soft underside of her chin, and her lips were drawn tight across her teeth, which had been bloodied by a slap, Jared suspected.

He averted her gaze, fearful that her terrorized expression might make him freeze.

Monty's eyes seemed wistful, tender even, seemingly unconnected to what his hands were doing. "Aren't you going to ask me to let her go?"

Jared studied his eyes for a few seconds more, trying to fathom his state of mind. He appeared to have a day-old laceration on his brow—was he delirious? "Yes, hoss, I'll ask that. I'll ask you to let Mrs. Nitta go."

"Civil even now." Monty began fighting back tears. "You were always the best among us. And the worst, I suppose."

Jared tried to keep his voice dispassionate. The rawness he could do nothing about. "I don't understand."

"The hell you say."

"No, what do you mean?"

"Your miscegenation!"

All around, the nutcrackers were startled into cawing.

Kimiko moaned, which made Monty dig the muzzle deeper into her chin. Here, at last, was the twisted, livid face that had stared down in triumph on the corpses of Masao Shido and Morris Wenge. Here was the seething monster Jared had refused to see.

He lofted his empty hand. "Please don't do that, Monty.

I don't blame you for what happened. The sons of bitches put you in a situation you just couldn't handle. They used you."

"No, friend."

"They stole your chance to heal. Bleecher dangled you on strings—"

"Wrong . . . I *submitted* to their will. As much as it tormented me at times, I submitted. Nicholas Bleecher saved my wretched life. So then he owned it. He still does."

"Bleecher's dead."

Monty arched an eyebrow and chuckled without cause, then asked, "How's that?"

"I had to kill him. Dunnigan, too."

"Oh, my dear boy . . . my dear boy." Monty's eyes tripped back and forth as he made some inward calculation. "Are you sure?"

"Yes." Jared shifted a few feet to the side, looking for a clear shot. He had read Monty's expression, and it said that he was going to murder Kimiko no matter what was said. The knowledge filled Jared with an overwhelming sadness, and then panic burgeoned out of his sadness. A man has only so much luck in gunplay this delicate, and he sensed that he had used his up long ago in rescuing another hostage, a baby with her fool daddy's gun to her head. And now he was afraid he would choke at the fatal instant. Success rested on a nearly impossible trick, and he didn't think he could bring himself to risk it. He wanted to beg Monty to release her, but he sensed that pleading would only fuel the man's rage.

"Then you must atone," Monty said placidly.

Jared sidestepped again, but Monty was instinctively shielding his own head with hers. It would have to be a single shot, with only inches for clearance. So far the opportunity hadn't presented itself. And then, all at once, he was positive that his luck had run out.

"Atone for what, hoss?" he asked, his voice breaking.

"Why, for the awful thing you just confessed doing to the colonel and the captain."

"I didn't set out to kill them. I had to do it to save my own life, Monty." Keep saying his first name, he coached himself. Keep scratching at this inhuman husk for the seed he has jacketed in madness. And the instant he responds to the old bonds of warmth and friendship, drive a bullet through his forehead. Shatter the reflex to pull the trigger while it's still humming around inside the fusebox. But don't let him see the impulse take shape in your eyes. An impulse this ruthless swells the eyes first. The attack has to come out of the blue. "So how's this farm boy supposed to atone, Monty?"

His eyes went icy. "*You* kill her."

Jared stared at him, speechless for a moment.

"Believe me—she's a demon," Monty went on, gesturing with his pistol for a split second. But before Jared could do anything, the .45 was thrust under her chin again. "She cast a spell on you. And few men alive could've resisted. They have an uncanny sensuality—and no qualms about using it to further the cause of their race. God, how many times I wanted to discuss this very thing with you!"

"Well, why didn't you?"

"I knew if I tried to warn you, she'd kill you. Fukuda and she had it planned from the beginning—to kill you as soon as you got wise to them. So I had to watch and wait. I had to suffer the torment of seeing my dearest and truest friend dance on *their* strings—"

"All right, Monty."

"Pardon?"

"I'll do it."

Elation brightened Monty's face. But then, in the next instant, it was replaced by suspicion. "Oh, how I wish I could trust you." His smile was dolorous. "But we both know she controls your every thought."

Jared couldn't bear to trade glances with Kimiko. This was her first brush with ferocious insanity. *What must she be thinking? Ignore her or you'll balk!* At least she knew enough to keep silent: one word would be enough to unleash Monty's rage. Lee was waiting for her to say something, any damned thing.

"Well, hoss, I can understand how you feel."

"Thank you." Shutting his eyes for an instant, he grinned. "I hate quarreling with you, Jared. Hate distrusting you. But what can I do?"

"How about if you train your pistol on me while I do her? If that ain't insurance I don't know what the devil is. And turn a bit . . . so my bullet don't get you, too."

Monty cocked his head while considering this, then rested the barrel across her shoulder. "Very well."

Jared looked into the mouth of Monty's .45, then glanced down and to the side. It had been his final check. Two inches of clearance, a hairsbreadth of a target just beyond her profile, which he fixed in his mind's eye while he prayed that neither of them would move; and then, still gazing listlessly at the ground, he swept his pistol up and fired once, blindly.

He didn't hear the shot, but felt the recoil ripple up the length of his arm.

Gazing at the spot where their heads had been, he saw only the tops of the trees and a turquoise void of sky. And then his spent brass casing tumbled down past his eyes.

It was some time before he could force himself to look where they lay.

He would have almost preferred never knowing.

CHAPTER 29

Being relieved of command was an ascent or a descent into purgatory. He just couldn't decide which.

The lean middle-aged man sitting in a white rattan chair in the unadorned main compartment of his C-47 transport asked himself what he could have done differently in the past two and a half years, and then kept answering himself—not a damned thing.

That, clearly, was the hell of it.

He wore wire-rimmed glasses so thickly corrective his eyes looked blurry behind the lenses. An ammunition dump explosion during the Great War had nearly destroyed his left eye; overwork and poor lighting conditions in the jungles of Burma and later Chungking had done the rest. Yet, despite the discomfort, he continued to plow through the mass of mail and piddling dispatches from the War Department. It had been held for him in Delhi when word trickled down that Chiang Kai-shek had finally persuaded Roosevelt to replace Joseph Stilwell with someone who wouldn't question the Generalissimo's holding back troops and materiel for the more important war he envisioned with the communists as soon as the Americans defeated the Japanese for him. And FDR had no intention of risking a breach with the Nationalists on the eve of the U.S. elections—Stilwell had orders forbidding him to discuss the Chinese situation with anyone.

He checked his watch: another hour to Karachi.

The country below reminded him of northern Mexico, parched and tawny-colored. He longed for the green foggy coast of California. Home.

Something in the bottom of his mail sack caught his eye. He dug out the manila-wrapped package and shook it, expecting the rattle of cookies. But the contents were too heavy for baked goods, unless his Winifred had lost her touch. On closer inspection, he saw that the return address was general delivery in Reno. His home was in Carmel. Had she hopped the train from San Francisco to Nevada to pull a few one-armed bandits? Not likely. And the damned script wasn't hers. Nor did it resemble the handwriting of any of his five children.

His long fingers began shredding the paper apart.

He read the contents for twenty minutes before his temper got the best of him. Later, he admitted that his first communication should have been to the Chief of Staff, his old colleague from the Infantry School at Fort Benning, George Marshall. But, perhaps because all his resentments of the past months suddenly had an outlet, he strode forward through the lurching C-47, a slightly misanthropic glint coming to his eyes, and roused the radio operator in his cubical.

"General?"

"I want a wire sent via our Karachi attaché right away."

The airman touched pencil to pad. "Ready to copy, sir."

"To the Commanding General, Headquarters Western Defense Command and Fourth Army. My return stateside imminent. Thinking of forming a pickax club to protect Japanese Americans fighting the war with us. Any time I see a barfly commando picking on these kids I'm going to bang him over the head with a pickax. If that doesn't work, I'm going to wrap guts around every lamppost in San Francisco. Respectfully, J. W. Stilwell."

♦ ♦ ♦

Hank Fukuda was wheeled into the conference room. The MP faced him toward a long table, then withdrew. Behind the table sat five Army officers, the most senior a lieutenant colonel, all with their hands folded before them. The only other person in the room was a stenographer, a sergeant. No one from the War Relocation Authority was present.

Warm autumn sunlight streamed in through the windows, dappling the floor with bronze, yet Hank felt cold. He smoothed the GI blanket around his legs and avoided the stares of the officers.

Finally, after a month of bed rest, he could walk. But the effort quickly exhausted him, and he was still dogged by bouts of vertigo and a sharp irritability that shadowed his moods.

The lieutenant colonel turned to the stenographer. "Make sure the record reflects the names of the members of this board of inquiry, date, and time. Note location as civilian administration building, Tule Lake Resegregation Center, by permission of the project director."

The soldier nodded that he already had it all down.

The lieutenant colonel then studied Hank for an unnecessarily long moment. "Are you Henry Yoshio Fukuda?"

"I am."

"I remind you that this board relies on your loyalty as an American citizen to answer all questions truthfully and to the best of your ability." Hank made no reply. "Now, Mr. Fukuda, are you acquainted with one Jared Campbell, formerly a first lieutenant assigned to the 319th Military Police Guard and Escort Company, Manzanar War Relocation Center?"

"Yes." Hank marked the officer's order of words—*formerly a first lieutenant*. Jared had been stripped of his rank, then. Or did this mean that he was dead?

"Would you please describe your relationship with Campbell?"

"No," Hank whispered.

"I beg your pardon—I couldn't hear you."

"I said *no*." The chief came close to smirking when he

glanced up into their stunned faces—none of them had heard the word in a long time. But then his anger took over. "When this all began," he began slowly, resisting his corrosive bitterness, "the rumors, the accusations, the hysteria—I was asked to prove my loyalty by answering questions just like the one you're putting to me now. I was encouraged to come forward with information." He laughed. "Information to clear up misunderstandings that might prove injurious to *my people*. Well, you—the military, the feds—twisted my information, built lies out of it, then dumped it at the feet of the public as proof the treacherous little Jap couldn't be trusted. . . ." His eyes began smarting, and he looked away, afraid that he might suddenly burst into tears. He had never talked like this in his entire life, particularly to the *hakujin*, and was afraid of losing control. But after a few moments, by recalling Manzanar, he was able to glare at them, to take satisfaction instead of unease from their discomfort. "I wasn't the only one, of course. You enlisted dozens of us to spy on our neighbors. You told us we could prevent a wholesale evacuation by pinpointing the bad eggs in our communities. Weed out the dangerous pro-imperial aliens, you said, and we'll remind the public that most of you folks are God-fearing, loyal Americans." His hands were now knotted into fists. "Well, you lied! You used our reports to dress up stories to feed to the Hearst papers and growers' associations, who then stirred up John Q. Citizen to distrust his Japanese neighbor—!"

"Mr. Fukuda," the lieutenant colonel interrupted, "you are instructed to limit your replies to the questions. I will now repeat the question: Will you describe your relationship with Lieutenant Campbell?"

"I don't know where he is. I don't know what you've done to him. But if you've harmed one hair on his head, you've proved what I suspected all along—this bullshit won't be confined to a minority who were too powerless, too friendless, too obedient and cooperative to resist. You can't quarantine injustice. So if anything's happened to Campbell, I will point to the first Caucasian victim of your evacuation . . . but only the first. . . ." Hank wiped his eyes with a swipe of his sleeve. "I've spent my entire adult life serving the law. Even in Manzanar, as nuthouse and confused as it was, I always tried to serve the law. Well, gentlemen, I'll answer your questions about Jared Campbell when you bastards can show me you're half as loyal to the law as he was."

Then he spun his wheelchair around and rolled himself out. The MP at the door didn't try to stop him.

♦ ♦ ♦

During his fifth week of solitary confinement, he stopped hoping. He consoled himself that he had lost *well,* which seemed fitting for a "peckerwood," as Dunnigan had summed him up. And with this thought, his anxiety lessened. Right and wrong, accusation and vindication, God and godlessness—these things quit shouting inside his head and soon echoed down to whispers, like the sound of the surf that drifted across the tip of the peninsula and through the high windows of the Presidio's stockade. Never once during those weeks was there an inkling that a court-martial was in the works, and from that he understood what would become of him. At first, naturally, the prospect was terrifying. But, when the terror became too much to bear, he stopped suckling his dry hopes and his fears withered, leaving him feeling empty and lonely but also mercifully apart from the world. He began trusting that whatever followed would be deeply good and quiet, although probably unfathomable to an ignorant kid from outside Shawnee who'd stumbled into the Promised Land wearing a denim jacket, a four-in-hand, and crossroads store shoes.

There were worse fates than being hanged, he supposed. He just couldn't name any, not off the top of his head, anyways. Which made him laugh a little each time he allowed himself to think about it.

The MPs gave him all the cigarettes he wanted, although they had orders not to converse with him. The on-duty sergeant safe-kept his matches for him so he wouldn't try to set himself on fire. He smoked away the hours, which—now that he had given up hope—seemed numberless yet no longer interminable. He shifted positions on his wall-mounted cot a thousand times in a day, but never quite got comfortable; that didn't seem to matter either.

Then one night after lights the steel door to the block clanged open and footfalls came leisurely down the corridor toward his cell.

A figure halted in front of the bars.

The only illumination was from the moon coming in through the high windows. The chevrons on the man's sleeves indicated him to be a master sergeant, but his face was concealed by the shadow thrown by the wide brim of his campaign hat. Supposedly, only one man in the entire United States Army still wore a campaign hat.

Silent, nearly motionless, he regarded Jared for some minutes, then turned and strolled back up the corridor.

♦ ♦ ♦

The impertinent colonel kept his service cap squarely on his head as he stood at ease before the huge desk. He was within the scope of regulations by remaining covered, for he was under arms with a holstered pistol strapped to his hip. But it was clearly an affront to the dignity of the Commanding General of Western Defense Command, as was packing a handgun like some frontier-town constable. These subtleties were not lost on James Van Zwartz, but the grave demeanor of the Washington-based colonel made him unsure what to do about them.

He unwound the twine and opened the packet stamped FROM THE OFFICE OF THE CHIEF OF STAFF.

His lips moved as he scanned the face page, then grew thin as he leafed through what he quickly realized to be photostats of pages from his own diaries. Yet there was no mention of disciplinary action: he was being offered the easy way out, and he knew he had no choice but to take it. Still, he whipped off his glasses and gave the colonel a grin that was contorted by rage.

"Tell me—is Joe Stilwell bucking for my job now that he bitched up his in China?"

The colonel chose not to answer.

"This is just lovely!" Van Zwartz batted the two upright pens out of their walnut holder as if they were sentries who had failed him. "And what the hell is *immediately and without prejudice to these orders* supposed to mean?"

"Air transport is presently awaiting you. I'm to personally see you to Crissy Field at once, sir."

"And what in the name of God is Mrs. Van Zwartz supposed to do?"

"She'll be rendered every assistance in vacating your present quarters. After your departure, I'm to remain here and see that she enjoys a comfortable relocation to temporary housing of the new commanding general's choosing."

"For crapsake!" Van Zwartz looked around for something else to fling off his desk, but finally settled for smacking a palsied fist into his palm. "Persia?"

"That is correct, sir—Teheran."

"George had to dig deep to find me an apple this sour, didn't he?"

"I wouldn't know, sir."

◆ ◆ ◆

After supper, two guards brought him an immaculately pressed blouse with polished silver bars on the shoulder straps and collar tabs for infantry, his original branch of service—a gesture he appreciated. The MPs even threw in a pair of "pinks," fancy beige trousers with a pinkish sheen to the twilled wool. Manzanar's lack of military social engagements had kept him from shelling out the cash after the moths got through with his original pair. But now he had some honest-to-God pinks to wear, and he muttered a joke about wondering if he'd died and gone to heaven. This so unsettled his teenaged guards that he added softly, "You're only doing your jobs, boys." He finished knotting his light tan tie. "How's she look?"

One of them nodded.

"You all mind leaving me alone for a couple of minutes?"

When the MPs hesitated, he stripped off his trouser belt

and handed it over. They declined to take his tie before withdrawing. A show of trust, he supposed.

Jared threw down his pillow to save the knees of his pinks, then knelt beside the cot. He hoped for a sudden return of the spirit, that flush so sweet and copious it had almost dripped off him along with the water as he climbed out of that baptismal irrigation ditch of long ago. But the spirit wouldn't come, and it felt hypocritical to beg for it, so he closed his eyes and simply tried to send a message through the night, down the length of California, over her orchards and fields, across her brushy southern mountains, to his mother. Somehow, he wanted her to know that he hadn't died in shame. He wasn't glossing over all the sins he had done, but they sure as hell hadn't been committed in shame.

The two young MPs came back for him.

"Let's get it over with . . ." And he truly meant it. From this point on, he wanted to keep moving. If they stopped, even momentarily, he was afraid he might break down. His last ration of courage was thin, and he didn't want to test it with a lot of standing around.

Yet, in the corridor outside the sergeant of the guard's office, they halted.

Jared had to bite his underlip.

A full colonel, looking official as hell in his service cap, stepped out, glanced briefly at him, then inclined his head for the MPs to follow him with the prisoner.

Outside, in front of the stockade, the colonel asked, "How are you doing?"

He thought it the devil of a thing to say, under the circumstances, but didn't feel like arguing. "All right."

"Good."

It was foggy. The headlamps of a staff car emerged out of the mists. The colonel gestured for him to get in the back seat first, then ducked in himself, sighing wearily as he doffed his cap. One of the MPs took the shotgun seat beside the driver; the other saluted and went back inside the stockade.

The Plymouth pulled away from the whitewashed curbstones. The driver kept his speed down as he drove through the fog. Nothing was said. Every few seconds, the driver clicked on the wipers to clear the moisture off the windshield.

Jared betrayed no surprise when they left the post through the main gate, the sentry jotting down their time of departure. He expected it to happen somewhere away from the Presidio, some small out-of-the-way post.

They headed south through the dimmed-out city. He found himself trying to glimpse inside windows, looking for signs of life within, envying each window that had light. Eventually, they entered the seaside neighborhoods where the blackout restrictions applied all the time, and there were no lights to be seen.

An hour and a half later, while the car sped through ragged fields of artichoke, the colonel snubbed out his third cigarette since leaving San Francisco and said, "I'm not being close-mouthed for the hell of it."

Jared's pulse picked up. "Sir?"

"My orders are to brief you only in the presence of your commanding officer. At that point, you'll be offered a choice. The most important choice of your life—believe me."

The colonel clammed up again, and Jared was left wondering if by CO he had meant Snavely. Was this car en route to Manzanar, or had Snavely come across the Sierra to gloat? Either way, none of this was making sense. It seemed a shabby, offhand way to kill a man.

Yet, when the driver turned off the Pacific Coast Highway north of Monterey, and then past a sentry house and under a wooden arch that read NINTH CORPS INFANTRY TRAINING COMMANDREPLACEMENT DEPOT, Jared froze before letting go a long breath and leaning back in the seat for the first time. His tension had snapped, leaving him spent, slightly giddy, and still a bit suspicious. But, through it all, he sensed that his days in the craw were over.

A bruin of a captain with a combat infantry badge on his

chest met the car in front of the headquarters building and opened Jared's door.

He stepped out, too dizzy for the moment to take a step.

"Joe Kelly," the captain said simply, offering his hand.

"Jared Campbell, sir." The fog had turned sweet with the smell of dripping pines.

"Welcome to the infantry, Campbell." He saluted the colonel, who was yawning on the other side of the car. "We can talk inside, Colonel. I got a fresh pot waiting."

CHAPTER 30

As the bus pulled away from the icy parking lot of the Truckee railroad station, snow began to fall again. The driver said he would pick the prettiest girl to put on the tire chains, if the need arose. All the passengers laughed, except Kimiko, who—in spite of her troubled resolve—decided to take a seat toward the back. She didn't want to feel *hakujin* gazes on her neck, as she had constantly during the past five days of coach train travel from Boston.

A man with shifty eyes shot up from his seat and helped her lift her suitcase into the overhead storage, but he didn't smile. This sent her spirits crashing.

It began to snow harder, big curls of flakes. All at once she was certain that the roads on the other side of the Sierra, which always were hit harder by storms, would be closed, and she'd arrive at Lake Tahoe to find herself alone in a somber white silence. Incredibly, she was feeling something akin to homesickness for Manzanar, perhaps the lost security of that artificial *nihonjin* world. This strange longing made her feel weak and ashamed.

The exclusion order barring unescorted Japanese from the

West Coast had been rescinded on January 2; still, she felt like a fugitive, and each humorless-looking man aboard the bus became a government agent in her imagination. She regretted having left the relative safety within the *pale* of Boston, and the distracting solace of her work.

After six weeks of unexplained internment at Tule Lake, she had been offered every possible assistance to resettle outside Western Defense Command. The chief of the WRA's East Coast regional office personally called on her former Stanford classmate, Jean, who eagerly agreed to sponsor Kimiko for employment, namely the previously promised clerking position with her father's Boston law firm.

Three months later, Kimiko was set up in her own Cambridge apartment, sparsely furnished but comfortable, and with a peek at the Charles River through the kitchenette window. In the autumn, when enough money was saved, she intended to return to school and finish her law degree. It was a quiet existence of lunch counters and long walks in the evenings, but her loneliness was salved by reminding herself that things would get better, especially when the war ended—it finally looked as if the war was winding down . . . if the newspapers could be trusted.

"Kings Beach!" the driver bawled, startling her. She used her coat sleeve to rub a circle in the steamed-over window, her imitation jet buttons clicking against the glass.

He was standing alone in front of a boarded-up hotel, the collar to his greatcoat pulled up around his neck, his hands jammed deep into the pockets. He scanned the windows of the bus but didn't see her at first. His face was much thinner than she remembered. And he looked tired. But then he found her and gave her a shy grin. He started to wave, but checked the urge.

She filed out behind a half dozen passengers, wondering what she could possibly say to him. *Ask him about his trip*.

He didn't kiss her, and she was thankful, what with so many *hakujin* milling about, the bus passengers and those who had come in ice-encrusted automobiles to pick them up.

"How was your ride?" he asked, ignoring the stares as he took her suitcase.

"Fine," she lied. "And yours?"

"Miserable. Snow all the way up from Placerville. Just got here myself. You eaten?"

She shrugged, meaning no.

They crossed the slushy road, and he helped her over a berm of dirty snow onto an unplowed lane. Breaking the drifted whiteness were two sets of tracks of the same shoe size, one going down the slope toward the lake and one coming back up. "Yours?" she asked.

"Yeah . . . I just had time enough to the shovel the snow away from the front door before your bus arrived."

The pines were lovely, their branches thickly blanketed with fresh snow. But she couldn't really see the lake; the clouds seemed flush with the hint of its gray surface. After they had walked some distance down the lane, he took her hand. None of the cabins along their way appeared to be occupied. The war, she supposed.

Even the promise of a brief silence between them unsettled her; he seemed such a stranger, although she didn't know why. "How did you hear of this place?"

"The exec in the training command owns it." He gestured at a log two-story, then let go of her hand and went ahead to stamp down the snow a little more. "Hear anything more from the chief?"

"No." Hank Fukuda, resettled in New York City, had helped arrange this meeting—in secret, according to Jared's wishes, so neither the Army nor the WRA would know. "But I think he's doing okay."

Although it appeared somewhat neglected, the cabin was, as she had hoped, perched just above the shoreline. There was even a shingled boathouse, and she began to resent the mists obscuring the water. She had never seen Lake Tahoe, only color photographs in which it shone transparently like a sapphire. Reportedly, it never froze, so if the sun would only come through . . .

Then, as if he needed to get it out of the way, as if he had to put Eddie behind them, he asked, "Any word from the major?"

Perhaps she needed to be done with it as well. "Yes, his sister writes me now and again."

"Did he leave Tule Lake with you?"

"No, he was taken directly to Letterman Hospital at the Presidio after . . ." She still hadn't been able to find the words to describe that horrible morning.

Jared nodded as if he understood, then kicked his shoes against a porch post. "Did he mend okay?"

"Fine."

"I thought he would . . . the bullet zipped clean through. So you mean he's done convalescing?"

"Yes, the Army invited him to teach at the Military Intelligence Service Language School in Minnesota."

"Did he do it?"

"Yes."

"Good . . . good."

"But he was only there a few weeks when they shipped him to the Philippines. MacArthur's staff. Eddie didn't say to his sister, but I think they're already putting together plans for the occupation of Japan."

Jared swung back the weather door for her. The inside of the cabin was stone-cold, and the smell of stale woodsmoke clung to the threadbare furniture.

"How long do we have?" she asked.

He averted his eyes. "I've got to take the first bus in the morning."

"But why?"

"I ship out from Frisco the day after. You should probably take the noon bus."

She hid her disappointment: she'd expected at least a couple of days here. Now, there would scarcely be time to warm the place up. He knelt at the box woodstove, cracked the door, and began sifting his fingers through the powdery ashes.

"May I ride the bus as far as Walnut Grove with you?"

There she would check on some real estate that had belonged to her father. The county was maneuvering to keep released *nihonjin* from reoccupying their property, but—with the blessings of her new employer—she was going to contest the restrictive covenants and ordinances. "It'd give us a few more hours that way, wouldn't it?"

He crumpled up old newspapers and stuffed them in the firebox. "Shame when a house gets this chilly. It gets deep into the walls and won't come out easy."

"Jared?"

"We can't go down the hill together . . ." He wiped his fingers on the hem of his coat. "I made a deal with them."

"What kind of deal?"

"I agreed that none of the things that happened would come to justice. They said I got my licks in, and I figure they're right about that. But still, maybe I sold out. Hell, I don't know . . ."

"Why do you think you sold out?"

"The truth. I went looking for it. It'd be different if I hadn't found it. But I did. I went and stumbled on the goddamned truth, Ki."

"I don't care about that now. I never expected them to do anything except hide the truth—"

"There's more." From an old steamer trunk he took kindling and the smaller pieces of limbwood. "I agreed not to see you again."

"For how long?"

"Forever—that's what they said. As far as me getting ahold of Hank . . . well, they must figure they've got a pretty tight squeeze on him, too. I can write him. But it's no dice with you or anybody else from camp who's not working for some kind of government outfit now."

"Then what about this?" A sweep of her eyes took in the cabin. "Are you in danger by coming here?"

"It's worth it." He smiled uneasily.

"*Why?*" she asked, not wanting to be flattered; she simply had to know why he was risking this.

His smile faded. "I need to change your mind before I ship out. I'll break their deal if I have to. Hell, I figure they'll send me over no matter what I do in the next forty-eight hours. They'll just be tickled to get me out of the country and into combat." He lit the newspaper with his Zippo, then glanced up at her, his eyes turning dour as he saw the look on her face. "Damn, but I hate your stubbornness. I swear to God, Ki—I hate how you won't step sideways for nobody."

She said nothing.

Finally, he turned away to adjust the flue damper.

◆ ◆ ◆

The second-story bedroom remained cold hours after he had lit the stove downstairs. His pillow doubled under the back of his head, he was staring out the window. The storm was beginning to clear, the light filtering through the overcast seemed less wan than it had earlier in the afternoon, and a breeze was stripping the snow off the branches.

"Marry me, dammit," he whispered.

It was time to tell him, she decided. "Eddie and I decided to wait on the divorce."

The crow's-feet deepened around his eyes. "Why?"

"A lot of things. Residency, his being overseas again complicates the dissolution process—"

"What are you telling me? Are you still going ahead with it?"

He sounded so alarmed that she felt the need to lay a hand on his bare chest. "Yes, eventually." Then, rising from the warm bed, she wrapped the topmost blanket around her nakedness and padded to the window. As she'd sensed, the surface of the lake lay exposed under a patch of open sky, which reflected bluely on the waters. There were forested peaks on the far side, and a setting sun that endowed the fresh snowfall with stark shadows—it was all coldly beautiful. But then, with a shift of the wind, the lake was gone again under the banks of mist. "I wonder," she said, "is it the *freedom* that makes us feel like such strangers?"

"What are you talking about?"

"I don't know."

"You mean you don't have Manzanar for an excuse any-more?" he asked harshly.

She came back to bed and kissed him, if only because she feared they would slide into a litany of question heaped upon answerless question. "I love you . . . more than anyone I've ever known. You're the best man I've ever known. All right?"

"Are you scared then?"

"Yes, I'm scared."

He sat up. "I'll watch over you. I can protect you. You know that."

"But you're going away." The truth made him compress his lips. God, he looked so grim she wanted to shake him by the shoulders—their time was slipping away in unhappiness. "You'll be gone in two days," she went on. "You need to go, to make yourself feel right about things again. Just as I need to go back to Boston."

"But you don't have anybody back there. My family can watch over you out here, in California where you belong."

"No, darling."

"You doubt their kindness?"

She shook her head. "You see—Morris Wenge, most of the staff at camp, were *kind*. But I, all the other evacuees, we were at their mercy. I can't put myself through that again. I can't be someone's ward."

"Please—"

"And my God, Jared—California has a statute that would nullify our marriage even if we went to a justice of the peace in another state. Don't you see? Whichever way we turn—don't you see?"

"Then go back East, for chrissake—but say you'll marry me before you go. Hell, I might like Boston."

"No. Neither of us should be tied to the other. Not now. Not during the coming years. You know that, darling . . . you know what I'm saying is right. . . ." Already her mind's eye was watching him troop away from the cabin at first light, his breath steaming over his shoulder, his shoes squeaking in the snow. And the images filled her with such loneliness, she could scarcely resist saying that, yes, she would do as he asked; she would find a way. "Please hold me . . . and don't talk. Don't talk, my love."

At dawn, he left precisely as she had visualized, although midway up the lane he turned and stared back at her. He didn't wave.

Still, she had not anticipated the raw hurt that showed in his face at that moment. It left her regretting that she had come out to the porch, that she had come west at all.

♦ ♦ ♦

The stocky man in the brand-new overcoat hesitated at the foot of the steps to the tired-looking brownstone. Flanking him were two cast-iron pillars topped with opaque glass globes stenciled 88TH PCT. Turning, he regarded the profusion of concrete on all sides of him, appreciatively almost, as if once he went inside the station the urban landscape might be swept clean into a California desert.

But he had put this off for two weeks now, and each day's fresh failure left him feeling increasingly restless and guilty. Of course, it had been his first priority to write something meaningful to Jared Campbell, who might already be on his way overseas. But he had struggled with the words and torn up a dozen drafts before finally trusting himself to simply scribble on the back of a five-and-dime postcard of Lincoln: *I remember, therefore I am. I'll never forget you. Keep your big head down. Hank.*

He took the steps two at time, passed through the double doors, and halted before a towering desk behind which loomed a police sergeant.

"I'd like to see Miss Dos Santos."

"Who are you?"

Trying to keep his fingers steady, he took the New York Police Department Bureau of Criminalistics ID from his wallet.

The sergeant scanned both sides of the card. "You new?"

"Started a week ago Monday."

"Here on your lunch hour?"

"Right."

"Say, you mind taking some burg evidence back to the lab with you when you go? It'll save one of my boys a trip."

"Not at all."

"You're a pal." The sergeant's tone of voice warmed considerably, although Hank tried not to make too much of it: he had resolved to stop divining for signs of acceptance in everything his new *hakujin* associates said and did. "Lucy's in dispatch. First Dutch door to the left. Knock if the top's closed, and she'll open up if she ain't busy."

"Appreciate it."

His stride shortened as he neared the door. All at once, he felt ridiculous and thought about withdrawing without bothering her. Her name, he'd discovered from the personnel roster, was still Dos Santos, but that didn't mean she didn't have someone. Perhaps it would be more fitting—and potentially less embarrassing—to wait for an accidental encounter.

But as he stood there vacillating, the top half of the door swung open and Lucille Dos Santos, her attention divided between her radio console and Hank, hollered, "Would somebody please bring me some more log sheets before—!" Then her normally high color drained from her face, and she bent her fingers against her forehead—her gesture when caught off balance by something. A radio car transmitted to her once, and then again more insistently. She turned her stunned gaze away from Hank's equally startled face and handled the traffic, her voice edged with irritability. The PBX portion of the console began buzzing, and she furiously patched a call to detectives before utterly ignoring everything the precinct continued to throw at her.

Then she glared at him. "Christ, I've missed you."

She said it accusingly. And from that he realized she didn't have someone.

◆ ◆ ◆

While the special sea-and-anchor detail was being piped in preparation for distant service, Lieutenant Francis Roper led a file of thirty *nisei* down two ladders and a long passageway to the general mess. Although they wore the uniform of the

U.S. Army, the faces of the men—which so clearly resembled that of the enemy—drew second glances from the crew. But no one had said a word to these unusual GIs since they had embarked at the last possible minute, and that was probably the difference between a battleship and a transport sailor.

"Very well, gentlemen," Roper said, turning them over to a Filipino steward on loan from the wardroom, "enjoy your sandwiches and coffee. I'll be at my desk in the personnel office should any of you require further assistance."

"What happens if we can't find the personnel office, sir?" one of them asked, a kid with a coppery complexion.

"Then you're S-O-L, soldier."

A couple of them laughed, but most remained silent and expressionless. Perhaps they rightfully sensed that the sandwiches and coffee were a ploy to keep them off the weather decks—and out of public view—until the *Nebraska* had cleared port. They were Military Language Specialists, fresh out of a special replacement depot, and in a few weeks they would be crawling into caves and bunkers, trying to talk Japanese defenders into bucking *Bushido* and surrendering. Some crappy job. The admiral had feared an incident if they were divvied up among the troop transports at this point; there had been problems before. Instead, they'd be transferred to their individual units at Ulithi Atoll, by which time the white GIs would be too weakened by seasickness and apprehension to bait them.

There was another passenger on the *Nebraska* whose reason for being aboard was not so evident: an infantry first lieutenant, whom Roper had deposited in junior officers' quarters prior to herding the *nisei* to mess. Now he hurried forward to make sure that this guest was settled in.

From the main deck came the rattle of the huge anchor chains drawing back into the hawser pipes, and the unique sound made it really sink in: he was going back out.

Roper found the lieutenant sitting on the lower bunk in his compartment, seeming at a loss what to do next and looking slightly awed by it all.

"Everything okay, Lieutenant Campbell?"

"I was wondering—"

He fell silent as the boatswain's mate droned over the PA: "Shift colors, the ship is under way." The national ensign would now be transferred aloft to the gaff and the union jack struck.

"I was wondering if I might go topside for a gander as we pull out."

"You bet—follow me." Roper led him up to the prow, which was curling back the glassy green swells at a leisurely twelve knots. The great ship was northbound out of San Francisco Bay, about in line with the Ferry Building. Roper had another reminder that they were under way when he saw the flagless jackstaff. "This your first time out?"

"Sure is. I'm supposed to join up with my company someplace out there."

"Which division?"

"Twenty-seventh Infantry."

Tenth Army. That meant he was slated for the invasion of Okinawa, although he probably didn't know that yet. And it wasn't Roper's place to tell him. West of Alcatraz Island, tuglike tenders were opening the submarine nets to let the *Nebraska* through. "You involved in some way with the MLSs aboard?"

"No." Campbell looked uncomfortable for a moment. "Well, one of them's assigned to my outfit." He offered nothing more that might explain why he was aboard, and Roper let it slide.

"If you need anything, give me a holler."

"Sure will—and thanks."

♦ ♦ ♦

Jared gaped upward as the *Nebraska* plowed under the center span of the Golden Gate. Its shadow fell across his face, but then—an instant later—the bridge was behind him. He let out a deep breath and refused to look back at the Presidio. And then Fort Point was behind him. The whole damned country was behind him, receding on the swells.

Soon the bows started cutting rougher waters. The open sea.

The *Nebraska* steamed through a formation of transports

and oilers, then slowed to take the van. Destroyers, like sheep dogs, raced this way and that to form a screen around the convoy, the waves shipping over their sleek noses, although on the prow of the ponderous battlewagon he felt nothing more than an occasional mist. He knew damned well why the brass had put him aboard this ship with the *nisei* troops: they weren't about to let him forget; it was only a truce he had with them. But, soon enough, there would be more urgent things to do than sort through the past. One thing that could probably be said about combat—it had a way of swamping a mind with the present.

"Lieutenant?"

Letting go of the top lifeline, he pivoted and was confronted by a pair of Japanese faces. The youths saluted. "Yes, soldier?"

"Begging your pardon, sir, but are you Lieutenant Campbell?"

"That's right."

A few moments passed in which the *nisei* said nothing and he was left wondering if they knew him from Manzanar, a notion he didn't relish.

"I'm Corporal Segawa. I've been assigned to your platoon, sir."

"Oh, yeah—proud to meet you, Segawa. I was gonna look you up this evening. And what's your name, soldier?" he asked the other MLS.

"Goshi, Lieutenant."

"You boys from Hawaii?" It was the polite way of asking them if they'd come out of the camps.

"No, sir—we're mainlanders."

"Where are your folks?"

"Poston, sir. Both our families."

"It's a relocation camp in Arizona," Segawa said.

"I know what Poston is," Jared said quietly.

Then a rumble swelled over the sound of the water folding around the hull. He glanced skyward into a vee of silvery bombers, the biggest planes he had ever seen, flying directly into the afternoon sun. He could feel the thunder of their engines reverberating against his ribs.

"The new B-29s," Goshi said, shading his eyes for a better look at the last plane in formation. It was lagging behind a bit, but seemed to catch the sunlight more brightly than the others. "Go, team, go." He chuckled under his breath.

"Save some for us!" Segawa cried, momentarily forgetting himself.

"Listen . . ." Frowning, Jared took a toothpick from his fatigue blouse pocket as they turned their faces toward him. "We'll take this job slow. One step at a time. Slow and easy. Everybody watching out for everybody else. And nobody getting killed trying to make a show. You understand?"

"Yes, sir," they both muttered, coming to attention and looking shamefaced.

Jared tried to smile, sorry for cowing them, but he didn't want anybody getting killed trying to please him. He wanted to sleep nights after this war. "Good."

"Will that be all, sir?" Segawa asked, eager to withdraw.

"Yeah." He returned their salutes. "That's all."

Yet, a moment later, he couldn't help himself from calling after them. "They got all the gold-star mothers they can handle down there at Poston. At Minidoka and Manzanar, too. You got nothing to prove to nobody—other than doing your jobs. You hear? You boys got nothing special to prove."

Then he faced back out to sea and began chewing on the toothpick, his eyes intent upon the horizon. "I've got to learn how to talk to people," he muttered to himself.